**Sabrina Sheldon. Burnett Clinton.
Alexandra Logan.**

They're at the end of their ropes—and no
one on *earth* can help them.

Who they gonna call?

Because sometimes, you don't need to see
to believe....

ANNETTE BROADRICK

believes in romance and the magic of life. Since 1984, when her first book was published, Annette has shared her view of life and love with readers all over the world. In addition to being nominated by *Romantic Times* as one of the Best New Authors of that year, she has also won the *Romantic Times* Reviewer's Choice Award for Best in its Series for *Heat of the Night, Mystery Lover* and *Irresistible*; the *Romantic Times* WISH award for her heroes in *Strange Enchantment, Marriage Texas Style!* and *Impromptu Bride*; and the *Romantic Times* Lifetime Achievement Awards for Series Romance and Series Romantic Fantasy. She currently resides in Texas, and has written forty novels for Silhouette.

CHRISTINE RIMMER

has written seventeen novels for Silhouette. Her 1992 Desire, *Midsummer Madness*, was a Romance Writers of America RITA finalist, and her books consistently top the bestseller list.

Ms. Rimmer makes her home in California's Gold Country, where many of her books, including *Earth Angel* and her popular JONES GANG series, are set.

When she's not at her computer, Ms. Rimmer can be found driving her children to sports events in her '79 Seville and cheering on her husband's senior softball team.

JUSTINE DAVIS

has written almost twenty books for Silhouette. Her notable achievements include a Romance Writers of America RITA award for *Angel For Hire*, which also garnered the *Romantic Times* Reviewer's Choice Award for Best Romantic Fantasy. Ms. Davis also contributed to *Silhouette Summer Sizzlers* 1994 with "The Raider."

Ms. Davis is currently branching out into mainstream fiction with NAL/Topaz and Berkley/Jove. In addition to her writing, she works as a police officer in Newport Beach, California, where she answers the 911 line.

Help Wanted: Angel!

Annette Broadrick
Christine Rimmer
Justine Davis

Published by Silhouette Books

America's Publisher of Contemporary Romance

SILHOUETTE BOOKS

by Request

HELP WANTED—ANGEL!

Copyright © 1995 by Harlequin Books S.A.

ISBN 0-373-20118-4

The publisher acknowledges the copyright holders
of the individual works as follows:
A LOVING SPIRIT
Copyright © 1990 by Annette Broadrick
EARTH ANGEL
Copyright © 1992 by Christine Rimmer
ANGEL FOR HIRE
Copyright © 1991 by Janice Davis Smith

This edition published by arrangement with Harlequin Books S.A.

® and TM are trademarks of Harlequin Enterprises B.V., used under
license. Trademarks indicated with ® are registered in the United States
Patent and Trademark Office, the Canadian Trade Marks Office and in
other countries.

Printed in U.S.A.

CONTENTS

CONTENTS

A LOVING SPIRIT

To Michael,
wherever you are

Prologue

Jonathan had been nervous ever since he had received the summons to leave his duties and appear before Gabriel. Very few associates at Jonathan's level had ever been in Gabriel's presence. There was seldom a need for personal contact. Gabriel's communications were unfailingly clear and concise. Misunderstandings did not occur in Jonathan's dimension. That was not always the case on the earthly plane where he spent most of his time.

There were days when Jonathan became frustrated in his efforts to communicate with his charge. He had known that the position of official guide and protector to Sabrina Sheldon would not be easy, but it had certainly had its compensations.

Jonathan was besotted with Sabrina. And why not? He had been with her since shortly before her birth, thirty-six Earth years ago. He had joined her in order to prepare her for the traumatic occurrence known as birth. He had ac-

cepted the assignment with enthusiasm and pride, grateful for the faith his superiors had in him.

Now he shook his head, remembering some of the difficulties he'd had in his efforts to guide, protect and gently nudge Sabrina onto the paths that would ease her way through life. Jonathan had a hunch that his imminent meeting with Gabriel would bring to light some areas where improvement was needed. He grimaced at the thought. He wasn't looking forward to the meeting. Not at all.

"You wished to see me, sir?" he inquired.

In this dimension, time and space had no meaning. Therefore, his appearance before Gabriel was brought about by no more than the conscious thought that he needed to be there.

Brilliant light flooded the area, effectively shrouding the hallowed presence. Jonathan felt the loving energy emanating from his superior and began to relax.

"Yes, Jonathan. I've been going over the records on Sabrina Sheldon. I see that you have been assigned as her official companion throughout her life."

"Yes, sir."

"I also see that she has often disregarded your guidance and direction," offered Gabriel in a wry tone of voice.

Jonathan could not control his smile. "That's true, sir. She's quite headstrong. Likes to have her own way."

"I note that by disregarding your suggestions, she's created some rather traumatic episodes in her life, wouldn't you say?"

"Yes, sir. However, she has grown considerably as a result of those experiences," Jonathan pointed out. He tried to focus on the personage before him, but the shimmering light created such a glare that he was able to see little more than an outline of the man before him.

"Yes, I can see that," Gabriel responded.

"*I've attempted to teach her the necessity for daily contemplation and reverie, sir, so that she would be more open to suggestions.*"

"*Have you had much success?*"

"*Yes, sir, I think so...particularly now that she is older. Sabrina has accepted the consequences of her decisions and has matured quite nicely.*"

"*But a marriage so young, Jonathan? Surely you could have persuaded her to wait.*"

Jonathan shook his head. "*Oh, I tried, as did her parents. But she was determined to marry Danny Sheldon.*"

"*I see she was a mother at eighteen and widowed at twenty.*"

"*Yes, sir. However, she has done an excellent job with Jessica. In addition, she's built up a business of her own at the Lake of the Ozarks in Missouri. She has a comfortable home, a wide circle of friends, financial security...*"

"*But outside of her relationship with her daughter, fine as it may be, I see no indication that Sabrina is learning about love.*"

Jonathan could find nothing to say. Both of them knew what the record stated.

"*There's no mention of a man in her life.*"

Jonathan felt like hanging his head at that statement. Who knew better than he how little Sabrina had listened to his suggestion that she needed more balance in her present existence.

"*Is there someone in particular that you feel would help her to discover the transforming power of love?*" *Gabriel finally asked when it became obvious that Jonathan was not going to respond.*

"*Yes, sir,*" *Jonathan said with a sigh.* "*He was transferred to the lake almost three years ago, and I felt at the time that he was just what Sabrina needed in her life. He*

has all the qualities that suit him admirably to her, but..."
He shrugged, unable to find the words to express his frustration.

"She wouldn't have anything to do with him?"

"Sabrina hasn't even met him."

"Who is he?"

"Michael Donovan. Sergeant Michael J. Donovan. He's been with the Missouri State Highway Patrol for almost twenty years. He's currently working in the drug-enforcement division."

There was a pause, and Jonathan realized that Gabriel was calling up the records on Michael Donovan.

"Hmmm. Interesting man," Gabriel finally said.

"Yes."

"I agree. He would be an excellent choice for her."

Jonathan sighed. "I know. The question is . . . how do I convince her that she needs someone in her life? She shows no personal interest in anyone, even though she has a great many friends."

"What have you done to bring about a meeting between the two?"

"Sir?" Jonathan couldn't believe his ears. "What have I done? Well, nothing, sir. I have always been under the impression that we were not to interfere with that plane of existence." When Gabriel didn't respond, Jonathan went on, reciting the creed from memory. "We are to protect. We are to counsel. We are to guide. We are to instruct." He paused. "And we are never to take an active part in our chosen one's life. Otherwise their free choice is removed from them and their growth is hindered."

"I'm aware of the principles of conduct, Jonathan. I wrote them," was the ironic response. "However, a gentle nudge is never amiss."

"It isn't?"

"Surely you could arrange an accidental meeting, couldn't you?"

"I've tried. You wouldn't believe how often they've been at the post office at the same time, or the bank. They don't seem to be able to see each other, even when they pass. Their homes are within a few miles of each other. They've even passed each other while boating, but other than a friendly wave to a fellow water enthusiast there has been no contact."

"Don't they have any mutual friends who might introduce them?"

"No one. They move in different circles and have no acquaintances in common. Believe me. I've searched for a link that would put them in touch with each other, but without success."

"Study the situation some more and see what can be done. Neither of them has much time left before their next test. Their chances of passing will be greatly enhanced if they have each other's support."

"I had hoped to get an extension for Sabrina, sir."

"I'm sorry, Jonathan. That won't be possible. But I have faith in you. Surely you will come up with a feasible plan that will bring these two people together. You've done a fine job thus far. I know you won't let her down now."

Jonathan felt a surge of warm, loving energy flow around him. He closed his eyes, savoring the experience, and when he opened them once more he discovered that he was alone, except for the soft shimmering light, which seemed to linger.

With a renewed sense of understanding of his mission and a sense of urgency about accomplishing it, Jonathan rejoined Sabrina, determined to do whatever was necessary to see that she learned more about love. Before it was too late.

One

"**I**'d like to see some identification, please, ma'am," the large, shadowy figure told Sabrina, holding the beam of a flashlight on an opened leather folder that identified the speaker as Michael J. Donovan, a sergeant of the Missouri State Highway Patrol.

After hours of driving in the late-October rainstorm, Sabrina decided that this had to be the logical end to her less-than-perfect day. She'd finally arrived back at her shop at one o'clock in the morning, only to be cited for some unknown infraction of the traffic laws.

Apart from his deep voice, she could tell very little about Sergeant Michael Donovan. His wide-brimmed hat protected his face from the rain, and a heavy raincoat shielded his tall body. She could only hope his mood hadn't been adversely affected by the lateness of the hour, the storm, and whatever it was she had unintentionally done.

She fumbled for her purse, praying that this wouldn't take long. "What did I do?" she asked, in as pleasant a voice as possible, handing him her driver's license.

He glanced at it briefly and asked, "May I have your permission to search your van, Ms. Sheldon?"

His unexpected request caught her totally off guard. Search her van? She must have misunderstood. Her attempted laugh sounded hollow, even to her.

"Is this some kind of joke, officer? If one of my friends put you up to this, I'm afraid I don't find it very amusing. It's late...I'm tired...I just want—"

Sabrina wouldn't have believed that his deep voice could drop even lower. "I'm on official business, Ms. Sheldon. It would save us both a great deal of time if you'd allow me to inspect the contents of your van."

What was going on? This couldn't really be happening, could it? She was not the kind of person the police would suspect of— Suspect of what?

"Are you arresting me for something?" she demanded, her voice shaking more than she would have liked.

"I would like to search your van," he repeated doggedly, praying she wouldn't demand that he show her a search warrant. He didn't have one, damn it, because he didn't have enough evidence to obtain one. All he had was an anonymous phone call and a report that included the fact that Sabrina Sheldon made trips on a regular basis between Hot Springs, Arkansas, and her shop in Osage Beach, Missouri. Such a routine could possibly be utilized to bring drugs into the area. He couldn't afford not to follow up on the nebulous lead.

"Well. I certainly have nothing to hide." After her initial shock, Sabrina was beginning to get angry.

"Then I'm sure this won't take long," he replied, for all the world as though she had just graciously given him her permission. She had no good reason to deny him permission, of course. She knew she wasn't doing anything wrong. But it was cold and rainy and she had no desire to stand outside and get soaked while he dug through all the boxes she'd brought north with her.

"Couldn't we do this another time? I'm going to unload this in the morning, and it would be much more convenient to look through them inside my shop." She nodded toward the back door of the Crystal Unicorn.

Michael knew that he would lose the admissibility of any evidence he might find if the contents of the van were inside the building. Unless he had a search warrant. He didn't have probable cause at this point, and he knew it.

"This won't take long," he said, striding around to the back of the van.

Thank God she'd worn a water-repellent coat, Sabrina thought to herself as she flung the door open and jumped lightly to the ground. The rain immediately drenched her ponytail, and water began to drip off the wispy ends that had come loose.

She stomped around to the back of the van, unlocked the door and threw it open. Crossing her arms, she said in a seething tone, "Go ahead, then. Let's get on with it."

Standing next to her, Michael realized that she only came up to his shoulder, but her suppressed anger seemed to make her taller.

"You don't have to stand out here in the rain, ma'am." He nodded toward the front of the van. "You can wait up there if you'd like."

"No, thank you," she replied in an icy voice. "I am just as eager as you to find whatever it is you're looking for that would cause you to be out here at this time of night and in this weather." Nodding her head regally, she motioned for him to begin.

Michael smothered a smile. Based on his years as an investigative officer and his ability to judge people, he would have been willing to bet that this woman had nothing to hide. But he couldn't take any chances. The drug traffic into the lake area was too serious for him not to follow every lead, no matter how slim.

He crawled into the small space in front of the door and efficiently began to unpack each and every carton. Every once in a while he would glance out into the rain, where she stood watching him. As the minutes passed and he found nothing that looked in the least suspicious, Michael's conscience began to eat away at him.

When he finished there was absolutely no sign of any contraband hidden away in the merchandise. Making sure that he had restored each item to its proper carton, he glanced around at the woman watching him from the open door.

"If you'll open your shop door I'll get these cartons inside for you." That was the least he could do for her.

"That won't be necessary."

Michael felt his frustration mount. Hell, he was just trying to be polite. Didn't she understand that tonight was the culmination of weeks of investigation that had led him exactly nowhere? There were times when he really hated his job with the drug-enforcement unit and longed for early retirement.

Tonight was one of those times.

Rather than argue with her, he lifted several of the cartons and started toward the door. Because of their lack of weight, he decided they must have been packaged for a smaller person to carry.

What a stubborn man, Sabrina thought, realizing that he was going to have all her merchandise as soaked as she was if she didn't open the door for him.

She ran ahead of him, unlocked the door and shoved it open. Then she flipped on the lights and pointed over to the far wall. "Just put them over there." She was ashamed that she couldn't force herself to be more gracious. She spun on her heel and went back outside. If she helped they would be through that much quicker.

On her third trip out to the van she dislodged a small box that had slipped between one of the larger boxes and the side of the van, knocking it to the wet ground. She groaned, recognizing the box, and hastily piled it on top of the others that she carried in.

As soon as she set the cartons down, she put the smaller box aside intending to put it in her car, which was parked beside the van. The contents of the box had nothing to do with the shop. She decided to let him bring in the rest of the contents and went in search of a towel to dry her hair with. She quickly untied her ponytail and briskly rubbed the moisture from her hair. The humidity caused it to curl in riotous confusion until she dragged a comb through it and ruthlessly tied it back once more. At least water was no longer dripping down her neck.

Picking up the small box that Rachel had given her, Sabrina walked back into the storeroom in time to see the highway patrolman place another load of cartons in the storage room. She could not see much of his face, because he still wore his hat. However, the added light confirmed her earlier impression. He was tall, with broad shoulders and long, muscular legs. She doubted that there were many people who would willingly tangle with this man.

She sighed. What difference did it make, anyway? They'd be through unloading in a few moments, and then she could go home. She felt as though she could sleep for a week.

Michael lowered a load of boxes to the floor, then straightened. The sight of Sabrina Sheldon standing there watching him stopped him in his tracks. Nothing in his investigation had warned him of her attractiveness. The vital statistics—red hair, green eyes, five feet eight inches tall— hadn't explained how that particular combination of hair and eye color, size and shape, could come together in such a beguiling fashion. Her eyes were shadowed with fatigue, but their green glitter threw sparks, and her hair seemed to catch fire under the fluorescent illumination.

Forcing his thoughts back to the job at hand, Michael nodded and strode past her into the cold, blustery night. When he returned with the last of the boxes he turned to her and asked, "Is this everything you brought back with you?"

"Yes." Then she looked down guiltily at the package she still held . . . the one that Rachel had given her.

"What is that?"

"Nothing that would interest you," she responded sharply. Sabrina could feel the warmth in her cheeks and lamented the fair skin that quickly betrayed her whenever she was embarrassed. "Just a gift a friend gave me."

He shrugged out of his raincoat and pulled off his hat. "May I see it, please?" he asked quietly, holding out his hand.

"No!" She put the box behind her and tilted her chin. Now that he'd removed his outer clothes, Sabrina saw the man clearly for the first time, rather than the officer of the law. She blinked, startled by her reaction to him.

She had already discovered that he was tall, but seeing him this close unnerved her. When she tilted her head back to meet his gaze she looked into his silver-gray eyes for the first time. His eyes were riveting, distinctive in his deeply tanned face. Thick black hair fell across his forehead, softening his face somewhat.

Michael couldn't decide whether this woman was one of the coolest smugglers he'd ever had reason to search or whether she was innocent, but for the first time since he'd approached her van she was showing signs that could be interpreted as evidence of guilt. He hadn't found anything large enough to contain drugs in the merchandise. Even the box she clutched in her hands might only lead him to search elsewhere. However, he had no choice at this point but to continue what he had begun. He had to know whether this woman was concealing evidence or whether she was as innocent as she appeared.

He held out his hand, uncomfortably aware of how her porcelain complexion glowed in the light. Michael had a sudden, totally inappropriate urge to brush his hand against her cheek, just to verify that her skin felt as soft as it looked. Jade-green eyes glared at him as her cheeks turned crimson. Out of guilt, perhaps. Michael was surprised to discover that he hoped he'd been wrong about this woman. He didn't want her to be involved in something as sordid as drug smuggling.

The silence seemed to beat all around them as they stood there facing each other, her with defiance, him with stubborn determination.

Finally Sabrina's shoulders drooped. "Oh, this is ridiculous! Here!" She handed him the package with a mixture of anger, embarrassment and disgust, watching helplessly as he lifted the lid and brushed the tissue paper aside.

A pale green nightgown lay nestled in the soft paper. Michael could feel the heat suffuse his face. No one could smuggle much of anything in something like this. Unconsciously he slid his fingers beneath the shimmering material, verifying how revealing it would be against her body.

When he glanced up, he saw that her cheeks glowed even brighter than before.

"Very nice."

"I doubt that you've been taking up our time looking for something like that," she said. Her voice shook slightly...whether from anger or embarrassment, he didn't know.

"I apologize for any inconvenience I've caused you, Ms. Sheldon." He returned the box to her.

"Exactly what is it you thought you were going to find, Officer?"

"There's considerable trafficking in drugs here at the lake, Ms. Sheldon. Your periodic trips caught our attention. We felt we had enough reason to search you this trip."

"Drugs! You must be out of your mind. I'd have nothing to do with anything like that."

He nodded. "I'm pleased to hear that, ma'am." He almost smiled. Almost but not quite.

"How dare you search my van without a warrant of some kind."

"You gave me permission, remember?"

She hated his reasonable tone and his bland expression. She was so angry that she was shaking. How dare he treat her this way? He had no right. He had— "Do I need your permission to ask you to leave now?" she demanded.

He shook his head. "No, ma'am, you don't. Once again, I do apologize for any inconvenience I may have caused." He looked around at the cluttered storeroom, then picked up his brimmed hat and placed it on his head. Without another word, he pulled on his raincoat, nodded politely to her and disappeared into the stormy night.

Sabrina stood there in silence, watching the patrol car pull away. She could feel the tension leaving her body and the fatigue that had been lurking take over.

She couldn't remember the last time she had been so angry. How dare that man investigate her? How dare he treat her like some kind of a suspect?

And the way he had looked at the nightgown that Rachel had teasingly presented to her! She could have died of embarrassment. Did he think she actually slept in things like that? Rachel had embarrassed her enough with all her suggestions about improving her love life. Now this! Thank God she'd never see the man again. She'd never be able to face him.

Michael returned the patrol car to the station, climbed into his late-model truck and started home. While he drove, his mind continued to mull over his present investigation.

After the search and the limited contact with Sabrina Sheldon he would have been willing to place his twenty years' law enforcement experience on the line and say that she had nothing to do with the drug traffic in and around the lake.

He had dealt with a great many people involved in such activity, and he knew he could rely on his instincts. Sabrina Sheldon wasn't capable of the deception, the toughness and the cynicism that accompanied a life of illegal trafficking. Accepting that mental verdict seemed to take a load off his shoulders, and he knew he had to face the reason why.

He was attracted to the woman.

Damn. Who needed that complication in his life? Not him. Of course there had been women in his life over the past several years. He wasn't a monk, after all. But the relationships had been clearly defined from the beginning. He and his lovers had known what they expected from each other, and when the relationships had ended there had been no hard feelings or harsh regrets.

His instincts already told him that Sabrina was different. Perhaps he knew too much about her. Information gathered over the past few weeks had painted a picture of a solitary woman who appeared to be self-sufficient. At first he had interpreted her independence as toughness, but then he had seen her vulnerability, and it had called out to him for understanding and protection.

What the hell was the matter with him, anyway?

He pulled into the garage of his multilevel home overlooking the lake and turned off the ignition with a sigh. God, he was tired. Tired of the long hours, the unsatisfactory results, tired of his life-style. For some reason, that made him shift restlessly. He realized that he was tired of being alone. His restlessness stemmed from the encounter with Sabrina Sheldon.

What was she doing now? Probably still cursing him. Then she would go home, shower, maybe, or soak in a steaming tub of bubbles, then put on that filmy concoction he had seen ... and touched ... and imagined against her body.

Disgusted with his imagination and frustrated that he couldn't seem to keep her out of his mind, Michael got out of the truck and walked down the steps to his house.

His home was too large for one person, but he had known the moment the realtor had shown it to him that he had to have it. Because of his inheritance, he'd been able to afford it.

The main floor was open, with a cathedral ceiling that soared two stories. One wall was glass and revealed the ever-changing moods of the lake. A small kitchen was nestled in the corner, separated from the large expanse by an island-bar combination. Michael ate most of his meals at the bar, when he didn't carry them out to the redwood deck to better enjoy the peace and tranquillity of the water and the oak woods around him.

A massive stone fireplace covered most of the third wall, and the fourth wall supported the stairs to the loft bedroom where he slept.

He walked over to the refrigerator and stared at its contents. Nothing looked appetizing. He grabbed a bottle of beer, then closed the door. After he twisted off the cap, he took a long swallow, enjoying the sensation of the cool liquid coursing down his parched throat.

He stared out the window and watched as the rain continued to batter the glass that protected him from the elements. What a night.

He'd watched and waited for Sabrina Sheldon for over four hours, after putting in a ten-hour day. He shook his head. And for what? A chance to admire fragile glass figurines and a filmy nightgown.

He wandered over to the staircase and took the steps leading downward. Flipping on the light switch, he looked at the large game room located on the lower level and the green expanse of the pool table.

Maybe he would shoot some pool. It might help him to unwind. He picked up his cue and placed the balls in the triangular rack on the pool table. He knew he was too tired to sleep—too tired and too wired. He hadn't known what he would find or how she would react to the discovery of contraband. He never did. He'd learned to be prepared for any eventuality.

Failure to find anything had been a letdown, but it was one he was used to. Now he had to unwind and relax enough to sleep. He glanced at the wall clock. It was after two o'clock. No wonder he didn't have a social life. When would he have the time? Or the energy.

Phyllis's complaints had been valid. She'd hated his job—the long and irregular hours, his exhaustion, his lack of quality time with her and with Steve.

He leaned over and lined up a double shot, then watched as the two balls went unerringly to their pockets.

Steve.

Would he ever get over the ache in his chest whenever he thought of his son? When Phyllis had told him she was divorcing him he'd experienced the pain of losing his wife, but when she and Steve had moved to California he had been forced to face the loss of his son, as well.

Thinking about Steve would have him crying in his beer if he didn't watch it. Deliberately he returned his thoughts to the evening's events. Another lead had fizzled out. Granted, it hadn't been much of a lead, and he was glad that he hadn't found anything to connect Sabrina Sheldon with the nasty business of smuggling drugs. He would close the file tomorrow. But first he wanted a few hours of desperately needed sleep.

It took another two hours, three more beers and an uncounted number of games of one-sided pool before Michael managed to accomplish his goal.

Michael sat in his office the next morning, his feet propped on his desk, and gazed out the window.

The flatness he felt wasn't unusual. The anticlimactic feeling generally hit him at the end of an investigation, regardless of the outcome. What was unusual was the fact that he couldn't get his mind off the suspect. Or rather the ex-suspect. He'd fallen asleep the night before thinking about that damn nightgown—and how it had exactly matched the color of her eyes. He'd pictured her with her hair loose, falling onto her shoulders, the fiery tendrils contrasting with the soft green of the gown.

So he shouldn't be surprised that he'd dreamed about her. He found the impact she'd had on him downright irritating.

He caught a movement out of the corner of his eye and glanced around. Jim Payton, one of the men working with him in the drug-enforcement unit, stood in the doorway.

"Any luck last night?"

Michael shook his head. "Not a thing. She was clean."

Jim walked into the room, and sat down in the chair across the desk from Michael and placed a file on the desk. "Think someone tipped her off that you were watching for her?"

Michael leaned his head against the back of the chair and closed his eyes for a moment. "No," he finally replied. "No, I don't. She checks out as exactly what she represents herself to be—the owner of a small gift shop. There's no sign of unaccounted-for wealth. The call must have been somebody's idea of a joke. She even hinted as much last night." He rubbed his eyes, wishing he'd had more sleep.

"Alice goes into her shop every once in a while," Jim offered, referring to his wife. "Says she carries quality merchandise."

Michael nodded. "I can attest to that. I went through her entire shipment."

Jim fiddled with the file he'd placed on the desk. Michael knew he wanted to say something, but he seemed to be having trouble getting it out. Michael waited, feeling no need to pursue the topic of the moment and hoping Jim's thoughts had turned to something else.

They hadn't. "So what did you think about her?"

Michael lifted his brows slightly. "I just told you. She was clean."

"No, no. I don't mean professionally. Personally. Alice says she's quite an attractive woman."

Michael glanced out the window again. "So she is," he agreed, without looking at Jim.

"She's single."

Michael wondered if Jim would ever give up his match-making tendencies. Just because he had a happy marriage he seemed convinced that everyone needed to be married. Michael knew better.

"I'm well aware of her marital status," Michael drawled.

"You've given her a clean slate. So why don't you ask her out?"

Michael just shook his head. "You never give up, do you, Jim? I've lost count of the number of women you and Alice have dangled in front of my nose since I was transferred down here."

At least Jim had the grace to appear sheepish. "Alice worries about you, Mike."

Michael grinned. "Alice does, does she? I had no idea I held her interest to such a degree."

"You know what I mean. You're always spending your spare time working around kids. You should be raising some of your own instead of helping with everyone else's."

Michael dropped his feet to the floor and stood. He walked over and refilled his empty cup with coffee. "You're wrong, Jim. Dead wrong. I made a lousy father. I sure as hell wouldn't inflict myself on some other innocent youngster."

Jim heard the pain in Mike's voice and knew that he was pushing the limits of their friendship. But, damn, he found the man frustrating at times.

Donovan would let very few people get close to him. Oh, he was great working with groups, professionally or as a volunteer. But very few people ever got to know the real person.

He was one of the best investigative officers Jim had ever worked with, and Jim admired him tremendously. He just wished he wasn't so damned stubborn. But Jim knew when to back off.

Jim straightened the papers in the file in front of him and, without glancing around, said, "I was wondering if you would be able to help me on this case I'm working on? I have a couple of theories I'd like to run past you."

Michael returned to his chair and sat down, looking relaxed and at ease. Jim knew the look was deceptive. He eyed his friend uncertainly.

"Sure," Michael responded with a nod. "What have you got?"

Within minutes both men were absorbed in their work. Michael's personal life was not open to discussion.

Two

Sabrina didn't get to her shop until almost noon the next morning. Unfortunately, the extra hours in bed hadn't contributed much in the way of rest. As soon as she appeared in the doorway of the store her assistant, Pamela Preston, swooped down on her.

"Hi, boss lady. Boy, were you ever energetic yesterday! I never expected you to unload when you got home last night. What gives?"

Sabrina almost groaned aloud at the realization that the cause of her restless night was going to become a major part of her conversation today. She stalled for time, slipping off her jacket and carefully hanging it in the storeroom before she faced her inquisitive friend and employee.

"Actually, it wasn't my idea to unload the van at one o'clock in the morning," she admitted ruefully. She glanced around the shop, trying to decide where to begin with her various tasks and hoping against hope that Pam would let the subject drop.

She should have known better.

Pam cocked her head, looking for all the world like a curious bird, her black eyes bright with curiosity. "What happened?"

Sabrina straightened her shoulders into a quasi-military stance and said in a solemn voice, "The long arm of the law finally caught up with me." Then, throwing her arms out in a dramatic gesture, she exclaimed. "The secret's out. My smuggling days are over."

Pam's eyes seemed to enlarge with each word. "What? What are you talking about?"

Sabrina grinned and turned away, shrugging. "I'm still not certain that I understand, but somehow my bringing a vanload of merchandise from Arkansas seemed suspicious enough to the state highway patrol to warrant a search of all the contents of the van last night."

She disappeared into the back room and returned carrying an armload of individually boxed merchandise. Surely Pam had all the information she needed. Sabrina didn't want to talk about her last night's activities. She didn't want to think about them. All she wanted was to forget everything that had happened.

No such luck.

"You're kidding me."

Sabrina set the boxes down on the counter and began to carefully unwrap the contents. Without looking up, she muttered. "Why would I kid you about something like that?"

Pam hooted. "You? A smuggler? Don't make me laugh."

Sabrina glanced up and grinned, appreciating Pam's unswerving loyalty. "Thanks for the character reference. Who knows? I may need one yet."

Sabrina started back into the storeroom with Pam on her heels, firing questions. When she started her return trip, she paused and looked at Pam. Why had she thought that Pam would drop the subject before she had milked every possible ounce of gossip from the situation? Holding up her hands, she said with a chuckle, "Look, if you're going to dog my every step you could at least carry some of these in at the same time."

Sheepishly Pam scooped up a few of the small boxes and hurried into the display room. "Tell me everything that happened," she demanded.

Resigned, Sabrina recited the details that had haunted her dreams the night before.

"Did he find anything?" she asked when Sabrina finished.

Sabrina rested her hand on her hip. "Of course he found something—a bunch of glass and crystal figurines, wood carvings and folk art. He didn't seem particularly enamored with any of it, though. Maybe he isn't the artistic type." She continued unpacking and arranging the shelves, humming under her breath.

"Are those things illegal, do you suppose?"

Sabrina took a soft cloth and carefully wiped the lint from a tiny glass hummingbird. "If they were," she responded, making a face, "I would probably be in jail by now."

Pam unfolded and stored the empty boxes beneath the counter for use when the merchandise was sold. "Did he ever say what he was looking for?"

"Drugs."

"Drugs? You mean he thinks you might be involved in— Why, of all the nerve. Why would anyone think such a ridiculous thing?"

"Who knows? He said that the regular trips I make back and forth between here and Arkansas would give me the opportunity to smuggle drugs."

"I hope you told him what you thought about the idea."

"Don't worry, I did." Sabrina shook her head. "The most embarrassing part of the whole episode was his insistence on searching the box containing Rachel's gift to me." Sabrina still squirmed at the memory.

"Which was?"

"Rachel's idea of a joke. She presented me with a very provocative, very sheer nightgown, and Sergeant Donovan insisted on inspecting that particular piece of evidence very carefully, as well."

Pam's amused expression changed to surprise. "Did you say Donovan? As in Michael Donovan?"

There was something in Pam's voice that made Sabrina look up from what she was doing. "I don't remember. To be honest, I was so nervous I may not have gotten any of his name correctly. Why? Do you think you know him?"

"Was he tall, with black hair and a build that causes women to gnaw on their knuckles when he walks by and a smile to die for?"

Sabrina laughed. She certainly didn't recognize the description. "Well, he was tall," she replied, "but I never saw a smile of any kind."

Pam gazed thoughtfully out the large display window. "There can't be two Michael Donovans in this area. Now that I think about it, Tommy did say something about his coach being a policeman."

Sabrina knew that Tommy was Pam's youngest child. "His coach?"

"Little League. Tommy developed a strong case of hero-worship last summer. Mike Donovan is quite good with kids. I really enjoyed watching him work with them. He's patient and lavish with his praise and encouragement." Pam looked back at Sabrina with a mischievous grin. "You should have seen how the attendance at the games increased when he took ⁄er coaching—older sisters of the players, single mothers . . . he developed quite a following that never missed one of his team's games."

Sabrina concentrated on carefully placing the new items to their best advantage. When she didn't say anything, Pam prompted her with "So what did you think?"

Sounding preoccupied, Sabrina murmured, "About what?"

"About Mike! Isn't he gorgeous? Weren't you impressed?"

Sabrina took her time responding. She didn't want to admit what an impact the man had made on her. "I'd just like to know why he was so suspicious of me. Surely I'm not the only person around who travels on a regular basis."

Pam thought about the question for a moment, but she couldn't seem to find an answer, either. "Maybe it was just a routine check."

"No." Sabrina was certain about that, anyway. He had been waiting for her—had, in fact, followed her the last few miles to the shop, now that she thought about it.

Pam grinned. "Maybe it was an excuse to meet you."

"Very funny." She disappeared into the back room.

Pam followed her. "Well, what's so strange about that? Men are always trying to find excuses to see you, and you know it."

Sabrina just laughed, refusing to dignify Pam's remark with a response.

A lack of response had never stopped Pam before, and it didn't this time, either. "I just don't understand you, I really don't. You're involved with so many things, but you never take time out for yourself. Why, your personal life is practically nonexistent."

Sabrina handed her a stack of boxes, and Pam continued, undeterred. "You're young, and more than just attractive. You're—"

Sabrina brushed past her. "Perfectly content with my life, thank you, Pamela. I enjoy my life very much. I'm not looking for complications."

"I'll say. The most exciting thing that's happened to you lately was having Jessica's college roommate mistake you for Jessica's sister. You glowed for days!"

Sabrina chuckled at the dig. "You're right. I'm the first to admit that my life may appear dull to others. But I'm content. That's all that matters to me."

"I just hate to see you waste your entire life because of one man," Pam said vehemently.

The room echoed in silence.

The problem with having a close friend was that eventually you told them more than they needed to know about you, Sabrina decided. Then they had the audacity to use the information against you. For your own good, of course.

Pam plowed on. "I know you don't like talking about Danny, but face it, you've allowed him to mess up your entire life."

"What nonsense. Danny's been dead for sixteen years. I've certainly managed to put the past behind me after all this time."

They both carefully unwrapped glass figurines and set them on the counter.

"Except that you insist on keeping every man you meet in the friendship category. You won't even consider the possibility of another marriage," Pam pointed out.

Sabrina smiled, trying to hide her frustration at the turn the conversation had taken. "You probably haven't noticed, but there hasn't been a line of men queuing up at my door with proposals, either. None of that has anything to do with Danny, you know. We were just a couple of kids back then. I'm not the same person who fell in love with Danny."

Pam had heard that before. "Yes. I remember what you told me about him. He drew your attention because he was so different from all the other boys you'd dated. He was wild, exuberant, a maverick, a rebel—and you found him exciting."

Sabrina paused, gazing unseeingly before her. "He would have settled down eventually. I know he would have. We were both too young for the responsibilities of marriage."

Pam drummed her fingers on the counter. "Maybe so. But the point I'm making is that you've allowed one painful experience to keep you from trying again."

"I had a child to raise, that's all. I was a child myself, in many ways. I didn't have time for another relationship."

"Fine. So you should have won Mother of the Year eight years in a row or something. But what about now? You've been absolutely miserable since Jessica went off to college. You devoted your entire life to her. Now your life's empty."

Sabrina turned and looked at her assistant. Leaning her hip against the counter, she crossed her arms and asked, "Is this conversation supposed to be cheering me up? Because if it is, I must tell you that I managed to miss your uplifting message."

Pam chuckled. "All I'm saying is that your life doesn't have to be empty, boss lady. Now's the time to get involved with someone again. Learn to enjoy yourself."

"I do enjoy myself. I'm involved in all sorts of activities."

Pam gave an unladylike snort. "Business activities, you mean."

"Well, since I'm a businessperson, that makes a lot of sense to me."

"But what do you do for fun?"

"I've worked with the Lake Area Performing Arts Guild ever since I moved here. That certainly takes up any extra time I might have."

Pam just shook her head. "You don't see it, do you? You're so busy rushing around looking after everybody else that you don't do anything to look after you. You've carried the nurturing process to the whole blamed area. But who looks after you?"

"I don't need anyone to look after me. I'm just fine."

"Of course you are. And your acting abilities were never more evident than when Jessica called from college the other day. Real Oscar material, you are. You almost made me believe that having her away from home hadn't affected you much at all."

Sabrina could feel herself flushing. "I don't want her worrying about me. Of course there's going to be an adjustment at first, living alone after all these years. But I'm doing fine. Really I am."

Pam tilted her head and looked at her doubtfully. "If you say so."

Sabrina threw up her hands. "All right. I give in. The next time Sergeant Donovan decides to search my van I will insist that he invite me out on a date. How's that?"

Pam laughed. "Now that I would like to see."

Sabrina picked up some of the Styrofoam packing that was lying on the counter and threw it at Pam, causing her to duck. Pam finally allowed the subject to drop, for which Sabrina was profoundly grateful.

Later that evening, as she was getting ready for bed, Sabrina reluctantly recalled their conversation. She couldn't fault the logic of Pam's argument. She just didn't know how to explain to Pam that it was fear that kept her from forming any but the most casual of relationships with men. She felt uneasy, because she had so little experience in relating to a man. It was as though she had stopped developing socially when she was a teenager. As soon as she met a man she knew was single, she could feel herself tensing, becoming stiff and formal, unable to relax and chat as she did with her women friends.

She'd learned how to be a mother through trial and error, eventually becoming comfortable with the role. She felt too old now to learn how to relate to an adult male. Even the thought of attempting to socialize and date filled her with a horrible sense of inadequacy.

No. She was content with her safe life, she decided as she crawled into bed and turned off the light. She had lots of friends, and she felt safe socializing in groups. She saw no reason to make any changes in her life.

Lying there in the dark, she could secretly agree with Pam that Michael Donovan was extremely attractive, even when he was being stern and starkly professional. Surely he had missed his calling. With his dark good looks, Sergeant Donovan should have been on some television series—*Men in Blue* or something.

So what if she had found him attractive? She wouldn't have the foggiest idea how to relax around a man like that.

She would end up a nervous wreck or—worse—she'd end up making a complete fool of herself.

As long as she was being honest with herself, Sabrina had to admit that perhaps Pam had a point about Danny, as well. She had loved him, and the pain that loving him had caused her had been more than she could cope with as a teenager. When he had died she had packed up all her feelings along with Danny's few belongings. She had returned most of his possessions to his family, except for a few things that she saved for Jessica. Her love she'd stored carefully away inside herself, afraid to offer it to anyone besides Jessica.

Sabrina turned on her side and curled into her pillow. Her present life was safe. She intended to keep it that way.

By Saturday Sabrina had distanced herself from the events of Sunday night. Following her weekly routine, she set out for the post office, the bank and the grocery store, wishing she hadn't overslept. Now she found herself rushing in order to make up some time.

As soon as she pulled into the post office parking lot she slipped out of her car and dashed to the entrance of the neat brick building. Just as she reached for the inner glass door, it moved away from her. Glancing up, she saw a pair of silver-glinting eyes in a darkly tanned face, thick black hair liberally sprinkled with gray and a frankly fascinating smile. White teeth flashed, and she heard the words "Good morning, Ms. Sheldon." It was as though they were coming from a great distance.

This dazzling specimen of manhood knew her? She quickly scanned downward, taking in the tan leather bomber jacket. the faded jeans that testified to the excellent physical condition of the wearer, down to a pair of scuffed but comfortable-looking boots. Numbly her gaze retraced its path, more slowly now, as though to make sure she hadn't missed anything vital.

The woman standing before Michael was a far cry from the pale and obviously tired female he had seen a few nights before, but he had no trouble recognizing her. None at all. He took his time inspecting her in the light of day. He definitely liked what he saw.

She wore a moss-green suede jacket and skirt, with matching pumps and a pale pink blouse peeking over the collar. Her hair was no longer tied back. Instead, it fell in waves around her face and onto her shoulders in a casual look that he found extremely enticing. Michael could almost feel his fingers twitching, eager to touch the fiery cascade of color...wondering if they would be singed...knowing it might be worth it.

When his gaze finally met hers, he was delighted to observe the heightened color in her cheeks. She was not unaware of him, either, if her flushed expression was any indication. Feeling more than a little overheated himself, Michael was pleased to know that his reaction was not totally one-sided.

Somebody brushed against his shoulder with a murmured apology, and Michael realized that he was blocking the door to the post office. He stepped back, holding it wider and waving Sabrina through with a flourish.

She nodded a little uncertainly. "Thank you."

Sabrina took several steps toward her post office box before she realized who the man at the door was. She spun around, but he was nowhere in sight.

Michael Donovan! The highway patrolman! Pam had been right. He had a devastating smile, but that was just part of his attractiveness. She had found him appealing in his uniform, but the leather jacket he wore this morning emphasized his broad shoulders to a distracting degree.

And those jeans! They should be outlawed in the name of decency.

However, it was the unexpected charm of his smile that lingered in her mind, causing her to fumble for her box key and drop several pieces of mail as she emptied her mailbox. Sabrina shook her head, trying to clear it. His potent smile dazzled and distracted her, making her feel like some easily impressed adolescent.

How out of character it was for her to act this way. Jessica was the one who noticed and pointed out good-looking men.

When Sabrina returned to her car, she was astounded to note that her hands were trembling slightly. What in the world was wrong with her? Hadn't she ever seen a handsome man before? One who spoke to her, calling her by name in a deep, velvety voice? One who smiled at her as though he found her the most attractive woman in his life?

Come to think of it... no, she hadn't. And she was more than a little uncomfortable with the turmoil that their recent encounter had produced inside her. She was no giggling teenager who was routinely infatuated. She was a mature woman, with a grown daughter. Was she going to allow her irrational reaction to a strange man throw her? Of course she wasn't. She had just been a little on edge lately, that was all. Maybe a little more emotional than usual.

Feeling somewhat more calm after the lecture she had given herself, Sabrina backed out of the parking lot and continued her errands. She turned in at the bank and pulled into a parking space next to a late-model pickup truck. As she started toward the door, Sabrina began to search for her checkbook in the depths of her purse; she didn't see the man coming out of the bank until she ran into him.

The impact was strong enough that she would have fallen if his quick thinking hadn't saved her. He grabbed her shoulders and steadied her, but her open purse went flying, strewing its personal contents along the sidewalk and in the grass.

Sabrina felt jarred by the impact against a leather-clad chest, and what little breath she managed to save escaped her when she glanced up into the laughing face of the man who held her in his arms.

Thoughts of apologizing for not having seen him flew out of her head when she recognized the man who held her. She had never felt so flustered in her life. Thoroughly rattled, she was mortified to hear herself blurt out. "Are you by any chance following me?" Without waiting for a response to her ridiculous question, Sabrina pulled away from him and knelt to pick up the scattered contents of her purse.

Michael obligingly knelt down beside her and handed her a set of keys, a lipstick, a comb and a half-eaten candy bar. Although he had carefully removed the smile from his lips, his eyes danced with amusement.

"How could I be following you, Ms. Sheldon? I was at the post office and the bank first. If anyone is following someone—" He paused, handing her a ticket stub, two grocery receipts, a compact and a tiny perfume atomizer, tactfully not finishing his sentence.

Sabrina had a fleeting thought about an unjust universe that did not allow a person to dematerialize on demand. She even considered the advantages of fainting or dropping dead. However, she had to admit that facing the humiliation of explaining her asinine comment was preferable to meeting her Maker at this stage of her life.

Or so she tried to convince herself.

"I'm sorry," she muttered. "That was a stupid thing to say, I wasn't looking where I was going, and—"

He waited, but when she didn't go any further with her explanation he asked, in a voice that seemed to affect her in ways she couldn't begin to understand at the moment. "Are you hurt?"

She pushed her hair out of her eyes, wishing she had taken the time to pin it up this morning, and looked over at him. They were still kneeling facing each other, only inches apart. She could see herself reflected in his clear silver-gray eyes. Absently placing her retrieved items into her purse, she could only continue to stare into his eyes and shake her head, unable to find her voice.

"That's good," he said, coming to his feet and lifting her, as well. He glanced around as though aware for the first time where they were. "Say, why don't we go across the street and have a cup of coffee? We seem to be on the same schedule today anyway." The smile he gave her almost caused her knees to buckle. "It would probably be safer for everyone concerned if we went together."

Sabrina panicked at the thought of spending any more time with this man. There was no telling what she might blurt out in her rattled condition.

"Oh, no, I can't," she replied, shaking her head vigorously. "I'm sorry, uh, really, but, you see, I'm already running late. I still have to go to the grocery store, and—" She paused as she caught a subtle change of expression on his face. An uncomfortable suspicion about the possible reason for this change caused her to sigh and ask, "I suppose you're going to the grocery store next, right?"

He nodded, trying hard not to smile. She could tell that he was having a difficult time, but she strove to ignore the grin that threatened to overtake him. She glanced up the street to the modern supermarket that had been built at the lake two years before. "Over there?" She was beginning to feel resigned. He nodded once again, chewing on his bottom lip, which kept insisting on curling upward into a smile.

She glanced at the bank, then back at him. "Look, I'll probably be in here for several minutes. That should give you plenty of time to get across the street and park. I promise not to pick the same aisle as you, okay?" She smiled brightly, secretly wishing that the man would refrain from looking at her as though she were a lovable but slightly backward child.

"What's wrong with a cup of coffee?" he asked patiently. "It wouldn't take that long or make such a difference in your plans for the day, would it?"

"I really can't—" she stammered. "I'm running so far behind already, and Pam—uh, that's my assistant—well, she's, uh, expecting me to relieve her, and—" Why was she blithering on like this? Her brain seemed to have melted into a blob of inert material.

His expression changed, and once again she was looking at the polite, aloof police officer she had first met. With a distinct pang, Sabrina realized that she missed the teasing, warm and very charismatic man whose smile had affected her so strongly. Too late she recognized that her cowardly behavior was depriving her of an opportunity to get to know this intriguing man. No doubt she would regret her behavior even more at a later date, but at the moment she just had an overwhelming desire to escape. She forced her stiff lips into the semblance of a smile. "Thanks, anyway," she managed to get out before she spun around and headed toward the bank and safety of sorts.

Michael watched her disappear inside before he turned toward his truck. Well, she couldn't make it any clearer than that. He knew his approach was less than polished, but she had acted almost afraid of him.

Perhaps it was just as well. Since he had met her the other night, Sabrina Sheldon had managed to become something of a distraction in his life. Now that he had a flesh-and-blood person to go with all the data he'd turned up during his investigation, he found himself unable to concentrate on anything else for very long. He'd be thinking about a problem at work and remember a piece of information he had learned about her.

He would lie in bed at night thinking about her. He felt as though he could almost drown in the green depths of her eyes, go up in flames from fiery contact with her hair, and now that he had come into brief contact with her body he knew that having her in his arms could easily turn him into a stammering schoolboy.

Michael climbed into the cab of his truck. He knew he should be grateful for her lack of interest in him. The emotions she had already stirred in him could create a turmoil in his life that he didn't need.

Let's face it, Donovan. The lady made her intentions clear. She isn't interested.

He pulled onto the highway and headed toward the grocery store. Despite that morning's encounters, there was no reason to think they would ever see each other again. Michael tried hard to convince himself that this was no big loss in his life. No doubt sooner or later he would believe it.

Three

———

"*I just don't understand it. I thought that once they met, felt the obvious attraction, saw how perfectly they suit each other, my work would be done. I thought nature would take its course. I thought—*"

"*Jonathan, old boy. You're talking to yourself. Not a good sign, you know.*"

"*Oh, hello, Harry.*"

"*Something bothering you?*"

"*I'm obviously not the person to be doing my present job. I don't know anything about matchmaking.*"

"*That's no problem, is it? There are always seminars going on around here on any subject. Why don't you sign up for one on matchmaking?*"

"*I don't think even that would help me at this point.*"

"*What seems to be the problem?*"

"*Sabrina shows no interest in forming a relationship, and a relationship is exactly what she needs in her life right now.*"

In fact, it's imperative. I managed to have her meet a man who would be perfect for her, if she would just allow herself the chance to get to know him.''

"And what happened?"

"Nothing! Not a thing. They keep walking away from every encounter with no intention of seeing each other again. I just don't understand human beings."

"Well, chemistry is a funny thing, Jonathan. It's hard to predict."

"But according to all my data their chemistry is exactly as it should be. She's just refusing to deal with what her sensory perceptions are telling her. She's going to ignore the whole situation!"

"How did he respond to her?"

"The way a well-adjusted red-blooded male would respond to an attractive female. He was already fantasizing about taking her to bed!"

"Well, I suppose that's a start."

"Not really. Well-adjusted males do that all the time, I understand. Doesn't necessarily mean a thing."

"So now what are you going to do?"

"I don't know. I just don't know."

"What does his guide say about the matter?"

Jonathan felt the jolt of surprise hit him. "But of course! I never thought about contacting Michael's protector. Thank you, Harry. You've been a real help!"

Harry looked at his friend in amusement. "Don't mention it."

But Jonathan didn't hear him. He was already looking for Michael's guide.

"Excuse me, I understand that you're known as Daniel and that you've been working with Michael Donovan."

"That's right."

"*I was hoping that we could work on a little project to-gether.*"

"*Project?*"

"*Yes. I'm Sabrina Sheldon's guide.*"

"*I see.*"

"*I've been trying to get Michael and Sabrina together.*"

"*Yes, I've noticed.*"

"*But I haven't been having too much luck.*"

"*Michael's been alone for several years now. I've done what I could to get him interested in a more balance   xis-tence, but he's never responded to my suggestions,*" Dan-iel pointed out.

Jonathan sighed. "*Another stubborn one. And I thought they would be so good for each other.*"

"*Yes. I must admit that I was encouraged by Michael's interest in Sabrina. Unfortunately, she's giving him no en-couragement.*"

"*I know,*" *groaned Jonathan.* "*It's enough to make me wish for another assignment at times.*" *He glanced at his companion.* "*Only kidding,*" *he added quickly.* "*Do you suppose that if we worked together we might be successful in bringing these two together?*"

"*Perhaps. It would certainly be worth a try. What do you have in mind?*"

"*That's the problem. I've exhausted most of my ideas. I was hoping you'd have one or two we could use.*"

Daniel was quiet for some time. "*We need to make sure that they keep running into each other.*" *He smiled.* "*I don't necessarily mean literally, of course.*"

"*I suppose, but I'm beginning to think that continuing to have them see each other in passing isn't going to fur-ther their relationship much.*"

"Perhaps he could do something that would make her grateful to him, that would be a great first step, don't you think?" Daniel asked.

"At this point, I'm afraid to hazard a guess. If they would just relax and get acquainted I know that they would eventually recognize how much they have in common."

"Michael's so used to being alone that I'm not sure he's going to risk being rejected again. It's a very painful experience, you know," Daniel pointed out.

"Yes. Sabrina went through some traumatic rejection, too."

"It makes them afraid to try again."

"Yes."

"But perhaps if both of us keep nudging them toward each other they will give a relationship a chance," Daniel offered. *"With both of us working on the project, I'm certain we'll be able to come up with a solution."*

"I hope so. I sincerely hope so. I'm getting close to being discouraged with the whole idea."

"We can do it. I'm sure of it."

Jonathan felt a little better, knowing that he would have some assistance. With renewed enthusiasm, he returned to Sabrina.

Sunday morning Sabrina came awake with a start, then lay staring at the ceiling in dismay. What had she been dreaming about that still seemed to be affecting her?

A pair of silver-gray eyes filled her inner vision with their steady gaze. Thick black hair tipped with gray beckoned to her, as though coaxing her fingers to thread themselves through it, to luxuriate in the tactile sensations of silky strands curling around them.

What was the matter with her? She had dreamed some stupid dream that she couldn't shake, that was all. During the past several months her sleep had been disturbed more than once by dreams that had quickly faded as soon as she awakened.

Glancing at the clock, Sabrina discovered that she had slept past ten, and she was on her feet before she remembered that today was Sunday. The shop was closed today. She sank down on the side of the bed and closed her eyes. That damn dream had unnerved her. It had seemed so real, the man so familiar.

What man? Who would she be dreaming of, who would she be so intimately, so passionately, so— Her eyes flew open. Oh, no! She had dreamed about *him*! She refused to think his name, as though he would then seem less real to her.

So why would she dream such an embarrassingly erotic dream about a man she had barely spoken to during two rather brief encounters?

"Whose fault is that, may I ask? You never gave the man a chance!"

"A chance! What do you mean, a chance? A chance to do what?" Sabrina wasn't aware that she spoke out loud.

"A chance to get acquainted. If you would relax and allow yourself to get to know him, you might discover the two of you have a great deal in common."

"Says who?"

"Says me!"

"But you're just my imagination, and I refuse to debate the issue with you."

"!?"

She continued bickering with Jonathan while she showered.

"It's Sunday. Why don't you treat yourself to brunch at one of the local restaurants?"

Sabrina paused in the midst of reaching for the coffee canister. Now where had that idea come from? She rarely went out to eat—especially on a Sunday.

Now that she thought about it, however, she found the idea appealing. Jessica was no longer home, and there was no reason to continue to follow their old routine.

Pam was right. She needed to get out more. She needed to enjoy life. Have some fun. A quiet Sunday brunch might be a tame beginning, but it *was* a beginning.

With a newfound determination, Sabrina returned upstairs to dress. When she stepped in front of the mirror, she was surprised to see a smile of anticipation on her face.

Her smile was conspicuously absent a short while later, when she was only a few miles from home, following the winding lake road that led to the main highway.

Sabrina had no idea where the deer came from. Perhaps she had been paying more attention to the passing scenery than to the familiar drive. Whatever the reason, the consequences were startling. As soon as she saw the large buck standing in the center of the roadway, she twisted the steering wheel sharply and slammed on her brakes. No doubt as startled by her sudden appearance as she was by his, the deer spun away, bounding neatly into the surrounding woods.

Headed in the other direction, the car finally came to a shuddering stop after plunging down a shallow embankment and delicately resting its front bumper against a slender sapling. Sabrina rested her head against the steering wheel, somewhat dazed by how quickly everything had happened.

When Michael came along and saw the car in the ditch, he automatically slowed down to offer his assistance. He was on his way home after having picked up the Sunday paper.

He pulled up and parked across the road from the car, trying to remember where he had seen it before. Nothing came to mind until Sabrina raised her head from the steering wheel and turned to look at whoever was approaching her car.

Michael felt as though he'd been slammed in the chest with a fist when he saw her pale face with its strained expression. Sabrina! He ran across the remainder of the way and tore open the door of her car.

Crouching in the doorway, he asked, "What happened? Are you hurt?" He reached out and ran his hand across her forehead and along her cheek in a light caress.

She fumbled for her seat belt. "I'm okay, I think," she mumbled, disgusted to hear her voice shaking. She swung her legs around to get out of the car and found Michael still blocking her way, although he had come to his feet.

"Are you sure you feel like moving? You may be injured and don't know it."

She smiled and slowly came to her feet. Since Michael hadn't moved, they were standing only a few inches apart. It felt very natural to both of them when he put his arms around her.

"I'm afraid the only injury is to my pride," she admitted. "I feel like such a fool."

"What happened?"

"When I came around the curve—" she nodded toward the road "—there was a deer standing in the middle of the road. Like a novice driver, I overreacted and jerked the wheel." She glanced around at the car. "I hope I didn't damage the car."

Michael didn't want to let go of her to find out what sort of damage might have occurred. The thought of what might have happened to her made his knees weak. Had she hit the deer, it could have been thrown into the windshield.

In his years of working state highways he'd investigated his share of bad accidents involving animals that had wandered onto public roadways.

He ran his hand down the slight indentation of her spine. She wore a light jacket that he pushed aside impatiently so that his hands slid around her waist, across her silky blouse, until they met at her back. The smooth material assisted the glide of his fingers as he reassured himself that she was all right.

Sabrina suddenly recognized that she was perilously close to allowing her head to rest on his broad, sweatshirt-covered chest. She wavered, longing for the comfort. Then her dream suddenly flashed into her mind, and she remembered some of the rather explicit things she had done with this man ... and to him! She almost flinched with embarrassment. Within hours after dreaming that frankly erotic dream, here she was throwing herself into his arms!

Sabrina stiffened, bringing her hands up to rest against his chest. What a mistake that was! She could feel the steady rhythm of his heart beating beneath the palm of her hand. Her other hand—without the slightest encouragement from her brain—smoothed the sweatshirt that covered the hard muscles of his chest. When she realized what she was doing, Sabrina jerked both hands away from him as though she had been scorched. That was exactly the way she felt.

Michael stepped back, devoutly wishing he hadn't worn such embarrassingly tight jeans. They did nothing to conceal his reaction to her. He turned away, hoping she hadn't noticed, and walked to the front of her car. Kneeling, he checked the undercarriage, then reluctantly returned to his feet, making sure the car concealed the lower half of his body.

"I don't see any damage. You may have picked up some tall grass and weeds. You probably weren't moving very fast."

"No, thank God." She looked around, only now recognizing that no other traffic had gone by. "I suppose I'd better see about getting out of here."

He heard the doubt in her voice and guessed that she didn't have much experience with off-road driving. "Would you like me to move it for you?"

He saw the quick look of relief on her face. "Thank you. I'd appreciate it." Sabrina stepped aside and allowed him to crawl behind the wheel of her car. The car seemed to shrink once he was inside, and she watched as he adjusted the seat to accommodate his longer legs.

Sabrina walked toward his truck to make sure she was out of his way. She watched him maneuver her car with a skill she envied until he had it out of the ditch. He parked it across the road from his truck, then got out, carrying her keys, and walked toward her. His boyish grin made her catch her breath. He looked so darned pleased with himself.

She held out her hand for the keys, but instead of handing them to her he asked. "Have you had lunch yet?"

She shook her head. "I haven't had breakfast, as far as that goes. I was going to the Lodge for Sunday brunch before I took my detour."

He glanced down at the keys, as though they might give him some vital information. When he raised his head she noticed the color in his tanned face had deepened, giving it a ruddy glow.

"Would you mind if I joined you? I, uh, really get tired of eating alone."

Although his tone couldn't have sounded more casual, Sabrina noticed that he seemed to be holding his breath, as if he were afraid of her answer.

She knew what she needed to say. There was no future in their seeing each other. Besides, she found him entirely too attractive. Her heart had already forgotten its normally steady beat, just at the thought of spending more time with him.

But how could she say no? Her eyes searched his, wondering if she could explain that she didn't know the first thing about dating. His steady gaze seemed to fill with light as he watched her, waiting, and she felt mesmerized by the glow.

"All right," she finally responded, her voice breaking between the two words. She hastily cleared her throat.

His pleasure at her positive response quickly covered his surprise. "Say, that's great! I'll follow you over there, okay?" He handed her the keys as though he were presenting her with a medal.

His enthusiasm flustered her. Ducking her head slightly, she walked to the car, hoping she didn't look as self-conscious as she felt.

Michael waited until she drove off before he got into the cab of his truck. Then he carefully turned around in the narrow roadway and followed her. Reaching over to the dashboard to adjust the volume of the radio, he discovered a slight tremor in his hand. My God, he couldn't remember the last time he'd been this nervous.

Sabrina Sheldon was going to have a meal with him, that was all. This was just a casual, accidental meeting. Look at him—dressed in old jeans and boots, wearing one of his oldest sweatshirts. She looked wonderful in her short jacket and tailored slacks. The trim fit of the pants had lovingly revealed the line of her curvaceous backside when she'd walked away from him.

He followed her toward town, pleased that he had thought up the idea of eating together. No matter what he tried to tell himself, he wanted this woman to be a part of his life. Michael was smiling to himself when he pulled into the parking lot behind her. After finding a parking space, he started toward Sabrina, who stood waiting for him near her car.

She turned her head, watching him approach, her expression hidden by sunglasses. Michael felt a sudden charge of energy run through him, like a bolt of electricity. Damned if he didn't seem to suffer the same reaction every time he saw her: his mouth went dry and his heartbeat seemed to triple.

There was something about the way she stood there, patiently waiting for him—the tilt of her head, the curve of her cheek, the soft wisps of hair fluttering around her face. He had a sudden feeling of having experienced this same scene many times before—walking toward her, returning to her, always knowing that she was there waiting for him. He wondered if he was losing his mind.

Sabrina waited for Michael to join her while she concentrated on hanging on to her composure. She wished she could understand her reaction to this particular man. Her heart and stomach seemed determined to change places with each other, and she was having difficulty taking a deep breath. What was it about Michael Donovan that created such an intense reaction within her?

Watching him cross the wide expanse of parking lot toward her, Sabrina thought of a sleek jungle cat padding soundlessly through its natural habitat—stalking its prey. She had a hunch he would be merciless in his quest. He was probably very good at what he did for a living.

He's probably very good at everything he does, her traitorous mind offered, just as he reached her side.

"I hope you're hungry," he said with a grin. "They serve a great buffet here." He guided her toward the front door of the restaurant by placing his hand lightly against the small of her back. "I seem to have worked up quite an appetite," he murmured in her ear as he opened the door for her.

Sabrina hoped he didn't expect a reply to that last remark, because her tongue had suddenly gone numb.

The restaurant was crowded, and they were asked to wait in line to be seated. She was aware of his presence close behind her and knew that if she were to lean slightly backward she would be resting against him.

A man coming out of the dining room with a group of people recognized Michael and waved, calling him by name. Michael acknowledged the greeting, and the deep sound of his voice reverberated through her body. She stared straight ahead, praying to be seated so that at least they would have the width of a table between them.

Another group of people entered, and the resulting jostling for room pushed Michael solidly against her. He chuckled, and she felt his breath against her ear. With a nonchalance she envied, he placed his hands on each side of her waist, as though to balance them both.

Her prayers for a little more space were answered when the hostess appeared before them and led them to a small table near one of the large windows. Sabrina sat down with a quick sigh of relief. Then she looked up and realized that he was watching her intently.

She brushed her hand self-consciously across her cheek. "What's wrong?"

He shook his head and smiled. "Not a thing. I suppose I was just wondering why I've never seen you before this week, since we seem to lead a similar life-style."

"Maybe you have."

"I don't think so. I'm sure I would have remembered." His gaze seemed to wander over her features, as though memorizing each and every one.

The implied compliment did nothing to steady her nerves. She glanced around, searching for another topic. "Perhaps we should get in line at the buffet. What do you think?"

He looked over at the laden table and the line beside it. "I suppose you're right," Michael stood and held out his hand to her. The gesture was so natural that she took his hand before she realized what she was doing, then allowed him to lead her over to the line that had formed in front of the buffet.

"Do you come here often?" he asked.

"This is my first time."

"Oh, I stop in every once in a while. I get tired of my own cooking."

Sabrina found it hard to picture this man alone. He was entirely too attractive, too personable, too friendly, to be alone unless that was his choice.

They filled their plates in silence and returned to the table.

Michael obviously had not been exaggerating his hunger, Sabrina decided, watching him methodically clearing his plate. She began to relax slightly. His nonchalant attitude toward her helped. Obviously he saw nothing eventful about the two of them having a meal together. He had no way of knowing that she never did this sort of thing. He, on the other hand, probably had a very active social life.

After the waitress refilled their cups with coffee, Michael leaned back in his chair with a sigh of satisfaction and picked up his cup.

"Did you get enough to eat?" His smile flashed again, and she could feel her relaxed mood slipping away. Did he have any idea how attractive that boyish smile was?

"I ate enough to keep me going for a week," she replied. She searched nervously for an innocuous topic of conversation. "Have you lived at the lake very long, Sergeant Donovan?"

"Three years. And the name is Mike."

"Do you like it here?"

"Very much."

He looked amused, and she realized that her nervousness must be showing. He looked very relaxed and at ease as he sat there sipping on his coffee and watching her. When she didn't say anything else, he spoke.

"I understand you've lived here for several years."

"That's right. Five. How did you know?"

He shrugged, reminding himself that he wasn't supposed to know much about her. "Somebody may have mentioned it to me. Your shop is quite popular, from all reports."

"Yes, I'm thankful to say." She glanced down at her hands, clasped on the table before her. Her thoughts had completely deserted her.

"Sabrina?"

She glanced up quickly. "Yes?"

"Do I make you nervous?"

Her gaze darted to meet his. "Oh, no. Of course not. I mean, well...it's not you exactly. It's the situation. I'm not very good at this sort of thing."

His face reflected his confusion. "What sort of thing?"

She waved her hand in a gesture that encompassed him, the table, the room. "I don't do much socializing."

He grinned, relaxing once again. "Oh. Neither do I. Guess that makes two of us."

"I guess so." She couldn't think of anything else to say.

"What gave you the idea of starting a gift shop?" he asked.

"I received a small inheritance that I wanted to invest. Glass sculpture and crystal figurines have always fascinated me—I've been collecting them for years—so I decided to turn a hobby into a profession." She paused, thinking about that first year. She forgot her shyness and went on to explain, "I had met Rachel one time when I was visiting in the Hot Springs area. She's such a creative person, and when I first got the idea for the shop I contacted her and asked for her help in collecting items that might prove to be popular. She has a shop where several artists work, turning out the products that I sell."

"How do you spend your hours away from your shop?"

Sabrina smiled at the casual way he asked the question, so different from the intentness of his expression. "During the winter Jessica and I watched our fair share of movies and worked jigsaw puzzles. We spent summers around the water."

Michael knew who Jessica was because of his investigation, but he didn't want Sabrina knowing how much information he had accumulated about her. He knew she would be offended to learn how thoroughly he'd delved into her life. He was just thankful that he'd found nothing in her background to warrant continued investigation, because that would have effectively prevented him from spending his off-duty hours with her.

He already knew he wanted to spend as much time with her as she would allow. So he pretended ignorance.

"Jessica?"

"My daughter. She's a freshman at the University of Missouri in Columbia."

"You must miss her now that she's away," he said, watching her expressive face reveal her feelings. He reached over and touched her hand, which was resting on the table.

Sabrina heard the understanding in his voice, and a sense of comfort stole around her like a cloak.

"Yes, I do," she admitted in a sudden burst of honesty, not only to Michael but to herself. "Jessica's father died when she was two. I suppose it was only natural that I planned my life around her."

"But it makes life a little rough when they leave."

Sabrina heard pain in his voice and impulsively asked, "Do you have any children?"

He nodded. "A son, Steve. His mother and I were divorced when he was ten. I'm afraid it wasn't one of those friendly divorces you hear about. Phyllis hated my job and the long hours. She felt I wasn't a stable enough influence on Steve. As soon as the divorce was final, they moved to the West Coast to get away from my influence."

"How old is Steve now?"

"Twenty. He's enrolled at Stanford," Michael's voice showed no emotion whatsoever.

"Do you see much of him?"

"No. I've tried to arrange visits between us, but his schedule has always been heavy. Phyllis saw to that. I flew out a couple of times to see him when he was younger, but we were both ill at ease." He shrugged, as though he wanted to shift some burden he was carrying. "We talk on the phone occasionally, but that's about the only contact we've had in recent years."

Sabrina turned her hand, which was resting beneath his, so that her palm touched his. She slid her fingers between his and squeezed. "No wonder you can understand what I'm going through now."

His silver gaze met hers. He saw her concern and understanding reflected in her eyes and realized that he'd shared with her feelings that he'd managed to keep buried for years. Instead of being embarrassed, he felt a sense of relief. She was a parent. She knew how it felt to lose a child from your daily life, to wonder how they were doing, to know they had another life now, one that didn't include you.

He looked down at their clasped hands and felt encouraged. They had found a bond of sorts, an empathy. It was a start.

Determined to lighten the mood, Michael grinned and said, "I warned you, I'm not very good at social chitchat. At the rate I'm going, we'll both be crying in our coffee in a few minutes."

She laughed, just as he had hoped she would.

Michael casually lifted their clasped hands and took her hand between both of his. "There's this guy I work with—Jim Payton—who's always pushing me to meet friends of his wife, trying to get me to go out more."

"Can I ever relate to that! Pam, my assistant at the shop, is forever nagging at me about the same thing."

They smiled at each other in mutual understanding. Michael was pleased to note that Sabrina no longer seemed to be nervous with him. He felt as though he'd achieved a major breakthrough.

"What we need to do is to convince both of them that we are perfectly capable of taking care of ourselves."

"You have no idea how often I've tried to point that out," Sabrina responded.

"So what I was thinking was..." Michael took a deep breath and prayed he wouldn't reveal how important her response to what he was going to say was to him. "...maybe we could do each other a favor and spend some time together."

He felt her stiffen, and he almost groaned. She pulled her hand away and placed it in her lap. He caught a hint of wariness in her eyes when she asked, "What did you have in mind?"

Michael heard caution, but he also heard interest, and relief swept over him. "Oh, I thought we might get together for a meal once in a while...or a movie. Something along those lines." He was quiet for a moment, and then he grinned. "Take today, for example. I've got the day off, with nothing to do that can't be postponed. Maybe we could do something to enjoy the nice weather before it gets too cold to stay outside."

"I'm afraid I can't today," she replied with what Michael considered to be an encouraging reluctance. "UPS delivered a large shipment of merchandise from one of my suppliers yesterday. I'll probably spend the rest of the day unpacking at the shop."

"Could I help? It's the least I could do after the mess I left for you to clean up the other night."

Sabrina knew that if Michael came to the shop she wouldn't be able to concentrate enough to get anything done. The longer she was around him the more potent she found his charm. There was no mistaking the fact that he was showing definite interest in her. She certainly couldn't deny her attraction to him, either, and that scared her. What had happened to her safe little world? All of this was new territory.

He sat across from her, waiting for her response. She had to have some breathing room. She had to have some time to deal with what was happening to her.

She needed some space.

"That's very kind of you," she finally replied, "but I really don't think so. . ." Her voice faded when she saw the look in his eyes and realized that he wasn't going to give up.

She found his determination a little unnerving—and exhilarating. Never in the past sixteen years had Sabrina been so actively pursued. She knew that she needed to learn how to cope with her reactions whenever she was around him. Perhaps if she started with small doses of him she could build up to longer periods of time, sort of acquire an immunity to his charms.

He saw the hint of fear mixed with excitement and rapidly decided to back off, at least temporarily.

Deliberately leaning back in his chair, he smiled his most disarming smile. "Okay. I'll let you work to your heart's content this afternoon if you'll have dinner with me tomorrow evening."

He waited for her answer with no sign of impatience, and Sabrina faced the fact that she could not resist this man.

"Yes. I'd like to have dinner with you tomorrow night."

His grin lit up his face. "Great. Give me directions to your place. Then I'll go back home today and do the chores I was willing to postpone."

She drew him a map of the route to her home, then glanced at her watch. "I really need to go."

"So do I."

Neither one moved.

"I can't believe I'm doing this," she finally admitted with an embarrassed laugh. "It just isn't like me."

"Maybe it's time for you to do something different, something that's nothing like you."

"That's Pam's advice. She thinks I'm in a rut."

"It can happen."

She leaned forward and said, "I've never seen anything wrong with a rut, myself," she confided. "It may look boring to others, but I find it rather comforting."

"Safe?"

"Exactly!" she agreed, pleased that he understood.

"I'm not trying to take you away from your rut, you know. I'm just offering to share it with you from time to time."

"I think I'd like that," she managed to say.

"I *know* I would."

She couldn't hold his gaze. Pushing away from the table, she said, "I really must go."

He came to his feet at the same time and walked her to the lobby, where he paid the bill. Then he escorted her to her car. Opening the door for her, he leaned down and kissed her softly on the lips.

"Thank you for trusting me enough to see me again. I'll pick you up tomorrow night at seven."

Startled by the unexpected kiss, Sabrina could only stand and stare as he strode toward his truck, whistling.

She rested her fingers against her lips and watched as he drove away.

Four

The late-afternoon sun was almost setting behind the western hills when Michael decided to call it a day and go inside. He had raked and burned leaves and split firewood until the restlessness that had plagued him since brunch with Sabrina appeared to have been conquered.

The woman had a powerful effect upon him. Michael couldn't understand his reactions to her. He found her attractive and intelligent, but it was that slight hint of vulnerability that caught him so off guard, that made him want to wrap her securely in his arms, protect her from any possible harm, and never let her go.

"Let's face it, Donovan. You're hooked, and you might as well admit it." He couldn't remember the last time he'd so eagerly anticipated seeing someone again.

Michael heard the phone ringing when he opened the door. He hoped it wasn't an emergency at work. All he wanted at the moment was a hot shower and a cold beer, not necessarily in that order.

He grabbed the phone. "Donovan."

"Mike, this is Rusty."

Rusty was the dispatcher of their unit. "What's up, Russ?"

"Weren't you investigating a Sabrina Sheldon?"

Michael tensed. "What about her?"

"She was admitted to General Hospital a couple of hours ago. Looks like she may have had a falling-out with her cohorts."

"What are you talking about?"

"A shopper at the mall happened to glance into her shop window and saw that the place had been ransacked. She called the police, and they went over there. They found this woman lying unconscious in the storeroom, apparently from a blow to her head. She was identified as the owner, Sabrina Shel—"

Michael didn't wait to hear any more. He dropped the phone, grabbed his coat and sprinted for the door, his heart pounding.

What in the hell was going on? Who could have done this to her? His mind raced as he took the curves between his home and the hospital as fast as he dared.

Sabrina! What could have happened? He should have insisted on going to the shop with her. But he'd wanted to give her a little space. Hell. They had both needed a chance to come to terms with what was developing between them.

Now this.

Michael pulled up in front of the hospital, turned off the ignition and grabbed the keys, then ran to the front door.

"Where is Sabrina Sheldon?" he asked at the front desk.

As soon as he was given her room number, he raced down the hallway.

The door was closed, and he glanced at the nurses' station. There was no one there. He pushed the door, started in, then abruptly halted just inside the room.

She was alone, her head turned toward the wall. The almost silent *whoosh* of the door as it closed behind him was enough noise to cause her to turn her head.

The first thing he noticed was how pale she looked—except for her bruised and swollen cheek. She was surprised to see him. Her attempted smile wavered, and she blinked the moisture from her eyes.

"You manage to turn up, no matter where I am." Her voice sounded hoarse, and his heart lurched.

Michael returned her smile, his silent steps taking him to her side. The blinds at the window were closed, leaving the room in shadows. He reached for her hand, needing the contact, and held it between both of his.

"I came as soon as I heard." Seen up close, her bruise looked livid and painful, and Michael could feel the rage grow inside him, at the thought that someone had dared to harm her. "How's your head?"

"Not too bad. They've given me something for the pain. I feel like I'm floating about six inches off the bed."

He lifted her hand and kissed her fingertips. "I'm so sorry this had to happen to you, honey."

"It wasn't your fault."

"I should have been with you. I should have been watching the store. I should have—"

"Michael, you aren't my guardian angel, you know."

"Well, you definitely need one. I don't dare let you out of my sight."

She smiled. "It was kind of you to come see me."

"Is there anything I can do? Someone I could call? Your daughter, perhaps, or your assistant?"

Sabrina started to shake her head, then winced at the slight movement. "No. I don't want Jessica to worry. I've already talked to Pam. She and her family plan to go to the shop and straighten everything before tomorrow. Everyone's being so helpful." She brushed her hand across her eyes, but Michael had already seen the tears. He leaned over and kissed each eyelid, feeling the quiver of her moist lashes against his mouth.

"I don't know what's the matter with me. I'm not usually so weepy."

"You've had quite a shock. It's only natural to have a reaction." He eased down on the edge of the bed, and she turned on her side toward him. Pulling her knees up, she curled around him. He smoothed the wisps of hair on her cheek back behind her ear, then continued to stroke his hand over her hair and along her shoulder. She wore a cotton hospital gown, and he found it as appealing on her as satin or lace on anyone else.

He really had it bad.

"I've never had anything like this happen to me before," she murmured. "I had no idea how frightening it would be."

"Do you remember what happened?" He kept his voice low and soothing and continued to stroke her gently.

"I parked in back like I always do. When I got to my shop I discovered the door was slightly ajar. I hadn't seen Pam's car, but I decided that one of the family must have dropped her off."

He could feel the tension in her. He squeezed her hand slightly. She returned the pressure before continuing. "I called out, so that I wouldn't startle her, then stepped inside the storeroom. It was a shambles. Boxes and shipping material were scattered everywhere. Unpacking is messy, but the place looked like a tornado had swept through. I called Pam's name, because I heard movement in the other room. When I started into the showroom I saw—" she paused as though searching her memory "—I saw a movement or a shadow and started to turn my head."

When she didn't say any more, he prompted her. "And that's when you were hit?"

She took his hand and raised it to the side of her head. He felt a large lump there. "I think I must have hit my cheek when I fell."

"That's quite a knot you're sporting, lady."

"The doctor thinks I may have a slight concussion."

"I wouldn't be at all surprised."

Her eyes were filled with apprehension. "Why would anyone be ransacking my store? We don't ever keep money there overnight."

"Perhaps whoever was there didn't know that."

Sabrina's eyes revealed her pain and confusion, and it was all Michael could do to refrain from gathering her into his arms and holding her close. She met his gaze steadily for a moment before she asked, "Does this have something to do with your searching my shipment?"

"God, I hope not, but I have no way of knowing at this point." He moved his hand down her back, which was left bare by the hospital gown. She accepted his caress, and Michael could feel himself relaxing for the first time since Rusty had called. Whatever was happening between them seemed to be mutual.

"Why did you think I'd have something the police wanted? I've wanted to ask you, but I never quite dared before."

Her hesitant voice touched him and, without giving the gesture much thought, he leaned over and lightly touched his lips to her cheek, brushing them against the velvety softness before he answered her.

"I received an anonymous call one evening. I've thought about that call a great deal since then. I was told to watch you, and I assumed the warning came because you were doing something illegal. Now I'm wondering if I was to watch you in order to protect you."

Her lashes quivered slightly at his touch, but once again she didn't pull away. Instead, she pursued the topic. "You have no idea who called?"

He shook his head, feeling the frustration of having asked that question many times himself. "Not a clue. I couldn't even decide the caller's gender."

"How strange."

Michael saw her worried frown and wished he hadn't allowed her to continue discussing the subject. She didn't need to be focusing on the case at the moment. What she needed was to rest, to get better and to get out of here.

Deliberately this time, he leaned down and kissed her on her mouth. Once again he caught the subtle scent of her perfume. Now he felt the tender curve of her lips, which steadily enticed him as they shaped themselves to his mouth, and without further thought he increased the pressure, tasting and exploring her soft warmth, familiarizing himself with the pleasure of intimacy with her.

"Young man! I don't know how you managed to get in here. Our patient is not to have visitors. You are going to have to leave immediately!"

Michael jerked away from Sabrina. Their eyes met, and he saw in hers the flush of newly awakened desire, mixed with amusement. He grinned in response. He hadn't heard that tone of voice used on him since Miss Casey, his third-grade teacher, had caught him with his pet frog in the cigar box he'd used to store his pencils in school.

He stood and turned to face the nurse, who stood militantly just inside the door. "I'm sorry. I didn't mean to disturb Ms. Sheldon. I'm the, uh, one of the police officers working on this case, and I had a few questions I hoped she could answer."

The nurse's studied gaze took in his jeans and sweatshirt before she sniffed and said. "Well, the police have already been here and gotten their statement from her. What Ms. Sheldon needs is rest, not harassment!"

He almost smiled at the stern countenance of the woman who had appointed herself Sabrina's watchdog. "Of course, you're right, ma'am," he responded. Turning back to Sabrina, he said, "I'll be by to see you in the morning, honey. Try to get some rest." Ignoring the nurse's presence, he leaned over and brushed his lips against Sabrina's cheek. He noted the slight agitation of her breathing and knew that it matched his. Straightening, he nodded to the nurse and slipped out the door.

The nurse turned back to Sabrina. "He didn't look like any police officer I ever saw! Why, he wasn't even in uniform!"

"He had today off," Sabrina murmured, still dazed that he had come to see her, that he had touched her so lovingly, that he had kissed her with so much warmth.

The older woman studied her with a speculative gleam in her eye. "And was the kiss routine police procedure?" she asked archly.

Sabrina could feel the heat in her cheeks but didn't comment. She was trying to come to terms with what had happened and how she had reacted to his touch. Was it the medication, or the blow on her head, or had she just lost her mind? Something was strange. He had treated her as though they were lovers, and she had responded, feeling comforted and comfortable with him. She had never reacted to anyone like that before. What was happening to her?

After a moment of fussing with the pillow and the covers, the nurse patted Sabrina's hand. "There now, that should do you for a while. Just ring if you need anything."

When she was alone once again, Sabrina played over in her mind Mike's visit to her. He had been so upset, and not in the least professional. He'd acted as though he thought he was to protect her, to care for her.

Once again, like some star-struck schoolgirl, she found herself touching her lips where he had kissed her. She grinned at the thought. She felt like a young girl with a crush, and at the moment she didn't even care.

She knew that she was feeling vulnerable and alone right now, knew that the pain from the blow on her head contributed to her emotional state, but for a little while she had felt safe, protected and cared for. Sabrina couldn't remember the last time she had felt that way.

Turning in an attempt to get comfortable, she closed her eyes. She would see him again tomorrow. He had promised.

Michael stopped by the Osage Beach Police department to talk to the officer who had answered the call about Sabrina's shop. Tom Hastings was in his office filling out a report. Michael paused in the doorway. "Do you have any information you can give me on the assault on Sabrina Sheldon?"

Tom glanced up and nodded. "Come on in, Mike. I was told you were investigating her."

"Yes," Michael replied, taking a chair across the desk from him. "What do you have?"

"The place had been ransacked. I'm not sure whether they found what they were looking for or not. Ms. Sheldon was in no condition to tell us anything when we found her." Tom glanced down at the report he was working on.

"Do you think she's involved in whatever is going on?" His gaze met Michael's.

Michael walked over to the window and stared out for a moment, then turned and looked at Tom with an unwavering gaze. "No, I don't. She checked out clean. I've talked with her a couple of times. I see no indication that she's involved in anything illegal."

"Then you've dropped your investigation?"

"Officially, but now that this new incident has occurred I intend to follow up until we can get to the bottom of what's going on around here."

Tom tapped his pencil on his desk in a sharp rhythm. "Have you considered that someone could be using her to transport drugs without her knowledge?"

Michael sat down again. "If they are, I didn't find a sign of it. And I went through everything carefully."

Tom leaned back in his chair and said, "We dusted the place for prints, but if these guys are pros they won't have left their calling cards."

Michael ran his hand through his hair. "What bothers me is that if the intruders didn't find what they were looking for they might be back."

"There's that possibility, all right."

Michael pursued his line of reasoning further. "Sabrina lives alone, in an isolated area of the lake. There's also the possibility that they might wait for her there."

"The problem for us, Mike, is that we don't have the manpower to give her protection."

"Yeah, I'm aware of that," Michael responded absently. They sat there in silence as Tom continued to fill out his report.

Michael finally nodded, as though he had made up his mind about something. "I have an idea that may give us some time."

"Which is?"

"While you're running down possible leads and my office is checking the local drug suspects, I'll find a safe place for Sabrina. Surely we can clear this up in a few days."

Tom grinned. "That's why I've always liked you, Mike. An incurable optimist."

"It's worth a try."

"You bet. Who knows? Maybe we'll get lucky."

As soon as he got home, Michael called his superior and filled him in on what had happened, then discussed his plan. When he hung up, Michael felt better, more in control of the situation. He hated to feel helpless. He needed to be doing something, taking an active part in what was happening.

He just hoped he could convince Sabrina to go along with his plan.

Sabrina came awake with a start and sat up, her heart pounding. The muted sounds of the hospital at night reached her through her closed door. When she realized where she was, she slowly relaxed.

Sinking back onto her pillow once again, she became conscious of the pain in her head. The doctor had confirmed that she had a mild concussion. She sincerely hoped she never found out what a severe one felt like.

From the faint light at the window it had to be close to dawn. She had spent two nights there. Hopefully the doctor would allow her to go home today. She could nurse a headache at home as well as she could here. Surely there was no reason to keep her.

Sabrina closed her eyes, hoping to find some relief from the dull ache echoing through her skull by sleeping for a while longer.

What had the doctor said? Something about her need-ing to rest. There was no chance that she would be running any races for the next several days. She would be more than content to rest and recuperate in the blessed peace and pri-vacy of her own home.

If only she would stop having these nightmares of being pursued, of hands grabbing at her from the darkness. For the first time in her life, she was experiencing fear about living alone. She knew she was being silly, but fear wasn't rational.

If only she knew who had wrecked her shop, and why. What had they been searching for?

Pam had come to see her yesterday with the news that nothing appeared to be missing from the store. Whoever had attacked her had probably been searching for some-thing valuable to steal.

A random coincidence? A burglary that she had just happened to interrupt? Surely it would not happen again.

Pam had cheered her with a couple of nightgowns to re-place the hospital haute couture, together with a saucy bouquet of brightly colored flowers and a cluster of bal-loons with silly faces on them. Sabrina couldn't resist Pam's high spirits. She had been smiling at one of her witty comments when the door had opened and Mike had walked in, wearing his uniform.

Thank God she'd taken the opportunity before he'd ar-rived to change into one of the new gowns, brush her hair and apply a touch of color to her face.

As soon as Pam saw him, she jumped to her feet. "Hi! You probably don't remember me. I'm—"

Michael stepped forward and held out his hand. "Of course I remember you, Mrs. Preston," he said with an enchanting grin. "You're Tommy's mother. I didn't connect the Pam that Sabrina has mentioned with you." He shook her hand. "How's Tommy doing?"

Pam had looked startled when Mike casually mentioned having heard her name, and Sabrina knew that her assistant would be demanding some answers as soon as they were alone. Sabrina wasn't looking forward to the inquisition, but she knew it was inevitable.

Pam responded to Michael with a chuckle. "Oh, he's having a great time, as always. Still in sports, of course."

She sank back into her chair when Michael walked over to the other side of the bed and, as though it were the most natural thing in the world for him to do, picked up Sabrina's hand, lightly stroking the back of it with his thumb. "Is everything all right at the shop?" Although the question had undoubtedly been aimed at Pam, his gaze fell on Sabrina and his eyes darkened.

Pam blinked at the tension that seemed to spring up between the couple in front of her. She cleared her throat, and in a voice that was a little heartier than necessary, she said, "Oh, everything's fine. I was just explaining to Sabrina that one of my neighbors, Mrs. Moore, has agreed to help in the shop for a few days, until Sabrina feels up to returning to work."

The look on his face was causing all sorts of responses in Sabrina. "You're looking beautiful, as usual. How are you feeling?"

She could feel her face flame at the tone, as well as the words. He spoke as though they were alone, and with a sinking sensation Sabrina realized that he was not going to hide what was happening between them.

Whatever that was.

She didn't dare look at Pam and found it almost as difficult to meet Michael's heated gaze. His eyes were very expressive at the moment, and if she was interpreting their message correctly he was contemplating leaning down and kissing her.

He wouldn't dare! Oh, please, not in front of Pam.

Michael must have been able to read her silent message because his grin widened, even though he contented himself with stroking the palm of her hand with one of his fingers. She could feel her body tighten at the provocative message.

"Has the doctor mentioned when he thought you might be able to go home?"

Sabrina moistened her lips, only to find his gaze focused on her mouth. She found she could hardly speak. "Possibly tomorrow, he said . . . depending on how I'm feeling by then."

Pam spoke up. "I've been trying to convince her to come stay with us. Of course, with three kids in the house it isn't exactly restful, but you know you're welcome."

Sabrina smiled. Pam sounded almost as nervous as she felt. "I know. But I'll be fine at home. The doctor said I need to stay quiet. I can do that with no difficulty. I can rest, read a little. It will be a nice change of pace from my normal routine."

Pam leaned forward in her chair. "Oh! Sabrina, I meant to ask you, have you talked with Jessica yet?"

"No. I'll call her later today. I don't intend to tell her I'm in the hospital. She'd just worry, and there's no need." Sabrina was very conscious of Michael's presence, and of his disturbing touch. Pam's bright eyes had not missed anything since she had walked into the room. Sabrina felt totally out of her depth. She didn't know how to cope with the charged atmosphere. She closed her eyes briefly, wishing she knew what to do or say to defuse the situation.

Pam came to her rescue. She got to her feet and said, "Well, guess I'll go back to Mrs. Moore so she doesn't have to spend too much time alone on her first day." She patted Sabrina's free hand. "I'll give you a call later."

"Thanks, Pam. For everything."

Pam grinned. "That's what friends are for." She glanced at Michael, her eyes twinkling. "It was good to see you again, Mike."

"Same here. Tell Tommy hello for me."

"Oh, I will. He'll be delighted to know I saw you."

They were both silent after she left the room. Michael continued to hold her hand until Sabrina felt she could no longer ignore his gaze.

"You never did answer me," he said softly.

"About what?"

"About how you feel."

"It's hard to tell, really. The medication keeps me feeling dopey, but without much pain. When it wears off I'm more aware of the pain, but I can also think more clearly."

At the moment, she had a strong need to have a clear head. This particular man caused her to do and say all manner of unexpected things.

"I can't stay long," he said after a moment. "I just wanted to check in with you, make sure you weren't feeling any worse."

She rubbed her swollen cheek. "I think my vanity has been wounded more than anything else."

His fingertips grazed her cheek as delicately as the wings of a butterfly. "The swelling and discoloration will go down in a few days."

"I know. I'm really being a big baby about all of this."

He leaned down toward her, taking his time, until his mouth was only a few inches away from hers. "You're doing just fine, honey. Give yourself a little credit. You've gone through a traumatic experience. It will take you a few days to bounce back." The warmth and desire in his eyes were unmistakable from this distance, and she almost groaned aloud. Then he kissed her, and Sabrina felt as though she had come into contact with an electrical current that sent tingling charges racing throughout her body.

Even remembering his kiss now could set up the same sensation of a current causing her body to throb. If she hoped to get any more sleep this morning, she would have to think of something more restful than her unprecedented response to Michael Donovan.

She recognized that she was a long way from gaining control over her reactions when, hours later, he walked through the door, just as the nurse was helping her into a wheelchair to check her out of the hospital.

He wore jeans, a leather jacket and a black-and-red plaid wool shirt that put Sabrina in mind of lumber jacks and the north woods. He looked wonderful.

"Hi," she said with a smile, unable to hide her pleasure at seeing him again. "You almost missed me. They're letting me out of here this morning."

He leaned down and kissed her cheek as though the greeting were routine, smiled at the young nurse—who was not immune to his charm—and picked up the small case that Pam had brought her clothes in yesterday.

"I know. I've been in touch with your doctor. He said he was letting you leave on certain conditions."

She sighed. "Yes. I've heard them more than once, I can assure you." She glanced around the room, not unhappy to be leaving. "Pam said she'd be by to get me."

"I've talked to her, as well. I told her not to worry about you, that I would see that you were taken care of for the next few days."

Her gaze flew to his face, which wore a carefully guarded expression. "You?"

"Um-hmm. I'm taking you home with me."

Five

Sabrina sat across from Michael at a small table in his kitchen, wondering what she was doing there with him, sipping coffee and trying to understand how this man had been able to step into her life and take over so completely.

She knew her thought processes were not working at full power, and she forced herself to concentrate on his explanations.

"We aren't sure what caused the attack on you," he explained earnestly. "I don't want to take a chance that there is someone looking for you personally. Rather than raise anyone's suspicions, I decided to have you disappear for a few days, if you don't mind."

"Do you think the secrecy is necessary?"

"Yes, I do. I'd like to play this one as safe as possible." He gave her his most engaging smile, and she wondered if he knew how susceptible she was to it. "It won't be so bad, will it? I'll be at work much of the time, and you'll have plenty of opportunity to rest and relax." He touched her hand. "It will also give us a chance to become better acquainted." *That's exactly what I'm afraid of*, Sabrina thought. *Having dinner occasionally or seeing a movie together is a far cry from living together!*

"Why don't you let me show you around the place? It's not as though we'll be stumbling over each other while you're here."

He stood and held out his hand to her, and Sabrina found herself responding. Perhaps she was overreacting. It was probably the pain in her head that kept her from coming up with logical alternatives to his suggestion.

She managed not to stiffen when he placed his hand at her waist. He had a beautiful home with a panoramic view of the winding lake that had at one time been the Osage River. Sliding doors opened onto a redwood deck that held a table, a few comfortably padded chairs and a couple of chaise longues.

"The master bedroom is up there. It has its own bath." Michael pointed to the balcony overlooking the living area. "I thought you might enjoy staying up there, although you may stay wherever you wish. There's another bedroom on this floor that I use as an office, and two more downstairs that are separated by a bathroom."

She nodded toward the balcony. "Isn't that your room?"

"Yes, but I don't spend much time there." He guided her downstairs, where she discovered a large game room. A pool table dominated the room. "When I'm too keyed up to sleep I come down here and shoot pool for hours. I'm afraid I might disturb you if you were down here, but of course it's up to you. I want you to be comfortable."

She rubbed her forehead. "Are you sure you want to do this?"

He turned her so that she was facing him. "I'm very sure."

"But what about my clothes? I only have the gowns that Pam brought me and what I'm wearing now."

He led her back upstairs. "Why don't you take your pain medication and lie down for a while? When you wake up I'll run you over to your place and let you pack a few things."

Lying down sounded like a terrific idea. She would think about all of this later. "All right."

"Great." He led her up to the balcony. The view was spectacular. When he walked over and drew back the covers, she willingly sat down on the bed and slipped off her shoes. He leaned over and casually kissed her, straightened and, with a smile that she found oddly reassuring, said, "Rest. I promised the doctor I'd see that you took it easy."

With that he turned away and disappeared down the stairs.

Sabrina stretched out on the bed and sighed. She wasn't sure about what was happening in her life at the moment. She would have to think about it later.

Downstairs Michael took a deep breath and quietly released it. So far, so good. He couldn't remember the last time he'd worked that hard to bring something to pass. Perhaps he'd been a little high-handed in picking her up and bringing her to his home without giving her a choice. Perhaps he was taking advantage of the circumstances a little. Perhaps, hell—he knew he was, but somehow he couldn't dredge up any feelings of guilt. None of what he had told her was a lie. He was worried about her, and he wanted to ensure that she was safe. If the bonus to having her safe was having her become a part of his daily life, he certainly couldn't complain about that. He just hoped she wouldn't insist on returning home.

Sabrina came awake three mornings later and was relieved to note that her head no longer ached. She lay in bed and thought about all that had happened in the few days she had been at Michael's.

Surprisingly enough, they had found a companionable routine, despite the fact that he was used to living alone and she hadn't lived around a male in years. Michael left early, long before Sabrina was awake. Sometimes he would not return until late at night. When he arrived home, she heard him, even if she had already gone to bed. Then she would join him, heat up his portion of the meal she had made earlier and chat with him about whatever he felt like discussing.

Sometimes she would sit and watch him shoot pool while he unwound from his day. What surprised Sabrina was how much she looked forward to sharing a few hours with him whenever he was there. Another surprise was discovering that she wasn't as anxious about not going to the shop as she had thought she would be. It was a relief to know that Pam would take care of things until Sabrina was ready to return.

She'd made her periodic call to Jessica, who had seemed to be enjoying school. For this little while Sabrina felt as though she had escaped her responsibilities and could do whatever she wished.

Michael had an eclectic collection of books, and she enjoyed reading them and discussing them with him. She'd also discovered that they had similar tastes in music. After being in his home for a few days she felt that she knew him better than friends she'd known for years.

She wondered if he ever slept. She would wake up some nights and hear the soft click of the balls on the pool table. There was comfort in knowing that he was there if she should need him, and she would drift back to sleep.

What she appreciated most was the fact that he had begun to share his thoughts, his feelings and some of his past with her. He told her about the pain he'd experienced as he'd watched his son grow more and more different from the ten-year-old who had moved away. He touched on the fights with his former wife about visitation rights and how he had backed off when he saw how much the situation was upsetting Steve.

She shared with him the horror of losing her brother in Vietnam when she was sixteen. He'd been three years older. They had been so close, and she had been devastated by the loss. Looking back, she sometimes wondered if losing her brother before he'd had a chance at life was the reason she had insisted on marrying Danny. Her parents had cautioned her to wait, but she had been afraid she would lose him if she waited. In the end she had discovered that he had never been hers to lose. But it had taken a great deal of maturity for her to understand that.

She told Michael so many things that she had never shared with anyone. The late-night chats took place in an atmosphere of intimacy created by the soft lights, Michael's weariness, her own sleepy sense that they were the only two people in the world who were awake—sharing secret parts of themselves, discovering how they had dealt with what had happened to them.

Somehow, in talking about the past, Sabrina found herself releasing much of the pain of the old hurts, recognizing that they were no longer a part of the person she was today. She felt lighter, somehow, as though she'd dropped unseen burdens that she'd carried for years.

Yes, there had been important revelations during the past few days, not the least of which was her discovery of growing feelings for Michael.

Sabrina heard a slight noise downstairs and remembered that Michael had told her this was his day off. He was home! She threw back the covers and hurried to take her shower, pleased to know he would be waiting when she got downstairs.

He was sitting at the kitchen bar, sipping a cup of coffee and gazing at the lake through the picture window, when she came into the kitchen.

"Good morning," she said with a smile, enjoying the sight of his freshly shaved face, the way his thick hair glistened in the sunlight and the warmth in his eyes when he looked around at her.

"As a matter of fact, I was thinking the very same thing," he replied.

She looked at him, confused.

"That it's an unusually good morning for this time of year," he explained. "I was wondering if you felt like taking a drive today. I have a feeling you might enjoy getting out of the house for a few hours."

She poured herself a cup of coffee and joined him at the bar. "That sounds like fun. Did you have any particular place in mind?"

"I thought we might go to Ha Ha Tonka." The state park was one of the most scenic spots around the Lake of the Ozarks.

He hoped she would agree, because he wasn't sure how much longer he was going to be able to handle being there alone with her without making love to her.

He hadn't realized what having her in his home was going to do to him. He couldn't remember the last time he'd had a decent night's sleep. As soon as he fell asleep he would dream about her, and those dreams were slowly driving him out of his mind.

During the day his thoughts would return to her; he would remember how she looked, what she wore, an expression on her face. She always seemed so damned glad to see him when he got home hungry and tired. Without asking, she would get something for him to eat and drink and would sit quietly with him, as though she were just content to be with him.

He wasn't used to someone who didn't make demands on him, who seemed to accept him and his life-style. He was finding it more and more difficult not to take advantage of the situation. Perhaps getting away today would help ease the tension for him.

"I haven't been to the park in a couple of years. I think that would be fun," she said, her eyes sparkling.

Michael fought the impulse to lean over and kiss her. She was such a temptation, and one he knew he wouldn't be able to resist much longer.

"I thought we might park near the island and go over by the rapids." He paused, studying her. "If you feel up to it, that is."

She laughed. "I feel like a fraud, actually. I'm really all right now. There's no reason for my not returning to work."

"Not right away, please. We're running down some fingerprints we found at the shop. We should be getting a report back in a day or two."

Sabrina felt that Michael was making too much of what had happened, and she discovered that she didn't want him worrying about her. Today she wouldn't think about anything but the fact that they were going to spend a few hours together.

Later she decided that the day would stand out in her memory as one of the loveliest she had ever spent. They explored several of the paths near the bluffs overlooking the island, enjoying the view and each other. Michael seemed to be more relaxed than she had ever seen him as they wandered around the Indian council area.

By the time they reached the rapids on the island, they were both ready to sit and rest for a while.

"I don't believe I've ever seen water this blue." Michael commented after a while. The source of the water was an underground river a few hundred yards from where they sat.

"I have a friend who grew up near here," she replied in a lazy tone. "She said that as a child she was convinced that there were little magic people who lived here at the park. She called them Tonkans. She decided that they came out at night, after everyone had gone home, and added bluing to the water to keep it looking like that."

Michael was stretched out beside her, leaning on his elbows. "Do you believe in the Tonkans?" he asked with a grin.

She shrugged. "It's as good an explanation as any. The color certainly doesn't look real, you have to admit. I think that whenever I come here I'm more aware of the Indians who lived in and around the area. Sometimes I feel as though—if I were quick enough—I would see one or more of them looking down at us from the bluffs up there." She pointed up to the towering bluffs, finding their sheer grandeur fascinating.

"Do you come here often?" she asked after a while.

"Whenever I can."

"I used to bring Jessica here all the time, but then her schedule became hectic and we got out of the habit of coming."

He sat up so that their shoulders were touching. "You really miss her, don't you?"

"Yes, I do, but I'm pleased that she's as independent as she is. I wanted her to be strong and self-reliant, willing to take chances, willing to grow and learn about life."

"And what about you? Are you willing to take chances?"

Sabrina caught her breath at the sudden intensity in his voice. "I suppose that depends on what I would be taking a chance on."

He reached out and cupped his hand around the back of her neck. Just before his lips touched hers, he murmured, "Us."

Although tender, the kiss held a hint of passion that teased her with its power over her senses. He nibbled at her bottom lip, then stroked his tongue soothingly across it. When she responded to him, his touch became more intimate and exploratory.

Sabrina hadn't realized how much she had wanted him to kiss her again until now. She felt as though she had just gone up in flames.

He slipped his hand beneath her sweater and brushed against the lace of her bra. Finding the front clasp, he slowly turned it until the bra fell open. He gently cupped one of her breasts, sliding his fingers slowly back and forth until she could feel a tightening within her body in response.

His touch made her tremble and press closer to him. He lifted the sweater and placed his mouth over the rigid peak, his tongue lightly flickering across the sensitive crest of her breast.

Sabrina forgot that they were in a public park, no longer aware that anyone looking down from the bluffs would be

able to see them. She was too caught up in the wonder of
what she was experiencing through his touch.

He lazily moved his mouth to the other peak, his hand
still gently holding the first. She could feel his hot breath on
her sensitive skin and could not hold back a soft moan.

Michael paused, forcing himself to hold on to his restraint. What the hell was he doing? The purpose of the
outing had been to release some of the tension that had
been growing between them. This certainly wasn't the way
to do it!

Reluctantly he refastened her bra and straightened her
sweater. "I'm sorry, honey. I don't seem to be able to think
straight when I'm around you."

He watched as her eyelids slowly opened, their slumber-
ous sensuality almost destroying his tenuous hold on his
willpower.

"Are you ready to go?" he asked, brushing a wisp of hair
behind her ear.

She smiled and nodded. He stood and pulled her to her
feet, then hugged her to him. They returned to the car in
silence.

By the time they returned home, some of the tension had
eased between them. More tired than she wished to admit,
Sabrina accepted Michael's suggestion that she rest while
he got some needed chores done outside.

He spent the afternoon raking leaves and chopping
wood, hoping to burn up some excess energy before evening. He wasn't sure how he was going to get through the
weekend without dragging her off to bed with him. He
supposed the best thing to do would be to tell her how he
felt, what he wanted, to be honest with her.

They were adults, weren't they? He was encouraged by
her response. Maybe she was as attracted to him as he was
to her.

Hours later, he still hadn't found a way to broach the subject of possible intimacy between them. They'd had dinner and, because the weather had turned cooler, he'd built a fire in the fireplace. Now they were watching a movie on cable television. He was stretched out on the sofa, and she was curled up in one of his overstuffed chairs.

The movie was all right, Michael decided, if you liked that sort of thing. *Terms of Endearment* was more of a woman's movie, he decided. The mother-daughter conflict didn't particularly interest him, but the acting was good, and he always enjoyed Jack Nicholson.

It was rather sad, too, so when it was finished he wasn't surprised to notice that Sabrina was crying. He had to admit it had brought a lump into his throat more than once.

He walked out into the kitchen to get something to drink and called back. "Would you like something to drink?"

"No, thank you. I think I'll go on to bed," she replied in a muffled voice.

He shrugged. That was probably the safest decision she could make. He walked back into the living room, flipped off the television and started downstairs to shoot some pool. Halfway down the stairway he paused, listening.

He heard muffled sobbing. She was crying. The movie had been sad, but would it have affected her so strongly? Was she comparing the relationship of the mother and daughter to her with Jessica? Surely not. She had mentioned earlier that she wanted Jessica to be independent of her.

What could be wrong?

He turned around and went up the stairway, past the living room and up to the bedroom. She was in bed, the covers pulled high over her shoulders, her head buried in her pillow.

He sat down beside her and touched her shoulder. "What's the matter, honey? The movie get to you?"

She caught her breath and lay there for a moment without moving. Then she slowly turned until she was facing him. "I'm sorry. I don't know what's wrong with me. I guess the movie brought back some memories I wasn't prepared for."

"About you and Jessica?"

She shook her head. "About my marriage."

That surprised him. "Care to talk about it?" He smoothed the covers over her and stroked her cheek with the back of his hand.

She sat up, placed the pillow behind her back and leaned against the headboard. Drawing a ragged breath, she sighed and shook her head. "I don't know why that story hit me so hard. I suppose I just got so caught up in what the daughter was feeling. It was so much like what I went through."

He took her hand. "Tell me."

She was quiet for several minutes, as though she were trying to collect her thoughts. "We were both too young to get married. Our parents tried to talk us out of it, but Danny was going away to school and I didn't think I could survive without him. Money really wasn't a problem—our college funds were intact—and they finally caved in." She gave him a rather watery smile. "I think they were afraid I'd get pregnant if they didn't. As it turned out, I got pregnant on our honeymoon, so didn't enroll in classes that fall. Instead I stayed home and played housewife and bride."

He took her hand and held it between his.

"Danny had a football scholarship. He was a good athlete, but an indifferent scholar. I used to do as much of his homework as he did. After Jessica was born I took a couple of classes when I could, but Danny was seldom home, and I hated going off and leaving her with just anyone.''

Michael shifted so that he was leaning against the headboard beside her. He slid his arm around her and held her close, wishing he could take away some of the pain he heard in her voice.

"The summer after she was born, Danny became interested in stock-car racing. When he wasn't in class or involved in sports, he was either working on his car or racing it.''

Sabrina suddenly realized that she was resting against Michael's chest, her hand idly smoothing the material of his shirt. She felt so protected in his arms, as though nothing could ever hurt her as long as he was there.

"At first I used to go to all the races to watch him, but the noise scared Jessica, and the dust and confusion didn't help. I began staying home more and more.''

She shook her head. "Looking back, I realize how ill prepared we were for the responsibility of marriage and children. I didn't know the first thing about being a wife and mother. But I tried. I really tried to do all the right things. Somehow they just weren't enough.''

"What happened?''

"It was a freak accident . . . a trial run. No one really understood how it could have happened. Danny lost control on a curve, hit the rail and flipped over. They said he was killed instantly.''

"It must have been a horrible time for you.''

"He had another girl with him that night. Someone he'd met at school. I guess they had been seeing each other for some time. I think everyone on campus knew about it except me. She witnessed the crash and became hysterical. Eventually I heard about it.''

He held her snugly against him. Now he understood why the movie had affected her so strongly. She turned and slipped her arms around him. "I've never told anyone else the truth about Danny—not my parents or his, and most especially not Jessica. I'll never really know, but according to the girl, Danny was planning to leave me. She said they had talked about it several times."

"Oh, Sabrina." He held her for a long time, content to have her in his arms, touched by her willingness to share something so traumatic with him. Her openness gave him hope about their relationship.

Michael felt that he understood her so much better now. Of course she would be shy of relationships. Like him, she had found only pain. So she had devoted herself to raising her daughter and filling her life with safe pursuits.

Sabrina felt drained now that she had shared with Michael such a painful memory. Maybe she had needed to look at that relationship once more to realize that she was no longer that terribly young, inexperienced girl overwhelmed by circumstances. Perhaps she had allowed those early experiences to color her view of herself where men were concerned. She'd assumed that she had been rejected, discarded, replaced. From her vantage point now, she could see many other ways of looking at what had happened.

Michael had come into her life, and he had taught her so much. She had learned not to be afraid of her feelings. Today at the park he had made her aware of how much she wanted him to make love to her. Unfortunately, she was too inexperienced to know how to let him know that.

She could feel his heart pounding beneath her ear, and she became aware of his ragged breathing. She lifted her head and looked at him. The message in his eyes was unmistakable.

With a boldness that surprised her, Sabrina slipped her arm around his neck, drawing him closer, and kissed him. Her kiss held all the pent-up longing of years, and by the time it ended she knew that Michael could be in no doubt of what she wanted to happen.

"Are you sure?" he whispered when their lips finally parted.

She couldn't look at him. Instead she reached for the buttons on his shirt and began to undo them. With a chuckle that was almost a groan, he began to help her remove his clothes. "Do you have any idea how badly I want you?" he asked softly, his voice uneven.

"No."

He slipped between the sheets and pulled her against his aroused body. "Then let me show you," he muttered, before his mouth found hers once again.

Six

Michael wasn't sure he was going to be able to hang on to his control. Afraid that he was rushing her, he forced himself to slow down. She wasn't helping his control any. He could feel her light touch as she ran her hands along his bare skin. He groaned when her fingers brushed against his arousal.

He shifted until his mouth found her breasts. He heard her slight gasp as he tugged gently against the fullness. Her skin felt satiny to his touch. When he slid his hand down across her abdomen, past the tight curls at the junction of her thighs, he found her moist and ready for him.

He forced himself to hang on to his control long enough to reach into the drawer beside the bed. With only a slight pause, he moved above her and took possession of her, easing himself into her warmth, forcing himself to go slowly until he was fully sheathed deep inside her.

She was trembling so much that he was afraid he had hurt her. Opening his eyes he raised his head from her breasts and gazed into her face.

She glowed with a radiance that defied description. Her long lashes brushed against flushed cheeks, and her smile caused him to catch his breath.

"Are you okay?" he murmured.

"Much better than okay," she responded, sounding breathless.

"I don't want to hurt you."

"You're not."

He couldn't wait any longer. His body demanded satisfaction, and he began to move, wanting to please her but afraid that his control was gone. He gathered her closer as he increased the pace. She met each of his thrusts with one of her own, her soft sighs of pleasure encouraging him.

He felt her convulsive shudders in the same instant that he fell over the edge of control and went tumbling into a maelstrom of intense pleasure and relentless completion.

For a few seconds he felt almost disoriented. Never had he responded to anyone the way he had just now. He realized that he must be crushing her, and with immense effort he forced himself to raise his head.

She tightened her grip around him, her ankles locked around his legs.

"I'm too heavy for you," he managed to say between breaths.

"No. You're just right." She slid her hands across the satiny sheen on his back, measuring the width of his shoulders with her hands, tracing the slight indentation of his spine down to his tailbone, gripping his buttocks and squeezing.

She felt dazed. Nothing in her experience had prepared her for what she had just shared with Michael. She had only made love with a boy, never a man. Never a man like Michael.

Sabrina couldn't believe what she had been missing all these years, and yet she was thankful that she had waited to share such a beautiful experience with him.

None of her dreams could compare with the reality of making love with Michael.

"Well, Daniel, it looks as though our plans are working," Jonathan pointed out with pleasure.

"So it seems. However, I was sorry that Sabrina had to suffer an injury."

"Yes. There are some things we can't control, no matter how much we wish we could. However, we managed to have her discovered quickly. She would have been much worse off had she been left there until her assistant showed up for work the next morning."

"I don't think Michael is conscious of the fact that he wants to marry her."

"I agree. Sabrina hasn't gotten that far in her thinking yet, either. But, of course, that is what each truly hopes for—that commitment, the long-term caring, the give-and-take of life."

"When do you think they'll discover how deeply they feel for each other?"

"Soon now, I'm sure. Our plan worked quite successfully. Now we only need to allow them to come to the natural and very normal conclusion that calls for a permanent and public acknowledgment of what they are feeling." Jonathan and Daniel smiled at each other, pleased with their joint efforts to help those on the earthly plane to experience the wondrous and transforming joy of love for another person.

* * *

Hours later, Sabrina surfaced from a deep sleep. She felt deliciously warm and very content. She attempted to move in order to stretch and discovered that she was effectively clamped by a muscular arm and leg to a very masculine body. Cautiously opening her eyes, Sabrina stared at a strong, firm jaw a couple of inches away.

Michael. She had spent the night with Michael. To put it more bluntly, she had spent the night making love with Michael. Gray light had been replacing the darkness of the room by the time they had finally fallen asleep.

She inched away slightly so that she could raise her head and look down at him. He appeared so vulnerable in his sleep. Thick lashes concealed his compelling eyes. His face looked relaxed, with only a few lines around his eyes and the edge of his mouth. His lips looked very tempting, and she ran her tongue over her own lips as though she could still taste him.

Sabrina had had no idea that she had such a sensuous side to her. The past several hours had been a rare education in lovemaking, in enjoyment of another person, in sharing herself fully with another human being.

She felt renewed, somehow... revitalized.

Carefully lifting his arm from around her, she wriggled out from under his leg.

"Where you going," he mumbled.

She smiled. "The bathroom."

"Umh." He rolled over onto his stomach, burying his head under the pillow.

When she came out of the bathroom, she discovered that he hadn't moved. *My hero*, she thought to herself, grinning. The sheet and comforter were tangled around his waist, revealing his muscular back and shoulders. One arm lay flung across her side of the bed.

Now that she was up, she was wide awake—and cold. The gray light hadn't gotten much brighter, because a cold front had moved in sometime during the night. Dark, lowering clouds swept the sky with more than a hint of snow.

How quickly the weather changed in Missouri. She was grateful for the warm weather that had been an amiable companion while they were at the park yesterday.

Shivering, she searched for a heavier sweater and some woolen pants, then went downstairs and started the coffee. She was glad to have this time to herself. She needed to think. She was still stunned by the decisions she had made in the past twenty-four hours. To decide to embark on a flaming affair after all her years of being carefully aloof from men was so out of character for her.

What worried her even more was that even now she didn't have any desire to go back and change her decision. Spending these days with Michael was like stepping out of space and time. It had nothing to do with the real world and her responsibilities there. She was taking time for herself for once in her life. Finally, after eighteen years, she was no longer responsible for anyone but herself. And if she chose to be irresponsible, then only she would have to deal with the consequences.

The fact was that she loved the man. She certainly couldn't have explained it to someone else, since she didn't understand her feelings herself. However, she no longer felt alone, battling life's daily challenges. Michael was there—reliable, stable, dependable.

She stood at the window and watched as the strong wind whipped the bare trees and listened as it howled around the corners of the house, accompanied by the rhythmic spatter of rain hitting the glass that towered two stories above her.

A perfect day to stay in bed.

How many times had she made that remark over the years? Today it took on a meaning that caused her to smile and glance up at the loft. She returned to the kitchen, poured two cups of coffee and quietly carried them upstairs. Placing one on each bedside table, Sabrina slipped out of her clothes and got into bed, tugging the comforter around her bare shoulders.

"I missed you." His voice was muffled by a pillow.

She smiled. "I brought us some coffee."

Slowly he stretched and rolled, gathering her into his arms. "I know. I smelled it. It smells wonderful. You smell wonderful," he added, nuzzling her neck.

"It looks like it may snow."

"Darn," he said without emphasis or inflection, nipping softly at her shoulder.

"What's wrong?"

"I can't do any of the things I planned to do today." He tugged at the comforter until she released it enough for him to slide it down to her waist. Leaning over, he lazily flicked the tip of her breast with his tongue. "Guess I'll have to find something else to do."

"We could always shoot pool," she said, fighting to maintain her concentration on the conversation.

"Mm-hmm." He moved to the other breast, kissing her, nuzzling and stroking the sensitive area.

"Or—" She gasped when his hand slid between her legs.

He lifted his head and looked at her, his eyes dancing with a mischievous light. "Yes?" He found his goal and began to stroke her. Her body responded automatically, her hips lifting toward him with each movement.

"Enjoy the— Oh, Michael!"

She couldn't think any longer. She could only feel what he was doing to her. He was driving her crazy! He seemed to know just where to touch her to create the most dizzying sensations.

By the time he entered her she was almost beside herself, pleading for release. She held him tightly to her, staying with him as he set the pounding rhythm that would take them both where they wanted to be. When they reached that pinnacle of sensation, they both cried out.

They lay in a tangle of sheets, pillows and comforter, her head on his chest. They were both trying to catch their breath, and Sabrina could still feel his heart thudding against her ear.

"That's quite a wake-up call you've got there, lady," he said between breaths.

"Me?" She raised her head, pushing her tumbled hair away from her face. "All I did was to bring you some coffee!"

He turned his head slowly, as though it took all the energy he could possibly muster, and looked at the cup sitting there. "Mmm. Coffee. Someday I might have enough strength to pick up the cup."

She giggled, and he grinned at the sound.

"It's probably cold by now."

He leaned up on his elbow and picked up the cup, took a sip and nodded. "Just right." Pulling himself up against the headboard of the bed, he tucked her next to him with one arm. "Thank you, love."

"You're welcome. For what?"

"For being you. For coming into my life. For being here with me now. For taking a chance on us."

"Not to mention bringing you coffee in bed."

"Especially for that." He kissed the top of her head, then lazily combed his fingers through her hair.

"Michael?"

"Hmmm?"

"May I ask you something?"

"Ask away."

"What's the real reason you wanted me to stay with you?"

There was a long silence before he answered. "Do you think this was what I had in mind when I suggested you stay here?"

She could tell from his tone of voice that he was hurt that she felt she needed to ask. She added sensitivity to the list of traits she was learning to attribute to him.

There was another silence before she decided to answer him honestly. "The thought obviously crossed my mind, or I wouldn't have asked." She leaned away from him so that she could see his face. He looked grim.

"I wanted you somewhere that I knew would be safe. This was the only place where I knew you would have some protection. I did not plot and plan to seduce you, if that's what you're asking."

"Don't you think we moved into this relationship a little fast?"

"Obviously you do." Michael reminded himself that she was the one who had let him know the night before that she wanted more than shared kisses. Otherwise he would be feeling as guilty as hell about now. The fact was that he had wanted her from the first night he'd met her. If he admitted that, would she consider him a lech?

"I'll admit my head is whirling, and the concussion I received has nothing to do with it. How could something like this happen so fast?"

He touched the end of her nose with his finger. "You're asking the wrong person, lady. I've never reacted this strongly to another woman. If I believed in them, I'd swear you'd mixed up some love potion that bewitched me."

She nodded her head. "That's exactly the way I feel. I consider myself very sane, sensible, practical, and I don't hop into bed with men." She waved her hand to encompass the bed. "Yet here I am."

"Are you sorry?"

She closed her eyes, thinking about the past several hours. Sorry? How could she possibly be sorry about what they had shared. She had to be honest with him and with herself.

She shook her head.

"Neither am I."

"I'm just afraid this is going to make my life very complicated."

He hugged her to him. "Not if we don't let it. Let's take it one day at a time, okay? So maybe we've rushed things a little. I won't push you for a physical relationship if you're not ready."

Easy enough for him to say, she decided, after the night they had just spent. But how could they ignore what had already happened between them? How could they go back to the platonic roles they had played all week?

She supposed it was possible. At least it would give her time to think some of this through.

"Maybe that would be better," she said quietly.

He almost groaned out loud. He'd been afraid she was going to say that! Why the hell had he been so quick to offer that option to her? *Because you don't want to lose her now that you've found her.*

Good point.

Lifting her chin, he kissed her. It was a long, leisurely, lazy kiss, just to show her that he could accept her suggestion without any ill will. At least that was his intent, but somewhere along the way he lost track of his original intention.

Sabrina eventually broke away from him. "Michael! What was that supposed to be?"

"A platonic kiss?" he suggested.

She moved away from him. "Hardly." She eyed him uncertainly. "If we're going to put this relationship back on a more casual basis, I don't think we can share those kinds of kisses."

He grinned. "Good point." He glanced around, taking in the dreary day. "Why don't we go have some breakfast, then play some pool?"

"Sounds fine with me. Just don't expect to get much competition from me. I haven't played for years."

She might not have played for years, Michael decided a few hours later, but she must have been one hell of a pool player when she had played. As the afternoon progressed, he watched her regain her eye for a shot, get her feel of the table and her cue and steadily begin to make each turn count.

"Where did you learn to shoot pool?"

"At home. We had a pool table, and my brother taught me." She glanced up. "But that was years ago."

"You couldn't prove it by me."

She sank three of her balls in a row and lined up her fourth shot.

Michael had to admit to himself that he wasn't much competition for her today. He was having trouble concentrating. He kept being distracted whenever she leaned over to check an angle or line up a shot. The jeans she wore fit so snugly that whenever she leaned over it was all he could do not to reach over and smooth his hand across her taut, saucy bottom.

He was acting like a lovesick teenager. Not since his college days could he remember feeling this way. He'd spent most of the night and morning making love to her and he still couldn't seem to get enough of her. She would walk around the table, intent on the game, the light shining on her hair, and his heart would suddenly bob up into his throat. Then he would forcibly remind himself about their agreement to cool things between them.

The bulky knit sweater she wore was the same color as her eyes, and he would find himself staring into her eyes as though hypnotized.

"Your turn, fella. You miss this one and you're through."

He glanced up, a little embarrassed to be caught day-dreaming, then looked at the table. She had one ball left, besides the eight ball. He had four, and she had left the cue ball in a lousy position for him to do anything. Quite intentionally, he was sure.

He managed to sink two before missing a shot, but she was right. She ended the game.

She looked so damned proud of herself that he almost laughed. They had been playing for hours, watching as the rain turned first to sleet, then, just before dark, to snow. It would probably melt by morning, but in the meantime it was a good evening to spend indoors.

"Had enough?" he asked.

"Me? You're the one who's losing."

"Yeah, well . . . you know how it is. I need to have some sort of incentive. Something to really make it worth my while to try to win."

"You mean a bet?"

"A little wager on the side never hurt."

"I don't have any money with me." She thought about that. "I suppose I could write an IOU."

"You're so certain you're going to lose, are you?"

"No, of course not! I'm just not one to gamble. I don't even buy state lottery tickets."

He grinned. "Quite the conservative, aren't you? Ah, well. You probably wouldn't care for my next suggestion, either."

"What?" she asked suspiciously.

"Strip pool."

"Never heard of it."

"Well," he explained with an innocent smile, "It's like strip poker. If you lose, you have to take off something you're wearing."

He stood there grinning at her. She knew what that grin meant. He was just giving her a bad time by inventing some preposterous wager. There was no such thing as strip pool. But then again, how would she know? And what would he do if—

"Okay, it's a deal."

She watched with a great deal of satisfaction as her response caught him off guard.

"I was just kidding, honey. I don't want to embarrass you."

She smiled. "Don't worry, you won't. However, you may find yourself red faced before long." It didn't take much to figure out that she was wearing a great many more items of clothing than he was. Perhaps he should have thought of that before making his brash suggestion.

The mood in the room changed. A sense of purpose and dedication began to settle in. They carefully followed the rules for picking the first player to break, and when Michael won Sabrina stood by and watched him run the table, winning the game without giving her an opportunity to shoot.

"Willing to call this off now?" he asked as she gathered the balls on the table for racking.

"Of course not."

"What are you going to take off?"

"My ring."

"What?"

She glanced up at him and smiled. Then she removed the ring from her right hand and motioned for him to shoot. Perhaps he was getting the idea. Whatever the reason, he didn't play the second game as well, although he managed to squeak by.

This time she took off her watch.

Michael set his jaw and began the third game. This time everything went against him and Sabrina won with no problem. She stood there, waiting.

"I'm not wearing my watch," he pointed out needlessly.

"I know."

"And I don't wear a ring."

"I can see that."

"Well, damn it, what am I supposed to do?"

"Be inventive."

Finally he smiled devilishly and pulled off one of his sneakers.

She nodded agreeably and proceeded to win the next three games in a row.

If nothing else, they had discovered that they both were highly competitive. The kidding around had stopped. They were taking each game—each shot—extremely seriously.

Michael was now playing barefoot, having lost the other shoe and both socks, while she was still fully clothed. He was determined to show her that he wasn't easily rattled.

They paused long enough to eat a couple of sandwiches, and she agreed to have a beer with him—an unaccustomed drink for her—but the tournament was the focal point of the evening.

Several more games were played and most of them went against Sabrina. She, too, was now without socks and shoes, and she had to decide what item to take off next.

After a silent debate, she reached to her waist and unbuttoned her jeans, then slowly unzipped them. She took her time sliding them down her legs, then carefully stepped out of them. Nonchalantly she smoothed the hem of her sweater and said, "I believe it's your shot, isn't it?"

Michael could only stare. The silk-and-lace panties she wore hid nothing. Cut high on her thighs, they were too thin to conceal. They teased. Her legs were long and shapely, and as she stood waiting for him to finish she leaned against her cue, as relaxed as if she were fully clothed.

Damn her! How could he possibly concentrate with her standing around looking like that? He closed his eyes, forced himself to think about the game, then opened them and leaned over to line up his shot. As he looked down his cue, his gaze was directed to the V of her pastel panties at the other end of the table. He could feel his body reacting. What red-blooded male wouldn't react to that sort of provocation?

Michael lost that game. And the next one.

He was now down to his briefs, a bright red pair that concealed very little. If Sabrina won once more, he would be nude. And the loser.

Sabrina was feeling distinctly uncomfortable. She had had fun watching him squirm, seeing his forehead bead with perspiration during the last two games. She had even enjoyed viewing his bare chest as she had played the last one.

She was certain it was only the bright color of his briefs that she found distracting. The problem was that no matter where she lined up to shoot he seemed to be at the other end of the table in her direct line of vision. If she changed her mind and moved to another ball, he would also move. She couldn't get away from him.

Neither one of them had said more than a half-dozen words for hours.

How could he be so nonchalant—now that he was practically naked—about his obvious arousal? There was no way she could ignore it. That tiny red excuse for underwear hadn't been intended to cover such a situation.

For the first time in almost an hour, Michael was beginning to enjoy himself once again. It had been hell watching her bend over, leaving her derriere bare except for a tiny piece of lace. Or watching her stride around the table, her long legs reminding him of how they had wrapped around him so passionately the night before. Or having to stare at the V nestled at the top of her thighs.

Now it was his turn to watch her squirm. And squirm she did. He made sure he was always in her view, letting her see the effect she had on him. And when it was his turn to shoot, he did so with deadly accuracy, winning the game.

She removed her sweater, leaving her clad in only her lacy bra and panties.

Sabrina lost the next game and reluctantly unsnapped her bra.

He didn't really think he was going to be able to get through that last game. He watched her frown as she tried to guide her cue past her breast, which was no longer hidden from his sight. It was almost as though he could feel that satiny surface as the cue slid past—back and forth—as she positioned herself for the shot. His fingertips quivered with the imagined sensation.

"Darn it!" She had missed the shot.

"What's wrong?"

"I can't play without a bra. These get in the way." With a look of disgust, she lifted her breasts with her hands, as though trying to decide what to do with them.

He could think of several things he wanted to do with them. Immediately.

"Do you want to concede?" he asked, his voice carefully casual.

"No! I can still beat you!"

He smiled. "Go ahead and try, lady. I'm not stopping you."

He grew hotter with every movement she made. He could tell that she was determined to beat him now that the moment of truth was at hand.

She had played brilliantly all evening, making some shots that he had seen professionals miss, and she had been under considerable pressure. He had seen to that.

What a woman. Somehow he had to convince her that what they had together was too powerful to ignore. Whatever Fates had brought them together, they had found each other, and what they had found could never be duplicated. Not for him, anyway. Surely she felt the same way.

She sank the eight ball and spun around, triumphant. "I won, I won! I—"

As soon as he saw that the ball was going into the pocket, Michael made his move. His briefs were gone and he was striding over to her by the time she turned around.

"Michael!" Laughing, she allowed him to pick her up and seat her on the side of the table. But when he started tugging at her one remaining piece of clothing, she protested. "Hey, that's not fair! I won! I don't...have...to..."

Her words were lost as he pulled her legs around his waist and plunged deep inside her without saying a word. His mouth found hers, his tongue imitating his movements. She had teased him all evening, taunting him with her luscious beauty. He had been forced to look without touching, to merely imagine, to remember, to fantasize.

Winner or loser, agreement or no agreement—he had to have her. Now!

Seven

During the past two hours Sabrina had become increasingly aroused as Michael had revealed more and more of his well-honed body to her gaze. She had begun to have second thoughts about their agreement, wondering if they were being realistic with regard to their new relationship. His shattering response to the end of the game put an end to her confusion and delighted her with his intensity and spontaneity. The sheer unexpectedness of his move took her breath away, and his driving possession left her helpless to do anything but hang on to him.

He felt good to her. She let her hands roam up and down his back, feeling the muscles tensing and working in his buttocks, experiencing him with a sensitivity that had only recently developed. She could almost feel his pleasure in making love to her; she almost knew how desperately he had wanted her.

Suddenly he raised his head and let out a cry as he made a final driving lunge deep inside her. She responded with a strong, convulsive movement that seemed to go on and on within, holding him, stroking him, loving him.

"Oh, Sabrina!" he moaned, his legs shaking so badly he was afraid they weren't going to hold him much longer. He eased her off the table and lowered them both to the floor, where they lay in a limp tangle of arms and legs, their bodies still joined.

Neither one knew how long they lay there like that, just as neither one knew who chuckled first. Or was it a giggle?

Once it started, they both laughed long and hard.

Eventually Sabrina carefully moved off him and stretched out by his side as he lay spread-eagled.

"So much for our platonic relationship," he finally managed to mutter.

"Maybe we'll be all right if we don't play any more strip pool."

He lifted a brow. "Think so?"

She couldn't find an answer to that at the moment.

"I wonder what we're trying to prove?" he muttered after several minutes of silence. "How many times a couple can make love in twenty-four hours without killing themselves?"

"Do you think we've set a record?"

"No. I think we just killed ourselves."

Sabrina sat up, looking indignant—or as indignant as she could, under the circumstances. "Speak for yourself. I realize that a man your age has to take it a little easy—"

Michael's head came up with a snap. "A man my age? What a snide thing to say! I'll have you know that I—"

She leaned over and kissed his protests into silence. When she raised her head, they were both smiling.

"I have an idea," he offered.

She groaned. "I'm not sure I can handle any more of your ideas."

"You'll like this one. Why don't we fill the Jacuzzi in the upstairs bathroom? That should help to revive us."

"Either that or relax us until we melt."

He came to his feet, ignoring his lack of clothing, and pulled her to her feet. "Come on. You'll enjoy it. I promise."

Standing beside him, she casually ran her tongue over his nipple. He jerked as though he had just received an electrical shock. "See? There's still life somewhere in there," she pointed out, pleased with herself.

He took her hand and led her to the stairs. "You knew what you were doing to me when we were playing pool, didn't you?" he demanded.

She shook her head. "No. Not at first. It was only after you, uh, revealed yourself that I realized something must be getting to you. Since I'd only taken off my jeans, I wasn't sure what it was, but—"

"But you played the scene out anyway, right?"

She giggled. "I suppose."

He paused on the stairs and hugged her, then continued upstairs. After filling the tub, they sank into the bubbling torrent of water with sighs of pleasure. When he tugged at her hand, she willingly allowed him to guide her over to his lap. "I'm not trying to start anything, believe me. I just want to hold you close to me."

She snuggled against him, content, enjoying the moment. The real world had never seemed so distant.

The steady ringing of the phone intruded into their sleep. Michael fumbled for the receiver.

Sabrina fought her way through layers of foglike sleep and forced her eyes open. There was no light coming from outside. She glanced at the digital clock beside the bed and noted that it was almost five o'clock.

She listened to Michael's side of the conversation but couldn't tell much from it. He asked a few terse questions, gave some instructions, then hung up and threw back the covers.

"Trouble?"

He started toward the bathroom. "That's a given in my line of work."

She heard the shower running. He was obviously going to work early. She slid out of bed, dressed hurriedly and went downstairs. At least he could have some coffee before he left.

A hot cup of coffee waited on the counter when Michael walked into the kitchen. No matter how many times she saw him in his uniform, Sabrina still reacted to him. She turned away, embarrassed that he might see how strongly he affected her.

"You didn't need to get up," he said softly, coming up behind her and slipping his arms around her waist. He hugged her to him.

She leaned her head back against his shoulder and closed her eyes. He felt so good to her. "I wanted to make you some coffee."

He kissed her neck. "You're spoiling me."

She turned her head so that her lips brushed lightly against his. "You're easy to spoil," she whispered against his mouth.

He turned her in his arms and kissed her—a long, leisurely kiss that made her knees wobble.

When they finally paused for air, he grinned and said, "How about a friendly game of pool when I get home tonight?"

"How friendly?"

He chuckled. His smile was dazzling. "Very friendly."

She stepped back from him. "Mike, I really need to go back to work. I've been gone a week. What if someone needs me? I can't continue to hide forever."

"All right. Let me see what I can find out on the fingerprint inquiry we made. Maybe something's turned up."

"At least let me get in touch with Pam."

He kissed her again, then abruptly turned away and walked over to the counter, where his coffee waited. He drained the cup in three swallows, then refilled it before he faced her again.

"I have no problem with that, but I don't want you leaving the house. As soon as I find out anything, I'll call you."

"Whoever it was probably left the area the same day he broke into the shop."

"Maybe," Michael replied. "I just don't want to take any chances." He picked up his hat and started for the door. "I'll see you tonight sometime."

She smiled. "I'll be here."

The house seemed empty after he left, and Sabrina glanced at the clock. It was too early to stay up. She turned off the light and went back upstairs to dream about Michael.

It was after ten o'clock that morning before Sabrina called Pam at the shop.

"The Crystal Unicorn, Pam speaking."

"Hi. This is me."

"Sabrina! Am I ever glad to hear from you! I tried all weekend to get in touch with Mike to find out where you were, but he had the weekend off and has an unlisted number."

"Why were you looking for me?"

"Well, it started out because Jessica called. I knew you didn't want her to know about what happened, so I made up some excuse about your being away at the moment. She said she'd tried the house the night before until quite late, and when you never answered she became worried. She knew you seldom, if ever, stayed out late."

"Oh, dear." She had talked to Jessica the day she'd left the hospital. They had agreed not to get into the habit of calling each other frequently. What could have happened? "Did she say what she wanted?"

"I got the impression she wanted to tell you about a fellow she'd met. Nothing major...until she couldn't find you, that is."

"Oh. When did she call?"

"Friday."

"I'll call right away."

"Also, there have been several calls from your supplier in Arkansas. Rachel mentioned something about an order being put in your shipment by mistake."

"Did she say what it was?"

"It was a special order that someone in her shop had made up, and she inadvertently packed it with your things. She seemed really upset. I guess the guy who was supposed to have gotten it is raising all kinds of hell."

"What did the order look like?'

"Like most of her merchandise, it was blown glass. There were two leaping dolphins coming out of an ocean wave. I swear to you, I've taken this place apart, piece by piece, and I haven't seen anything remotely resembling that."

"Oh, Pam! I know what she's talking about. I came across it the morning after I brought all that stuff back. It's absolutely beautiful. The crystals in the wave catch the light so that the water actually seems to be moving. I took it home, thinking I would give it to Jessica for Christmas.'' She was quiet for a moment. ''I remember thinking at the time how peculiar it was that there was no listing for that piece on the statement. I was going to ask Rachel for more of them the next time I go down.''

''Well, maybe you should call Jessica and Rachel and calm them both down. It sounds as if it would only take a phone call to each of them.''

''No problem.''

''Now are you going to tell me where you've been?''

Sabrina smiled to herself. ''Just taking your advice.'' Before Pam could ask any more questions, she said, ''I'd better make those phone calls and find out what's going on. I'll call you later.''

''But, Sabrina . . . Where are you? Are you at home?''

''I'll call you,'' she repeated, hanging up. She sat there for a moment, looking out at the lake. Her life was suddenly readjusting itself once again, and she realized more fully how out of character her behavior this past week had been. It was just not like her to completely lose touch with her work and her family. Was it the blow to her head or being around Michael that had caused such a lapse?

She shook her head. Nothing in her life had been the same since the night Michael had approached her van upon her arrival from Arkansas.

Arkansas. That reminded her. She had to call Rachel. She found her address book in her purse and quickly flipped it open to Rachel's number.

As soon as Rachel heard her voice, she exclaimed, ''Oh, Sabrina, do you have any idea how glad I am to hear from you?''

''From the sound of it, I could ask for a special discount on merchandise for the next twenty years and get it.''

Rachel laughed. "You got that right. I tell you, I've really been in a dither. I have a new artist working with me these days. Wouldn't you know I would do something stupid with one of his creations and get him and his client furious? Please tell me you know where the dolphin figurine is."

"I do, I do, never fear. It's sitting on my dresser at the house. I was so impressed with the craftsmanship that I intended to give it to Jessica."

"Oh, thank God you have it. Look, the client is up in Osage Beach right now, trying to find you or someone who knows something. Would you mind if I call him and have him pick it up from you?"

"No problem. Since it's at the house, you might as well have him meet me there." She gave directions to her home, then added, "Do you think you can have your new guy make up some more like it? I could sell those little jewels like crazy up here."

"I'll talk to him about it. I'm afraid I'm not his favorite person these days. Finding his treasure will no doubt redeem me, at least a little, in his eyes."

"I hope so. I'm really sorry about all of this, Rachel."

"Hey! It wasn't your fault. I'm the one who messed up. I'm just sorry to create such a hassle for you. Look, I'll call him right now and have him meet you in an hour or so. Will that give you enough time?"

"Sure. I'll be seeing you in a few weeks, Rachel."

"Oh, Sabrina?"

"Yes?"

"Modeled your new sleepwear lately?"

"More than you can possibly imagine, my dear. I can't tell you how much I appreciate your gesture!"

"Sabrina! What's going on with you? You were shocked to the gills when you first opened that package."

"Maybe I'll tell you the next time I'm down. Goodbye, Rachel," she added, laughing at Rachel's protests as she hung up the phone.

It was only after she hung up that Sabrina remembered her promise to Michael. She looked up the local number for the highway patrol in the phone directory and dialed hurriedly.

As soon as the phone was answered she asked, "May I speak with Sergeant Donovan, please?"

"I'm sorry, ma'am, he isn't in at the moment. May I give him a message?"

Darn. What was she supposed to do now? No doubt Rachel was already in touch with her irate client. Making up her mind, she said, "Yes, thank you. Would you please tell him that Sabrina Sheldon called? Tell him that I have to go to my house for a few minutes and that I'll be in touch with him later."

"Sure thing."

"Thank you."

Then it hit her that she had no transportation! Obviously her brain wasn't functioning full-time yet. Shaking her head, she called the shop again.

"Hi, Pam," she said as soon as Pam answered. "I really need a favor from you."

"That was quick. Did you get in touch with Rachel?"

"I did. The client who ordered the figurine is in town and wants it immediately. Unfortunately, I'm not at home and I don't have my car."

"No problem. I can come get you. Where are you?"

Here it comes. She gave directions, then said, "I'm at Michael Donovan's house."

The silence after her comment seemed to echo with questions.

"Mike's house," Pam repeated, her voice an octave higher than normal.

Sabrina chuckled. "That's right."

"Sabrina, I only suggested that you date the man, not move in with him. I mean, I could tell there was something going on between you two that day at the hospital...but let's face it, you hardly know the man."

"That's true."

"Well, far be it from me to give you advice about how to live your life...."

"Why? It never stopped you before."

"Oh, you!" Pam began to laugh. "I'll be there soon, okay?"

"Thanks, Pam. I really appreciate it."

"Don't worry. I intend to hear all the details."

Sabrina hung up and started upstairs. She needed to change clothes. At least now she could get something different to wear.

She wondered if Michael had gotten her message. Hopefully he wouldn't be too annoyed with her. She was sure that once she explained what had happened he would understand.

Fifteen minutes later, she heard a horn honk, grabbed her purse and ran downstairs. Waving at Pam, she locked the door behind her, then realized that she had just locked herself out of his house. Oh, well. There was nothing she could do about it now. She would call Michael later from her place and explain what she had done.

She climbed the wooden stairs from the front door to the driveway, where Pam waited in her car. As soon as Sabrina got in, Pam exclaimed, "My God, Sabrina, you look marvelous! If I'd known getting involved with Mike Donovan would do this for you I would have recommended it ages ago."

Sabrina felt her cheeks growing warm. "Don't be silly. Jeans and a sweater do not make a person look marvelous."

"No, but that glow about you certainly does. You just radiate vitality. My imagination is running overtime. Tell me all."

"There's not much to tell, actually. Mike wanted to be sure that I was somewhere safe while they were investigating the attempted burglary and assault on me, so he had me stay at his place. I haven't seen much of him all week. He works long hours."

"But I happen to know he had the past two days off. Surely you saw more of him then."

Sabrina could feel herself blushing, a sudden picture of their pool game flashing into her mind. "You could say that."

Pam glanced at her, then grinned, her eyes returning to the road. They had gone a few miles when Pam began to laugh.

"What's so funny?"

"I was just thinking about what Jessica's going to say when she finds out about you and Michael."

"Would you stop making it sound as though Michael and I are having some torrid love affair?"

"Are you going to sit there with a straight face and try to tell me that you have lived with that man for a week and he hasn't made love to you?"

Sabrina decided to sidestep the question. "What do you mean about Jessica saying anything, even if I am seeing Michael?"

"You have to admit that she's not used to sharing you with anyone and she's very possessive of you. She's grown up having your undivided attention."

"Was that so wrong?"

"Who knows? I'm just saying that she might not take too kindly to having to share you with anyone."

"She'll just have to learn how, then," Sabrina murmured.

Pam chuckled. "Good for you, boss lady. It's time you had a life of your own."

They pulled up in front of the house. The last time she'd been there she had been with Michael, and once again she felt a twinge of conscience. She shook it off. Now she would have her car. He'd have to let her know when he was home before she could get back into his house.

She also intended to dress very carefully to make sure that she wore a number of items of clothing that could be discarded without revealing herself, just in case he was serious about another game of pool.

After waving goodbye to Pam, she fished into her purse for her keys and let herself into the house.

The first thing she needed to do was to call Jessica. Even if she was in class, maybe someone would hear the phone and take a message. Sabrina didn't want her daughter worrying needlessly about her.

Pam's comment came back to her as she waited for the call to go through. She had never thought of Jessica as possessive. Why would Pam see her that way?

The phone was picked up on the second ring.

"Hello, darling. This is your mother speaking."

"Mom! Oh, I've been so worried. I've had visions of you being kidnapped or bashed over the head and left for dead or something. Are you all right?"

Was it possible that her darling daughter had a touch of the psychic in her? "Really, Jessica. You're either watching too much television these days or you should put that creative imagination to work. Have you ever thought about being a writer?"

"Mother, you're changing the subject. Where have you been?"

So now it was "Mother," was it? Jessica only called her that when she was irritated with her. So much for being concerned about her safety.

"I'm fine, darling. Really. I understand you were looking for me. What's your big news?"

"Oh, it wasn't all that great. Jeff Malone asked me to go to the dance after the next home game. He's in one of my classes, and I never really thought he'd noticed me."

"I take it you've noticed him."

"You bet. He's a doll. Blond, blue eyes. Wears his hair shorter than most. Somebody said he's been in the service. They thought he was a marine."

Sabrina's heart sank. Her daughter dating an ex-marine. Oh, dear God. Now what? "That sounds really, uh, well...what can I say? You like him, he noticed you, asked you out. Things must be looking up for you."

"Mom? Are you okay? You sound kinda funny."

"I'm fine, honey. Really. Look, I've got to go. I'll talk with you again soon. I'll want to hear about your date with Jeff." Actually, what she would like to do was to *accompany* her on her date with Jeff. Of course, she knew better. Jessica had to make her own decisions, use her own judgment, make her own—heaven forbid—mistakes.

It was at times like this that she wished there were such things as guardian angels.

"Wait, Mother. Don't hang up! You never told me where you were the other night. I called until two o'clock in the morning!"

"Since when have I had to report in to you, young lady?"

"Don't try to sound like a parent now, Mom, it's too late. You're hedging, you're dodging the question, and, frankly, you sound guilty as hell."

"Jessica."

"Am I supposed to guess?"

"Jessica!"

"You don't want to tell me that you spent the night with some guy, do you, Mom?"

"Jessica!" Her voice sounded strangled.

"That's okay, Mom. I understand. You dedicated your life to raising me. Now I'm gone. It's time for you to have a life of your own. If you've found someone you want to spend time with, I think that's wonderful."

"You do?"

"Of course I do. You're a mature woman. You know how to behave. You understand the pitfalls of modern dating. You—"

"Wait a minute. Isn't this the speech I gave you just before you went to college?"

"And you have a great memory! Yep, I think I got it down fairly accurately."

"You're making fun of me."

"Not at all, Mom. Actually, I'm pleased for you. And I know that when you're ready to talk about him you'll tell me everything. So just remember whenever you're out with him that whatever the two of you decide to do together your daughter is probably contemplating a similar decision."

"Jessica!"

"Bye, Mom. Just remember. Don't do anything I wouldn't enjoy."

When Sabrina put the phone down she stared at it as though it were a snake about to strike. What had happened to her sweet-natured, obedient, loving daughter? After two months at school she had developed an outlook that could take a person's breath away. Especially if that person happened to be her mother.

Don't do anything I wouldn't enjoy, my Aunt Minerva! A sudden picture of her and Michael lying beside the pool table the night before flashed into her mind, and she flinched. Would she want her daughter doing something like that?

Of course not. She was too young, too vulnerable—and her mother was being a hypocrite.

Sabrina knew that what had happened between her and Michael was premature. Had the circumstances been different, they would probably have dated for months before becoming intimate.

She hoped.

Sabrina wasn't at all sure, not when she considered the way she reacted to him. She didn't know where their relationship was headed. But there was a sense of rightness about the two of them being together. Meeting Michael had forced her to face so many of her fears. She hadn't been conscious of the fact that she had hidden behind her role of mother to Jessica all those years.

Thank God Michael had come into her life when he had. He'd taught her so much. About life... and love... and sharing herself with another person. He was right. They would take it one day at a time. After all, they had all the time in the world.

Eight

She didn't like the man the minute she laid eyes on him—
and that was before he opened his mouth. As soon as he
started speaking, her opinion of him rapidly deteriorated.

The doorbell had rung only minutes after she'd hung up
the phone. Sabrina had hurried to answer the summons.
When she opened the door, he stood there in a rumpled suit
and a food-stained tie, greasy hair and a few days' stubble
of beard.

"You Sabrina Sheldon?" he demanded.

For the first time it occurred to Sabrina that she had ne-
glected to ask Rachel the name of the man who was coming to pick up the figurine. What if this man had nothing
to do with Rachel? Michael's warning flashed into her
mind. This person certainly didn't look like anyone who
would appreciate the delicate beauty of the leaping dolphins.

"That's correct," she said, praying that her voice wouldn't betray her nervousness.

"You've got something I want."

"And that is?" Who was this man?

"Don't get smart with me, lady. You've wasted enough of my time. Just give me the dolphins and cut out the chatter."

At least he was the right person. Regardless of who he was, she was not going to allow him to put one foot inside her house. She forced herself to smile as pleasantly as she could under the circumstances and said, "Just a moment and I'll get it for you."

She turned away and began to shut the door behind her when he shoved the door open. She stumbled back against the wall. "I'm not playing games with you, lady. You ain't shoving no door closed in my face. Now go get it."

The ease with which he had moved her and the door frightened her. She was no match for this man. She almost ran to her bedroom and picked up the figurine from her dresser.

She had only taken a couple of steps away from the dresser when he appeared in her bedroom doorway. "I told you I would get it! There was no reason for you to follow me in here."

As soon as he saw the little figurine, he jerked it out of her hand and studied it intently. Slowly he began to relax. He smiled, displaying the fact that he had more than one tooth missing. She tried not to shudder.

"Yep, that's it, little lady. I've had a hell of a time tracking this thing down."

"I'm glad that you're pleased. I'm sorry to rush you, but I have several things to do today...." She motioned toward the door and felt a rush of relief when he started out of the room.

He walked into the hallway, with her following a safe distance behind. "Yep. Everything's worked out all right after all. I hate mistakes, you see. Just hate 'em. People learn not to make 'em around me." He glanced over his shoulder as he reached the door. "You know what I mean?"

She must have made the right answer, because he continued through the doorway without stopping. As soon as he stepped outside, she closed and locked the door, her heart racing. What a horrible man. He made her flesh crawl.

"Oh, Michael. I should have listened to you. I should have waited for you to come over here with me."

She peeked out the window to make sure the man was really leaving. He was crawling into his car, thank God. She was shaking. Now that it was all over and she was safe, she was falling apart.

The sound of another car pulling up drew her back to the window. A highway patrol car pulled up and stopped in front of the other car. Michael. Oh, thank God, he was here. She stepped outside to welcome him.

She watched as he got out of the car. Never had she been more pleased to see anyone in her life. Let him be angry at her. She didn't blame him. She would promise never to be so thoughtless again.

He came around the front of his car, and she waved, but he didn't see her. He was looking toward the other car.

Sabrina heard a double explosion and with a sense of horror saw Michael fall against the front of his car and slide to the ground.

Michael! She screamed and began to run. She heard another loud report and saw the man in the car pointing a gun at her. She fell flat on the ground and heard tires squeal and a car engine driven at high speed. Carefully raising her head, she saw the car disappearing down the road.

"Michael!" She jumped to her feet, but her legs didn't seem to want to move. She stumbled up the path to the driveway. He lay where he had fallen without moving. "Oh, dear God! Michael!" She touched his face. He felt clammy, and blood was spreading rapidly across his chest. She had to get help!

She looked up and down the road. There were no close neighbors at home this time of year. She ran back down the steps, burst into the house and dialed the emergency number.

"Highway Patrolman Michael Donovan has just been shot in front of my house," she said, then quickly gave directions. "Please hurry. And call the police!"

Then she ran into her bedroom, pulled the blankets and comforter from her bed and dashed back outside. She had to keep him warm. She had to keep him alive. *Oh, Michael. Don't die. Please don't die.*

The ambulance was there within minutes, and she rode with them to the hospital. Everything that could be done for Michael was being done. A surgeon was already preparing for surgery by the time they got him to the hospital. Both city and state police officials were there, asking for details of what had happened.

Sabrina felt numb. This really couldn't be happening. She was going to wake up in a moment and find herself curled up next to Michael in that big bed of his and realize that all of this had been a nightmare.

"Ms. Sheldon, I know you're upset, but we need some answers. You've got to help us catch the man who did this. Nobody shoots a law-enforcement person and gets away with it. We'll hunt him down, but you've got to help."

Haltingly she described the man and told them everything she could. She gave them Rachel's number, hoping that Rachel wasn't somehow involved in what had happened. She had no idea who the man was or why he had shot Michael.

Finally one of them said, "I think we've got enough to get started." To Sabrina he said, "Why don't you go on home, Ms. Sheldon, and get some rest? I know this has been an ordeal for you, particularly since you haven't been out of the hospital all that long yourself."

"I can't leave. I've got to stay here with Michael. I can't leave him."

One of them patted her shoulder. "We'll check back on his condition later."

The other one said, "I'm really sorry about all of this, Ms. Sheldon."

"So am I," she murmured. "So am I."

The time seemed to drag by as she waited. No one seemed to know anything. Had he ever regained consciousness? Was he still in surgery? Couldn't anyone tell her anything?

One of the nurses paused beside her. "Dr. Jordan will no doubt come and speak with you when he's finished in surgery. He knows you're waiting for some word."

Sabrina could scarcely see the woman for the tears that kept flooding her eyes. "Thank you."

However, when Dr. Jordan found her, his news wasn't good. "We've done what we could, Mrs. Donovan. I'm not going to pretend that he isn't in very grave danger. We removed the bullets, but they did considerable damage." His gaze held hers. "We'll do everything in our power to keep him alive for you."

"Can I see him?"

"Not for several hours. He's still in recovery, and will be for sometime. Then you will only be able to see him for a few minutes."

"I'll wait, if you don't mind."

"Suit yourself. I'll let you know if anything changes." He walked away, and only then did it register that he had called her Mrs. Donovan. He thought she was Michael's wife. His family.

His family! She had to let Steve know. She didn't know anything about Michael's parents. But maybe Steve would know.

All she knew about Steve was that he attended Stanford. She went to the bank of phones. It was a start. Sabrina didn't know how long it took before she finally had Steven Donovan on the other end of the line, but she was fairly certain that she had talked to everyone who worked at Stanford, taught there or attended as a student.

When she heard his voice, her knees almost gave way in relief.

"This is Steve Donovan."

"Uh, yes. Steve. My name is Sabrina Sheldon, and I live at the Lake of the Ozarks, in Missouri." He didn't need her life history, for heaven's sake. Get on with it. "I'm, uh, a friend of your father's, and— Oh, Steve. Your dad is in the hospital, and they don't know—" She stopped and tried to swallow. "They don't know if he'll—" Her voice broke.

"What? My dad's ill? What happened? How long has he been sick? Why didn't someone call before now? Why—?"

"No, Steve. He was in good health until somebody shot him today."

"Shot him! Oh, God, no!"

"Yes."

"Is he still alive?"

"Yes, but the doctor isn't too encouraging. I didn't know who to call. Are your father's parents—"

"Both dead. He doesn't have any family—" his voice cracked slightly "—except me."

"Steve, can you come?"

"Do you think he'd want me to?"

"Oh, yes, Steve. Your father loves you very much. He's so proud of you. He misses you, and—"

"I miss him, too," he said gruffly.

"It's a little tough to get here by air. If you fly into Kansas City you can catch a commuter bus."

"Yes. Yes, I'll be there as soon as I can. What did you say your name is?"

"Sabrina. Sabrina Sheldon." She gave him her home and work numbers. "I will probably be here at the hospital when you get here." Unless he arrived too late. But she wouldn't say that. She wouldn't even allow herself to think it.

"Thank you for calling me, Sabrina. You'll never know how much I appreciate it."

His deep voice sounded so much like his father's that she had to bite her lip—hard—to keep from sobbing.

"I'll see you, Steve."

"Mrs. Donovan?"

Sabrina opened her eyes and saw the nurse standing in front of her. Coming to her feet, she asked, "Is he—?"

"He still hasn't regained consciousness, but he is now out of recovery and in a private room. The doctor said you may see him, but only for a few minutes."

Forcing herself to stay calm now that she was going to be allowed to see him, Sabrina followed the nurse down the quiet hallway. She glanced at her watch. It was after midnight. She had been at the hospital since around three. Nine hours. It seemed like a lifetime. But not Michael's life. Please, God, don't take him now.

The nurse pushed open the door and motioned for her to go inside, leaving her alone with him. A night-light placed the room in shadows, and she slowly approached the bed. She saw why there was no one with him. He was hooked up to so many machines that there was no reason for anyone to hover over him. No doubt the nurses were watching the signals bleeping across the various screens at their station.

The covers were pulled up over his chest, and there were tubes going into his arm. So many wires and machines working to keep him alive until his body could take over the job.

Would his body do that? Please? Please get well. His hair looked stark against the white pillowcase, and she remembered how he had looked the other morning, with his head buried beneath his pillow.

There was no color in his face, except maybe gray.

"Oh, Michael. I'm so sorry for what happened. If I hadn't called and told you where I was, you wouldn't have come to the house. This is all my fault." She fought back a sob. "I don't want to lose you, now that you've come into my life."

She touched his cheek. "I love you, Michael. I want you to know that. There's so much I love about you...your kindness, your gentleness, your understanding. Even your protectiveness. I've never felt so comforted as I have this past week. You're such a good, kind man...filled with compassion. Please get well."

He was so still.

"I called Steve today. He's coming to see you. He loves you, too. It was so obvious in his voice. We have that much in common, anyway." She tried to swallow around the knot in her throat. "I want you to get well to give me hell for leaving the house."

The tears were sliding unheeded down her face. She didn't care. "I'm going home now for a couple of hours. I can't go back to your place, because I locked myself out. It's just as well. I couldn't stand to be there without you. But I'll be back. I want to be here for you. I want you to know how much I love you." Tears ran down her cheeks.

She heard the door open and turned her head. The nurse stood silhouetted in the doorway, and Sabrina slowly walked to the door, leaving Michael with the machines watching over him.

"Surely there is something that I can do, isn't there?" Jonathan asked his exalted leader.

"No, Jonathan. Your mission is to counsel Sabrina. What happens to Michael is not your concern!"

"But, sir. I don't think he's going to make it."

"I know."

"I don't understand."

"What has happened was something that was scheduled into his life program. What happens now will be up to him."

"But, sir, surely he won't let himself die at this point in his life! Not when he has so much to live for!"

"Die, Jonathan? Where did you get such an archaic expression? Nobody dies, Jonathan. You know that."

"Yes, sir. I was thinking in Earth language. But they've just found each other, after all this time."

"And I want to commend you on your inventive schemes. I thought the deer a nice touch."

"But shouldn't they have some time to spend together?"

"Time? Another Earth expression. They've been to-gether before. They'll be together again. My, but you've gotten quite caught up in the drama of the situation, haven't you? If Michael makes his transition now he will find many things to do while he waits for her to join him."

"It just seems so unfair, sir. I mean, Sabrina is just now beginning to truly understand herself and her relationship to her daughter, to find meaning in a relationship with Michael. This is such a cruel blow for her to have to endure."

"But you and I know that there is no such thing as 'los-ing' love. Love is a permanent condition, one that we carry with us at all times. She will always experience the love she feels for Michael. Sabrina will never be deprived of that."

Jonathan shook his head sadly. Gabriel certainly saw the overall picture better than anyone, but this time Jonathan hoped that something would happen to prolong the hap-piness that Sabrina and Michael had discovered on Earth.

Jonathan felt so helpless. All he could do was sit with Sabrina, wait and watch, and console her whenever he could.

"Excuse me...the nurse said you're Mrs. Donovan?" He sounded young, uncertain and bewildered.

As soon as she heard his voice, she looked up. Now she knew what Michael had looked like twenty years ago. She stood, holding out her hand. "You must be Steve. I'm afraid I've never bothered to introduce myself here. Since I arrived with your father, they just assumed..." Her voice trailed off.

The young man nodded. He was dressed fashionably in baggy pants and jacket. He wore his hair short in front and down to his collar in back. He was as tall as his dad, but not as filled out. Even though his eyes were blue, they were shaped like his father's, with the same unwavering look.

It was all she could do not to throw herself into his arms and just hold him.

"How is he?"

"His condition remains unchanged." She shrugged. "Whatever that means."

"Has he been conscious at all?"

"No. I must warn you that when you first see him with all those machines you may wonder if he's even alive."

Steve nodded, swallowing. When he ran his hand through his hair in a gesture she'd seen his dad use often she felt the tears well up in her eyes.

"Do they let you see him very often?"

"Once an hour. For just a few minutes."

"But he doesn't know you're there?"

"Maybe he does. I don't know. But I talk to him anyway. I tell him everything I want him to know. I want him, on whatever level he happens to be at that moment, to know that he is loved and wanted right here."

He took her hand. "I'm glad he's got you. I'm sorry to say he's never mentioned you."

"We haven't known each other very long."

He looked relieved. "Oh, well. That explains it. I haven't talked with him since August."

The nurse paused at the door of the waiting room. "Mr. Donovan? If you would like to see your father now?"

"Yes. Thank you." He squeezed Sabrina's hand before releasing it.

She sat down and waited for him to return. Now she didn't feel so alone. They could wait together.

Steve let himself into the room and stood by the door, staring at the man lying so still on the bed. Seeing him made the news become more real, somehow. He moved closer, looking at the man who had been a part of his world for the first ten years of his life.

What could he say to him? If his father were conscious and could hear him, what would he want him to know?

Steve looked down at his father's hand, which rested so quietly on his chest. He'd always remembered his dad's hands—their strength, their gentleness.

Only then did he realize that tears were running down his cheeks. He reached over to a box of tissues beside the bed and wiped his face.

He cleared his throat and began to speak in a low, hoarse voice.

"Hello, Dad." His voice sounded harsh in the quiet room. He cleared his throat again. "I guess you're kinda surprised that I showed up here after all these years." He reached down and touched his dad's hand and found its warmth reassuring.

"I had several hours to think on the plane flying out here, remembering things about you. It was surprising, all the things that came back to me. I remember when I was little, how you used to always let me sit on your shoulders, during parades and ball games and things. I remember thinking how lucky I was because I had the tallest father around."

He sank into the chair beside the bed and studied his father's face.

"You know, Dad, you always stood tall to me. I remember being so proud of you in your uniform. And sometimes when you'd come home you'd look so tired, and maybe, you know, sad, as though things didn't always work out the way you hoped they would on your job."

He paused, listening to the steady blips of the monitors, wondering if his father could hear him. He squeezed his hands together, praying that somehow his father knew what he was trying to say.

"Do you remember how you'd always let me crawl up in your lap, even after I was in school, no matter how tired you were, or how many hours you'd been working? You'd let me sit there with you. I always felt so safe there in your arms. I knew that nothing could ever hurt me because you were there."

Steve reached for more tissue and wiped his cheeks once more.

"And you came to all my ball games whenever you could get away. Did you ever know what a thrill it was for me to look over at the stands and see you sitting there watching me, smiling, giving me that thumbs-up signal?"

His voice cracked, and he paused, swallowing a sob before it became audible.

"I remember when Mom and I left and moved to California. I didn't think I could stand leaving you. I didn't want to go. But there was Mom. She was always so upset. And she needed me. She said that you didn't need anybody. But I wasn't sure about that. I'll never forget the sad look in your eyes, even though you didn't say anything to me about wanting me to stay, not wanting me to leave. You hugged me and told me you loved me."

He fought for a calming breath.

"You know what I realized coming out here on that plane, Dad? That I'm twenty years old and I don't even know if my dad knows I love him. I couldn't remember the last time I told you. It was easy when I was little. We used to make a game of it. Then when I got older I was embarrassed about saying it, and you didn't seem to mind. You just seemed to know how I felt and it was okay."

Steve could no longer sit still. He got up and paced across the room and looked out at the night. His throat felt raw.

It ached from the effort at control. Finally he turned back to Michael.

"So I flew two thousand miles to tell you that I love you, Dad. I always have. I want you to know how sorry I am that I haven't spent more time with you during these past ten years." He placed his hand over Michael's hand. "I have no one to blame but myself. You offered to pay my way, but I was always so busy with my own activities. You never put any pressure on me. You always seemed to understand."

Steve shook his head in bewilderment.

"It was me who didn't understand. I guess I thought I would have all the time in the world to see you, to be with you, to get to know you better. I mean, as far as I'm concerned you're invincible. Right up there with Superman. It never occurred to me that you couldn't stop bullets. That you were mortal. That you could die and leave me. That I might never have the chance to tell you how much I love you."

He could no longer hold back the sob that shook him. He turned away, trying to gain control over his emotions. He managed to take a couple of deep breaths, then turned to Michael again.

"I have no idea if you can hear me or not, but Sabrina said she talks to you anyway. I liked that. I like her, Dad. She's real and she's loving. You need someone like her in your life. We all do. I want to be a part of your life, Dad. I want us to spend time together. I want you to be around when I get married. I want you to help spoil your grandchildren."

Steve lifted Michael's hand and placed it between his hands. He closed his eyes and whispered. "Oh, Dad. I don't want you to die."

Nine

"Doctor, this is Sue Brown, supervising nurse in ICU. Mr. Donovan is showing some increased activity on the monitors. It appears that he may be coming out of the coma." She listened for a moment. "Yes, sir. I'll tell them."

With a smile, she went to find the two people who had been living in the waiting room for the past few days. As usual, she found them talking quietly in the corner.

"There are indications that Mr. Donovan is regaining consciousness. The doctor will be here shortly to check him. He wanted you to know." She returned to her desk and left Sabrina and Steve staring at each other, afraid to believe what they had just heard. Then Steve gave a whoop and grabbed Sabrina, swinging her around in a circle.

"Did you hear that? He's going to make it. I knew it! He's too tough to let a couple of slugs in the chest stop him."

Sabrina shuddered at the graphic reminder and the memories it evoked. She had gotten to know Steve quite well during these past few days, since they had had little to do but wait and talk. One thing she had quickly discovered—subtlety was not one of Steve's long suits. He said whatever was on his mind, with little regard for the consequences. How ironic that he had chosen the field of communications in which to work toward a degree.

He went charging after the nurse. "Can we see him?"

She shook her head. "Not until the doctor arrives."

"But wouldn't he want to see someone he recognizes when he comes to?"

"You'll have plenty of time to be there when that happens. He's far from being conscious. But he is rousing, and that's an excellent sign."

Sabrina felt a wave of weakness wash over her, and for a moment she thought she was going to faint. Michael had somehow faced the crisis stage and had hung on. Surely now he was going to be all right.

He had to be. Things would be different for him now that Steve was here. Steve had spent all these hours sharing his feelings about his father. He wanted a second chance to get to know Michael better.

She just wanted him to live and be a part of her life in whatever way he chose to be. She was no longer afraid to face her feelings about life and about him.

Three days passed before Michael was fully conscious. He sometimes stirred and muttered, but he didn't seem to be aware of his surroundings.

On the fourth day Sabrina and Steve were standing beside his bed watching him when he finally opened his eyes and looked around. He blinked several times, as though the light bothered him. Then his eyes narrowed and he looked at the man standing there.

"Steve?" His mouth formed the words, but no sound came out. He licked his lips and tried again. "Is that you?"

Sabrina thought Steve's smile was going to split his face. "Yes, Dad. It's me."

Michael looked bewildered. His gaze wandered to Sabrina. "Hi," he whispered.

"Hi yourself."

"How long have I been here?"

"I lost track of time. I honestly don't know."

"I vaguely remember somebody telling me I was shot."

"Yes. I understand that they caught the man who did it."

He lay there, a puzzled frown on his face. "I don't remember much about it."

She smiled. "Don't worry about it. The important thing is that you're getting better. You've amazed the doctors with your rapid progress."

He looked at Steve as though he were having trouble believing his son was there. "Shouldn't you be in school?" he finally asked.

Steve shrugged. "I can make it up."

"It's good to see you." He closed his eyes. He felt so damn weak. He could feel tears forming. The last thing he needed was to let his son see him cry.

"You're tired. We'll let you rest," Sabrina said, touching his hand lightly.

He opened his eyes once more. "You'll come back?" His gaze went to each of them.

Steve nodded. "You couldn't keep us away."

"I wouldn't want to try."

A week later the nurse had him sitting on the side of the bed. Dangling, she called it. Michael couldn't get used to feeling as weak as he did. He hated it. The pain in his chest still took his breath away. But at least he could breathe.

The doctor had told him that his chances had been slim. They weren't sure what had pulled him through. The doctor mentioned his strong constitution, his relative youth, his good overall physical condition.

He didn't mention love.

Michael wasn't sure where he had been. But he had been safe, hiding from the pain, waiting to see what would happen next. While he had waited there in the place of safety, his son had joined him. They had reminisced, reviewed their lives together and apart. Discussed their feelings about life in general, shared their philosophies. He had been comforted and warmed by his son's obvious love and tenderness, his compassion. They had discussed his choices. Did he really want to confront the pain? Wouldn't it be easier to ignore it?

Sabrina had kept visiting his safe place, as well. She had reminded him that he had taught her so much about love and that she wasn't through learning yet. She needed about thirty more years of tutoring, and he had to be the one to teach her.

When had all that happened? And where?

The nurse complimented him on managing to sit on the edge of the bed without falling off—as though he were a toddler in need of praise—plumped up his pillow, helped him to lie down again and promised him his lunch before she disappeared out the doorway.

When he heard the door open again, he thought he was going to be exposed to some more cheerful chatter. He almost didn't open his eyes, hoping she would leave him alone, but something different had entered the room, a new energy, almost as though the very air around him hummed.

Sabrina stood at the foot of the bed.

"Did I wake you?"

He smiled. "No. I was pretending, in case you were Chatty Cathy coming back for something." When she looked puzzled, he explained. "You know, the friendly nurse."

"She has a terrific crush on you."

He groaned and rolled his eyes.

"She does. She envies me."

"I do, too. You get to walk in and out of this place. I'm trapped here."

"Not for much longer. The doctor is extremely pleased with your progress. He's muttering something about miracles under his breath."

As soon as she got close enough, he took her hands, pulled them to his mouth and kissed each palm. He felt the slight tremor in her fingers and glanced up.

She smiled but didn't say anything.

There was so much he needed to say—so much that he needed her to know.

"Did Steve get off all right?"

"Yes. We made it to the airport with time to spare."

"I really appreciate your driving him into Kansas City."

"I wanted to do it." She brushed her hand across his forehead, gently brushing his hair back. "He's quite a guy. A son to be proud of."

"I know. It's still hard for me to realize that he actually came all this way to see me."

He hated the way his voice kept breaking, as though he were an adolescent whose voice hadn't quite found its true register.

"He loves you very much, you know."

Michael couldn't restrain the smile that appeared on his face. "Yeah. He told me."

"Do you remember my telling you that?"

His gaze met hers. "That you love me?"

She nodded.

He glanced down. After a moment he said, "I was afraid I dreamed it." His voice was so low that she barely heard him.

"I'm not sure I'll ever forgive myself for putting you in danger," she murmured, wanting to hold him in her arms and revel in the fact that he was alive and with her once more. "It just never occurred to me that the man Rachel told me about had anything to do with the break-in at the shop."

He pulled on her hand with a steady pressure until she was seated on the bed beside him. "You're changing the subject." He watched, fascinated as the color rose in her cheeks. "Do I still make you nervous, Ms. Sheldon?"

"A little."

"I find that hard to believe. A pool hustler like you nervous?"

Her soft laughter seemed to wrap him in a soothing warmth.

"Sabrina?"

Her eyes seemed to hold the light in the room. He was mesmerized.

"Yes?"

"I love you."

Because her hand was still between both of his, he felt more than saw her reaction.

"And you love me."

She nodded, as though she were unable to speak.

"And usually..." He paused because he felt her tense. But he couldn't let her reaction stop him from saying what he had to say. "Usually," he went on, "when two people love each other, they decide to get married."

He waited, but she still didn't speak. Her eyes seemed filled with emotion, and he could only hope that he would hear the answer he wanted.

"So what I've been wondering is, would you consider marrying me? That is, once I get out of here."

"Oh, Michael," she whispered.

He waited. And waited.

"Is that a yes?"

"I love you so much."

He grinned. "Must have been a yes."

"But it's so soon."

"To get married? Or to know that's what I want?"

She shook her head. "This has been such a traumatic time for you."

He frowned. "Do you think it's because I'm laid up here and don't have anything better to do that I decided to propose to you?"

"Not exactly, it's just that—"

"You know where I was when you called the day I was shot?" He didn't wait for her answer. "I'd taken my lunch break and was looking at engagement rings." He lifted her hand and looked at it. "I was trying to get some idea of what you might like, although, of course, I didn't know your ring size. But I did know I was going home that night and tell you that I didn't want any misunderstandings between us, that my intentions were strictly honorable, but that I was willing to wait as long as you needed in order to be sure about your feelings."

She leaned over and kissed him. "I'm very sure about my feelings."

"Then you'll marry me?"

"Yes."

"When?"

"Whenever you say."

He grinned. "That's what I like. A docile, accommodating woman."

"I'll let you get away with that because you're still in a delicate condition."

"Speaking of which—" He paused, as though searching for the right words.

"What do you mean?"

"Uh, delicate conditions. The one thing we didn't discuss was the possibility of pregnancy."

Sabrina's gaze didn't waver. "I know."

"It would be foolish of me to assume you were protected."

"Michael. I'm not pregnant."

"Oh."

She studied him for a few moments. "You look almost disappointed."

"Well, it wouldn't really be fair to you to have you start off our marriage being pregnant."

"You *are* disappointed!"

He'd had many long hours to think about Sabrina and their relationship, to remember the time they had spent together. It was only when he smilingly relived their unusual pool game that he realized he had not taken time to protect her as he had the night before. He'd been so caught up in what was happening at the moment that he hadn't given a thought to the possible consequences.

Lying in the hospital had given him plenty of time to think—and to consider what those consequences might be.

He'd fantasized about having another child, maybe more, with Sabrina. He would lie there when the pain seemed to gnaw at his chest like a starving rodent and visualize what it would mean to him to have another chance at being a husband and father.

Ten years was a long time to contemplate the mistakes he'd made. He knew what he would do differently if given the chance. But that was how he felt. He didn't know how Sabrina felt about the possibility of motherhood again. After all, she had raised her daughter. Perhaps now she wanted her freedom. Reluctantly he had allowed his dreams of a family to fade, at least until he knew for sure if she was pregnant and how she felt about the possibility.

"No," he finally replied. "Not really." Not exactly.

They looked at each other for several minutes without speaking. "I would very much like to have your child, Michael," she said quietly.

"You would?" He couldn't hide the hope in his voice.

"Yes."

He watched her expression as he asked, "So if you got pregnant right away—"

"I wouldn't complain."

He glanced around the room as though assessing their chances for privacy.

She began to laugh. "But I want you a little stronger than you are right now, my love."

He smiled, liking the idea that he was her love. "I was just bluffing," he admitted. "I'm so weak I can hardly feed myself."

She leaned down and kissed him very gently on the mouth. "We have plenty of time."

"I wonder what Steve and Jessica will say," he said after a moment.

"I won't try to guess. We'll let them surprise us."

"You really don't care, do you?"

"I care. But their opinions won't change what I do with my life and how I live it. I love you. I want to marry you, and if our marriage is blessed with a child I will be delighted. Whatever reaction that causes in the family they can deal with."

He groaned. "God! This is frustrating, lying here, wanting you so badly I ache with it and not being able to do a damn thing but look at you."

"Well, you could fill me in on what's been happening regarding that man who shot you. Did you get any more information about the shooting? I never understood why he shot you when he already had the figurine."

She was right. They needed to change the subject for the time being. But at least he knew where he stood with her now, knew he could spend his time lying there making plans for their future. He liked that thought very much.

He kissed the tips of her fingers and tried to concentrate on her questions. "He thought I was there to arrest him, according to Jim Payton, one of the men who worked on the case with me."

"Was he wanted for something?"

"He was part of a ring of jewelry thieves who had worked out an ingenious plan to smuggle diamonds out of the country. Unfortunately, through a quirk of fate, one of the shipments was sent to the wrong place."

Sabrina stared at him in disbelief. "Are you saying that the dolphin figurine contained diamonds?"

"That's right. They were scattered in the wave that had been shaped around them."

"That's what made the water glitter so! I thought those were crystals, since Arkansas has so many of them."

"That's what they were hoping anyone looking at the figurine would think."

"No wonder that was such a beautiful piece of work. It must have been worth a fortune."

"Several hundred thousand, anyway."

"So he was the one who broke into the shop, wasn't he?"

"Yes. He was a little careless. He left a print that helped us to identify him. When I got your message I had just found out the man's identity, but we had no idea where to look for him."

"How strange that you should have turned up at my house at the same time. Do you have any idea how upset I was when he shot you because of me?"

He pulled her closer. "You should have been. If you'd done what I asked, you would have still been at my home, safe. I was more then a little irritated with you by the time I got to your place."

"You had a right to be. I kept thinking about that all the while you were unconscious and we didn't know if you were going to pull through. I had no idea that there was any connection between Rachel's client and the break-in at the shop. Did Rachel know about the diamonds?"

"No. We discovered that he had blackmailed the artist to hide the diamonds in the figurine. The artist was more than cooperative once he knew about the arrest."

"I'm so glad that Rachel isn't in trouble."

"Me too. She has great taste in sleepwear."

She leaned over and kissed him. "I haven't even worn it yet."

"I know. I can hardly wait."

"Soon, love. Soon."

"I would like to have a word with you, Jonathan," Gabriel intoned.

"Yes, sir?"

"I understand that you contacted Michael Donovan while he was in a comatose state."

"Well, yes, sir. I did. I couldn't find anything in the statutes that forbade it, sir."

"Your behavior was highly irregular. What did you say to him?"

"Oh, I, uh, just introduced myself, and we chatted, sir. I explained my role in Sabrina's life, shared with him some of the more hilarious moments I've had trying to work with her independent streak. I told him how long I had worked to finally bring about a meeting between the two of them. You know, just chitchat.

"We also talked about Steve and all he meant to him. I, uh, even apologized for not being able to warn him about what happened."

"How did he take the information?"

"Quite well, actually. He was aware by that time that he was in a position to make a choice about whether to return to his earthly existence or whether to complete his transition."

"I suppose you did your own persuading."

Jonathan shone with a radiant light. "No, sir. I didn't have to. Sabrina and his son did all the work, sir. Their strong, steady love for Michael gave him the energy and strength to face the return to pain and a lengthy convalescence. My visit was more a getting-acquainted one. As you know, sir, he will never consciously remember anything we talked about. It is all deeply buried in his subconscious."

Gabriel was silent. "I know that, but his not remembering it is not the point, as you well know," he said finally. "He had Daniel working with him, and you should never have interfered."

Jonathan waited, not knowing what he could say to redeem himself in his superior's eyes.

"Well," Gabriel went on after a lengthy silence, "I must say your behavior has been more than a little unorthodox, but given the situation I suppose it was understandable."

"Yes, sir."

"I suppose I should be pleased with the enthusiasm you have shown for your job. All in all, you managed to pull the whole thing off quite nicely."

Jonathan beamed. "Thank you, sir. Daniel was also a great help."

"So he was. But Daniel wasn't the one breaking all the established traditions for conduct. I sincerely hope that this doesn't happen again."

"Oh, yes, sir! I mean, no, sir. What I mean to say—"

"I'm aware of what you're trying to say, and I heartily concur. We both know that Michael is going to have his hands full trying to deal with Sabrina's spirited ways. He doesn't need to deal with your well-meaning interference again."

"Yes, sir."

"Yes, well, get back to work, then."

"Yes, sir."

"Oh, and Jonathan?"

"Yes, sir?"

"Congratulations. You have certainly earned your promotion."

Jonathan watched as the brilliant light dimmed around him and knew that Gabriel was no longer there.

Promotion or not, he would be with Sabrina for some time to come. He was rather looking forward to it, actually.

He rubbed his hands together. Twins. Just what they needed for a new little family. This was going to be fun.

Epilogue

When he walked into the bedroom he found her standing before the sliding glass door that led out to the lanai. The only light came from the full moon that coated the nearby gently rolling waves and the white beach with silver dust.

She wore the gown that he had first seen the night he had met her, and she looked as good in it tonight as she had when she'd first worn it for him—on their wedding night, five years ago tonight. It cupped her full breasts and skimmed her trim body but did nothing to conceal what lay beneath it.

Her hair tumbled around her shoulders, framing her face. It was longer now than when they had first met. Its glorious color lit up any room she happened to enter.

As usual, when Michael saw her he seemed to need more air and his heart began thudding in his chest. After all this time he still had trouble believing that she was his. He felt as though he had waited for years—no, a lifetime—for this beautiful woman.

Silently approaching her, he slipped his arms around her waist and pulled her against his bare body.

"It's all so beautiful, Michael," she whispered, as though afraid to disturb the scene before them.

His lips found the soft, vulnerable spot just below her ear and caressed her, causing her to shiver.

"I've always wanted to visit Hawaii. You always seem to know what to do to please me." She turned in his arms and slipped her hands around his neck. "Thank you, my love."

"The pleasure is all mine, believe me," he replied, just before his mouth found hers.

He could spend the rest of his life holding this woman, kissing her, making love to her…and that was exactly what he intended to do.

Without removing his mouth from hers, he picked her up and carried her to the bed, which was already turned back for them. Placing her in the middle, he found the hem of her gown and slowly raised it until he was forced to pause in his kiss so that he could lift it over her head.

The brilliant moonlight spotlit her where she lay, highlighting the peaks and curves, leaving provocative shadows to entice him to explore.

He sank down beside her, determined to make love to every inch of her body, from the tips of her toes all the way to the crown of her head.

By the time he had reached her knees she was shivering, her breath coming in small, shallow pants. He shifted so that he was lying between her knees as he continued his progress.

Her fingertips lightly caressed him, and he was reminded of fragile butterfly wings fluttering against his sensitive skin. He felt her tense as his lips followed an invisible path up her inner thigh. A muscle quivered, then was still.

He paused and raised his head. Her eyes sparkled in the moonlight. "With my body I thee worship," he said softly.

His next intimate kiss made her shift restlessly, but he relentlessly pursued her pleasure. Patiently he kissed and caressed her, until at last she cried out, her body rippling with the intensity of her reaction. Only then did he continue, still tracing an invisible path up her abdomen, her stomach and her breasts.

Once again he paused, teasing the tips with his flickering tongue until she moaned. His playfulness was having a strong effect on him, and he knew he could not prolong this much longer.

She took the choice away from him by blindly searching for his mouth as she boldly reached for his aroused masculinity. Lifting her hips to him and pulling him hard against her, she completed the union, holding him tightly.

They clung to each other, celebrating life. He began a steady pace that she matched. Slowly but inexorably he increased the intensity of the pace until the emotional storm they generated became a frenzy of passionate expression.

His cry echoed hers as they found the peak together, tumbling down the other side with whispered sighs and endearments. They were so much in tune with each other, each intuitively knowing and fulfilling the other's needs, wants, and desires. Unmeasured time drifted by as they lay there, still entwined, and watched the brilliant moon move across the heavens.

Sabrina kept her hand pressed lightly against his chest, enjoying the feel of his heart beating, of his lungs first filling with air, then releasing it. Her fingers traced the scars on his chest. Even after all this time she felt an ache whenever she remembered the time when she had almost lost him.

What a difference he had made in her life. She looked back on that poor woman who hadn't understood the fulfillment of a loving husband, a truly intimate relationship with someone who loved and accepted her, who made her feel so cherished.

"It seems almost impossible that we've been married five years," she said softly.

He stirred slightly and moved his hand lovingly across her hip. "In some ways, perhaps. Every time I make love to you I'm as excited as if it were the first time. And yet there are times when I can't remember what my life was like without you."

She placed a kiss on his jaw, wordlessly thanking him for his words.

"Are you sure Jessica has the number here?"

She grinned, though she knew he couldn't see it. "Yes, darling. She has our complete itinerary. She'll know where to contact us at any moment of our trip." She waited a moment. "Why do you ask?"

As if she didn't know.

"Oh, no reason in particular." He sounded very unconcerned. He didn't fool her a bit.

"I don't mind if you want to talk about them, you know. I miss them, too."

He lifted his head so that he could peer down into her moonlit face. Her warm smile and understanding expression made him feel more than a little sheepish. "It's just that they're so young, and we've never left them for this long before."

"I know. We discussed all of that before we left. But Michael, they're almost four years old. Besides, David and Diane have grown up with Jessica in their lives. She's like a second mother to them. In fact, she could be their mother."

He grinned. "I happen to know better. I remember the exact night they were conceived, not to mention being there when they made their entrance into our lives."

Sabrina remembered their conception quite well. Strip pool had become one of Michael's favorite forms of entertainment! She also remembered how wonderful he'd been to her all during her pregnancy, labor and delivery. He was there for them, all of them, whenever they needed him.

"Jessica was right, you know," he offered after several moments of silence. "Once she takes that job in New York, we won't have an opportunity to get away so easily."

"I know. I'm going to miss her."

"So will I. She's been a joy to be around."

"I wish that she and Steve got along better."

He looked down at her in surprise. "What do you mean? They seem to get along all right, don't they?"

"Well, with Steve's schedule he hasn't been home all that often, maybe twice when Jessica was home, but she always seems to change the subject whenever I bring him up."

"She's probably bored with listening to you rave on about him. To hear you talk about him, a person would think he walks on water."

Sabrina looked at him indignantly. "Well, I'm proud of him. Look what he's managed to accomplish in a few short years."

Michael nodded. "I know. He graduated with honors, got a job with a national television company and is currently working out of their London news office."

"You have to admit he's done well."

"I do. I have. But I've also caught Jessica rolling her eyes a couple of times when you start bragging about him."

Sabrina laughed. "Really? Then maybe that's why she changes the subject." She curled up against him. "I'm glad to know it's not Steve, then."

"Why?" He wasn't sure he wanted to know the answer.

"Well, he's such a wonderful person. He'd make any woman a marvelous husband."

"Sabrina! You know how much you hate matchmakers."

"I'm not matchmaking."

"What would you call it?"

"How could I matchmake with those two? They're seldom home at the same time. They barely know each other. He's in London, and she's going to be in New York."

He groaned. "Knowing you, you'll come up with some idea."

She smiled. "Let's just say that I'll enjoy watching their careers progress. It's interesting that they're in related fields."

"She's accepted a position writing for a travel magazine, and he's a television news reporter. How can that be related?"

"They're both in communications. Don't you see?"

He was quiet for a moment, but the hands moving across her body gave her a clue to what he was thinking.

"Sabrina?" he whispered.

"Hmmm?"

"I'm a great believer in communicating."

She smothered a chuckle. He certainly had a way of communicating his desires to her.

"Yes, Michael, I know."

There was no more need for words.

Jonathan and Daniel nodded to each other, shook hands and smiled, content with their success.

* * * * *

EARTH ANGEL

For Dharmaraja, always my heart's home.
And with special thanks to Matthew Reynolds
who loves my sandwiches, brings me ice water
and helped with the map.

For Downieville, always my heart's home.
And with special thanks to Matthew Reynolds,
who loves my sandwiches, brings me ice water—
and helped with the map.

Chapter One

Out in the frozen world beyond the kitchen window, a flicker of movement caught Frannie's eye.

Curious, she approached the window. She had entered the kitchen to refill her cup of hot cider, and she'd already done that. Now she took a cautious sip. As the sweet heat slid down her throat, Frannie searched the icy landscape before her.

She scanned the clean carpet of new snow, which rolled out from under the posts that held the back of the old house above the river during flood times. At first, the pure whiteness below lay still as a held breath. Perhaps, Frannie thought, the flutter she'd seen out of the corner of her eye had been an illusion.

But then she shifted her glance upward slightly so she was looking past the gate and her own truck parked beside it, half buried now in the snow. She looked across the unpaved road that ran by the back fence. Beyond the road rose the levee, and on the other side of that, the river ran icy and swift.

At the base of the levee, Frannie saw what had moved. It was a man—there in the shadow of a cedar tree by the side of the road.

A very tattered-looking man. Even from several hundred feet away, Frannie could see that his clothes were old and worn: a pitiful plaid wool jacket, torn denim pants that probably extended to overalls beneath the jacket, and bulky brown boots. He was a big man, well over six feet.

As Frannie watched, he came out from under the shadow of the cedar tree. She could distinguish the color of his hair then; it was a deep black-brown, surprisingly rich looking, even in the flat light from the gray winter sky.

Shuffling and lurching, he began to climb the levee. The foot of snow that had fallen since dawn was still loose and powdery. It impeded his progress, imprisoning his feet with each step he took.

But Frannie suspected that the new snow wasn't the real reason the man was having such difficulty negotiating the short climb to the top of the levee. The man reeled. Frannie would have bet her favorite Christmas record that he'd spent the better part of the afternoon bending his elbow in one of the two bars on Main Street not far away.

Frannie shrugged and sipped again from her mug. The man was none of her business. In the living room at the front of the house, she'd been in the process of decorating her Christmas tree. She should get back to it.

Yet she didn't move. The man intrigued her. There was something in the set of his broad shoulders that drew her. Something determined and proud that completely contradicted his lurching walk and pitiful clothes.

With some difficulty, he made it to the top. He stood, large and tattered, silhouetted against the winter sky. He swayed on his feet for several seconds, and then seemed to gather himself to stand tall.

He took something from his rear pocket—probably a wallet, Frannie decided, because he paused, his body swaying once again, to fiddle with it for a moment. Then he shoved his hand into the side pocket of the old jacket, as if sticking something from the presumed wallet in there.

That action almost cost him his balance—he teetered like a falling tree. Frannie smiled in spite of herself, and then felt her smile melt away. He was sad and silly. And yet there remained that other quality, which was serious and solemn and full of noble purpose.

Once again, he collected himself and slid his free hand to his breast beneath the jacket. He pulled his hand out again, clutching something flat and palm-sized.

For a moment he was very still, arms at his sides, looking out over the surging gray river before him. The quality of grave determination that Frannie had sensed in him seemed suddenly stronger than before. His big shoulders were set, his head high.

Frannie felt a little catch in her throat, a quick thrill of fear. Could he be thinking of tossing himself out into the rushing water? Was she standing sipping cider at her window, witnessing a man attempting to end his life?

Slowly, with great and somber dignity, the man raised his hands straight out to his sides, still clutching in each fist the objects he'd found in his clothes. He rocked, his body swaying toward the river.

"No!" Frannie heard herself gasp, sure in that moment that he intended to hurl his body into the pounding torrent below. She slammed her mug on the counter, slopping cider across the ancient Formica, and reached for the window latch. The latch was old and stubborn. She struggled with it.

Sounds of frustration escaped her. She had to get the window open, call out to him, beg him to reconsider. True, life could seem a pointless thing, each day a wasteland, each night an eternity where the best you could hope for was just to get through it—to face another meaningless day. But even the emptiest of lives could be turned around. It had happened for Frannie Lawry. It could happen for the raggedy man on the levee, she knew that it could!

Frannie glanced up from her struggle with the window—and her fingers stopped fighting the latch. She watched, unmoving, as the man flung the objects in his hands, one at a time, into the river below. That done, he planted his fists on his hips and stared at the river once more. His entire stance shouted grim satisfaction as the river carried away whatever it was he'd tossed into it.

He showed no inclination whatsoever to throw himself in next.

Frannie let go of the window latch, feeling more than a little foolish. The man was no potential suicide. He was just a poor guy on a bender, behaving oddly, throwing the contents of his pockets into the river for reasons he himself would probably wonder about when he finally sobered up. He was a total stranger, doing nothing threatening to anybody—not even himself. His actions should be no concern of Frannie's.

She cast an irritated glance at her spilled cider, and started to reach for the counter sponge. But the man was turning around now and starting back down the levee. Once again, Frannie found herself observing his unsteady progress.

He didn't get far. Two steps down the slope, his legs shot out from under him. He went sliding on his backside, plowing the powdery snow as he went. He landed at the base of the levee, faceup to the lowering sky.

Once he stopped sliding, he didn't move.

Frannie waited for him to stir. He remained utterly still.

There was really no reason to be concerned about him, Frannie told herself. He was just—resting for a moment, before he dragged himself to his feet and went on his way.

From the front of the house she could hear the festive sounds of the Christmas carols she'd been playing while she trimmed her tree.

Halfway through a chorus of "Jingle Bells," the man still hadn't moved. But of course, he would get up soon enough. She should get back to the tree and her private holiday celebration.

Yet she didn't. She kept watching him, thinking vaguely that as soon as he stirred and she knew he was all right, she would turn and forget about him once and for all.

As the seconds stretched out, Frannie became aware of the popping sounds made by the fire in the cast-iron stove a few feet away. She heard the muffled crunch of a log collapsing within. She smelled the tart sweetness of the steam escaping from the pan of cider on top.

She remembered the spilled cider on the counter, turned, picked up the sponge and mopped it up.

That done, she shot a look out the window again. The man was perfectly still, spread-eagled, like someone who'd been staked out to die there, in the snow.

Frannie made a low, disgusted sound in her throat. She just had to stop imagining tragic things about him. He was no victim. He was just a drunk who had passed out in the snow. And if he didn't get up in a little while, someone would go down there and help him. He was in plain sight of other houses than Frannie's, so eventually someone else would notice him and do something about him—someone other than a single woman staying alone.

She glanced at the wood basket beside the stove. It was almost empty, just a few sticks of kindling and one lone pine log left. She might as well refill it before returning to the front of the house.

Resolutely veering from the window and the sight of the inert figure at the bottom of the levee, Frannie took the heavy work gloves that were hung on the side of the basket and then headed for the basement stairs.

When she reached the foot of the stairs, where the cut wood was stacked neatly against the dirt wall that supported the front of the house, she reminded herself that her kindling supply was low. Tomorrow she'd make time to split some.

The door to the one finished room beneath the house was slightly ajar. She'd left it that way after lunch, when she came down to get the box of decorations stored in there. Frannie pulled the door closed and then put on the heavy gloves.

She made three trips up and down to refill the basket. Each time she entered the kitchen, she was scrupulously careful not to let her glance stray toward the window. When at last the box was full of wood, she removed her gloves and laid them on the rim of the basket again.

Now she would turn and march back through the dining room to the living room, where another fire crackled in the grate and her tree stood proudly before the front window, already strung with lights and ready for some serious bulb-hanging. All she needed was her cider. She strode past the window to reach it—and, in her peripheral vision, saw that dingy plaid jacket again.

Sighing, Frannie turned and once more stared at the motionless figure still sprawled in the snow.

How long had he been lying there now? Ten minutes, maybe?

And how cold was it out there, actually? And how long till dark—a half hour or so?

She allowed herself to wonder if, beyond being drunk, he might be hurt or ill?

Frances, a cynical voice in her mind rebuked, *must you romanticize even an insensible drunk?*

Though it was only in her mind, Frannie recognized the voice. Kenneth's. He'd dominated her life for so many years, that in moments of indecision she still imagined him pronouncing his opinions in that haughty, preemptive way of his.

The voice continued, cold and full of mounting disdain, *There's nothing wrong with that lowlife out there that a trip to a detox unit wouldn't cure. That man is not ill, except in that he's poisoned himself with alcohol. That is his responsibility. Let him live with it.*

Outside in the snow, the raggedy man lay unmoving. By dark, it would be getting even colder. The weather forecast was for more snow and a low in the mid-twenties.

Maybe she *should* go down there and—

Are you insane, *Frances?* Kenneth's imaginary voice cut her off before she could finish her thought. *The man is obviously a bum. Notify the sheriff if the sight of him bothers you, but there is absolutely no reason to become involved yourself....*

Frannie lifted her chin. She and Kenneth had parted a year and a half ago. Their divorce had been final for over six months. She was no longer the child bride of a successful older man. At thirty-three, she was her own independent person at last. What Kenneth Dayton might have thought in this situation didn't matter.

What mattered was what Frannie Lawry thought—and just what she intended to do about it.

The man, whoever or whatever he was, had been lying too still for too long. Who was to say he wouldn't get frostbite—or worse—before one of the neighbors became concerned enough to check on him?

Frannie needed to do something. Unfortunately, since she used the old house left her by her dad only for holidays and vacations, she didn't keep a phone here.

Of course, she could trudge next door to borrow her Aunt Bonnie's phone. But that prospect didn't fill her with enthusiasm. She and her aunt seemed to be forever disagreeing on things lately. They'd parted this very morning on a sour note. Now Bonnie would be full of her own opinions about what to do concerning the man in the snow.

The other option was to troop on out the back gate and rescue her raggedy man on her own.

A small chuckle escaped her. How strange. Thinking of the poor man as *hers*. Of course, he was nothing of the kind.

But he did need help.

Frannie whirled from the window and made for the side door, pausing only to lift her red down jacket off its hook on her way out.

Chapter Two

"Can you hear me?" a gentle voice asked.

Though it caused him considerable discomfort, Burnett Clinton opened an eye and willed the world to come into focus. What he saw made him force the other eye open, too.

An angel hovered above him. She had pale skin and shell-pink lips, and her dark brows were drawn together with concern.

Her hair was another story, not angelic at all, Burnett thought. She had hair that cried out to be spread on a pillow. Thick, wild, long, curly hair. It was chestnut-brown.

"Are you injured?" she asked.

Her eyes were blue. A very light blue at the center, with dark blue rims around the iris. The dark rims made the light centers somehow mesmerizing, Burnett thought.

Amanda, Burnett's ex-wife, had blue eyes. But Amanda's eyes were a uniform, flawless blue. Not an odd, arresting contrast between light and dark the way this woman's were.

"I went for a walk," Burnett told the angel, with a dignity that he himself found amazing, considering his position, sprawled faceup in the snow. "I thought the cold air might sober me up a little."

"I see," she said.

"But I fell in this snowbank, and then... I didn't get up."

"I saw you from my kitchen window." Her warm breath came out on a silvery plume. "I thought maybe you were ill."

"No, just drunk." He shook his head, which caused all manner of minor explosions in his brain. Then he added, feeling defiant, "And it's not even dark yet." Truth to tell, Burnett Clinton could never remember being drunk in his whole life, let alone so drunk he could topple into a snowbank at five in the afternoon and not be able to get up.

Beyond the chestnut halo of the angel's wild hair, the pewter winter sky seemed to vibrate. Burnett's stomach churned. He closed his eyes once more, hoping that when he dared open them again, the world would stop pulsing in rhythm with the pounding in his head.

He felt someone pulling on his arm. "Come on," the angel urged, "Let me help you."

She was strong, for an angel, and she managed to get him to a sitting position before he knew what was happening. He opened his eyes again.

The harsh winter light found its way to his pounding brain. It hurt—both having his eyes open, and sitting up.

"No, no," he shook his head—a mistake because it intensified the pounding. "I'm too disgusting." With a groan, he fell back upon the blanket of white, shut his eyes and turned his cheek against the icy coldness.

"You can't just lie here," she said.

"Watch me."

"Please, Mr..."

He realized she was waiting for a name. He wished he was someone else, anyone but Burnett Clinton, a man who'd sunk so low that he couldn't drag himself out of a snowbank on his own steam.

"Ned," Burnett heard himself say. "Call me Ned." His first name was Edward, after the father he'd hated, and everyone used to call him Ned years ago, until he'd grown old enough to reject the name and adopt his middle name, Burnett, as his own.

"Do you have a last name, Ned?" the angel asked.

A last name. Did he have a last name? He thought of the bar he'd recently staggered from, the St. Charles Place bar. "St. Charles," he said. "Ned St. Charles."

"Ned St. Charles," the angel said. The name sounded wonderful on her lips. "Please let me help you. The temperature's dropping. It'll be dark soon, and it's going to snow again, too."

"I could freeze to death," he said matter-of-factly, keeping his eyes clenched shut. Right then, freezing didn't seem like such a terrible fate. If he froze to death he wouldn't have to live through the hangover he was going to be experiencing soon.

"I doubt you'll be allowed to freeze," she said, her voice suddenly tart. "You're in plain sight of the Riverside Motel, as well as half the houses on Commercial Street. Someone will come down and pull you out soon enough— probably the sheriff."

"Oh." Burnett pondered this information.

"In fact, since you're too big for me to carry, maybe it's better if I go hunt down someone larger to help you up."

He heard the crunching of the snow as she rose from her kneeling position beside him.

His angel was leaving him.

"Wait!" he said, oblivious to the ringing echo the word set off in his aching brain. He opened his eyes and lifted his head off its pillow of snow.

She towered above him, miles away, incredibly beautiful. She had her hands stuck into the pockets of the red jacket she was wearing. "What is it, Ned St. Charles?"

"You came down here. To help me. You don't even know what kind of guy I am. People don't do things like that anymore."

"This is Downieville," she said. "It's a small town. People help each other here. It's understood."

"Oh," he said.

"I'll be back soon. Don't worry," she assured him, starting to turn away.

"Wait!" he said again.

She stopped. "What?"

He gazed at her for a moment, his mind a blank. Then words finally came to him. "Today's the day my divorce is final."

"I'm sorry," she said.

He let his head fall back, but held on to her bewitching gaze. "No," he told his angel. "That marriage was no good. I couldn't give her what she wanted. And maybe I never really loved her anyway. She was perfect. She was exactly what I thought I should want. But we were never happy. I don't think I know how... to be happy."

The angel said nothing, she just looked at him, her head tipped in an attitude of listening.

Beyond the levee behind him, Burnett could hear the river's hollow roar. "Why am I telling you this?" he said at last.

She shrugged, her slim shoulders lifting and dropping in that blindingly red jacket. "Maybe you need someone to talk to."

"But I don't want to talk about it. I want to forget about it."

"Fine," she said. Then, "I'll be back soon."

"No, please." He just couldn't let her walk away.

"Yes?"

"Don't leave me here for the snow to fall on."

She smiled then. The smile lit up her already incredible face. Burnett's stricken senses reeled.

"Then you're going to help me?" she asked.

"Help you what?"

"I'll need you to work with me to get you up. You're a pretty big man. I'm strong, but I doubt if I can do it unless you help."

Burnett considered her words. Then he said, momentously solemn, "I am going to help you to help me. Indubiously."

She actually laughed. Her laughter was like bells. "You mean indubitably."

"Right. Absolutely." He managed to nod—with great dignity, he thought.

"All right, Ned," she said. He wondered for a moment who Ned was, and then he remembered that *he* was Ned. He'd always been Ned; he'd just made everyone call him Burnett for the last twenty-seven years of his life.

It had been a mistake, he realized now, to have ever changed his name. Burnett Clinton had lived an empty, meaningless life. Burnett Clinton was rich. Burnett Clinton had everything—except love and laughter and someone to call his own.

He supposed, if he were fair, that he must admit his family loved him—his mother and his brother and his brother's wife and his little nephew, Mike. They loved him *in spite* of how difficult he'd made it for them to love him. To them, he was someone who insisted on making them all rich—whether they really wanted to be rich or not—and then tried to run their lives. He was someone they put up with because they understood that he *meant* well.

His angel had swooped down to his level again. She grabbed his hand in her slim one, and yanked him up to a sitting position once more. He heard a groan, and realized it came from him.

"Lord, that hurts," he said.

"Your arm?" she asked, since that was what she'd been pulling on.

"Everything. My stomach, my head, my eyebrows, my hair..."

"You should have considered that earlier," she muttered dryly.

"I've been a fool," he said with becoming gravity.

She said nothing, only wrapped his arm around her slim shoulders and then wedged herself against his side.

"Okay," she told him. "Let's get you to a crouch first. Pull up your knees and put your feet flat on the ground." She waited while he did that. "Now, when I say the word, you rock up onto your feet."

He could feel the warmth of her all along his side. It was wonderful. He hadn't realized how damn cold it was until right then.

Lightly, the snow began to fall again. Big, fat flakes drifted down. They fell on his angel's unruly hair and melted on her dark brows.

"What's your name?" he asked.

"Frances. Call me Frannie. You ready?"

"As I'll ever be."

"Oomph," they said in unison, and Burnett found himself kneeling on his feet.

"Halfway there," she told him. "Okay, when I say now..." He took in a breath, and held it. "Now!" she said.

The breath he'd drawn came out in a hard rush as, with a superhuman effort and the help of his angel, Burnett surged to his full height.

Being upright was not a pleasant experience. The world went spinning. He staggered.

"Whoa..." she said, and steadied him.

Burnett sucked in another breath and let it out with great care. His surroundings ceased whirling crazily and settled into a slow, stomach-churning slide.

"We did it," she announced, her soft voice full of pride.

Burnett said nothing; he was trying not to disgrace himself all over his angel's red parka.

"Now," she went on. "Ned, where did you come from?"

He swallowed, forced himself to think. Where did he come from? He remembered.

"The bar."

She shook her head, her hair picking up static against the scratchy wool of the ancient jacket he wore. "No," she tried again, "I mean, where do you live? You aren't from town, are you?"

He considered. Where did he live? *Burnett* lived in Sacramento, in a big house off of Fair Oaks Boulevard.

"Town?" he asked.

"From here, Downieville," she elaborated, with a look that said she wondered if he'd actually managed to do some permanent damage to his brain.

"No, not from town," he said.

"Where, then?"

Then it came to him. The cabin in Graeagle. Where he'd gone to be alone. His family's cabin, where he'd found the disgraceful clothes he was wearing in a dusty box upstairs and put them on because . . . why? It was something about wishing he were someone else. Anyone else but Burnett Clinton who had it all, and still had nothing.

"Ned?" his angel prompted again. "Can't you tell me where you're from."

Where I'm from, he thought. "Graeagle," he said.

"Graeagle? But that's up past the summit, through the Lakes Basin."

"Right. I went for a drive this morning. I ended up here." She was giving him an exasperated look. He attempted a shrug and explained as if it were worth something, "The bar was open."

"Yes." Her tone was wry. "I think we've already established that."

She was quiet for a moment—trying to decide what to do with him, no doubt. He experimented with squinting his eyes, to see if the houses across the road would stop moving around so much.

"Well," she said finally, "you'll have to check into the motel, then. The roads are going to be rough going tonight—and it would be illegal for you to drive in your condition anyway." Her breath, scented faintly of apples and cinnamon, was warm against his cold cheek.

She was tall for an angel, he realized, only four or five inches shorter than his own six-three. He liked that. No wimpy little dinky angels for Burnett Clinton—correction, Ned St. Charles—no sirree.

"Ned? Did you hear me?"

"Um. Yes. Every word."

"We're just going to struggle down this road here, okay? I'll take you to the motel."

Burnett remembered what he'd recently done with his wallet and his money clip. All he had in his pockets now was his driver's license. He'd saved that because, even so drunk he could barely stand, the solid citizen inside him couldn't bear the thought of walking around without identification. If it really became necessary, he'd wanted the means to prove who he was on demand.

"Ned? Are you phasing out on me again?"

" 'Scuse me?"

"I said we're going to walk to the motel now."

He shook his head. "So sorry. Can't do that."

"Yes, you can," she said gently. "I'll help you."

"No, not that. I don't mean I can't walk. I can walk, more or less."

"What is it, then?" she asked.

He looked at her very seriously, drawing his brows together, but forgot to say anything.

"Why can't you go to the motel?" his angel prompted.

He understood he needed to answer then. "No money," he said gravely.

"No money," she repeated after him. She said it more as a confirmation than a question, and she didn't sound the least surprised.

"Not a red cent," he announced with an absurd flare of pride. Of course, even in his inebriated state, he knew it would take no more than a single phone call to line his pockets once again. But he wasn't going to tell his angel that.

To her, he was Ned St. Charles, from Graeagle. A pitiful case. A loser at the game of life. Ned St. Charles had hit rock bottom. He was the kind of guy God just might send an angel to help.

Burnett Clinton needed help, too. But God, rightfully, wouldn't worry about him. Burnett Clinton had everything. It wasn't God's problem if Burnett Clinton couldn't make himself happy.

"Not even a credit card?" his angel asked.

"Threw my wallet in the river," he replied.

"Why?"

"I had this crazy idea that money meant nothing," he told her.

Her haunting eyes shifted once, and he knew she was thinking that there couldn't have been much in the wallet to begin with. It was logical that she'd come to that conclusion, given his condition and the old clothes he was wearing.

She was watching him, her head against his shoulder as her body helped to brace him upright. Her magical eyes gazed into his. It occurred to him that anyone glancing at them from a nearby house might think they were lovers out for a stroll, cuddled up close against the winter cold. Burnett smiled at the thought; it held definite appeal.

She saw his smile and became stern. "So you have no money."

"Nope." Well, he didn't—not *on* him.

"And nowhere to go."

"Right." Or at least, nowhere that mattered.

"What in the world am I going to do with you?"

He tried to look as appealing as possible—given the circumstances. "Take me home?"

Her strange eyes narrowed at him. "Give me a good reason why I should take a drunk stranger into my house."

"Pity?" he tried.

She was silent.

"It's Christmastime," he reminded her hopefully.

She shook her head.

He said a word he'd rarely uttered in his thirty-eight years. "Please."

She was silent again. He held his breath. At last, she said warily, "All right. I do have a room in my basement . . ."

"A room," he said, still hardly daring to breathe. Somewhere warm to lie down, he was thinking. A place where, when he woke up tomorrow, she'd be there. That seemed even more important than a warm bed to pass out in right now—to make sure she would still be there when morning dawned. Having found his angel at last, he had to be careful she didn't fly away.

"I suppose you could stay there," she offered. "For this one night. To sleep it off." Her voice was reluctant.

"Yes, to sleep it off," he said too eagerly.

Her eyes narrowed further. When she spoke, it was in a warning tone. "There's a deadbolt lock on the door between the basement and the house," she told him. "I plan to use it."

He looked at her seriously, and slowly assimilated that she was telling him that her door would be locked against him, should he have any sinister plans.

"Fine," he said.

She didn't look completely convinced. She glared at him measuringly, and then pointed to one of the houses opposite where they stood on the snow-covered road. "See that house right there?"

He squinted where she pointed. "You bet."

"See that woman looking out the kitchen window?"

He saw the outline of a head in the window she was pointing to. "I see someone," he allowed.

"That's my aunt, Bonnie Lawry. The house to the left of hers is mine."

"Oh," he said, not sure what she was getting at.

"What I'm saying is, Aunt Bonnie's seen you. If I take you to my house, there'd better not be any funny stuff. Because she'll know you were there."

Burnett wondered, with some irony, exactly what Aunt Bonnie would *do* were he to commit some transgression. By the time she found out, it would be too late. He opened his mouth to inform his angel that the threat of her Aunt Bonnie's wrath probably wouldn't add up to much if he were really intent on *funny stuff*. But then it occurred to him that such a remark wouldn't help his case much.

He raised the hand that wasn't slung over Frannie's shoulder. "I swear. No funny stuff," he said. Even if he were the type of man prone to funny stuff, he was in no condition for it. In his current state, he'd be lucky to stagger to the basement room his angel had offered him and collapse on the first piece of furniture that presented itself.

She was looking at him doubtfully, shaking her head. "I've got to be out of my mind," she sighed.

"No," he said, "not out of your mind at all."

"Then what?"

He considered, and the answer came. "You're good. A good person. Generous and kind." And an angel, he added silently. *My* angel. At last.

She smiled just a little. "Thanks."

"Welcome."

They looked at each other for a moment through the thickening fall of the snow. Then her gaze slid away, and she gestured at the house she'd said was hers. "Let's get started. There's a basement entrance, so it won't be too far."

"Ah," Burnett said, nodding. He looked where she pointed, and tried to estimate the distance he was going to have to walk.

The distance was rather hard to judge, actually. The snow was falling harder, like a softly swirling veil between himself and the white clapboard structure that she had pointed to. And, of course, there was the cruel glitter of the snow on the ground to further confuse him, not to mention the way stationary objects just refused to *stay* stationary. Everything rippled and swayed. Except his angel. She was warm and firm—and yet soft at the same time—braced at his side.

She took a step.

His stomach lurched. "Oh, God," he said. "I can't do this."

"One foot in front of the other," she told him.

"Oh, God," he said again, and they started across the road.

She took him, one stomach-churning step at a time, across the road. They had to stagger around a parked truck to reach the gate. Once through the gate, they lurched past a lot of bare bushes sticking up through the fiercely brilliant snow. When they reached the house, they went beneath an overhang between supporting posts. She guided him around the side, to where there was a rough wooden door with a padlock on it.

"Rest here." She propped him up against the wall and removed the lock, which had only been turned but not engaged.

He thought to reprimand her for not keeping it locked. She was much too trusting, he decided. Leaving her doors open, taking in strange men she found in the snow. But then the door swung open, creaking loud enough, it seemed, to make his head explode, and he knew right then that if he tried to lecture her, he would be sick.

"Come on." She hooked his arm around her shoulder, and bolstered him once more. They stepped down into the dark basement, which was as cold as it was outside and smelled of frozen earth.

Burnett felt the contents of his stomach rise up alarmingly. He distracted himself from the certainty that he was going to be sick by exerting a superhuman effort to study his surroundings.

They tottered across a concrete floor, past stacks of firewood on one side and a washer and dryer that had seen a lot of loads on the other. They stopped where the concrete ended.

He paused, swaying. "Oh, no. Stairs," he groaned.

"Only four steps," she reassured him. "To that door there."

"Oh, no," he said again, but she was already guiding him upward.

He managed—Lord knew how—to negotiate those four steps. They stopped at a small landing in front of the door she'd mentioned. To their left, the stairs turned and continued up—to the main house, he presumed.

His angel pushed open the door in front of them. He saw a low-ceilinged cell of a room with a window on the outside wall, a battered chest, a closet—and a single bed.

Nothing in his life had ever looked as wonderful as that bed. His weary body yearned for it.

They made it up the last step and over the threshold. His head grazed the low ceiling as she helped him stagger to the bed and sink down upon it.

"Now, don't you dare lie down yet," she said. She'd dropped to the bed with him, and was still tucked beneath his arm, keeping him from doing what he most longed to do—fall over on his side. "We've got to get your coat and boots off," she continued. "But first I want to turn the heater on."

"Yes, ma'am," he humbly replied, and then found himself grinning, almost forgetting that if he didn't stretch out flat he would probably die.

He wished his brother could have heard him say *yes, ma'am* like that. Casey would never believe Burnett capable of sounding so meek and obedient unless he heard it with his own ears.

"What's so funny?" his angel was asking.

"My brother, Casey," he said without thinking, "would not believe what a mess I'm in now."

She pulled away from him and stood looking down at him. Her eyes looked sad. He could see she felt sorry for him, for pitiful Ned whose life was out of control. "You're often in trouble, then?" she asked.

He couldn't speak for a moment as he looked up into her face. God, she was beautiful. Her pale skin seemed to glow. He thought it was about time he told her who he really was. But then, who was he—really? Ned *was* his real first name, and he *had* come from Graeagle. Calling himself Ned *St. Charles* might have been pushing it a little too far...

"Ned?" she asked, concerned at his extended silence.

Hell, he thought. I'm drunk. I can't explain it all now. Plenty of time for that later, when I'm sober, when I can lay it all out for her, in simple, clear terms.

She was looking worried. He realized he needed to say something. To answer her question . . . what was the question?

He remembered—was he often in trouble? That was what she had asked.

How to answer that—without lying, exactly, but without having to explain everything right now when he just wasn't in any condition to explain.

How, he found himself wondering, would Ned answer that question?

Ned was on the skids—but he still had his pride. And Ned was every bit as drunk as Burnett was right at the moment.

So, he decided, Ned wouldn't want to take on the question of the trouble he'd been in any more than Burnett did. But how would Ned avoid it?

He thought of a manager he'd been forced to fire—a once-dependable fellow who hadn't been able to pull himself together after a series of personal setbacks. The day Burnett had let him go, the man wouldn't look at him. He'd been silent and withdrawn, the few things he did say hesitant and unsure. Perhaps Ned was like that...

Burnett looked away from his angel. "In our family, Casey was the wild one," he said, telling the truth about his younger brother. "And I was the *good* boy. But lately..." He didn't finish, as if it was just too painful to go on.

He heard her soft sigh. "Never mind. I guess now's not the time to go into that anyway."

He glanced back at her, putting on a brave smile. She smiled in return, and his heart did something strange inside his chest. He felt himself swaying, and quickly braced his fists to either side.

She put up a hand. "Don't fall over yet."

Then she whirled, so quick and lithe he had to close his eyes to keep his head from spinning. He heard an electric whine and realized she'd switched on a portable heater against the inside wall opposite where he sat. He felt the heat from it immediately in the small space.

Then she was back in front of him, busy and purposeful, making his brain reel from the force of her sheer, focused energy as she pushed the old coat off his shoulders.

He tried to be helpful, he really did. But the minute he lifted one fist off the bed, he crumpled to that side and lay there, bent at the waist, his face smashed into the nubby softness of the pink bedspread.

"Oh, well," he heard her sigh. "I'll get the one side off while it's easy to get at." She made a few soft little noises as she worked the jacket off of his left side. And then she pulled on his arm to try to get him upright again. He felt himself being lifted, his cheek leaving the soft, tufted spread for a moment.

But then he must have been too heavy. She let him back down. He heard a moan, and barely recognized it as his own. As it had out in the snow when he landed at the base of the levee, the soft, blessed void of unconsciousness enticed him. It was like a warm pool of darkness, a place he could drown in and forget everything for a while.

But then his angel was pushing at him from the other side, until she got him sitting again. He hung there, and then toppled the other way. He felt the jacket leave him.

And then she was levering his legs up on the bed. His booted feet hung off the end. He remembered, for some inexplicable reason, his custom-made bed at home. It was a super king-size and extra-long, so that he could sleep on his back and have all of him on the bed.

Home, his foggy mind scoffed. Was that empty showplace of a house he owned really anything that remotely resembled a home? Even Amanda, who had done most of the decorating herself, hadn't wanted to live there in the end.

"It's much too traditional," she had said. "After all, I chose every last stick of furniture with you in mind." There had been that tone of noble reproach. "No, darling, I'll take my share in money. Ashford prefers a more contemporary style." Ashford was the man Amanda lived with now, a lawyer. He'd had eight children and a lovely wife when Amanda had met him. Now, since Amanda was pregnant, he was about to have nine children—and a *new* wife, as soon as his own divorce was final next month.

"Now, the boots," he heard his angel say. He forgot all about Amanda and Ashford as he felt nimble fingers working the laces, and then, at last, pulling the boots off his feet.

He heard her step away. The closet door opened and closed. And then a heavy quilt that smelled faintly of mothballs settled over him. It was big enough that she could tuck it in beneath his stockinged feet. She said something like, "I'll bring down a big bowl, just in case..." He managed to nod, vaguely understanding that he was to use the bowl should his stomach rebel in the night.

Burnett sighed, and, even as blackness beckoned again, he felt his cold body warming and thought that it was good. "Wonderful. Thank you," he mumbled, and covered his eyes with his arm.

She might have said, "you're welcome" but he wasn't sure, because unconsciousness was coming at him like a huge wave, rising up and tumbling over him. He surrendered to it, as he had never in his life surrendered to anything, passing into oblivion like a swimmer swallowed by a midnight sea.

He didn't see her turn and leave, nor was he aware of her return with the promised bowl. Neither did he observe the way she hovered at his side, her mouth turning suddenly soft and tender. He also missed the flush of excitement that chased the softness away.

Beyond that, he didn't hear the way her breath caught when she realized what she'd been thinking. And he didn't see her whirl and flee the room, barely pausing to drop the bowl by the bed and whip the door closed behind her.

Chapter Three

Her breath coming too rapidly into her chest, Frannie turned the deadbolt that effectively sealed off the basement from the rest of the house.

She shivered, though the fire in the stove kept the kitchen toasty-warm. What in the world had she let herself imagine down there?

The sound of knuckles tapping on glass across the room saved her from having to answer her own question right then. She collected her scattered wits and turned for the side door, which was set with small glass panes in the top half. Through the panes, Bonnie Lawry's sharp dark eyes peered at her.

Putting her private thoughts away, Frannie went to let her aunt in from the cold. Since the shadows of twilight had darkened the high-ceilinged room, Frannie flipped on the light switch as she pulled open the door.

The two women regarded each other for a moment, and then Bonnie began busily brushing snow from her bare head, and stomping it off of her rubber boots onto the mat. That done, she stepped inside so Frannie could close the door.

The two stood close together. Bonnie leveled a piercing look at her niece. "I thought I should at least check on you," she said, "after I saw you pull that strange man from the snow."

Frannie looked away. "I'm fine, Aunt Bonnie." She busied herself shrugging out of her own red jacket and hanging it on the peg beside the door. That done, she held out her hand. "Here. Let me take your coat."

"No, I'll just keep it on." Bonnie wrapped her plump arms around herself and gave a shiver. Frannie felt guiltily relieved, thinking that if she wouldn't take off her coat, perhaps her aunt didn't plan to stay long enough to start asking uncomfortable questions. But then Bonnie sniffed. "What's that delicious smell?"

"Hot cider," Frannie allowed, then paused. Her aunt's bright eyes burned through her, and Frannie's ingrained good manners won out over her desire to avoid the coming interrogation. She asked, with a touch of irony, "Won't you have a cup?"

"Why, thank you, dear." Bonnie now looked quite serene. "Shall I get it myself?"

"No, no," Frannie said, handing out the rote courtesies more elaborately than necessary. "You sit down. Make yourself at home."

"Thank you. I shall."

Bonnie went to the scarred walnut table in the center of the room and pulled out a chair. Frannie opened a cupboard, saying no more, waiting for her aunt to begin asking the questions that Frannie knew would come.

Bonnie kept her peace until Frannie had poured the last of the cider into a mug, set it before her, and carried the pan to the sink. Then she asked, suddenly brusque, "Well, then, what did you do with him?"

Frannie ran water into the pan. "I put him to bed in the basement."

"He's down there now?"

"Yes, he is." Frannie glanced over her shoulder in time to see Bonnie shoot a look at the basement door. "It's locked," Frannie assured her.

"I should hope so."

Frannie flipped off the tap and went to sit in the chair at the head of the table. "I also told him that you knew what he looked like. So if he tried anything, he'd live to regret it."

Bonnie clucked her tongue. "I'll just bet that terrified him."

"Aunt Bonnie, he's harmless."

"Why do you think that? Because he told you so?"

"No, I just, well, I just know it."

"Ah, you've recently become psychic?"

Frannie looked away, and then back again. "He's staying the night. I said he could and I won't go back on my word."

Bonnie sipped from her cider and looked out the window at the darkness and the snow for a moment. "Has he got a name?"

"Ned. St. Charles."

"St. Charles?" Bonnie scoffed. "What kind of name is that for a man?"

"There's nothing wrong with it."

"It sounds phony."

"It does not."

"And it's also suspicious. Think about it. There's that big marker over town, where the St. Charles hotel once stood—not to mention that it's the name of one of the bars. It's just the kind of thing a drunk up to no good would do—give a name he's recently seen on a window somewhere instead of saying who he really is."

"Oh, Aunt Bonnie. That's ridiculous. St. Charles is a perfectly acceptable name. You're just looking for any excuse to get me to put the poor man out in the cold."

"Mark my words. He made it up."

"I mean it, Aunt Bonnie. Stop it, now."

Bonnie subsided against the straight back of her chair, crossing her arms over her full bosom. She studied her niece, her head tipped to the side, like a bantam hen seeking a new place to peck.

During the brief silence that ensued, Frannie told herself that her aunt's opinion about Ned would naturally be biased. Bonnie was "an old maid, and proud of it," as she defined herself. She lived alone, and would never allow a strange man to sleep the night in her house. Besides that, Bonnie hadn't talked to Ned the way Frannie had, or seen the lonely sadness in his dark eyes.

Yes, Frannie found herself thinking. Ned did have fine eyes. There was a sensitivity in them that even his being so drunk couldn't completely mask.

"Frances, what are you thinking?" Bonnie suddenly demanded, apparently having decided that the silence had lasted long enough.

"Nothing important," Frannie answered right away.

"Are you sure? All at once, you began to look positively moony."

"I'm sure."

Bonnie narrowed her eyes suspiciously, and then decided to return to the original topic. "All right, answer me this. Just where is this Ned St. Charles from?"

"Graeagle."

Frannie was granted a look of utter disdain. "There are no people named St. Charles in Graeagle."

"Oh, Aunt Bonnie. How can you be sure of that?"

"I have lived in these parts all my life."

"You don't even know anyone who lives in Graeagle."

"Of course I do. I know several people from Graeagle— and none of them are named St. Charles."

"Aunt Bonnie, no matter what you say," Frannie stated slowly and with great care, "I'm not kicking him out tonight. He's a poor guy with a lot of problems and he tried forgetting them in the bar. He's run out of money and has no place else to go."

Frannie decided against mentioning that Ned had thrown what little cash he possessed in the river, although it was entirely possible that Bonnie had seen him do it. If her aunt asked about it, Frannie would be honest. But Frannie had no intention of volunteering the information. Bonnie would only see it as more proof that Ned should be booted out the door posthaste.

"There are many people with problems in the world, Frances," her aunt was saying in her most patient voice. "Do you plan to let them all spend the night at your house?"

"No," Frannie told her. "Just this one."

"It is foolish and dangerous."

"My mind is made up."

"Change it."

"No."

"Frances—"

"I mean it, Aunt Bonnie. He is going nowhere tonight."

Bonnie glared and fumed. "You're being as foolishly obstinate about this as you've always been about working things out with your mother," she muttered in disgust.

At that, Frannie decided she'd had enough. Earlier in the day they'd been arguing about that subject, and Frannie had told her aunt in no uncertain terms that her relationship with her mother was her own business. "Ned St. Charles stays," she said after a heavy pause, her voice hard as rock. "I absolutely refuse to kick the poor man out." Frannie took a breath, then added honestly, as she'd learned to do in the past eighteen months, "And I resent the reference to my problems with my mother."

Bonnie's pugnacious expression slackened. She was caught off-guard by the new forthrightness in her niece. Beyond that, she seemed to realize that she'd gone too far. "I apologize for bringing Alicia into this," she nobly intoned. "That is a subject for another time." She even uncrossed her arms and tried to look sheepish. But she hadn't given up the battle over where Ned St. Charles would be spending the night. Frannie knew her aunt's quick mind was ticking away, conceiving the next line of attack.

When Bonnie spoke again, she had assumed a wounded expression. "I won't sleep a wink, worrying over you all night." She took a small, pained sip of cider.

Frannie said softly, "That's emotional blackmail, Aunt Bonnie. And it isn't going to work."

Bonnie huffed, "Emotional blackmail, indeed. Where did you get that, in that support group of yours down in Sacramento?"

"Maybe, but it doesn't matter where I got it." Frannie had joined the group when she left Kenneth. Just having a regular forum to discuss what she was going through had been invaluable. "What matters is that I believe you're using emotional blackmail on me right now."

"Oh, and don't you know everything lately," Bonnie muttered, suddenly finding the lights across the river of great interest.

"Aunt Bonnie—" Frannie tried. Bonnie stopped her with a curt wave of her hand, which she then let fall to the edge of the table. Frannie covered the hand with her own and pushed on. "Do you disapprove of my support group, is that what you're trying to tell me?"

"No." Bonnie was still looking out the window, but she didn't pull her hand out from under Frannie's. "I'm sure it's good for you. It's only..." Silence fell again.

"Go on," Frannie prompted.

Bonnie's eyes, full of confusion and concern, looked into Frannie's at last. "You're different, dear."

"Yes..." Frannie smiled. "I am."

"You're so... opinionated, lately."

"Thank you."

Bonnie groaned. "That was not a compliment."

"To me it was."

"Oh my, I just don't understand you."

"I think you do, Aunt Bonnie. I think you understand me just fine."

"What is that supposed to mean?"

"Only that you are a very strong person. And that I am becoming that way."

"Strong, you mean."

"Yes. And that makes things a little strained between us, for a while. As we both get used to the change."

Bonnie was quiet. Then she made a humphing sound. "You used to be so sweet." She grinned suddenly, the fine wrinkles in her round face deepening. Frannie was struck again with why she loved her bossy aunt so much when Bonnie added with charming frankness, "You used to be so delightfully easy to order around."

"Exactly. And when I married Kenneth, and *he* started ordering me around, you and I hardly saw each other—since the two of you never got along."

"But now, since you're becoming so strong," Bonnie concluded, her head tipped to the side, "no matter who you get involved with, he won't be able to keep you from visiting your dear old Aunt Bonnie. Is that what you're telling me?"

"Exactly."

"So I am expected to be grateful that you never do what you're told anymore?"

Frannie laughed. "Yes."

"Well," Bonnie conceded, "I *am* grateful to have you near again, dear."

Frannie squeezed her aunt's plump, calloused hand. "Me, too."

Bonnie's expression grew reproving once more as she pulled her hand from Frannie's warm clasp. "But I still don't like it. A man you don't even know—"

"Aunt Bonnie. Ned St. Charles is okay. There's nothing to worry about. He's locked out of the house, and he's too drunk to make trouble, anyway."

"But Frances . . . why?" Bonnie showed her bewilderment at last.

Frannie glanced away. The question made her nervous. "He needed help," she said after a weighted moment. "And it's Christmas, after all." She knew that neither of those answers was the real one, but she just wasn't ready yet to examine her own motivations more thoroughly—or to reveal them to her disapproving Aunt Bonnie when she did.

"I don't like it," Bonnie said.

"You've made that very clear."

"He will leave tomorrow?"

"Yes, that's what I said."

"Frances, you are wearing an evasive expression."

"Because there's nothing more to say."

"You have become stubborn about *everything* lately."

"This is my house, Aunt Bonnie. I can invite anyone I like to stay in it."

"It's foolish."

"You've said that."

Bonnie sighed, and Frannie realized that her relentless aunt had at last run out of new lines of attack.

"You absolutely refuse to listen to reason?" Bonnie asked sourly.

"He's staying," Frannie replied.

Bonnie shook her head. "What in the world ever happened to my sweet little girl?"

"She finally had to grow up."

The fire popped in the stove as the two women looked at each other.

"Now you listen here," Bonnie instructed at last. "If that man gives you a bit of trouble, you just tell him I live with a sumo wrestler and that I keep an arsenal in the front hall."

"I promise," Frannie chuckled, not so much at her aunt's attempt at humor as with relief that Bonnie was finally allowing Frannie to make her own decision about this. "I'll tell him."

"Good enough." Bonnie drained the last of her cider and stood up. "It's getting late." She slid her chair back beneath the table before she went to the door. "I saw the tree in the front window. It looks beautiful."

Frannie grinned. "Wait till I get some bulbs on it."

"Whether we get along as we once did or not, I do enjoy it when you're here, Frances."

"So do I." Frannie opened the door. Both women shivered, and Bonnie stepped out onto the side porch.

"I mean it," Bonnie said. "You warn him."

"I will." Frannie watched Bonnie's retreating back as her aunt stepped off of the side porch and approached the gate between the two houses.

When she retreated back inside, Frannie glanced at the clock and thought about dinner. But she wasn't really hungry. She'd fix a sandwich later.

In the front room, her tree was waiting. She might as well get back to it.

But perhaps she should check on Ned first, make sure the electric heater was warming things up properly and see that he was covered up. He was probably very vulnerable to a chill in his condition. She'd just go down there and—

Frannie caught herself before her hand turned the lock.

The man had been down there for less than half an hour. It was not likely that much could have occurred in that amount of time. The space heater was working fine, and if he'd kicked off his blankets, he would only be likely to do it again should she tuck them around him now.

She simply had to get her mind off Ned St. Charles and back on her own activities.

Resolutely, Frannie marched through the wide door to the dining room and through that to the front parlor. She turned the Christmas record over on her old portable turntable and dug into her box of decorations with a vengeance.

In another hour, when the night outside was pitch-black save for the shimmering patterns the whirling snow made in the glow of streetlamp and porchlight, the tree was finished. Frannie climbed her stepladder to balance the star on top and then climbed down and stood back to admire what she had done.

The tree was a silver-tip fir, majestic and symmetrical, its branches rising in flat, perfect tiers. Rather than peeking out, as they would in bushier trees, the bright bulbs and holiday figurines hung between the branches, sometimes spinning with slight movements in the air, twinkling in the light.

"Nothing like a silver-tip," her dad used to say. "A silver-tip's the queen of Christmas trees. Any other tree's just a substitute in my book."

Frannie looked up, tipping her head to study the star, to see that it didn't tilt as it presided over the splendor below.

It was a homemade star, created by Frannie's own hands the Christmas she was nine. She'd shaped it from a wire hanger and wrapped it with a silver garland.

Frannie's dad had said the star was beautiful. "It's beautiful, sweetheart. You've done a fine job." He'd set the star on top of the tree with great ceremony, making sure it was placed just so, and he swore it would be their star for all the years to come.

But, of course, it hadn't been. Because that was the last year they had together. The next Christmas he was gone.

Over a decade later, she'd brought the star out again. That was during the one time she'd dragged Kenneth up here, the first year they were married. Then he was still infatuated enough with his young bride that he occasionally did things to please her.

Frannie had lifted the star out of the box, bent the crooked wires back into reasonable shape and held it up to the light, grinning proudly.

"Oh please, Frances," Kenneth had said. His handsome, distinguished face had worn no expression. His tone had been utterly flat.

There was no need to say more. The three words had said it all: the star was tacky, crudely fashioned by a child. Not the kind of thing one displayed on top of a tree. So far from perfect that it was beneath recognition.

Frannie had put it away quickly, her face flaming.

Now, a decade later, Frannie felt her face flushing all over again at the memory. But this time the flush wasn't from embarrassment. The flush was from anger.

What a cold bastard Kenneth was. But worse than that, what a weak-kneed little yes-girl she had once been. So easy to order around, just as Aunt Bonnie had said.

"But not anymore," she whispered under her breath. "Never, ever again will any man dominate me."

And she saw, in her mind's eye, the man in the basement. She saw him first as he'd been outside, when he'd begged her to take him home with her.

"Please," he'd said. And something had happened inside her, a melting kind of feeling— Kenneth had never said please. The next minute she'd heard herself offering poor, helpless Ned the basement room for the night.

Frannie closed her eyes, as if blocking out the sight of the crude star would stop the next image that came unbidden to her mind. But shutting her eyes did no good.

Against the velvet darkness of her inner eyelids, she saw Ned St. Charles as he'd been just before she left him, passed out beneath the old comforter in the bed that was too short for him.

He'd had an arm flung over his eyes, as if the slightest bit of light caused him pain. He'd groaned and then sighed. And she'd known he was asleep.

His body lay slack. Right then, for all his size and strength, he'd been completely helpless, felled by his own excesses, at the mercy of the woman who'd allowed him shelter for the night.

Frannie had stood there, rooted to the spot, and looked at the shape of his raised arm—beneath the soft, old shirt, the bulge of his bicep was clearly defined.

She'd thought how hard and strong that arm looked, how physically powerful, like the strength in his big thighs beneath the frayed overalls when she'd raised his legs onto the bed.

She had wondered, then, what it would be like to make love with a man like Ned. A simple man, with simple desires.

The idea had excited her—a hot, pulsing kind of excitement. The kind of excitement the more candid women in her support group sometimes talked about, the kind of excitement Frannie herself had never really known. Until that moment.

She had run from it. Whirled and fled up the stairs and bolted the door.

A few minutes later she'd told her aunt that Ned St. Charles represented no danger at all.

And he didn't. Ned St. Charles, of himself, was no threat to Frannie Lawry at all. She didn't need to be careful of him. The person she needed to watch like a hawk was herself.

Frannie opened her eyes and stared blankly at her tree and her wire-hanger star.

Of course, she hadn't actually fallen for Ned in the brief moments she'd spent with him. She'd only been dangerously attracted, that was all.

Frannie slumped to the sofa and leaned back on the pillows, still gazing at the star she had made as a child.

No, she hadn't fallen for him. Yet. And the *yet* was the problem.

Ned St. Charles absolutely had to go. In the morning, without fail.

Chapter Four

"**M**r. St. Charles?"

Hating to do it, Burnett opened one eye. The diffused light from beyond the drawn shade sliced into his brain. He perceived that a tall woman with a lot of brown hair was bending over him. That was all he could take. Before the light could finish him off, he shut the eye he'd opened. "God. Go away." He rolled onto his side and yanked the comforter over his head.

She shook him. "It's morning. You have to get up."

He would have laughed at such a suggestion—but every cell in his body was screaming in hung-over agony. To laugh right now was something from which he doubted he'd ever recover.

"Mr. St. Charles. Please."

She yanked on the comforter. He held onto it, though even his fingers were in pain. "Have mercy. Get lost," he managed to croak.

But the woman, whoever she was, had no pity. She kept pulling the comforter. "It's morning," she said again, as if he hadn't become excruciatingly aware of that fact when he made the mistake of opening that eye a moment ago. "And you have to go." Cruelly, she ripped the comforter away. He groaned and brought up his hands to shield his hapless eyes. She grasped his shoulder—to turn him faceup again, he assumed.

But then he forgot everything as his stomach seemed to rise, inexorably, toward his throat.

"Oh, God." He surged toward the edge of the bed, knowing everything was coming up way before he could get his aching body to go anywhere.

She must have understood what was happening, because suddenly she had a big bowl in her hand and was guiding him over it.

He was sick, repeatedly. Thanks to the merciless woman, though, it was mostly in the bowl.

When he was done, he flopped on his back and wished he was dead.

"Is that all?" the woman asked.

"Isn't that enough?" he somehow got out in response.

He was nebulously aware that she left—probably to empty the bowl. But he didn't waste a lot of time thinking about the woman. He mostly cursed his own self-indulgent idiocy and lived through the agony that being in his body right then represented.

His whole self was raw, just raw. Every muscle seemed to spasm and quiver. He imagined that criminals flayed alive in the Middle Ages probably hadn't felt this bad; at least they hadn't been skinned *inside,* which was what he felt like after losing the contents of his stomach—as if most of his internal organs had come up with yesterday's Scotch.

He was distracted from the gruesome contemplation of his own pain by the sound of the door opening. The woman spoke again. "Now just what am I going to do with you?"

Burnett groaned.

"We had an agreement that you would leave in the morning," she said. "But I suppose now you'll say you don't remember it."

"Could you please stop talking?" he whispered.

"What?"

"The sound of talking hurts."

She fell blessedly silent, but not for long.

She said, "All right. I'll be back to check on you in a couple of hours. We'll try to get some liquids in you then."

He said nothing. The ability to speak had left him, or so it seemed. He breathed, slowly, trying to slip the oxygen in without letting his body know. His body didn't want to move; even the slight expansion and contraction of breathing was too much for it. At some point a little later, he gratefully lost consciousness once more.

"All right. Let's try a few spoonfuls of this broth."

She was back.

"You said a coupl'a hours," he made himself complain in that hoarse croak that was all he had for a voice right then.

"It's after nine," she said, as if that explained anything.

"Do you...have to answer so fast?" he grumbled. Then, "Oh, God" again, as she shoved her hands under his arms and began pushing him upright. "Oh, please..." He felt the wall at his back. He was sitting. He kept his eyes tightly closed, thinking that right then the pain was just bearable, but if he let the light in through his eyes, the pain would be too much. "Whoever you are, I hate you," he said.

She chuckled.

"A man is dying—and you laugh," he nobly accused. "And I refuse to open my eyes."

"Fine. Just open your mouth. I'll spoon it in."

"What?"

"I told you. Beef broth."

He smelled it then. His stomach began to rise. "I can't..." he warned.

"You can. And you will. Open your mouth."

She sounded so sure that his stomach wouldn't dare make trouble again, that he did as she said. In went a spoonful of broth. He dared to swallow, then held his breath.

"It's staying down," he ventured after a nervous count of ten.

"Good. Open again."

She patiently ladled several spoonfuls into his mouth, waiting each time until he swallowed before dipping up another. Once, while she fed him, he opened his eyes. He saw pale skin and wild hair, and decided that he had been right before. The pain of the light was simply too much at this point. For the rest of the time that she fed him, he kept his eyes closed. He felt her hand brush the side of his face once; it was a cool hand, and slightly rough. He wondered what she did with her hands that made them rough. But he didn't wonder long. Wondering, like thinking in general, just caused his head to pound.

"Okay, good," she said finally. He heard her set the soup bowl down. Then she pushed on his shoulders, guiding him back flat.

He sighed. He still felt like hell, but he no longer wished he was dead.

"Who are you?" he asked.

"We covered that yesterday."

"A name, that's all," he complained. "I'd like to know what to call you while you torture me."

"Think about it," she said flatly. "It'll come to you."

He tried to remember, though it caused his brain considerable pain. He thought of a red jacket, of strange blue eyes. "Frannie," he muttered. "Frannie." He actually felt himself smile. "Right?"

"Right." Her voice was distant.

He opened his eyes again, and actually looked directly at her for the first time that morning. She was not smiling back.

"What's the matter?" he asked, a little bewildered. Though the recollection was fuzzy, he remembered she'd been sweet and good and kind yesterday. She'd patiently assisted him across the road to her house, where she'd helped him off with his jacket and boots and gently tucked him into this lumpy little bed.

He'd imagined her an angel, he recalled now. *His* angel, sent to save him from the empty wasteland that had become his life.

Right now she didn't look too angelic. She was glaring at him like a female drill sergeant with a rebellious recruit.

"Nothing's the matter," she said coldly. Her strange eyes were as expressionless as her voice. "Sleep some more. I'll be back down at noon. You'll get some solid food in you. Then you are out of here. Understand?"

Burnett frowned. Even flat on his back, nobody talked to him like that. "I'll leave now," he said, and sat up. Hot needles pierced his brain. "Sweet Lord..." he groaned, and closed his eyes.

"Down." She shoved him flat, surprising him with her strength. "You couldn't walk if you tried, and it's still snowing out. Noon will be soon enough. Sleep." Before he could tell her that he thought she was a bitch, she left.

He lay there and practiced opening and closing his eyes for a while, rather pleased that he could do that now without feeling as if a cruel hand had just shoved a burning stick into his head. And then, though he didn't plan to, he went to sleep again.

He woke the next time on his own, feeling impatient. It took him a few minutes to realize the feeling was physical; he needed to relieve himself. Bad.

He sat up, though his head protested, and threw back the comforter. He swung his legs to the floor and grimaced at his stockinged feet. He shot a glance at the battered boots he'd been wearing, then groaned. Lace-up boots. No way. His need was way beyond fumbling with lace-up boots.

He stood up, his head pounding and his stomach pitching. But when he got on his feet, he stayed there. He pulled open the door to a wall of frigid air, and confronted the basement.

In his mind, he replayed the grueling walk across the concrete floor the evening before and decided it was unlikely there might be a bathroom down here. He glanced up the stairs and saw the door that must lead to the main house.

He thought of his angel, who'd become a real harpy in the harsh light of day. Hadn't she warned him last evening that she was going to dead-bolt that door? Now, if he pounded on it, she probably wouldn't answer. She'd wait, smirking, until he disgraced himself in his overalls and then she'd come flouncing down here crowing *I told you so*, and order him out into the snow.

"No thank you," he growled aloud, and faced the opposite wall and the rough wooden door that led outside.

Outside, he concluded, was going to have to do. He stepped down to the concrete.

Even through his thick socks, it was like walking on a slab of ice. He made it quickly to the wooden door, and yanked on it.

Thank God, it was open. She hadn't gone down there and padlocked it from the outside just to torture him further, after all.

Squinting his poor, abused eyes against the glare of daylight on new snow, he stepped out of the basement and onto more, even colder concrete, beneath the overhang of the side porch.

He heard a continuous roar, and wondered what it was for a moment. Then it came to him. He was less than a hundred yards from the levee that held back the Yuba River.

All that water. Flowing.

The thought made him groan. He quickly took care of his problem, and the relief was a wonderful thing.

He stood there for a few minutes afterward, staring toward the levee, registering the fact that the snow had finally stopped, the sun was out, and he would soon, the good Lord willing, feel like a human being again.

From over on Main Street, he heard a loud, long siren go off. He had no way of knowing that the siren sounded every day at noon, or that behind him, in the basement, Frannie was just reaching the foot of the stairs.

Seconds later, Frannie stood before the entrance to the little room. She stared at the open door and saw that Ned St. Charles wasn't in there.

She glanced down to the other end of the concrete floor and saw that the outside door was open. For a moment Frannie was sure that Ned St. Charles was gone.

She didn't move. She felt...what? A sort of sinking feeling, a gray feeling, as if all the color had gone out of the day.

But then she glanced into the room again and spied his boots and coat. He must have only gone outside for a moment, she reasoned. Before she could stop it, a pleased smile was curving her lips. Her heart picked up a faster rhythm.

Frannie shook herself, and ordered herself to stop behaving like a lovesick fool. She'd come down here to get him up and make him eat. After that, she was going to give him a few dollars and send him out of her life once and for all.

Shivering, Frannie stepped into the little room and shut the door to seal out the cold. She went to the electric heater and let it blast some hot air around her ankles, feeling absurdly anxious and on edge. Her glance, as agitated as the rest of her, flickered around the tiny room as if there might be something new to look at there.

She noticed again the dingy jacket, which was draped over the lone straight chair in the corner. And she recalled that yesterday afternoon, out on the levee, he had put something from his wallet back into the jacket pocket. She wondered now—what could it have been?

It was none of her business. She knew it. But after the attraction she'd felt toward him last night, after the silly, impossible feelings she was having right now, she longed for any proof that showed her aunt's opinion of him to be the right one.

She longed to find out he'd lied to her, that he wasn't really Ned St. Charles at all, but some rat up to no good, who'd given her a false name and taken advantage of her sympathy for him.

If he'd lied to her, it would be easier to keep on being cold to him, easier not to smile back if he smiled at her, easier to tell herself she had the problem of his questionable fascination for her thoroughly under control.

Frannie tiptoed across the room, swift and silent, and scooped up the jacket, hardly pausing to think that it wouldn't take much time at all for a man to take care of his business in the snow.

Out behind the house, Burnett was enjoying his first positive thoughts in days. He found himself thinking that maybe getting so plastered he hardly knew his own name hadn't been such a big mistake after all. Now that the hangover was receding a little, and the natural health of his big body was reasserting itself, he could feel rather grateful just to be alive.

His divorce from Amanda was final, and actually, that was a good thing. Even yesterday, when he'd felt so damned despondent, he hadn't regretted the ending of their so-called marriage. No, his depression had been more about his failure to find love and happiness, when everything else seemed to be going so well.

He owned and operated twelve ice-cream stores that his family had started back when he was eleven. Sometime after the first of the year, he would be signing on twelve new franchises, which would double his holdings. He was well-to-do now. By next Christmas, he would be rich.

And yet it all felt kind of hollow at the core. That's why the realization that his marriage was at last truly and finally over had hit him so hard; in the family, he'd always thought of himself as the stable one, the responsible one. And yet here he was, divorced with no children. Thirty-eight, with no one to call his own.

Burnett shook his head, and turned away from the hard glitter of the new snow. Better not to start dwelling on it all again. Better to take this new day and make the most of it, whatever it might bring. He'd get his angel-turned-drill sergeant to lend him her phone. He'd call the office, and have some money wired to him right away.

He realized that his feet were freezing as he ducked into the basement once more. He took the concrete floor in six big steps, in a hurry now, flush with the intention to get back to his life—lacking in real meaning as it might be—in Sacramento.

Tomorrow was Christmas Eve. He'd spend it and Christmas Day with his mother and brother and his brother's family. And he'd be grateful for all of them, that they had continued to care for him in spite of all he'd put them through over the years.

He remembered, just as he reached the closed door to the small room, about the old Jeep parked on the street across the bridge, opposite the St. Charles Place bar. Chances were, he didn't even need to wire for money, he realized. Given half a tank of gas, he could make it the hundred miles to Sacramento, and worry about money when he got home.

He pushed open the door, not remembering that he had left it ajar behind him until he heard the gasp of the woman who'd tortured him all morning. She whirled to face him, clutching his jacket in her hands.

"Oh!" she said, her wild hair flying out, her pale skin flooding with guilty color. It didn't take a brain surgeon to figure out that she'd been just about to go through his pockets.

"Looking for anything in particular?" he inquired.

Frannie stared back at him, her heart racing in her chest, all too aware that her face wore an obvious hand-in-the-cookie-jar expression. Worst of all, she hadn't explored his pockets yet, so she wasn't going to find out what he'd stuck in there yesterday.

"I...well..." she stammered, sounding just as culpable as she knew she looked.

"Yes?" he asked on a pointedly rising inflection.

Nothing to do, she decided, but brazen it out. She smoothed the ragged coat and laid it neatly back on the straight chair. "Well...there you are finally," she said, doing her best to drum up a little disapproval of him for leaving the room, in order to take the pressure off of herself for rifling his clothes. "It's time for lunch."

He folded his arms over his broad chest and studied her for a moment, a knowing smirk on his lips. Then he shrugged, apparently deciding not to challenge her further about snooping.

"Lunch?" he asked.

"Yes. It's ready now."

"Am I to be allowed inside the house for this event?" he quizzed with heavy irony.

She belligerently scowled at him. "Do you think you can behave yourself?"

"I will sincerely try, ma'am." He didn't sound sincere at all, but she decided to let it pass. To get him fed and out of her house, that was the goal.

"Put on your boots and come upstairs, then," she instructed, and then boldly took the few steps to where he stood blocking the door. "Excuse me," she said, keeping her head high.

"Certainly, ma'am," he told her, stepping to the side. She marched right past him and up the stairs, very careful with every step not to falter or look back.

Chapter Five

Burnett dipped up a spoonful of the hot, brothy vegetable soup and brought it to his lips. It was damn good. He told the silent woman across the table from him as much.

"Thank you." She delicately sipped from her own spoon, and then looked out the window at the pine-covered mountains across the river.

He shrugged, and spread creamy butter on the hot rolls she'd provided. Then he silently ate, drinking the cold milk with as much determination as he devoured the soup and rolls.

After the first few shaky bites, the food went down fine, and he was glad for it. The queasiness was passing. He felt better almost by the minute now.

What he could use, he thought, was a good workout. That would clear out the lingering fuzziness in his head, banish the faint sour taste in his mouth, burn off the shakiness from his legs and arms.

He grunted. Time enough for that when he reached home. There, he'd retreat to his private gym in the back of the house and jump rope until the last cobwebs in his brain had been completely swept away.

"More?" the woman, Frannie, was asking.

"Thank you, I'd like that," he said.

She ladled him up another helping from the big white tureen between them. He ate some more, aware that across the table she had finished eating and was watching him.

He glanced up. Her gaze slid away to the mountains again. He studied the fine line of her jaw and the pink perfection of her mouth in profile. He also noted that sometime before they sat down, probably while he was washing his face and hands, she'd pulled back her unruly hair and anchored it at her neck with a big tortoiseshell clip.

Still studying the western hills, she reached up a slim, short-nailed hand to smooth her hair. He recognized the action as a nervous one; she had felt his gaze on her hair. He watched her hand, and remembered the touch of it on his skin earlier—cool and slightly rough.

He wondered again what she did that made her hands rough—and it no longer made his head pound to ponder that. He realized he wanted to know more about her, but wasn't sure how to go about finding out. He'd never been good with casual conversation.

Since he was big and reasonably good-looking, Burnett knew most women—and men, too—perceived him as purposely remote. That had always been fine with him. Much better, he thought, than that they should know the truth; that he was shy and socially inexperienced.

He'd been the man of his family since the day his father headed off for a little fun in Lake Tahoe—and never came back. Burnett had been eleven. He'd gone to work behind the counter of the ice-cream store his mother bought, determined to do everything in his power to see that his family survived and prospered. Maybe he'd carried his dedication to duty a bit far. He'd had little time to make friends—and no time at all for girls.

He'd met Amanda when he bought his house off of Fair Oaks Boulevard. She'd been the real estate agent—and she'd taken one look at his financial statement and decided that here was the man for her. She'd pursued him relentlessly, always somehow making it seem as if he were the one chasing her. That had been fine with him, Burnett realized now. He'd felt masculine and commanding. He'd never had to confront his own shyness as long as Amanda was around. She'd hung on his arm and looked up at him adoringly and told him he was wonderful. The day they were married, he'd thought he had everything.

Remembering his own foolishness, Burnett chuckled aloud.

"What's so funny?" Frannie snapped, looking at him directly for once and narrowing her eyes.

"Nothing." He glanced at the fat, black stove in the corner, and decided to try breaking the ice by asking her something truly harmless. "You use only wood heat here?"

She looked at him, just a glance, as if checking to see if he was up to no good. Then she answered, grudgingly, "There is gas heat throughout the house, but yes, I mostly use wood."

"Wood can be expensive."

"My dad was born here and I have several distant relatives in town. Someone's always clearing trees off their property. I get wood for free, or nearly so—and I don't actually live up here anyway." She fell silent, and her mouth grew tight, as if she thought she'd revealed too much.

"Where *do* you live?"

"Why?" The word was suspicion personified.

"Just making conversation." He grinned, absurdly proud of himself because he was doing just that.

She looked even more suspicious at his grin, but allowed, "I live in Sacramento."

He started to say he lived there, too. But then he remembered that he'd given her some wild story about being from Graeagle the night before. Maybe it would be better, since he'd be leaving in a little while anyway, to just let her go on thinking that what he'd told her of himself last evening was the truth.

But then a thought struck him. Out on the levee, he'd been proud as only a drunk can be of having the foresight to salvage his driver's license before he threw his wallet in the Yuba. He'd stuck the license in the pocket of his old coat.

A little while ago he'd caught her with that coat in her hands. If she'd seen the license, then she might already know where he lived—as well as that he'd lied to her about who he was.

Burnett stared out the window himself for a moment, wondering if he owed her some kind of explanation, and not really feeling up to providing one. When he returned home, he'd send her a check for her trouble, along with a little note explaining why he'd pretended to be Ned St. Charles. In the note, he'd remind her how drunk he'd been, and point out that his reasoning had been completely skewed.

You're not drunk now, a chastening voice in his head suggested.

So?

So, the responsible thing to do would be to tell the truth before you leave here...

"Ned?" she asked softly from across the table, putting an end to his internal dialogue. He looked at her, registering the lack of irony in her use of the name, and deciding she must not have seen the license after all. She still believed he was who he'd said he was. He felt relief, but refused to examine the feeling.

He looked at her, raising a brow. "Yes?"

She swallowed, and her eyes slid away once more. "Nothing. I don't know." Her voice was soft. He realized that the icy facade she'd maintained between them had melted away sometime during his extended silence. She pushed her empty soup bowl away a little and folded her hands on the table. "You seemed far away," she said. "And tense, just then." He could see that she was concerned for him, worried perhaps that his being quiet for so long might mean something grave. "You're going to be all right, aren't you?"

"I'll be fine," he said.

"Good. I'm glad," she said. Then she smoothed her hair again and stood up. "Finished?" She gave him a forced, bright smile, which he saw as an attempt to reclaim some of the distance between them, distance that had dangerously dissolved in the past few minutes.

He nodded. "Thank you," he said, picking up her formal tone. "It was delicious."

She began gathering the bowls and spoons. He rose and helped her, carrying the remaining rolls to the counter, and after that the big white tureen.

When he set the tureen down beside her, she turned to reach for the sponge. Her arm brushed his.

It was nothing, really. Hardly enough even to be called a touch. But his breath caught, briefly, in his throat at the warmth that radiated from her. He was inordinately aware of the way she stiffened and pulled back.

"Excuse me," she said, as if she'd done something impolite.

"No problem," he responded, his own face reddening at how utterly inane that sounded.

They both cleared their throats then, and she busily began wiping down the counters, while he stood back, stuck his hands into his pockets and tried not to stare at her skin and her hair and the way her lashes brushed her cheeks whenever she lowered her eyes.

When at last the evidence of the lunch had been cleaned away, she asked him with diffident courtesy, "Won't you sit down again, Ned?" She smiled, fleetingly, as their eyes met.

The slight flush that came to her cheeks before she glanced away told him that he hadn't imagined her reaction to their quick, brushing touch. She was attracted to him—or at least, to Ned—even if she didn't want to be.

As he took his chair, she disappeared through the door to the dining room. She returned in no time at all and sat down herself. Then she cleared her throat, the way people do when sneaking up on a delicate subject.

She looked at him through those incredible eyes—how could he have forgotten, even while she was torturing him earlier, what unbelievable eyes she had?

And had she really been so rough on him? Of course not. She'd done what she had to do with him to help him get sober.

And now he *was* sober, thanks mostly to her. And he could look at her beautiful face and hear her soft voice and completely comprehend why he had thought her his angel the evening before.

"Ned?" she said hesitantly.

"Yes?"

"I want you to take this money." She pushed a few bills across the table at him. "I know you need it."

He looked at the bills for a moment, and then pushed them back to her. "I can't take that," he said, just as he imagined Ned might. With proud restraint. A good, responsible man fallen on hard times, who was still above charity.

"It's okay, really. You can pay me back," she said, sounding strained.

He put his hands in his lap and looked down at the beat-up surface of the table. He knew what was coming next. She was getting ready to ask him to leave.

And he just wasn't ready to leave quite yet. Suddenly his life in Sacramento was seeming empty again. While here, in this big, old-fashioned kitchen, there was warmth and nourishment and a pretty woman who blushed when her eyes met his.

But how was he going to convince her to let him stay for a while?

An idea occurred to him immediately, and he put it to use without even stopping to think; he decided to do what he imagined Ned would do—go on the offensive, because of injured pride.

He looked up, setting his face in defiant lines. "What do you mean, I can pay you back?" he demanded, and watched as she gasped, surprised at his sudden wounded vehemence. "You don't ever expect to see a penny of this money again. It's charity, pure and simple. And I don't want it. Understand?"

She looked stricken. "I didn't mean to insult you," she said. "I only thought . . ."

"What?" he demanded. "What did you think?" Her gaze slid away. "And stop looking out the window. Look at me."

She straightened up and faced him. "All right. I thought you could use a few dollars to get you back to Graeagle. If you won't take the money, that's your business. But now I want you to go."

"Why?"

The word hung between them for a moment. Then she said, "It was what we agreed."

"I was drunk," he said.

She glared at him. "It was a perfectly reasonable agreement, no matter what state you were in. This is my house and you are taking advantage of my hospitality—for as long as I choose to extend it. And I told you from the first that you were only here until morning. Well, morning has come and gone. Your welcome is worn out."

He looked at her flushed face and guarded expression, thinking that, while her argument was completely acceptable, there was much more to her urgency that he be gone than what she was telling him.

She felt the same attraction he felt, he was sure of it—and she didn't like it one bit. He couldn't fault her for that; she was displaying nothing less than sound judgment. To her, he was a down-and-out drunk she'd pulled out of the snow. Pursuing an attraction to him would be foolhardy.

He understood that he should say *thank you for all you've done* and get up and go. But he didn't. Some perverse part of him wanted her to admit the *real* reason she was so anxious to see him leave.

He prodded, "You still haven't answered my question."

"What question?"

"Why you are so anxious to see the last of me?"

She squinted at him as if he weren't very bright. "Didn't I just explain that?"

"You said I'd worn my welcome out."

"And you have."

"Because I was drunk and disorderly and you've been having to play nursemaid all morning?"

"Yes. That's right."

"And that's all?"

"What are you getting at?"

"Is it? All?"

"It's enough, I should say."

"But it isn't everything."

She was quiet for a moment. Then, "I don't choose to go into this any further." She stood up. "Take the money, Ned. Send me a check general delivery, care of Bonnie Lawry when you have it."

"No," he said.

Her face was cold and set again, her voice hard. "All right. That's up to you. But I do want you to leave now."

He stood up, slowly, and they faced each other across the table. Her strange eyes commanded—yet seemed to plead at the same time.

Burnett began to feel like a heel. She'd been nothing but generous to him, and here he was baiting her to confess an attraction that all wisdom demanded she should deny.

"I want you to leave," she said again, her gaze locked with his. He said nothing. He was thinking how beautiful and vulnerable she looked. He was wondering what she would do if he reached across the table and—

"Don't..." It was a plea, as if she'd read his thoughts in his eyes.

He didn't move.

"You must leave." Now she truly sounded desperate.

"Please..." he said, thinking vaguely that, since he'd met her, he'd been using that word as if he said it all the time.

"Ned, I mean it..."

"What?"

"You can't stay here."

"I know," he said, though he didn't know. Not at all. "But I'd just like to..."

"Yes?"

"There's one more thing I'd like to say."

"All right."

"Don't answer too fast, okay?" he urged. "Give it just a little thought."

She promised she would.

He began hesitantly, "You pulled me out of the snow, put me up for the night. Then you nursed me this morning. I've caused you nothing but trouble. At least let me do a little something for you around here. To work off what I owe you."

"Ned, I..."

"Please."

She started to shake her head, and then stopped at the sound of a sharp knock that came from behind him. Burnett turned his head. Through the glass at the top of the side door, he saw a gray-haired woman with a round face, a prim mouth and a downright antagonistic expression.

"It's Aunt Bonnie," Frannie said, then louder, "Come on in."

The stocky little woman bustled in the door. "I made some fudge." She held out a plate veiled in plastic wrap. "I knew you'd want some, dear."

"Thanks," Frannie said, dryly, as if she were well aware that her aunt had more than fudge on her mind.

"I'll just set it right here on the counter," the little woman went on.

"Great."

"And then, I can only stay for one cup of coffee."

"There's some in the coffeemaker." Frannie's voice was resigned.

"Well, I know that. I can see. And I'll just help myself." Aunt Bonnie did precisely that, scurrying to the coffeepot and then to the head of the table between Burnett and Frannie. Frannie sighed and sat back down. Burnett, wary of the way the woman's small dark eyes bored through him, but glad of the reprieve from being told again to leave, followed suit.

"Well now," Aunt Bonnie said pointedly as soon as they were all three settled in their chairs. "This must be the man you pulled out of the snow last evening, Frances." She looked from Frannie to Burnett and then back again. "He looks well enough now."

"Aunt Bonnie, this is Ned St. Charles," Frannie said, her voice studiously bland. "Ned, Bonnie Lawry."

Burnett held out his hand. "Pleased to meet you, Mrs. Lawry," he said with a slight drawl that surprised him a little coming out of his mouth. Burnett Clinton never drew out his words. But somehow, he was realizing, Ned St. Charles did.

Bonnie Lawry looked at his hand a long time before taking it. "It's *Miss*," she said at last, condescending to shake. The she looked down at the hand that engulfed hers. She looked up again, her expression more distrustful than ever. Right then, Burnett was sure that Aunt Bonnie had noticed what her niece hadn't: his hands were smooth, the nails trimmed. Hands like his didn't belong on a man who couldn't even afford a motel room for the night.

Bonnie began tartly, "I hear you're from Graeagle, Mr. St. Charles." She put just the slightest emphasis on the name St. Charles, and Burnett was sure that it was her way of telling him she knew very well what the bar on Main Street was called.

"Yes," he said, dreading whatever she would ask next. "I drove over from Graeagle yesterday, that's right."

"Not a lot of work in Graeagle," she remarked. "Especially in the winter, when all the tourists go home."

"That's true," he said noncommittally, "it's mostly a tourist town, from what I hear."

"From what you hear? I thought you lived there."

"Aunt Bonnie, that's enough," Frannie said, her face pinkening.

"It's all right," Burnett said, loathing the quizzing aunt, but keeping sight of his objective: to get Frannie to allow him to stay. He wasn't going to get what he wanted by being surly to her relatives. He smiled at Bonnie. "No, ma'am, I don't live there. I've just been staying there for a couple of days."

Burnett was aware of Frannie across the table, of her tense regard. The aunt's questions, he realized, were probably ones she herself had wanted to ask, but hadn't quite managed. The attraction between them had kept her too wary and nervous around him to pry.

Bonnie, however, had no such problem. She wanted to know about this Ned St. Charles, and she had no compunction about coming right out and accusing, "You told my niece that you were from Graeagle."

"He was drunk, Aunt Bonnie," Frannie answered before he could. "And it was true. He'd come from Graeagle, and that was where he would have returned, had he been in any condition to drive." The aunt made a humphing sound. Frannie bristled, "It was a simple slipup in communication, that's all."

Burnett held back a fatuous grin. The last thing he'd expected was for Frannie to leap to his defense. Maybe he was closer to being allowed to stay than he imagined.

He glanced at Frannie. She met his eyes briefly and then looked at Bonnie once more. Burnett realized he'd lose whatever ground he'd gained if he didn't join in his own defense. He put on an abashed expression and said to the aunt, "I've been having a rough time lately. And a...friend offered me the use of his family cabin there, to kind of pull myself together."

"What friend?"

"Burnett's his name," he said, almost without thinking. It was, in a strange way, the truth. "Burnett Clinton."

"This Burnett Clinton is a *close* friend of yours?" Bonnie asked.

Burnett swallowed. "Very close. We grew up together."

"Where was that?"

"Sacramento."

"Is that where you actually live, then?"

"Yes. It is." He felt the quick flick of Frannie's glance and feared she was finding it suspicious that he hadn't mentioned he lived in Sacramento when she told him she lived there. But then, he reasoned, that had been an emotionally charged moment. He'd fallen silent. And she'd asked him if he was going to be all right. If she thought about that exchange, she could interpret it any number of ways.

"And exactly what kind of work do you do?" the relentless aunt continued.

"I'm a . . . manager, among other things."

"Manager of what?"

"Aunt Bonnie, you are being downright rude," Frannie said rather hotly.

Her aunt tossed her a pugnacious little scowl. "*Somebody* has to find out who this person is that you've taken under your roof."

"It's my roof, and my business," Frannie shot back, every bit as belligerent as the little woman to her right.

"Ladies . . ." Burnett began.

Both women glared at him. He decided to say no more, realizing that there was more going on here than he understood, some kind of conflict between the aunt and niece that had been in progress well before he landed in the snowbank out back.

"In any case," Bonnie said brusquely after a moment of heated silence, "It's past noon, and you said he would be gone in the morning."

Burnett longed to tell Aunt Bonnie exactly what he thought of women who spoke of him in the third person when he was sitting right there. But he didn't. He counted to ten, and tried to remember that he was supposed to be an unassuming guy named Ned, who probably put women on a pedestal and who was surely accustomed to having people talk about him as if he wasn't even in the room.

He was grateful he'd kept his mouth shut when he heard what Frannie said next. "Well, I changed my mind."

"You *what?*" the aunt demanded, puffing up her already considerable chest so that she resembled an enraged mother hen.

"You heard what I said," Frannie flatly announced. "There's kindling to split in the basement, and logs that need to be cut down to size. Ned's going to take care of it for me. He'll be here at least until dark, the way I see it."

"But, Frances . . ." Aunt Bonnie sputtered.

Longing to throw back his head and crow in triumph, Burnett stood up before Frannie could think twice and change her mind.

"And that reminds me," he murmured in the soft-spoken drawl that was beginning to seem like a natural way to talk. "I'd better get to work. Nice to meet you, Miss Lawry. And Frannie, thanks for the lunch. It was mighty fine."

A half hour later, beneath the back porch where the chopping block was, Burnett sunk the ax into the hard hunk of oak, worked it out, and then brought it down again. Once cut in two, the log would be about stove-size. With the next stroke, one half of the log fell to the concrete beside the block.

Burnett laid the ax carefully against the block, hoisted the fallen half of the log, and tossed it onto the pile he was making of stove-ready wood to stack in the basement. He tossed the other half right after it.

Then he brushed his bare hands off—they were already a little tender, and tomorrow they would have blisters. The thought gave him some satisfaction, though he wasn't sure why. Maybe he wanted to punish himself for deceiving a woman who'd only been kind to him—though he wasn't willing to do the right thing and tell her the truth. Maybe he wanted to toughen his hands a little, since the sharp-eyed aunt had seemed to notice them as too smooth for the kind of man he claimed to be.

Hell, Burnett thought. Who could say why he was out here chopping wood without gloves? Who could say why he'd done *anything* he'd done in the past twenty-four hours?

He chose another log, set it on the block. Then he hefted the ax again, bringing it down with a resounding thwack.

He worked for a while steadily and smoothly; Burnett was no stranger to chopping wood. The cabin in Graeagle was heated with wood, and both he and his brother had learned to cut logs and kindling as soon as they were old enough to lift an ax.

Though the temperature in the shade was in the thirties, sweat had started on his body beneath the old flannel shirt he wore. He was content with that. After all, he'd wanted a workout, hadn't he? His blood, which had felt sluggish in his veins after the way he'd abused himself yesterday, had started pumping hard and clean again.

The tumbled pile of stove-ready logs grew. When it was high enough to fill the holes in the neat stacks inside the basement, he found some pine and a short ax and began to cut kindling, shaving it off the logs as a chef might slice a pineapple, turning the logs, paring them down to their pale cores.

The job was somewhat mesmerizing and pleasant in the hypnotic way of work that becomes mindless once the rhythm has been established. He was almost done when he heard Frannie's voice, gently chiding, from behind him.

"You could have asked for gloves."

He smiled to himself. Here it was, another opportunity to be honest. He could tell her just what he'd been thinking a while ago, that he'd set to work gloveless for at least two possible reasons—both of them reprehensible.

He set down the short ax, turned and gave her a broad smile, wiping the sweat from his brow with the back of his hand.

She was wearing her red jacket and holding out a pair of heavy gloves. Her hair was loose and wild around her face again. He reached out and took the gloves without letting go of her gaze, thinking that the last thing he was willing to do right now was be honest. If she knew that everything about him was a lie, he'd lose what little ground he'd gained since he'd broken the ice at lunch.

Later, he thought. He would tell her all of it later. After he knew her better, after he was sure of the right way to go about explaining it.

"Thanks," he said, still lost in her eyes. "I'm almost done with the ax, but these'll help for stacking."

"You'll have blisters." He felt the light brush of her hand on his—a swift touch, quickly withdrawn. Her face pinkened enchantingly.

"Doesn't matter."

They stood in tableau for timeless seconds. On the cold winter air, he got a whiff of her scent. It was light. Fresh and floral. He stepped back, feeling suddenly awkward and earthbound, musty with sweat.

She looked away, toward the levee and the drawn-out sigh of the river beyond. "She left, finally. Aunt Bonnie, I mean." She looked back, and gave a nervous chuckle. "But not before she told me you were nothing but trouble, and I was a foolish, foolish girl." Her voice pretended to accuse him. "You certainly didn't waste any time flying down those stairs when I told her you were staying to chop wood for me."

"I've learned a few things in my life, appearances to the contrary."

"Such as?"

"In this case, when opportunity knocks, open the door and grab it, before it gets away."

She laughed, and then grew pensive. "I know hardly anything about you."

He looked at her—steadily, he hoped. "What do you want to know? All you have to do is ask."

"All right." She paused, then queried, "How long have you been out of a job, Ned?"

"I'm not," he told her, absolving himself of some of his guilt by trying to stretch the truth without actually lying.

"You do have a job?"

He nodded. "I work for that friend of mine I mentioned to your aunt."

"Oh, yes. Burnett—"

"Clinton," he supplied the last name she'd been searching for.

"What do you do?"

"Well, Burnett owns a chain of ice-cream stores, and I help him out. I do...odd jobs for him."

"Like?"

He shrugged, trying to look unconcerned while he frantically sought a believable list of duties to report to her. Then it occurred to him, the things a guy like Ned might do.

"Fix equipment, maintenance, things like that," he said.

Once again he'd told a half-lie. As a kid, Burnett had always loved to figure out how things worked, to fix what was broken. Until well into his teens, he'd done the repairs at his family's ice-cream stores himself.

But then he'd wanted to attend college, and after that he'd gradually taken over complete control of the business from his mother, who was more than happy to relinquish it. It had become economically unfeasible for him to spend his time fiddling with the equipment, so from then on he'd hired professionals to do that kind of work.

"You're a repairman?" she was asking.

"Partly." He remembered what he'd told her aunt. "And sometimes I run individual stores, manage them, you know, when one manager leaves before a new one hires on."

"And this friend, Burnett, gave you some time off?"

"Yeah. I've been . . . kind of depressed lately. And he suggested I take off until after the first of the year."

"Depressed because of your divorce, you mean?"

"Partly." He longed to change the subject, because the more he told her about himself, the more danger he would be in of contradicting himself later. "Frannie?" he asked softly.

"Yes?"

"I've wondered, since this morning . . ."

"What is it?"

"What do *you* do for a living?"

She grinned. "All you had to do was ask."

"Well, that's what I'm doing."

Her smile turned proud. "I'm a stagecraft teacher. At Sacramento River Junior College." At his puzzled frown, she elaborated. "I'm a drama teacher, but on the technical end. I teach scene design and stage lighting, and set construction. And I design most of the sets for productions—as well as helping to build them."

He thought of the slight roughness of her hands, and understood now how they got that way. "You like your work," he remarked in reference to her proud smile when she talked about it.

"I do," she said, and the two words held a hint of defiance. "I would never give it up."

"Has someone asked you to?"

"I was married myself once. My husband found my job an inconvenience . . . at best."

"Married?" he asked stupidly. It took a minute to digest that information. His angel had a life before him. He'd known that she must have, of course. But hearing her say it suddenly made it real.

"I'm thirty-three," she told him. "I haven't lived in a vacuum, you know."

"You look younger."

"I'm a grown woman." Now she seemed almost angry. "And don't you forget it."

"I won't." He tried that charming smile that Ned St. Charles seemed to do so well.

"I run my own life. No one tells me what to do."

"Hey." He raised a hand. "Truce. Please?" At last, she smiled. A slow smile, one that looked somewhat embarrassed. "I . . . like you, Frannie," he added then. "I'm just curious about you."

She cast her gaze toward the sky, and then looked back at him. "I understand. I get defensive about my independence. It's very important to me."

"Because you lost it once?"

She was silent, considering his question. Then she said, "Because I allowed someone to take it from me once."

"Your ex-husband?"

"Yes—and I'd prefer to change the subject now."

He put in quickly, before she could start quizzing him about himself again, "How about if I get this wood stacked in the basement?"

"Good idea." They shared another long look, and he wondered if she was thinking what he was; their second agreement—about his staying until he'd replenished her wood supply—had almost played itself out. She'd probably be insisting he leave again, when he was done. And when she did, what excuse would he find to stay this time?

He wasn't sure. But he *was* going to stay longer. Somehow. Some way. The means to that end simply hadn't occurred to him yet.

Chapter Six

"Er, excuse me…" Frannie whirled around at the sound of his voice, her heart tripping into high gear and her cheeks burning as if they'd been set on fire from within.

"Oh!" she heard herself exclaim, like a giddy, breathless schoolgirl. "You surprised me."

Actually, she'd been staring dreamily out the window above the sink at the side wall of her aunt's house. She'd been thinking of things she had no business thinking about—like the way Ned looked when he smiled, so sexy and yet sincere at the same time.

"All finished," he said.

"Finished."

"With the wood."

"Oh. Oh, yes. Of course."

"Here." He held out the work gloves. "Thanks."

She took them. "Thank *you*."

"You're welcome." He stepped back and looked down at his boots. "Listen, I..."

"Yes?" Her voice sounded ridiculously eager to her own ears.

"I was wondering—"

"What?"

"If I might..."

"What? What is it, Ned?"

"Well, I'm a mess."

She grinned at him, thinking he was right. The old shirt clung to him, wet with sweat, while the shadow of new beard darkened the bottom half of his face. At lunch, he'd scrubbed his hands and splashed some water on his face. But he needed a good, hot shower.

"I realize it's a lot to ask, after everything else you've done for me," he began, "but I wonder if I could possibly..."

Frannie hid the smile that threatened to curve her lips. He was so polite and unassuming. Except when she hurt his pride by offering him a handout, Ned had never so much as raised his voice in her presence. She was sure he came from a down-to-earth, working-class family, where he'd learned good manners and respect for authority right from the first.

In fact, the more she was around him, the more Frannie was sure that he was utterly harmless. She'd be willing to bet now that yesterday's binge had been uncharacteristic for him. He was a good man for whom things had simply been very rough lately, and he'd felt so hopeless that he'd tried to forget it all in the bottom of a bottle.

She tipped her head and studied him, not thinking that her fond thoughts would be mirrored in the softness of her eyes. "You wonder if you could possibly what?"

"Well... Do you think I could use your shower?"

He looked so agonized over having to ask such a thing, that Frannie was hard put to keep a straight face. "Of course you may."

Gratitude lit him up like a beacon. "Thanks."

"You're welcome." How could she have ever imagined he might be dangerous to her?

You didn't, a voice in her head reminded. It was never *him* you were worried about . . .

Frannie ignored the nagging voice of her wiser self and gestured toward the bathroom, which was just off the kitchen on the other side of the heat stove. "Help yourself. There are fresh towels on those shelves in the corner."

"Great."

"And . . . why don't you toss your clothes outside the door when you get out of them. I'll wash them, and I'm sure we can come up with something for you to put on until your own clothes are dry."

"I couldn't," he said.

"You can and you will," she told him with firm authority.

He was quiet, smiling appreciatively. And then he turned for the bathroom and his shower.

Frannie stood there for a moment, staring after him with a half smile on her face. Then she shook herself and went up the back stairs to the attic to rummage through some boxes of old clothes she knew were stored there.

What she found wasn't much of an improvement over his threadbare overalls and torn shirt, but they were reasonably clean. She returned to the kitchen to find his dirty clothes neatly folded by the bathroom door. She traded them for the ones in her arms and then went down to the basement, humming, to put his things in the washer. She paused, before remounting the stairs, to approve of the way he'd stacked the wood, ends out, packed tight and even.

And then she thought of his old jacket, just a few feet away in the little basement room. It would be such a simple thing to sneak in there now and see what it was he had kept back from the river when he threw his wallet and money away. He would never catch her at it now. He was soaking wet in the shower; she could hear the water running in the pipes. She'd be in the room and out before he could dry off and put on the clean clothes she'd provided for him.

Frannie reached for the door to the room—and then dropped her arm.

Over lunch, and in the few exchanges they'd had since then, she and Ned had almost become *friends*. One didn't go through a friend's possessions. It simply was not done.

Frannie smiled to herself and turned away from the door. Ned's secrets were his own business. She wouldn't pry into them.

When she entered the kitchen again, she noticed that the sun hung just above the mountains. Soon it would be night again. And it was time for Ned to leave.

But then the bathroom door opened, releasing a cloud of warm steam. And he emerged, wearing the clothes she'd left by the door: patched jeans that hugged his hips and another old flannel shirt—this one a solid navy blue, frayed at the collar and cuffs. His hair was wet and his face was shaved. Frannie had never seen anyone look so handsome in her entire life.

He rubbed his smooth, square jaw. "I think I completely destroyed that little pink razor of yours."

"It's all right. I have more."

"That's good."

There was another of those silences that seemed to occur all the time when he was around—those silences where they just stared at each other, smiling inanely.

"Well," he said.

"Yes?" she asked.

"I have a Jeep," he told her, as if making a confession.

"Oh."

"It's over on Main Street."

"Where on Main Street?"

"In front of the restaurant."

"Cirino's at the Forks?"

"Yeah, across from the bar." He seemed to hesitate, then continued, "The St. Charles Place bar." Did his eyes shift away? No, Frannie told herself. That his name and the name of the bar were the same was merely coincidence, that was all. Aunt Bonnie and her suspicions could go take a hike.

Ned laughed, then. And Frannie knew she was right about him when he said easily, "You know, it seemed real meaningful to me yesterday—that I found a bar with my name on it."

"I'll bet," Frannie muttered, playfully grim.

"Don't give me that look, Frannie Lawry," Ned commanded with mock severity.

"What look?"

"The disapproving look."

"I'm not."

"You are."

"No."

"Yes."

"Uh-uh."

"Uh-huh . . ."

Frannie, who could have stood there looking at him indefinitely, didn't miss the marveling expression that crossed his face.

"What is it?" she asked.

"Oh, nothing . . ."

"Come on. Tell me."

"It's just . . ."

"Yes? Please, Ned. I want to know."

"My brother . . ."

She remembered last evening, he'd mentioned a brother. "Casey, right?"

"Yes. Casey," he said.

"Well? What about him?"

"He's happily married."

"Oh?"

"He married his best friend just a few years ago. A woman we both grew up with."

"Yes. And?"

"Just now, you and me . . ." His face went red. He was blushing.

Frannie thought it was wonderful to see a man do that. He looked so handsome, and . . . vulnerable. Something way down inside of her went very warm and soft.

"You and me what?" she prompted.

"Well . . ."

"Come on, you can tell me."

"I can?" He was half teasing and half serious.

"Yes. Tell me."

"We sound like them." He looked away. "That's all. It's silly."

"No," she said softly. "You don't really think it's silly, do you?"

He didn't meet her eyes, and he spoke with difficulty. "I've always envied what they had, though I used to pretend otherwise. My brother was sort of a runaround when he was younger. He had a reputation for being wild. But he always had this best friend, Joanna, who just happened to be a girl. And when they'd get together, it was always like they each knew what the other was thinking, and they'd always kind of tease each other, back and forth, like kids do, like you and me just then. And I used to almost hate them for having that, something so comfortable and *fun*, something I was sure I'd never have with anyone, let alone a girl . . ."

"Do you still almost hate them?" she asked when she was sure he wasn't going to go on of his own accord.

He shook his head. "We had a . . . family crisis, at the time the two of them were married. And since then Casey and I—and Joanna, too—have worked a lot of things out between us." He was quiet again.

Though her mind was filled with questions about his family and the family crisis and the "things" he and his brother had worked out, she didn't ask him. She felt he'd said more than he'd ever intended to and that was enough—for now.

She said, lightly, "So you've left your Jeep across from the St. Charles Place bar. And?"

He looked relieved, as if she'd rescued him from a conversational hole he'd fallen into. "And do you think it's been towed away by now?"

Frannie chuckled. "I doubt it. Around here, they give a little more leeway about things like that. Generally, they will try to find the owner of the vehicle first, and tow later. The winter population here is under four hundred. So that means we're all neighbors. And neighbors tend to want to stay on good terms with each other."

"Lucky for me."

"Yes. But, of course, you never know for sure until you go and find out."

"Yeah. And I think that's what I'd better do right now."

Outside, the sun was going. The corners of the kitchen darkened, while the light from the window cut a glaring swath through the heart of the room. Frannie, in the shadows, looked across the harsh path of light at Ned and found it hard to see his expression. He was in shadow, too.

It had been twenty-four hours, Frannie thought, since she'd pulled him from the snow. He was sober, cleaned up and ready to return to his own life. It was time for him to go.

She said, "Please let me lend you that money, Ned."

"No."

"Then take it for chopping wood."

"No." He smiled, his teeth flashing white through the shadows. "I'll get my coat." He turned and disappeared down the basement stairs, reappearing in no time at all.

"What about your clothes?" she asked as she watched him slide his arms in the old jacket.

"What about them?"

"They're still in the washer."

"They aren't important," he said quietly, after he had the jacket on. "Are these that I have on important to you?"

"No," she said. "No, they aren't important."

"Then, that's all. Isn't it?" There was a challenge in the question. He stepped out of the shadows and into the light in the center of the room. "Isn't it?"

"I suppose..."

He moved closer, skirting the table, until he was only a few feet from her. "You suppose what?"

That soft, liquid something was happening inside her again. She sounded like someone in a trance when she made herself tell him. "I suppose that's all."

"Over and done?" He said it very gently, so gently that she didn't even feel like backing away when she realized he had taken that one more step that put him right in front of her.

She could smell the soap on his skin, see the little nick on his jaw where her razor must have slipped once. "Ned?"

She breathed, thinking of how broad his shoulders were, how deep his chest. How he was big and strong . . . and yet vulnerable. Someone who would never try to tell her how to run her life.

"Frannie," he whispered, smiling, as if it gave him pleasure just to say her name.

"Ned, please don't . . ."

"What? Don't what?"

Don't leave, she thought. "Don't do this," she said.

"What? This?" he asked as his fingers tipped her chin so lightly, just the barest of touches, enough to guide her face up to his.

"Ned?"

His lips brushed hers, once across and then back. She sighed.

And then he dropped his hand and stepped back.

"Ned?"

"Sorry," he said, looking away. Then he looked back. And he smiled. "Hell, no. I'm not. I'm not sorry at all. I've wanted to do that forever—or at least since lunch."

The kiss had been so brief, and so achingly tender, that Frannie could find no regret for it inside herself. She returned his sweet, abashed smile with a tremulous one of her own.

He said, "Your lips are soft. Just like they look." Then he chuckled. "Does that embarrass you, for me to say that?" She shook her head. "Then why are you blushing?"

"Because . . ."

"Yeah?"

"All right," she confessed. "It embarrasses me a little." She felt warm and wonderful . . . and kind of silly, too. She glanced down bashfully. He put his finger under her chin again, to coax her eyes to meet his. She reached for his hand, and he winced, ever so slightly, when she touched one of the blisters he'd acquired while chopping wood for her without gloves. They stood for a timeless moment, hand in hand, eye-to-eye.

Then, reluctantly, he pulled free of her gentle grasp and stepped back.

Their eyes still held. And then Frannie heard herself suggesting, "I'll walk with you. To your Jeep."

They turned for the side door as one, pausing briefly while Frannie put on her jacket and tucked her hair under a fleecy wool hat.

Outside, it was below freezing. Frannie quickly shoved her feet into the rubber boots that she kept on the side porch, and they walked, hands stuffed into their pockets, to the front of the house, which faced Commercial Street.

The snow lay smooth on the front yard, an unbroken blanket of white covering the lawn and the walk all the way to the low wrought-iron fence. Beyond the fence, the slate sidewalk was covered with a layer of gray snow, while the street beyond had a scraped-raw look, the work, Frannie knew, of the county snowplow.

Frannie and Ned stood on the wooden boards of the porch for a moment, and the streetlamp on the nearby Pearl Street corner came on, as if lighting their way. They turned and grinned at each other. Then he was taking her arm and tucking it through his, and to Frannie it seemed the most natural thing in the world that he should do that.

They stepped off the porch into the foot and a half of snow together, and trudged to the front gate. At the sidewalk, they went left, down the sloping street to a bridge that crossed the Downie River, which converged with the Yuba on the west end of town. Across the bridge and down the street a ways, they came to another corner, the intersection of Commercial and Main. Both streets were adorned, all along the covered sidewalks, with live Christmas trees tied to the posts that held up the overhangs. Each tree had been decorated in a different style—some with bright bulbs and tinsel, some with paper chains, some with ornaments of cloth or straw.

Ned's battered Jeep, wearing a high cap of packed snow on the roof, waited right where he'd left it. They stopped when they reached it, and just stood there for a moment, still arm in arm.

Then Ned said, "Well. This is it."

Frannie's eyes burned suddenly. And the colored lights on the trees along the street blurred a little. But she took herself in hand. There was no way she was going to cry over a man she'd hardly known a day.

Behind her, the door to Cirino's restaurant opened, and a man and a woman who looked vaguely familiar came out. The couple nodded. Frannie said hello, and as they passed on down the street, she brusquely slid her arm from Ned's and stepped back.

"You, um, take care of yourself," she muttered awkwardly.

"Thanks. For everything," he said.

"Glad I could be of help."

"You were, more than I can say."

Then, too soon, they'd run out of all the standard phrases. He held her gaze for a moment more—and her heart jumped a little; she thought for a second that he was going to tell her he just couldn't leave, *wouldn't* leave....

But that was only the hopeless romantic inside her imagining things. He said nothing, only went around behind the Jeep to the street side and then climbed behind the wheel. He bent for a moment and groped under the seat, coming up with a key, which he inserted in the ignition.

Frannie stood on the sidewalk, bereft, her arms wrapped tightly around her body, while he fiddled with the choke and tried to get the ancient machine to turn over. At last, there was a groaning rumble, a sputter or two, and the thing was running, more or less.

There was a lump in Frannie's throat. She could hardly see for holding back the silly tears. She clutched her arms tighter around herself, as Ned, blurry through the moisture in her eyes, leaned across the seat toward her and pushed open the passenger door.

"I'll drive you back," he said over the ragged roar of the old engine.

Frannie had never jumped in a vehicle so fast in her life. She slammed the door firmly behind her. He pulled out of the space and turned around up past the community hall. They were back in front of the house her dad had left her in minutes.

He turned to her. "Here you are."

She looked at him. "I suppose you threw your driver's license in the river, too."

He shrugged.

"You could get a ticket, driving without it."

"Worse things have happened to me, believe me," he said.

She glared at him, feeling angry suddenly at what she knew she intended to say next.

She said, "All right. I've got an extra steak. Stay for dinner?"

His smile took her breath. "I thought you were never going to ask."

Chapter Seven

They ate in the dining room, which opened onto the front room. From where he sat, on the right side of the table, Burnett could see her Christmas tree in the front window. The lights on the tree were the big, old-fashioned kind, the color on the bulbs faded from years of use. Many of the ornaments looked homemade.

Frannie offered red wine with the steaks. Burnett declined even a glass. After yesterday, the thought of liquor, even of wine, made him a little queasy. But that wasn't the only reason why he refused when she tipped the bottle toward his glass. He also did it because he wanted his head clear. He did it because he had a specific goal now, and he wasn't going to allow himself to get fuzzy and mellow and put his foot in his mouth.

His goal was to stay here. At least for a few days, in this old house by the river in this charming small town. He wanted to share a white Christmas with the angel who'd dragged him from a snowbank yesterday evening. He was willing to sleep in the basement, if that was how she wanted it—though he didn't mind hoping that she might decide they could share even more than the short winter days.

Most important of all, he fully intended to tell her, before the night was over, who he really was. Because he wanted this time with her to be without lies or subterfuge.

But how exactly to go about telling her was the problem. It seemed that every time he opened his mouth to begin explaining, the words just wouldn't come out.

While he sought the proper moment to reveal all, he encouraged her to open up about herself. She told him that her dad had died when she was ten, and that her mother had remarried within a year.

"Downieville was my home," Frannie explained. "But as soon as my dad was gone, Mother moved the two of us to Tulsa, where her own family was. The man she married was..." She hesitated oddly over that and then continued. "...Someone she'd known before, a widower. They started having more kids right away. I have three sisters." She took a sip from her wineglass, her eyes far away and sad in the soft glow of the big red Christmas candle she'd lit in the center of the table. "I don't feel close to any of them—my mother or my sisters. My..." There was another of those strange hesitations, "...stepfather's okay, I suppose. A fair man. But not a warm man." She set the glass down, thought a minute, and then took another sip. "The years I was in Oklahoma, all I ever wanted was to come back home, to California. When I turned eighteen, that's what I did.

"I went to Sac State, majored in business at first. I took a drama class as an elective—and just fell in love with it. I mean, with the whole idea of building sets and lighting them and making—I don't know—magic, I guess. I switched my major to Theater Arts. And then, in my senior year, I met Kenneth . . ." Her voice faded.

Burnett prompted, "Your ex-husband?"

"Yes." She refilled her own wineglass. "It was a mistake from the first," she said.

"What?"

"Everything. I was never interested in the performance end of the theater. But one of the teachers talked me into taking a bit part in one of the shows—to round out my perspective, I was told. It wasn't much of a part. I had about five lines. Mostly, I stood around in a cocktail dress looking decorative. Kenneth saw that play. He's a land developer, and he was in Sacramento putting together a deal, and the son of the man he was buying the property from just happened to be in that play, too. Kenneth came backstage after the show, and he asked me out. I couldn't believe a man like that would be interested in me."

"A man like what?"

"A rich man. Older—he was forty-one to my twenty-two. Very sophisticated. In two months we were married and living in his house in the Bay area. For the first five years of our marriage, he completely dominated my every thought and action. He chose my clothes, my friends and the books I read. He made me into his ideal woman. . . ."

"And then?"

She fingered the nest of holly at the base of the red candle and took another sip of wine, sighing as she set the glass down. "And then one day I looked in the mirror and realized I didn't know who I was."

"What did you do?"

"Nothing, for a while. Then I went back to school. Kenneth was furious at first, because he wanted me at home. He wanted me *available* at all times."

"He missed you, you mean? Because you were gone all the time?"

"No, he didn't miss *me* one bit."

"Then what?"

"The way he saw it, I had a job already. I performed a very necessary function. I was Kenneth Dayton's perfect wife. That was a full-time career, as far as he was concerned."

Burnett flinched at her use of the word *perfect*. Amanda had been *perfect*. And she'd made of her wifehood a full-time career. He asked, trying to keep his voice merely curious, "What about children?"

"Children weren't part of it," she said. "Kenneth had a family by his first wife. He wanted a hostess. A dinner companion. An ornament to wear on his arm—when he needed me, which wasn't all that often, really."

Burnett realized he'd been tensing up when he felt himself relax. Perhaps he *had* thought of Amanda as an ornament at times. But they had both wanted a family. In fact, it had been the lack of children, more than any other issue, that had ended their marriage.

Strange. For a moment there he had begun to see a little of himself—the self he was *supposed* to be revealing to Frannie tonight—in the man she had once married. But, of course, that wasn't the case. Not at all. Not in any way that really mattered....

Frannie said, "I'm talking too much, boring you..."

"No," he told her quickly. "I was just thinking, that's all." She was sitting to his left, at the head of the table. He leaned toward her, coaxing. "So you went back to college..."

"Yes." The dark rims around her irises looked smoky black; the blue centers like a summer sky. "Ned?" she giggled, a sound both husky and nervous.

"What?"

"You're staring at me."

"You noticed. Go on about college."

"Well, I went. To San Francisco State, this time."

"And?"

"And, by the time I had my Master's degree, Kenneth and I were hardly speaking. Eventually, I got my job in Sacramento. I told him I wanted to take it, and he told me that was . . . convenient."

Burnett frowned, puzzled. "Convenient that you wanted to move to Sacramento, when he was based in the Bay area?"

"No, convenient that I was ready to move out of his house. He'd found someone else—someone who appreciated him and the kind of life he was willing to provide for a woman. He'd been planning to tell me for months, he said. He wanted me out so he could move her in."

The summer-day blue of her eyes was cloudy now. Burnett caught her hand. "I'm sorry, Frannie," he said, hurting from the pain he saw in her face. "He was a damn fool."

She bit her lip and shook her head. "You don't understand. I'm not sad because he cheated on me, or even because he replaced me like—like a piece of furniture he'd become dissatisfied with. I'm sad because I was willing to settle for so little when I married him." Her face changed, became less sad and more reflective. She went on. "And now, for the first time, telling you, I feel a little sorry for *him*—believe it or not."

"Why?"

"Because he was the kind of man people envy. He had success and money—and power, too. And yet, I never really knew him in the eight years we were married. I think deep down inside, he was afraid . . ."

"Of what?" Burnett, feeling uncomfortable once more, released her hand and picked up his fork.

Frannie drank more wine. "Something—I don't know for sure." Her tone was musing; she stared into the candle flame. "I really don't believe he ever loved me. Maybe he didn't know how."

Burnett chewed the last of his steak slowly, telling his tensing stomach muscles to relax. But relaxing wasn't easy. The man Frannie described was just too familiar. In fact, Burnett felt he understood Kenneth as well or maybe better than the woman sitting next to him did—because Kenneth could have been himself. A man good at giving orders, good at taking charge. But empty at the core. A man incapable of loving.

"In any case," Frannie spoke again, setting her glass down and picking up her own fork, "we were divorced, and I moved to Sacramento. And I joined a support group. I'm working on my problems, so I won't make the kind of mistake I made with Kenneth all over again."

"What mistake, exactly?" he asked, his voice gruffer than he meant it to be.

But she didn't notice his tone, only his question. She was still pensive, still absorbed in the why and wherefore of the choices she'd made in the past.

"I found someone distant and domineering," she answered after considering. "A wheeler-dealer who was willing to tell me how to run my life. Then I married him and did what he told me to. It was totally irresponsible of me. I've learned my lesson, as far as that goes. I'll never fall for a man like that again."

The tension in Burnett's stomach twisted into a knot. It had been bad enough to hear her seeming to describe himself when she talked about her "ex." But now she was, all unknowingly, giving him notice: if he told her who he really was, he wouldn't have a chance of getting close to her.

Harmless, ineffectual Ned might be allowed to sit at her table and chow down on her steaks. Sweet, unassuming Ned might kiss her gently in the kitchen and pull her arm through his for a walk to town in the snow.

But Burnett Clinton might as well face facts: if he told her about his real self tonight, he was out of here. And fast. She'd learned her lesson about men like *him*.

"Ned?" Her voice was apprehensive now. She had sensed that his mood had changed.

"What?"

"Is everything okay? You seem a little—"

"What?"

"Are you angry? Is it something I said?"

"It's nothing," he said, wishing to hell she'd just let it go.

"Please, Ned. That's not true." Her voice was quiet, full of steady conviction. "If something's bothering you, I'd appreciate your being honest about it."

Honest. She wanted him to be *honest*. The word turned like a knife inside him.

"Ned . . . ?"

"All right," he said, and stood up. "You really want to know what's bugging me, huh?" He was surprised at his own voice, at the drawl in it. Ned's drawl. He thought, vaguely, that he was sometimes beginning to feel more like Ned than like himself.

Because *she* wanted Ned. And, damn it, of his two selves, Burnett and Ned, he knew damn well which one might have a chance for that fantasy white Christmas he'd been dreaming about.

"Yes." She looked a little frightened at his vehemence, but she didn't glance away. She stared him straight in the eye. "I want to know."

"Fine—you say you'll never love some rich bastard again. Some guy who'll tell you what to do, dominate your life."

"Yes," she told him levelly. "That's what I said. And I meant it, too."

"Then who will you love instead?" he demanded, moving closer and looming over her, anger and frustration clear in every taut muscle of his big body. "Who will you love instead—a penniless beggar?"

Chapter Eight

Frannie stared up at him. Since she didn't know his secret, she misread him completely. She saw his guilty anger as proud defensiveness. She said, "Money isn't the issue, Ned. Not at all."

"Don't give me that," he said. "Money means power. And power means control."

Frannie was bewildered. He spoke with such certainty. Almost as if he understood the things that drove men like Kenneth, loveless men, who lived to dominate and command. But of course he couldn't understand, not in the concrete sense, at least. Not him. Not her sweet, diffident Ned St. Charles.

No, his anger was only a display of frustration, the same frustration he'd displayed when she'd tried to give him a few dollars to help him get home. His pride was wounded. Because, in the world, he was a powerless man, a man who thought himself a failure.

A yearning came on her—to grab his head and pull it down until their lips could meet, to melt his baffled fury with the sweetness of shared passion. She blinked, to try to push away that yearning. Then she said in a torn, breathy voice, "No. It isn't about money. Really, it's not. At least not anymore. I can—and do—take care of myself now. I don't need a man to support me financially. If I loved someone, money wouldn't matter..."

Something was happening in his dark eyes. Like the lighting of a flame, she thought inchoately, as if the husky sound of her voice was a signal, and now both of them knew what would come next. His hand closed around her upper arm.

"Ned..."

Slowly he pulled her to her feet. "Money wouldn't matter," he murmured, "if you loved someone?"

She shook her head, because right then she felt herself incapable of speech.

"What does that mean?" he asked. "Your shaking your head like that—No, that's wrong? Or, no, it wouldn't matter?"

"No, it..." she got out.

"Yeah?"

"It wouldn't matter."

His mouth was slightly parted. In the sculpted male perfection of his face, his lips looked to be the one vulnerable place. They were firmly cut—yet full and soft now, with what she knew in her woman's heart was desire. "If money wouldn't matter, then what would?" he whispered, and he pulled her against his chest.

Frannie felt his warmth and his solidity. Her nipples, beneath the heavy sweater and the bra she wore, grew taut, as if they strained to touch that warmth, to rub against it.

She struggled to remember his question, and it came to her: what would matter, if money didn't?

"A lot of things," she murmured.

"Like?"

"If I could talk to him..."

"And?"

"If we had fun together..."

"Yeah?"

"If he were gentle..."

"What else?"

"And if he had patience, when things got..."

"What?"

"When things got tough. If he were..."

"Tell me."

"...vulnerable."

"Vulnerable."

"Yes, that's what I said."

He made a little chuckling noise deep in his throat. And she felt his chest move against her breasts. He still held her arm. The pressure of his clasping fingers was firm and sure through the wool of her sweater.

"Vulnerable." He seemed to find the word amusing. He chuckled again. "And sensitive, too, I suppose. You'd want this fantasy man of yours to be sensitive."

"Is that funny?" She tugged on her arm. He didn't let go.

"No, not really," he said.

"Then why did you laugh?"

"I think you're one romantic woman, Frannie Lawry."

"I am not," she said much too quickly. He'd said it just the way Kenneth used to. Romantic. With a sneer.

"And, what's more, I don't think this fantasy man you're describing is the kind you'd put up with for long."

"What do you mean?"

"The guy sounds like a whiner to me."

"A *whiner?*" She jerked her head back so she could glare at him.

"You bet. So far, we've got this vulnerable, funny, gentle, patient guy..."

"Yes. So?"

"Well, what about reliable? Loyal? What about *responsible?*"

"Yes, well, that too..."

He pulled her close again. "What about *sexy?*"

Frannie swallowed. "Ned..."

"What about sexy?" he asked again, this time in a velvety tone.

"Well, I...yes, of course. Sexy."

He smiled then, slowly. And his grip on her arm loosened. "Of course."

Frannie knew that it was time to step back, away from him. He wasn't even holding on to her now, so it should have been easy. But it wasn't. She stared up at him, thinking how beautiful his mouth was, thinking of the things he'd just said, thinking that perhaps he was shrewder than she'd allowed herself to admit up till now.

He began, very gently, to stroke her arm where he'd been clasping it. It was as if he were petting her, soothing her. And she loved the way it felt.

She quivered, and then drew in a slow breath. "I don't, oh Lord..."

"You don't what?" He stroked her arm again.

"This wasn't supposed to..."

"What?"

"Happen. It wasn't—"

"Yes, it was," he argued sweetly as his hand kept softly stroking her arm. "From the first moment. In the snow."

She felt weak at the core, and remembered she'd drunk three glasses of cabernet. "I never should have drunk that wine." She shook her head. He caught her chin, held it still.

"Okay," his voice was tender. "Blame it on the wine." His hand smoothed her hair. "The moment I first saw you, I thought..." He let his voice trail off.

"What?" she coaxed, and then knew she shouldn't have.

"How beautiful you were. I thought you were an angel. My angel. Sent from heaven to save me from my empty life." His hand traveled in tender exploration down her back, molding her against him, until she felt the strength of his thighs against her own.

"But I'm not," she protested. "Not an angel. Just a woman..."

"Everything's different with you."

"How?" she wondered, not even stopping to think that she was pressing herself against him now, as much as he was holding her near.

"Exciting," he said. "But comfortable, too." His hand continued to caress her back in long, sweeping strokes. "I'm usually pretty... reserved around women."

Reserved. It was an odd word for him to use, she thought. She would have imagined a man like Ned would choose a simpler word—shy, perhaps. Or maybe nervous.

"Angel?" Ned was asking.

"Um?"

His arm held her close, and his free hand toyed with her hair, coiling and uncoiling a long lock of it on his index finger. "Are you still with me? You looked far away all of a sudden." He brought the lock of hair to his mouth and kissed it.

She forgot what she had been wondering about. "I'm with you," she sighed. "Yes."

"Show me," he whispered into the lock of hair.

"How?" she asked, though she knew that was foolish.

He let the lock of hair fall between them, down onto her breasts, which were pressed so firmly into his chest. "Show me with a kiss."

She knew she should tell him no. She asked, "Now?"

He nodded, his face solemn, his dark eyes full of humor and desire. "Now."

"Show you I'm paying attention," she said carefully, as if reciting the terms of a contract so that both interested parties would completely understand what the contract contained. "By kissing you?"

"Yes. By kissing me."

"Now?"

"Now."

"All right," she agreed. It seemed, right then, utterly logical. He lowered his head as she raised hers. It was less than an inch in distance, anyway.

Their lips met; they sighed in unison.

Her heart beat faster. All wisdom hung suspended on a slender thread of delight.

She slid her arms up around his neck. She stroked his hair, holding him close as she felt his tongue tease her lips.

Frannie sighed again, pressing herself ever closer to his body, rubbing her breasts against his chest, so that her already sensitized nipples hardened even more.

His tongue slid lightly along the line between her lips. She parted for him. His tongue slipped inside, just a flicker for a brief moment—and then it was gone.

"Ned..." She opened her mouth wider, inviting him. And he accepted the invitation with a low groan, pulling her tightly against him, kissing her harder and more hungrily.

Then, for just a fraction of a second, her heavy eyes fluttered open and she caught a glimpse of the two of them in the old, gilt-framed mirror above the sideboard. Herself and Ned. Locked in a passionate embrace.

Beautiful. Dangerous. Exactly what she had told herself must never happen. It had to stop now....

She slid her hands to his shoulders and gave a push. "Stop..."

He groaned, very low, but lifted his head. His dark eyes came open, charged with heat and hunger.

"Please. Ned..." she managed to whisper, a hollow, raspy sound. She was still pressed against him, though her hands were braced at his shoulders. "Please. Stop," she made herself say.

Very slowly, he slid his hands along her arms. When he had her by the wrists, he gently backed away.

As soon as the solid warmth of his body no longer supported hers, Frannie let her knees give way and sank into her chair. Ned released her completely and stood there, unmoving and silent.

Frannie sighed and closed her eyes, feeling infinitely weary—weary with herself, because she seemed to keep telling herself how she intended to behave, and then doing the opposite the minute she got the chance.

Frannie opened her eyes again, and found herself looking at the braided pattern of the big, oval rag rug beneath the table, as well as the toes of the beat-up boots that belonged to the man who'd just kissed her. She forced herself to lift her head and face him.

Watching her, Burnett ached for her, for the confusion he saw in her eyes. He longed to reassure her—almost as much as he longed to reach out and grab her and pull her against him once more.

"I don't know what's wrong with me," she said.

"Angel, there's nothing wrong with you. Nothing at all."

"I hardly know you." She looked away, and then back. "I...don't normally throw myself at men I hardly know."

As if he were an actor playing a role that had begun to fit him like a second skin, Burnett said what Ned would say. "What you mean is, I'm not good enough for you."

She made a protesting noise, but he put up a hand. "Let's get real about this," he said. "You'd be a fool to get involved with me. I'm some loser you helped out—but not someone you'd ordinarily *kiss.*"

"Oh, Ned..." There was real pain in those beautiful eyes.

"Angel, it's all right," he said gently, and he meant it. Both as Ned and as himself. "I don't blame you for being confused. Damn it, I'm confused, too." He raked his hand through his hair, considering, wondering how to convince her she could trust him without telling her the truth about himself and losing any chance he might have with her.

The moment of thoughtful silence cost him dearly. Because it gave her time to remember her original objective.

She said, "Ned, you have to go. Now." Her voice was flat and final.

His heart felt suddenly dead and heavy as lead. "Frannie—"

"I mean it. No more whys or wherefores. You're right. I don't want to get involved with a man who's got the kind of problems you have. Even you yourself just said that would be foolish of me. But I *am* attracted to you." She made the confession in a self-castigating tone. Then she hurried on, "So the best way to solve the problem is for you to leave as you promised you would."

For agonized seconds Burnett had no idea what to do. For the man he'd always been, after all, there were few options at this point. He held no power over her, so he couldn't demand she allow him to stay. And if he simply refused to leave, he was sure it would get him nowhere at all. She had the look of a woman who'd made up her mind. If he tried stonewalling her, he wouldn't put it past her to contact the authorities and have him forcibly removed.

But then it occurred to him—Ned was *vulnerable*. Ned was *sensitive*. Ned could do things that Burnett would consider blatant displays of weakness and irresponsibility. Ned could beg, plead, *throw* himself at a woman's feet . . .

And, to Frannie Lawry, he *was* Ned.

Burnett allowed all the anguish he was feeling to show clearly on his face. He said, in a tormented growl, "Damn it, Frannie—"

And he dropped to his knees before her.

"Don't!" she said, too late.

He looked up at her, pleading with his eyes. And then he reached out, wrapped his arms around her, and laid his head in her lap.

She stiffened. He felt her intention to shove him away. He held his breath and clutched her tightly, holding on for dear life.

He didn't allow himself to breathe again until he felt the hesitant touch of her hand on his head.

"Oh, Ned," she sighed. And her fingers combed, gently, through the hair at his temples.

For a time they were quiet. She continued tenderly to stroke his hair. Then at last, without lifting his head from the cradle of her lap, he said, "I have nowhere to go."

As the words left his lips, he despised himself for saying them—they were an outright lie. Or were they? If he really thought about it, maybe he didn't have anywhere to go— anywhere that mattered anyway.

"Oh, come on, Ned," she said. Her voice was kind, but it carried reproof. "What about that cabin in Graeagle? Are you telling me you can't return there?"

Leaving the cradle of her lap reluctantly, he rocked back on his heels and looked in her eyes. "I need...a friend right now," he said.

Her smile was gentle. "Go home to Sacramento, then. You have a friend there—what's his name?"

"Burnett." He uttered his own name grimly.

"You could share with him how you're feeling."

He tried to keep from looking pained. "I don't think I really explained about Burnett," he said carefully. "He's done a hell of a lot for me, but he's not the kind of guy anyone can talk to. I might as well...lock myself in a room and talk to myself as talk to him."

"Why do you say that?" She looked bewildered. "If he's your friend—"

"It's simple," he said in a preemptive tone, wanting to leave the subject of his real self behind before he got himself into more trouble than he could get out of. "Burnett's done all he can for me. But he's pretty fed up with me now."

"You've been lying to me, haven't you?" she asked then, causing his heart to leap disturbingly inside his chest.

"What do you mean?" he stalled.

She sighed. "Oh, Ned. Earlier, you said that Burnett had given you time off until the end of the year."

"Yes," he said warily. "I said that."

"Tell me the truth. Do you still have your job with him?"

His heart settled back into a regular rhythm. She only thought he was lying about having a job. "Let me put it this way," he hedged, "if I come back in better shape than I left, he'll give me another chance."

She shook her head. "Set your stubborn pride aside and be straight with me. What you mean is, you really don't have a job at this point, right?"

Instead of answering, he took her hand and raised it to his lips. He spoke against her fingers. "I'm sorry, damn it. I know I misled you before." *Just as I'm misleading you now*, his conscience whispered.

He pushed the nagging of his better self from his mind. "Let me stay. For a while. Please."

He watched her face soften. She drew a deep, unsteady breath. Then she shook her head, slowly, and pulled her hand from his grasp.

"I told you. No." She started to stand up.

"Wait!" He cast about desperately for his next move.

"You have to go."

"Just listen, please. Just hear me out. . . ." If he hadn't been so frantic to get her to listen to him, he probably would have laughed out loud at himself about then. Burnett Clinton had always made it a point of honor never to beg anyone for anything. Yet, with this woman, he was on his knees most of the time. With his angel, he had no shame whatsoever.

He held her gaze desperately, doing his damnedest to communicate with his eyes and his imploring expression that there had never been anyone as vulnerable and sensitive as he was—not to mention patient, fun to be with, easy to talk to, and kind. . . .

He had to restrain himself from crowing in passionate triumph when she finally said "All right" and sank back to her chair.

Burnett realized then that he had absolutely no idea what it was he just *had* to say. Casting frantically about for something—anything—he played the moment for all it was worth.

Still sitting on his heels, he laid his hands on his thighs. He looked down at them, as if contemplating the weight and deep meaning of what he was about to say. He closed his eyes, praying as he never had in his life that an idea would come to him. Absolutely nothing did.

When he felt he could stall no longer, he looked up and captured her gaze once more. He said the first thing that popped into his head.

"I need you right now—"

"Ned, I—"

He raised his hand for silence, opened his mouth and forged boldly on. "But, er, not the way you might think."

She gave him a puzzled look, scrunching up her adorable nose. "And what way is that?"

"What?"

"What way do *you* think *I* think you need me?"

He blinked, and tried his absolute best not to show her that he had no clue himself of where he was going with this. He said with great sincerity. "What I mean is what I said."

"But you haven't."

"What?'

"Said it yet." She looked now as though she wondered if he were mentally impaired as well as flat broke and a failure at life.

It came to him, then, where to go with this. He said, with simple honesty, "What I mean is, I'm not talking about any kind of man-woman thing. I want you to understand that. I need you, but in a way that has nothing to do with that."

She made a low, scoffing sound. "Ned, don't treat me like a fool."

"I'm not. I'm telling the truth." He allowed himself a slow grin then. "I have to be honest, though, and say I wouldn't fight too hard if you suddenly invited me into your bed."

She cleared her throat. "That is not going to happen."

"Fine. Like I've been trying to explain, sex isn't the important thing, anyway."

"No?"

"No."

"Then what is?"

He tipped his head, wanting to put this part just right. "That it's Christmas," he finally told her. "And that we're both alone when we could be together—as friends only, if that's what you want. I could keep the fires going, and do any odd jobs you can think of to pay for my keep. I can stay in the basement room, just like I did last night." She still looked at him doubtfully. He added quickly, "And it would only be for tonight, tomorrow, and Christmas. I'll leave on the morning of the twenty-sixth, before noon."

Frannie was silent. He knew he was reaching her. She still felt she should keep saying no, and yet she was a kind person, and generous, too. To a giving person like his angel, what he asked wasn't that unreasonable.

"Look," he went on, shamelessly playing on her tender sensibilities. "Lately, I've had to start facing all the ways my life just isn't working out anymore. I need to change some things, but I'm not really sure yet exactly what they are. I feel that if I can just get through Christmas, I'll make it out the other side. I'll be able to pick up the pieces of my life and start over. But I just don't know how I'll stand it, if I have to spend this holiday alone." He subsided, looking noble, he hoped—and yet needy at the same time.

He thought he'd convinced her. But he discovered he wasn't home free yet, when she asked, "What about your brother? Can't you spend the holiday with him?"

He thought about that, and decided to stick as close to the truth as possible. So he said, "Yes. Casey would welcome me. And so would his wife. And my mother—she'll be there, too. They'll be glad to have me."

"Well, then?"

He considered, and went on, still more or less honestly, "They'll spend the whole holiday worrying about me. I'm having enough trouble right now trying to deal with all the ways I've messed up my own life. Having to watch the people I care about agonizing over my problems, too, is more than I can take...." He let his voice trail off, and then decided he had no more to say, so he bent his head—humbly, he hoped—and looked at the rug he was kneeling on.

Frannie, trying diligently to be sensible, gazed down on his bent head. She knew she absolutely must stick by her resolution that he should leave—and yet she wanted, more than anything, to allow him to stay.

All her instincts told her, as they had from the first, that Ned was a good, gentle man. And she completely sympathized with his need to share Christmas with someone on this first year as a single man again.

Last year, her first as a single woman since her marriage, had been hell for her during the holidays. She'd been grateful to have this old house to come to, and Aunt Bonnie to share Christmas dinner with. She understood how Ned could feel the same way on *his* first Christmas on his own.

Also, she *did* like him. Her own Christmas would be much improved, should she have a friend to share it with....

Friend, that warning voice in her head scoffed. *There's a lot more than friendship going on here.*

Well, so what if I'm attracted to him, she argued back in her thoughts. That doesn't mean I have to do anything about it. He said it would be as friends only, and that's just how it *will* be.

Don't be an idiot, Frances, she could almost hear Kenneth jeering. *He's a nobody who can't even hold a job. Send him away now....*

And, of course, she knew what Aunt Bonnie was going to say. *What has happened to you, Frances? Have you lost your mind?*

Christmas dinner would be held at Bonnie's house. Like last year, Bonnie would roast a huge bird, and invite a few of her friends from Downieville and Sierra City, too. That would be an experience—Aunt Bonnie and her lifelong friends. And Ned, the raggedy man from Sacramento, by way of Graeagle and the St. Charles Place bar.

"And where are you from, again, Ned?" one of Aunt Bonnie's friends would politely inquire.

"Oh, Frannie found me drunk in a snowbank three days ago. She took me in and sobered me up and then said I could stay in the basement for a while—would you pass the peas, please?"

"Frannie?" Ned asked softly, interrupting her imaginings. "Are you all right?" He'd raised his head and was looking at her with mingled entreaty and concern in his eyes.

"Yes. I'm fine. Just thinking."

"And . . . ?"

She studied him as he knelt there before her. He looked hopeful and vulnerable and utterly harmless.

"All right, you can stay," she told him at last.

Burnett, stunned for a moment that his fervent wish had been granted, almost blurted out, "Are you *sure*?" He stopped the words just before they escaped his lips and murmured instead, with humble and quiet dignity, "Thank you."

"But there is a condition," she said.

"Name it."

"I don't want to control your behavior for you," she began hesitantly, "but I'm not willing to have someone around who can't stay away from the bar. How bad a problem is alcohol for you?"

There was no hesitation in his reply. "Tell you what," he said. "I freely give my word not to have a single drink while I'm staying in your house. And if I do, then you promise me that you will kick me out right away."

"As if it were that easy getting rid of you," she said with good-natured grimness.

He looked at her levelly. "I mean it, Frannie. I won't have a drink. If I do, you ask me to leave and I will."

She shook her head. "Why is it I believe you when the things you say about yourself seem so vague and hard to pin down?"

"Because, about this, I'm telling the absolute truth."

"Meaning there *are* things you're not being honest about?"

"Everyone has secrets, Frannie," he said soft and low.

He was thinking, though she couldn't know that, that his deception was fully justified. Right now, his angel wouldn't be able to accept his real self. Later, after she knew him better, he would tell her everything.

But not now. Now he would be the penniless, unassuming Ned St. Charles, willing to chop wood and fix anything that broke for a comfortable place to sleep and some nourishing food.

He'd be a nobody, a failure. And as he looked into his angel's glowing face, he found himself thinking that being a pitiful loser for a few days might be the best thing that ever happened to him.

Chapter Nine

"Come in, dear." Bonnie pulled open the door and gestured Frannie into her house.

Frannie held out the empty plate. "No, I won't stay. Here. The fudge is incredible—as always."

"You ate it *all*," Bonnie demanded in disapproval. "Already?"

Frannie understood that her aunt was still sulking from their last confrontation the day before and spoiling for a fight. Frannie chose not to give it to her.

"No, Aunt Bonnie," Frannie said. "I ate two pieces, put the rest on a plate of my own, and washed this plate, so I could return it. But even if I *had* eaten it all, that is why you gave it to me, isn't it? To eat?"

"Well, yes, of course," Bonnie said. Then, "Oh, why are we arguing?"

"Are we?"

"I don't want to argue."

"Great. Let's not."

Bonnie's little mouth pursed. "Fair enough. No more arguing."

"Fine." Frannie steeled herself for what she planned to say next. Returning the plate wasn't the main reason she was standing on her aunt's front porch. It was Christmas Eve morning, and she could waste no more time in informing Bonnie that she wanted to invite another guest for dinner tomorrow night—Ned St. Charles.

"Is *he* gone yet?" Bonnie asked right then, causing Frannie to wonder if perhaps her aunt could read minds.

"Aunt Bonnie—"

"It's a simple question. Answer it."

"All right. No."

"Good God."

"Aunt Bonnie—"

"Have you lost your mind? What's wrong with you?"

"Nothing, I—"

"Some bum off the street. It's a downright scandalous shame."

"Aunt Bonnie."

"I swear, I just don't know what has happened to you. First Kenneth Dayton, now this. It's...self-destructive, that's what it is. You have no respect for yourself, to get mixed up with—"

Frannie had had enough. "Stop," she said, her voice carrying an unmistakable note of command. Bonnie actually fell silent.

"Now," Frannie continued, "I am allowing Ned St. Charles to stay for Christmas at my house." Bonnie gasped. Frannie gave her a sharp look, and Bonnie remained silent—much to Frannie's surprise. "I understand that you don't approve of that, Aunt Bonnie. And your approval is your business. It's still my house, as I've already told you. And I choose to let Ned stay in it for a few days.

"Now, as for Christmas dinner, I would like to spend it with you and your friends, as we did last year. But I want Ned to be included. He's a man alone, who could use a little human kindness—especially considering the real meaning of the day. May I invite him?"

Bonnie's mouth was hanging open. She snapped it shut, then sputtered, "Why, I...I—"

"A simple yes or no will do."

"I don't...can't..." Bonnie began sputtering again, but then caught herself. She drew her stout body up as tall as it would stretch and declared, "All right. Bring him along, then. Though heaven knows I think you are making the biggest mistake of your life."

"Thank you, I will," Frannie said with a pleasant smile, and then turned and marched back down the steps before her aunt could say more.

At her own house, she found Ned down in the basement just screwing the back onto the old clothes dryer, which had given up the ghost sometime yesterday in the middle of drying his shirt and overalls.

"It's the belt," he explained as he pushed the dryer into its place against the wall. "It slipped loose. I readjusted the pulleys and the thing should work—for a while. But what you're going to need is a new belt sooner or later."

"Okay." She stood at the base of the stairs as he turned the dryer on and showed her that it did, indeed, work—for the time being at least. After it ran for a moment, he pulled open the loading door to toss in his clothes, which were waiting in a wet heap on top of the washer. He punched the start button and the dryer began spinning once more.

"How'd it go?" He straightened up and then leaned against the dryer, crossing his hands over his chest. "With your aunt?"

"She's concerned that I've lost my mind—and you're invited for Christmas dinner."

"That should be interesting."

"At the very least." She chuckled, and then fell silent. The rumbling of the dryer seemed to swell to fill the space. "Ned?"

"Yeah?"

"If you think you could trust me, I'd like to know. About you. And your family. And even what happened in your marriage...." Frannie spoke haltingly because across the concrete floor, he was scowling at her. She rushed on, before his dark look could intimidate her into silence. "I've been thinking about what you said last night, that everyone has secrets. Maybe that's true. But it seems to me that you've got more than most people."

"What do you mean?" he asked. His tone was cold, as if it could freeze her out of asking more questions.

She forged ahead. "Well, I can't put my finger on it exactly, but when you talk about yourself, I feel like you're hiding something."

"I am," he said flatly and held his hands out, palms up. "I told you that yesterday."

"It's not enough. If you won't trust me, it makes me wonder if there's something about you I really should know. Have you done something illegal? Or is someone after you?"

He glared at her. When he finally spoke, he didn't answer either of her questions. "My hands are dirty, and it's cold down here. Let's go upstairs. I'll wash up."

"But Ned—"

"We'll talk," he said with a sharp wave of his hand. "Upstairs. After I'm cleaned up."

"All right," she agreed, "that's reasonable."

"Let's go, then." He came away from the dryer and started toward her for the stairs. She turned and went ahead of him, feeling apprehensive at how brusque and cryptic he had been when she'd only asked him to talk a little about himself.

He spent several minutes in the bathroom. When he emerged, he was smiling.

"How about if we sit in the front room?" he suggested. It was as if, she thought nervously, he'd given himself time to think about what she'd asked of him, to decide how much—and what—he was going to tell her. And now that he had decided how far to go, he could relax a little, smile, be friendly with her.

Frannie pushed away the ugly idea that he might be planning to give her nothing but lies. "Sure," she said, and they went through the dining room together.

They sat on either end of the old, fat sofa. He hitched up a leg and turned toward her. "Okay, what do you want to know?"

A part of Frannie didn't want to push him, wanted to simply say *never mind* and let it go. But she'd gone this far. She boldly inquired, "How about your ex-wife?"

At the other end of the sofa, Burnett considered her question.

He'd resolved, as before, to try to stick as much to the truth as possible, and not to volunteer any more than was necessary to keep his angel from deciding he was too secretive about himself for her to risk having him around. Now she was looking at him expectantly, licking her lips a little, nervous and adorable. He stalled, "What do you want to know about my ex-wife?"

"Well . . . who divorced whom?"

The truth, as much as possible, he reminded himself. "She divorced me."

"Why?"

"She wanted kids. I couldn't give them to her."

Frannie now wore a sympathetic expression. "You aren't able to father children?"

He shook his head. "With most women, according to all the doctors we saw, there should be no problem."

"I don't understand."

Burnett was beginning to wonder if he should have stuck so close to the truth after all. The medical explanation for his and Amanda's fertility problems was complex.

"Can you explain?" Frannie prompted.

Burnett dragged in a deep breath. "It's real . . . complicated."

"Just try. Please."

"All right." He paused for a moment to organize his thoughts. Then he began, "What we were told is that our body chemistries were too similar. See, an embryo is actually a foreign body within the mother's body. And the natural reaction of her body is for her white blood cells to attack and destroy it. But, in normal cases, when pregnancy occurs, the mother's body also begins producing what are called blocking antibodies—antibodies that wipe out the attacking white blood cells, so that the embryo is protected from destruction by its mother's immune system."

Frannie, Burnett noticed, was looking a little dazed. He allowed himself a shrug. "I warned you it was complicated . . ."

"Go on, I'm following. More or less."

"In our case—Amanda's and mine, I mean—the doctors believed that our body chemistries were just too similar. Amanda's blocking reaction was never triggered, because her system didn't recognize enough difference between the embryo and her own body. But her immune system *did*. So it attacked and destroyed the baby in the first trimester whenever she got pregnant."

"And how often was that?"

"Twice, that we know of for sure. She had two miscarriages before she was three months along." Burnett was silent for a moment, watching Frannie's face, wondering if he'd made a mistake trying to explain all this. Ned was supposed to be a simple guy, not at all the type who tossed around words like *embryo* and *antibody*.

But Frannie, as usual, was more concerned for his pain than his inconsistencies. "Oh, Ned. I'm sorry."

The tender understanding in her voice struck a chord deep within him. He found himself opening up perhaps more than was safe. "She wanted to be perfect," he said. "The perfect woman. The perfect wife. And part of being perfect was producing perfect children."

"Adopting wasn't an option, then?"

He thought about that, and found himself telling a little more of the truth. "When my sister died, leaving her son, Mike, alone, Amanda wanted him. But my sister had wanted Mike to be with Casey. Amanda and I fought pretty dirty in an effort to get Mike."

"That was the 'family crisis' you mentioned before?"

"Yes. But Casey won. Mike stayed with him in the end. And it was the right thing. I understand that now."

"Why?"

"Casey was—is—a much better guardian than I ever would have been."

"Casey has money?" Frannie's look was full of gentle compassion.

"Money enough," he answered, knowing what she'd assume from that. She'd be sure that Ned hadn't been able to afford a lawyer to take the battle to court. It hadn't been like that at all, of course. The real issues had been about emotional suitability as a guardian. In the end, Burnett had been forced to realize he lacked certain qualities that Casey possessed in abundance—qualities like patience, tolerance and a sense of humor.

"In a way," he said, pondering out loud, "that was the real end of our marriage. When I stepped aside and let Casey have Mike, Amanda never forgave me for that. She'd had one miscarriage before the fight over Mike. And then she had the other afterward. That was the final blow. I was a complete failure in her eyes. I couldn't get my sister's boy for her to raise, and I couldn't give her a baby of her own."

"So she left you?"

"Yes."

"Where is she now?"

He shrugged. "Planning to remarry, from what I understand. She might even have done it by now. He's a lawyer, the one who handled her divorce from me."

"So this one's a lawyer. He has plenty of money, I imagine," Frannie commented. Burnett said nothing, though he understood her remark was predicated on the assumption that *he* didn't. She added, "And I imagine she's pregnant."

Surprised at her perceptiveness, he shot her a look. "How did you know?"

A sad smile curved her mouth. "The woman you've described would want to get pregnant *first* this time around. She'd learn from her mistakes."

"Mistakes like me, you mean?"

She reached down the length of the couch and gave him a playful nudge. "Don't get all gloomy on me."

"I'm not gloomy," he said. "Why should I be gloomy? My family considers me unfit to care for my nephew, and my ex-wife was scouting out new sperm donors before the ink was dry on our divorce papers. But that's okay. I'm cheerful. I refuse to let it get me down."

She laughed. "That's the spirit." Then she grew serious. "You said day before yesterday, when I found you in the snow, that maybe you never loved her."

"Amanda?"

"Mmm-hmm."

"I don't know..." He had to struggle to find the words. "I have this...problem about love."

"What problem?"

"Well, I mean, what is it?"

She laughed. "Love?"

"Right."

She looked away, at the Christmas tree across the room in front of the window. Her legs were folded beneath her and her slim body turned toward him. She wore black stir-rup pants, a big red sweater and red socks. She must have left her boots outside on the porch, because she'd been in stockinged feet since she came to find him in the base-ment.

A spark popped in the grate. She jumped, gathering her tucked-under legs even closer.

He asked, "Did you forget the question?"

She looked at him again. "No. No, I didn't forget."

"Well?"

"I don't know if I could give you a...definition of love. But I could tell you what I think of, when I think of that word."

"What?"

"My dad. When I think of love, I think of my dad. He loved me, I'm sure of that. And he knew how to show it, too."

Burnett made a low sound. "What about your mother?"

"We aren't close," she said, and the words had such a final sound that he didn't pry further along that line. She gave him a playfully warning glare. "Don't dare ask about *my* ex. Remember, I told you I don't think Kenneth knew how to love."

"I remember."

"What about *your* mother?" she asked. "She's still alive, right?"

"Yes?"

"Does she love you?"

Burnett thought of his mother, Lillian, of her honesty and her strength. Though she'd loved his father deeply, she hadn't let it destroy her when he left. She'd taken her children and a small trust she'd received from a bachelor uncle, moved to Sacramento and opened an ice-cream store, the first Chilly Lilly's. He admired his mother. "Yes," he said, and couldn't resist smiling as he added, "My mother loves me. There must be some hope for me, right?"

She chuckled at that. "And your father?"

"He's dead," Burnett said. "Long dead."

She straightened her spine a little. "You should hear your voice. You sound like you hated him."

"I did," he said flatly.

"Why?"

He told the truth; it could have been Ned's truth, as well as his own. "My father left us when I was eleven. Deserted my mother and brother and sister and me. He left a note that I found. It said that married life was stifling him. *Stifling*. And that he was through with it, for good and all. I never saw him again. Occasionally he would write to my mother. She never divorced him, so she was notified when he died."

Frannie, quiet understanding in her eyes, reached across the distance between them to put her hand on his arm. Her touch was warm. And welcome.

He put his hand over hers. She didn't pull away.

At that moment he was absolutely sure that they would be much more than friends before he left her house. He could see it in the softness of her face when she looked at him, in the way her body yearned toward his—as his yearned toward hers—across the cushions of the old couch.

He squeezed her hand, she squeezed his back, and then she seemed to realize that perhaps she was getting too close. She pulled her hand from his with just enough reluctance that he had to hide a knowing smile.

"What else do you want to know about me?" he asked after a minute.

She shrugged. "I guess that's enough—for now."

They were quiet for a while, then. Frannie rested her head against the back of the couch, and she stared beyond him into the dancing fire in the grate.

Eventually she spoke. "I'll go down and check on your clothes."

"No." He moved to stand. "I can do it—"

She smiled, already up and moving. "Stay there. Enjoy the tree. I'll be right back."

He sank back on the couch as she disappeared around the corner. He thought about what had just happened between them—by mingling truth and lies, he had brought her closer to trusting him. The idea did not make him proud.

Yet, he told himself defiantly, it was the only way. She would never let him get close if she knew the whole truth.

What he needed to do, he realized clearly now, was to get her to make love with him. For a woman like Frannie, making love with a man would be a turning point. She wouldn't give her body without her heart coming along, too. After they made love, she would feel committed to him. Then, very gently, he could reveal the whole truth. She might be upset with him for his deceptions, but she would come to accept him as he really was. After she'd given herself physically, her feeling of commitment would be stronger than her fears.

"They're still damp, but the dryer's working great." Frannie cut short his tender scheming as she came back into the room. She held out his old coat, and had hers over her other arm. "I have some last-minute shopping to do. Want to come along?"

He nodded and stood up, thinking that if he could slip away from her for a few minutes, he might call his brother and Leland Fairgrave, his lawyer. The call to Casey would reassure his family that he was all right. And Leland could assure Burnett himself that all was going smoothly in his business while he was gone.

Burnett reached out to take the coat from Frannie. She extended it—and with it several folded bills. It took him a moment to register that she was trying to give him money again.

"I told you. No," he said.

"For fixing the dryer," she coaxed.

"Frannie—"

"Oh, come on. It's no big deal. And you have to have a little pocket change, after all."

He looked at her, ready to tell her no again—and then decided she was right. Even the perennially poor-but-proud Ned would probably give in and take a few bucks from her at this point.

"All right," he said. "But I *will* pay you back."

"Fair enough."

He stuck the money in the back pocket of the jeans she'd given him and felt the bent corner of his driver's license as he slid his hand in there. He'd taken the license from the jacket yesterday afternoon, thinking it would be wiser to keep it on him, where she wasn't likely to find it and discover just how *close* he and Burnett Clinton actually were.

"All ready?" She was lifting her wonderful, unruly hair out from beneath the collar of her jacket. He watched as she tried to smooth the wild tangle of curls, and he smiled.

He nodded. "You bet."

They went out to the porch, where she paused for a moment to pull on her boots. He waited, looking out at the glittering, ice-pure diamond of a day.

Frannie finished putting on her boots and reached for his arm. As they had the day before, they set off arm in arm for the bridge that would lead them to Main Street.

Chapter Ten

As they went out the gate to the slush-covered sidewalk, Frannie was scheming. She needed to get rid of Ned for a while.

She'd had a brainstorm. Unfortunately it hadn't come to her until *after* she'd invited Ned to come along to town with her. She'd held out that hideous coat of his—and it had hit her like a bolt out of the blue....

It was Christmas! She could get him a present. And the perfect present for him right now would be some decent clothes. She'd get him a new shirt and some jeans and socks and underwear—and a nice winter jacket, for heaven's sake.

And she was reasonably sure he would even accept what she offered. Because she would be firm that he must not hurt her feelings and reject her gifts. It was Christmas, after all.

The problem was, how to escape him long enough to slip into The Ruffled Goose, the store at the west end of Main where such things were sold.

Once they'd crossed the bridge, Frannie smiled and said hi to everyone she passed. Ned walked beside her, not saying much, nodding at the people to whom she gave greetings. Frannie held on to his arm companionably, enjoying the warmth that radiated from his big body—and plotting how she was going to get rid of him for long enough to do what she needed to do.

A possible approach came to her. She paused and looked over at him. "I have an idea."

"Yeah?"

He was so handsome, she thought. And he'd be even more so in clothes that didn't look ready for the ragbag. "We could speed this whole process up a little, if you do the grocery shopping and I do the rest."

"The rest?" he asked.

"Mmm-hmm," she rushed on. "I need some wrapping paper from the hardware store, and a few things from The Ruffled Goose down the street. So what do you think?"

He shrugged. "Fine with me."

She had to hold back a smug smile. This was *easy*. He went right along with her. He hadn't a clue, she could tell by his open expression, of what she intended to do.

"Here." She took his hand and put her grocery money and the list she'd made into his palm, then wrapped his fingers around it. "Thanks. I'll meet you at Downieville Grocery. It's the building over there on the right. Half an hour."

"I'll be there," he said.

Frannie pulled her arm from his and crossed the street, stopping once on the other side to wave and smile back at him. Then she turned and made for The Ruffled Goose at the corner end of the covered sidewalk.

Burnett, watching her rush away down the street, lifted his hand, waving in return too late for her to see it.

After he let his hand drop to his side, he stood for a moment, wondering vaguely what she was up to. But then he decided not to examine the reason for his good luck.

She'd played right into his hands, after all. He had some time alone, and there was a phone kiosk right behind him, against the brick wall of a store.

He charged the call to his home phone, and dialed Casey's house first. Casey picked up in two rings.

"Big Brother?" Casey's voice came at him over the line, a voice with lazy humor in it as well as affection and, right now, carefully masked concern. "You doing all right? Still up at the cabin?"

"I'm doing fine. I'm in Downieville," Burnett explained. Casey would know of the town. They often drove through it when they took Highway 49 to Graeagle.

"What for?"

"I got in the Jeep day before yesterday. I started driving. I wound up here."

Casey chuckled. "That bad, huh?"

"Yeah. Pretty bad. But better now."

"You coming home for Christmas? Joey—" he used his wife's nickname "—made me buy this bird that would feed an army. And Mike's bought you something—I don't know what, but it's wrapped in three different kinds of paper and he swears you're gonna love it." Burnett cleared his throat, touched at the news that Mike had chosen him a special gift. "Also," Casey went on, "Mother's made divinity."

"Divinity," Burnett repeated, rather stupidly, he thought, as he realized that he *did* love his family. If it weren't for his angel, he'd hop in the Jeep and head home.

"Big Brother? You still there?"

"Yeah, I'm here. And I'm staying here for Christmas. And hopefully longer."

"Hopefully?" Casey chuckled again. "Come on, what gives?"

Burnett coughed.

"It's a woman," Casey said.

"All I did was cough."

"What's her name? What's she like?"

"Frannie. Frannie Lawry. She's an angel, I swear. My angel. She pulled me out of a snowbank, so drunk I couldn't walk. And she took me in her house and she's letting me stay. She thinks I'm flat busted. She thinks my name's Ned."

"Whoa, hold it."

"Yeah?"

"You sure you're okay?"

"That's what I called to tell you. I'm fine. I'm in Downieville at Frannie Lawry's house until sometime after Christmas Day. She doesn't have a phone, but all you have to do is ask someone who lives in this town. They'll know her. Everyone seems to know everyone else around here."

"I don't get it, Big Brother. You *told* her your name was..." After all the years of training, Casey couldn't quite say it.

"Ned. Yeah," Burnett finished for him.

"But you hate that name. After Dad left, you used to beat me up every time I called you that."

"I know, but it happened. I was drunk and I said my name was Ned. And now..."

"What?"

"That's who I am to her. That's who she thinks I am."

Casey was silent. Then he said, "Advice and a dollar fifty will get you a ride on the bus, but Burnett..."

"Yeah, what?"

"If you aren't honest, get that way. Okay?"

"I will."

"When?"

"Soon. Listen, freeze me some of that bird and save me some divinity, and tell Mike I'll get that present from him the minute I hit town again."

"Burnett—"

"Really, I gotta go." Burnett depressed the hook before his brother could say more.

Then he stood for a moment, clutching the handset, staring at the silver tinsel on one of the decorated trees that lined the streets. The tinsel moved in the slight cold wind, flickering and glittering beneath the winter sun.

Get honest, Casey had advised.

I will, Burnett swore, both to his brother and to himself. As soon as we've made love and she really trusts me. As soon as I know she won't send me away.

"Excuse me," a voice asked from behind him. "Are you through with the phone?"

He turned to face an old man with a cane. "Just one more call, sir," he said automatically, not even aware that his voice was a soft, gentle drawl and his face wore a solicitous expression. "Will that be all right?"

"You go right ahead, son. I'll get me my smokes from Yo-Ho's here." He pointed with his cane at the brick building. "And maybe when I come out you'll have your business all done."

"Thanks." The old man tottered off, pretty spryly, Burnett thought, for a guy who looked eighty if he was a day.

When the old man had disappeared into the corner store, Burnett dialed Leland Fairgrove. The secretary put him right through.

"My God, Burnett," Leland swore the moment he got on the line. "Where the hell are you?"

"Away. Is there a problem?"

"Jordan McSwain and four of the other franchise buyers are here."

Leland was talking about the key man in Burnett's upcoming franchise expansion plan. McSwain, who years ago had managed a store for Burnett, had done well for himself since then. Now he wanted to invest in Chilly Lilly's. He had a friend who was head of site development for Randall's Supermarkets, a national chain. The plan was that twelve franchise Chilly Lilly's would be built adjacent to twelve new Randall's Supermarkets.

Leland went on, "McSwain and his people need some paper from us. Now. Randall's has decided they want a firm commitment from us before the first of the year, and McSwain needs something official to take to his man in site development."

"Where is McSwain now?"

"I told you. Here." Leland's voice rose a notch.

"Settle down, Leland," Burnett warned. "Everything will be fine. Are you saying McSwain is at your office?"

"No. He was. They came into town last night, and I took them to dinner. I said you were out of town on an emergency, and would be back today."

Burnett looked at his wrist out of habit—before he realized that he'd left his Rolex in Graeagle with his pin-striped suit. "What time is it, anyway?"

"Quarter to noon."

"On Christmas Eve. It's too late to do much today anyway. Is McSwain taking the others to Tahoe for Christmas and the weekend?" It was a logical question. McSwain had originally come from Lake Tahoe. Some of his family still lived there.

"Yes," Leland said.

"I thought so. Where's he staying? Give me a number."

"A phone call isn't going to do it, Burnett. What's the matter with you? This is a hell of a lot of work on the line here."

"Give me the number."

The voice on the other end grudgingly complied.

"Thanks, Leland. Unless you hear from me, I'll be back Monday morning, in your office at eight sharp. We'll get together with McSwain and the others then. We'll write something up to satisfy all of them, and I'll put my name on it and things will be fine."

"Burnett, we need to get together. Go over this. Decide on the wording and—"

"Write it up, Leland. I'll go over it Monday. It will be fine."

"But—"

"Your office, Leland," Burnett said in a voice of steel. "Monday morning. Eight o'clock. Have you got that?"

Leland cleared his throat. Burnett's tone had told him more clearly than words ever could that he was wasting his breath to try to get Burnett to return early. "Yes. All right. I have it. But can you at least give me a number?"

"There's no phone where I'm staying."

"No phone?" Leland sounded as if he might have a stroke. "How can you go someplace where there is no phone?"

Burnett allowed himself a dry laugh. "Merry Christmas, Leland. See you Monday."

"Yes, of course, but—"

Burnett hung up the phone.

He turned, grinning a little, to find the old man, a carton of Pall Mall's under one arm, leaning on a cane and watching him.

"One more call?" Burnett asked sheepishly.

"Well, you just go right ahead." The old man nodded in a rather courtly fashion, and made himself comfortable on a nearby bench. He opened his carton of cigarettes and lit one, drawing on it with obvious relish. Then he coughed into his fist and gathered his heavy coat closer against the chill.

Burnett set about reaching Jordan McSwain at his hotel.

"Jordan? This is Burnett," he said when the hotel's front desk put him through.

"Clinton? What the hell? Where are you, buddy?"

Burnett smiled. Though he and Jordan were as near opposite as two men could be, Burnett had come to like the other man over the years. Jordan was a huge blond giant who loved two things equally—a good time and big deals.

"Gone till Monday," Burnett said. "Unless you absolutely have to have that piece of paper before then."

"So Leland filled you in, huh?"

"Yeah. And it's no problem. He says you're heading up to Tahoe for the weekend. And so I was thinking we all could go ahead and enjoy the holiday—and take care of business come Monday morning."

"Put business on hold and have a good time?" McSwain sounded truly baffled. "Is that really you, Clinton? And if it is, are you feeling all right?"

"Yes, Jordan. It's me. I'm feeling fine. Terrific, as a matter of fact. So what do you say? If you insist, I can be there in two, maybe three hours. We'll get you what you need today and—"

To Burnett's relief, Jordan cut him off. "Aw hell, no. If Burnett Clinton's gonna put pleasure first for once in his life, who the hell am I to spoil the party? I don't have to see my guy at Randall's until Tuesday, anyway."

"Good enough, then. Say, ten on Monday?"

"You got it, buddy. And Burnett?"

"Yeah?"

"Kiss her once for me, okay?"

Burnett chuckled and hung up.

Down on the bench, the old man stubbed out his second cigarette and rose shakily with the aid of his cane.

"Thanks for waiting, sir," Burnett said as he stepped out of the way. "And Merry Christmas to you."

The old man gave the greeting back. "Sounds like some big deal you got cooking there, son." There was a distinct glint in the old codger's pale eyes. Burnett realized he must present something of a contradiction, wearing clothes salvaged from the next rummage sale, and babbling on a pay phone about million-dollar franchise deals.

He winked at the old man, whom he was sure he'd never see again, and allowed his good spirits to carry the day. "Yeah, they can't do without me in the world of high finance."

The old man gave an approving cackle in answer and picked up the handset to make his own call.

Burnett strolled the few steps to the corner of Commercial and Main and then stood for a moment, in a kind of pleasant shock at what he had just done. For the first time in his life, he'd put his personal desires above his professional responsibilities. And it had felt fantastic.

Grinning like an idiot, he calculated that he probably had about twenty minutes until he was due to meet Frannie at the grocery store. He glanced at the list she'd handed him; only a few things. His guess was he could get the things she wanted, and still have a few minutes to spare.

Idly, he scanned the street, noting the post office across the road, and the hardware store next to it. Above the street, as probably could be seen in any number of small, western towns, hung silver tinsel looped in garlands. Down

at the entrance of town a silver star wrapped in colored
lights hovered proudly between the grocery store and the
building across from it, spreading holiday cheer to a win-
try world.

Tomorrow was Christmas Day. And he'd be spending it
with an angel. The thought brought a warm glow to his cold
skin.

Christmas. Tomorrow, he thought. And then it occurred to him that he had no gift to give her.

The noon bell sounded loud and long as he turned
quickly toward the gift shop down the street to his right.

The place was called The Mine Shaft, and he went down
rough-hewn wooden stairs to get to it, in a basement beneath Cirino's bar. The little shop had two rooms. Burnett
concentrated on the shelves and glass display cases in the
space immediately beneath the stairs.

He found what he wanted almost immediately—as if it
had been waiting for him. A Christmas angel in a snow
bubble.

She stood very still and proud in there, her hands tucked
in the folds of her belled sleeves. Her robe was white,
trimmed with gold. When he turned her bubble upside
down, the swirling tiny storm around her sparkled with
flecks of golden glitter.

"She's lovely, isn't she?"

Burnett detected the note of nervousness in the clerk's
voice. He looked down at his old coat and frayed borrowed jeans, and he understood that the woman was probably wary about a man like him, someone she didn't know
who appeared to be down on his luck.

He tried a hesitant smile, and watched her wariness fade
somewhat. "She's beautiful, ma'am. How much?"

The woman told him. With tax, it was just a few cents less than what Frannie had pressed into his hand before they left her house.

Burnett beamed, happier at that moment than he'd been in years and years. "I'll take her. Can you wrap her for a gift?" The woman agreed that she could.

Five minutes later Burnett emerged into the thin, bright sunlight with the wrapped angel tucked safely in the inside pocket of his shapeless old jacket. He hurried to the grocery store and was almost through the list Frannie had given him, strolling contentedly down the narrow aisles, when she caught up with him.

She was grinning, and her cheeks were stained pink, whether from the cold or excitement, he couldn't be sure. "How are you doing?" she asked.

"Almost finished," he told her. She was clutching a big shopping bag. He gestured at it. "Why don't you put that on the cart?"

"No, no... I'll just hold onto it."

He shrugged and opened the refrigerator case for a half gallon of milk. "Did you get everything you needed?"

"Absolutely. I did."

He turned and gave her a look. "What gives?"

"Nothing. What do you mean? Nothing gives."

They looked at each other for a moment. Then he said "Right" and rolled his eyes in a signal that he had a pretty good idea what she was up to.

They both burst into an absurd fit of laughter.

Nearby shoppers turned to look, smiled indulgently, and moved on down the aisles.

When the shared laughter faded, Frannie said. "It says on the bulletin board by the old theater that there's a candlelight service tonight at the Methodist church. I haven't been to one of those since I was little. Would you mind if we went?''

"I'd love to go," he told her, and meant it, though he was not a religious man. He'd have gone to church every day of the week, as long as Frannie went, too.

"I feel like . . ." she began.

"Tell me," he coaxed.

"It was a good idea," she said, her gaze sliding away and then back. "For you to stay. A good idea for me, as much as you. I'm, well, just glad you're here."

Her lips were slightly parted. He wanted to bend down and claim them with his own. But he didn't. Not yet. Soon enough, he told himself. He was absolutely certain now that his angel was near to being his in every way.

Chapter Eleven

The church was across the street from Frannie's house, and the service began at eight. Burnett felt strange at first, in his old clothes, but Frannie assured him that people came as they were.

They picked up candles at the door, and signed the open register on the podium inside. Burnett felt more than a little reprehensible signing his name as Ned St. Charles—especially within sight of the rugged cross on the altar and the looming pictures of Jesus and his lambs. But he did it anyway.

They sat in a pew near the back, and Frannie waved and nodded at everyone. She had an especially big smile for that mean mother hen of an aunt of hers, who took a seat a few pews up and across the center aisle. The aunt granted her a curt nod—and Burnett a disparaging frown.

There were perhaps twenty-five people there when the service began. Burnett and Frannie shared a hymnal, though they didn't really need to because there were more than enough to go around. Her singing voice was sweet and high, and she kept sliding him glances, coloring sweetly when he intercepted them.

A tide of mingled sentimentality and desire rose up and washed over him. He found himself thinking that sitting in that old oak pew next to his angel and sharing a hymnal was closer to heaven than he'd ever been in his life. When he tipped his candle to hers, spreading the light of the world, he felt himself transfixed by the light that shone from her eyes. It was all he could do not to kiss her right there, in front of the whole congregation.

When the service was over, they left the church arm in arm. In the darkness, a light, picture-postcard snow was falling. He started to cross the street to her house, but she tugged on his arm.

"Not yet. I want to show you something."

"What?"

"A surprise."

He went where she led him, down the sidewalk and around the corner to Pearl Street. He heard the music way before they got there. Tinkling Christmas music.

"What is it?"

"You'll see."

Soon enough, they reached the source of the sound. It came from a two-story house that backed onto the Downie River. The second floor of the house possessed a large balcony, accessed by a sliding glass door. Beneath the gabled roof and framed by the intricate curlicues of gingerbread trim that embellished the eaves, children in costume moved jerkily, like wind-up figures, in time to the chimelike music.

"What is this?" Burnett asked, enchanted.

"Shh, watch," Frannie instructed, shivering a little and holding tighter to his arm.

Up on the balcony, an angel in a filmy dress rode a rocking horse in the middle of a teeter-totter with an elf at either end. Toy soldiers paraded, up and down, in and out. Mrs. Santa sewed a Christmas quilt, and a red-nosed reindeer pawed imaginary ground. Lights of all colors were woven in the eaves and threaded on the railings, while lacy cut-out snowflakes hung from the rafters, turning slowly in the slight, cold wind.

The tinkling tune ended. The costumed children on the balcony froze in a Christmas tableau. The handful of spectators, including Frannie and Burnett, applauded. Then the music started up again, and the children once more came to jerky, wind-up life.

Burnett pulled Frannie even closer and inquired of her glowing upturned face, "Now will you tell me what this is?"

"The Music Box," she explained. "The lady who lives in this house puts it on every year. The local kids perform in it. It's always a big hit."

They stood for a while longer, watching the children on the balcony as the snow drifted down around them, like a billion tiny frozen feathers, falling slowly to earth. Then they looked at each other.

"Ready to go back?" she asked.

He nodded. They turned together and went back to Frannie's house, pausing briefly on the porch to remove their snow-crusted boots.

Inside, the old house seemed doubly warm after the cold outside. But still, the fire in the front room was low. Burnett added more logs while Frannie chose a Christmas record. Then they settled on either end of the couch, as they had in the afternoon.

The carols played on the old turntable for a while, and neither of them felt any need to fill the space between them with words. Burnett liked that, that he felt so comfortable being quiet with her. Just sitting here as they were, listening to the Christmas songs, he could almost let himself pretend that there were no secrets between them, that she knew him as he really was. And wanted him that way.

Of course, that wasn't true. She wanted him, all right. But she wanted him as Ned. So Ned was what he'd give her, in hopes that in the end she might learn to want his real self.

He watched her, taking in her dreamy expression, her half-open eyes. When she spoke, he let her gentle voice flow over him, knowing a sweet ache of pleasure from just the sound of it.

"When I was a little girl," Frannie told him. "We exchanged our presents on Christmas Eve. Dad would find some excuse to get us out of the house. We'd go to the Forks for dinner, or to church if there was a Christmas Eve service that year. And when we'd come back, Santa would have been here and we'd open our presents." She'd been gazing at the tree. Now she glanced at him, a glint of humor in her eyes. "I always secretly suspected that the reason Santa came early to our house was because my parents liked to sleep in on Christmas morning."

Burnett made a noise of agreement. "Makes sense." He thought of the gift he'd hidden behind the tree in the late afternoon while she was busy in the kitchen. He leaned a little closer, putting his arm along the back of the couch. "And what about now?"

"Now?"

"When do you open your presents now—Christmas Eve or Christmas Day?"

"Oh," she pretended to think about that, though he suspected she'd had her answer ready all along. "Christmas Eve. Definitely. How about you?"

"I'm easy," he told her.

"Oh, really?" He saw her foot in the red sock inch toward the floor, and he knew she was going to produce whatever it was she'd sneaked upstairs to wrap earlier in the afternoon.

He decided he wanted her to have his gift first. "Stay put," he commanded.

She looked puzzled, but did as he said. He went to the tree, reached behind it, and came up with the box that the lady in The Mine Shaft had obligingly wrapped for him. He went to stand before Frannie.

"Merry Christmas, Frannie Lawry."

He handed her the little box. She looked at it for a moment, as if he'd pulled it from a hat. And then she sighed, "Oh, Ned."

"Open it."

She did, slowly, untying the gold ribbon and carefully peeling away the red foil wrapping paper. When she took the bubble from its nest of tissue, she held it reverently and turned it upside down once. Then she looked through the round wall of glass as the gold and white storm swirled around the figure within.

"She's beautiful." Frannie met his eyes over the globe in her hands. "But she isn't smiling. Do you think she's happy in there?"

She sounded so sad, Burnett thought. He said, "I don't know," feeling hurt himself, suddenly, and far away from her when he longed to be so close. "I didn't think about that.... You don't like her?"

"Oh, Ned..." She reached out in a gesture that he read immediately as one intended to reassure. "She's a wonderful gift, and I love her." She took his hand and put it to her lips, then held it against her soft cheek, not even stopping to think that the last boundaries between them were dissolving, the walls crumbling away.

"I only wondered," she whispered, still with her cheek against his hand, "what an angel trapped in a bubble would feel like."

He looked down at her shining, wildly curling hair, and tried to hold himself back. But he couldn't, not completely. He laid his free hand on her hair. It felt like spun silk. He stroked it, and she rubbed her cheek against his other hand.

Beneath the buttons of the old jeans he wore, he felt desire stirring. He yearned to tip her head up, cover her mouth with his and guide her gently backward onto the couch.

But he also knew it was probably too soon. He sensed that the way to win her was to allow her to believe she was the one making the moves. And she wasn't quite ready to go that far yet. She wasn't quite ready to take the lead in lovemaking.

But she would be soon, he knew it with every fiber of his being. And she would be his.

The thought excited him more, at the same time as it terrified him. He was not the surrendering kind. But then he remembered that Ned St. Charles was, and he knew that it would be all right.

Frannie turned her mouth against his hand and sighed. Then she pulled away. She looked up, her light eyes shining. "I have something for you, too."

He'd known it, of course, ever since she'd come into the grocery store, flushed and happy, and refused to put her shopping bag in the cart. "You've done too much for me already."

"It's Christmas," she said, both solemn and teasing. "You got me something and I got something for you." She very carefully set the snow bubble on the small table by the couch and then stood up to approach the tree herself.

"This first." She held out a box that looked just about the right size for a shirt.

And it was. There were two plaid flannel shirts inside, one red and one green. "Festive, don't you think?" she asked when he held them up.

He thanked her. But that wasn't all. There were two pairs of new jeans, a quilted jacket, underwear and socks, and a new pair of leather boots, as well.

He shook his head when all the boxes were opened, positive that she couldn't have carried all this in the bag she'd refused to set on the grocery cart earlier.

Frannie laughed at his puzzled expression. "Except for the shirts, I brought everything back here before I even met you in the store," she announced.

"It's too much," he said flatly, knowing exactly how Ned would react and remembering to play his part. "I can't accept all this."

"Ned, please—"

"No, Frannie. This is just too much."

But she refused to hear him. "It is not. It's Christmas. And if you don't accept my gifts, I will be very hurt."

"Frannie—"

She grabbed up the green shirt, a pair of jeans and some socks. "Try these on. Now. And don't argue. I want to see how well I judged your size." She pushed the clothes into his hands, turned him by the shoulders and gave him a shove in the direction of the kitchen bathroom.

He went, to his own surprise, though he was reasonably sure that as Ned, he should have put up more of a fight. But he was tired of wearing rags, and also pleased beyond belief that she would do all this for him, choose him all these clothes, pay for them with her own money, and then wrap them herself in bright paper and shiny ribbons.

It moved him, the way hearing that his eight-year-old nephew, Mike, had chosen him something special and wrapped it in three kinds of paper moved him. It showed thought and care for him alone, a gesture expecting nothing in return but his pleasure in receiving.

For years, in his bitterness and his fear after his father deserted them, he'd been unable to accept with any grace the gifts his family tried to give him. He worked, hard and doggedly, because he somehow felt responsible—the man of the family now—for his father's desertion. He envied his brother and his sister and Joanna, who lived next door to them. He envied their laughter and their freedom and their easy camaraderie with each other—at the same time as he pushed them away whenever they tried to include him in their childish games.

Over the years, when time for exchanging gifts came, he became the one no one knew what to buy for. He received conservative ties. And monogrammed handkerchiefs. Briefcases and wallets and leather appointment books.

After he married, Amanda had him tell her exactly what he wanted, and then she went down and picked it up—at the same time as she bought his gift to her. After all, she reasoned, she knew what she wanted better than he possibly could.

But with Frannie, everything was different. She went down and bought out the store for him, guessing boldly on his sizes, choosing what she thought he'd like.

In the wavy mirror over the claw-footed sink, Burnett adjusted the collar of the new shirt, then he tucked the shirttail into the jeans.

He turned, to look over his shoulder at the top half of himself, which was all he could see in the cabinet mirror. His conclusion was that the clothes fit as well as things off the rack ever fit him. The shirt sleeves were a little short. He solved that problem by rolling them to below the elbows. The jeans were snug, but long enough, thank God. There was nothing at all wrong with the underwear and socks.

He smoothed the tuck of the shirt and readjusted himself inside the jeans. Then, feeling suddenly anxious, wanting her to think him attractive the first time she saw him out of rags, he returned to where Frannie waited on the couch.

In the living room, Frannie sat looking at the angel in the bubble. She was thinking that she would treasure it always, at the same time as it made her a little sad. The angel was trapped in there, in a way, in her bubble of glittering snow.

But Frannie put aside her melancholy thoughts as she heard the soft whisper of Ned's socks on the bare floor between the rugs. She looked up to see him standing there.

Her breath hitched and caught for a moment in her throat. Lord, he looked wonderful. So handsome. Her raggedy man. Sober. Cleaned up. And dressed in new clothes.

She had the oddest feeling, then. As if she had created him whole. As if he never would have existed except for her. She'd pulled a drunk stranger from a snowbank, and in the space of two short days, discovered in him the man of her dreams. It was wonderful. Magical.

She had sensed it from the first, of course. Ned St. Charles was exactly what she needed in her life. She'd fought it in the beginning. But as each hour melted into the next, it became less and less clear to her how she ever could possibly have been afraid of the attraction he held for her.

"Well?" he asked, sounding apprehensive. She realized he was nervous, as if his peace of mind hinged on her approval.

Something inside her heated at the thought. This big, beautiful man was anxious that she would like what she saw when she looked at him.

She rose, slowly, from the couch, and approached him.

He cleared his throat. "Well?" he said again.

A mysterious, purely feminine smile teased Frannie's lips. "You know—"

"What?" It was more a growl than a word.

She couldn't resist touching him. Though the hair above his ear was neatly trimmed, she smoothed it anyway, tracing the hairline. He tensed when she did that, and she found that arousing. His dark eyes grew smoky. His whole body seemed to gather and flex.

"You're so handsome, Ned," she gave out on a long breath.

His eyes narrowed, as if he gauged her intention. As if he wondered how far she was planning to go with this.

And Frannie knew then, with a delicious hollowing-out feeling inside her, that she fully intended to go all the way.

All her arguments and fears and bargains to the contrary, it was as Ned had said. It was meant to be between them. From that first moment in the snow.

She had lied to herself thinking she could—or even wanted to—escape it. He was a good man. And she sensed he would make love to her as she'd never been loved before.

And she wanted that. She was ready for that. For a man like Ned, who was vulnerable and sensitive. A man with whom she could let herself go.

"Frannie?" Ned was asking, his eyes burning into hers.

"Ned," she breathed, coming up on tiptoe. "Ned, what I said before . . ."

"Yeah?" His breath was sweet on her skin.

"I lied. About us never being lovers. I want . . ."

"Yes. Say it."

"I want . . ."

"Come on, Angel . . ."

"You, Ned. I want you."

"Now?"

"Yes. Now. Tonight." She brushed her mouth against his, once, her body yearning toward his. But they both held back, swaying there, on the brink of surrender to mutual desire.

"Frannie?" He sounded so desperate and hungry, but unwilling to make the move unless she was sure.

That made her only want him more. "I mean it, Ned." She put her hand on his shoulder, clasping it, feeling the strength and hardness beneath the soft, new fabric of the shirt she'd bought for him.

"You have to take the lead," he got out on a ragged breath. "I don't want to wake up tomorrow and hear you say I pushed you into it. It's gotta be what you want, freely given. Nothing else will do."

"It *is* what I want, Ned." She slowly slid her hand over his chest, molding him, feeling him, memorizing his body, because soon it would be hers. "I'm just a little—"

"What?"

"Scared, I guess."

"I understand."

"You do? How?"

"Because I'm scared, too," he confessed. Frannie thought that was wonderful, that he could admit, as so many men never could, his own fears and doubts.

Frannie kissed him, then. She pressed herself against him as she probed at his mouth with her soft tongue, until he allowed his lips to part. She tasted him, sighing as she felt his arms encircle her at last.

He moaned a little, and she held his head, kissing him long and deeply. And then she pulled back and boldly began unbuttoning the green plaid shirt.

He caught her hands. She looked up into his eyes. "What is it, Ned? Don't you want—"

"You know I do." His voice was rough with the promise of what was to come.

"Then what?"

He lifted his head toward the big front windows, where the Christmas tree stood still and proud. "I want more privacy."

She felt her face coloring. "Oh, yes. Of course."

"My bed in the basement's a little small for two."

She laughed then, a husky laugh, and took him by the hand. "Come with me." She started for the stairs in the dining room. He followed behind her, asking nothing more, willing as ever to let her lead the way.

Chapter Twelve

The room she led him to was tucked beneath the eaves above the kitchen. She left him alone there for a moment, explaining shyly that she would take care of contraception.

"We talked about it in my support group," she said. "And I realized that a woman has to be responsible in every way. By that I mean, I'm *prepared*, not that I, um, make love to every guy that comes down the road."

He didn't know whether to chuckle or hug her. "Frannie," he said. "It's all right."

"Okay, good. Well. I'll be right back."

"Good."

She disappeared back down the stairs. He stood in the doorway, waiting for her, gazing at the room where she slept.

The single tall window looked out on the back road and the snow-covered levee where she'd found him—could it have been only two nights before? He saw that he would only be able to stand to his height near the door, because the slanting of the eaves whittled away the headroom all along one wall. The pink, slightly faded wallpaper had tiny flowers on it. The quilt on the bed was a crazy quilt. It reminded him of the ones that were kept on the foot of the beds upstairs in the Graeagle cabin, random swatches of cloth stitched every which way in a patternless mishmash that had always offended his strong love of order.

This quilt, however, didn't offend him. It seemed whimsical, yes, and dizzying. But not the least offensive.

He was still considering the quilt when he felt the touch of her hand on his neck. He turned. Her arms encircled him, and she started kissing him again, pressing her soft body into his, so he once again felt he would explode with the heat and need that pulsed along his every nerve.

Dimly, through the swimming of his senses, he was aware that she was pulling away again. With a soft little sound of pleasure, she tugged him into the room.

She guided him to the double bed, a plain bed with no head or footboard, covered with its ancient crazy quilt.

She gently pushed him down onto the bed, and took up where she'd left off downstairs, unbuttoning his shirt. He watched, hardly daring to breathe, looking down at her slim fingers as they worked the buttons free of the holes.

When she was done and he felt the night air on his skin down the center of his chest, she peeled back the shirt to his shoulders.

She bent, hesitantly, and put her lips to his chest—high up, just beneath the wing of his collarbone. Her lips were incredibly soft against his skin. He hitched in a pleasured breath.

She glanced up, her light-within-dark eyes as starry as a clear summer night. And then, smiling a little in a secretive, feminine way, she tugged his shirt from the waist of the new jeans. She slipped the shirt down his arms and away.

She looked so busy and adorable taking off his shirt, that he dared to reach for her when she was done. He pulled her down on his lap.

She sat across his knees, giggling a little, as if her very boldness was a source of limitless amusement to her. He held her against his bare chest, and guided her head into the crook of his shoulder. She rested there for a moment, and he felt her sweet breath play over his heart.

Then she moved, tipping her head to look into his face. He smoothed her fabulous hair, feeling beneath it the tender shape of her head.

"I don't feel scared anymore," she said, her look as open as an innocent child's.

"I'm glad," he said, and lowered his mouth, covering her lips with his own. She sighed, and her body seemed to relax even more against him. He kissed her, long and searchingly.

And as he kissed her, his hands roamed her smooth flesh, seeking the warmth of her beneath the big red sweater, and finding the marvelous curve of her waist, the individual shape of each rib, and at last, the full, firm swell of a breast.

He cupped the round globe, and when she sighed and pressed herself closer to his hand, he gently slid his thumb between the cotton fabric of her bra and her silky skin. Lightly, with his thumb, he touched the budding nipple and felt it harden more in sweet response.

"Oh, Ned . . ." She moaned the name against his parted lips.

For a moment he froze, remembering with a cold clarity just how he had deceived her. He was not the man she thought him at all.

But then she asked, sensing his withdrawal, "Ned?" and he melted inside.

"It's okay, Angel," he murmured, raining kisses on her upturned face.

"You seemed to pull away. Are you—"

He didn't let her finish. He covered her mouth with his own again, and she moaned and murmured something impossible to decipher and relaxed fully in his arms once more.

He wanted to get closer to her. He wanted nothing between them. So he began working her sweater up over her rib cage. She assisted him eagerly, lifting her arms, pulling away with a sigh so that he could slip it over her head and off the ends of her outstretched arms.

He paused, then, to look at her, at her slender, pale arms and the full breasts beneath the practical bra, and the wild halo of hair around her sweet, flushed face.

"Angel," he murmured again, and tossed the sweater on the floor by his discarded shirt.

She flung her arms around him, pulling him against her, straining her head back, taunting him with the tender, exposed skin of her neck. He put his lips there and kissed her, as she sighed and pressed herself closer to him still.

His hands roamed her soft curves freely, making short work of her bra, tossing it away to join the growing pile of discarded clothes on the floor. Her unbound breasts swelled into his seeking palms. She groaned aloud when he cupped them, lifting her body avidly so that he could do as he wished.

He bent his head and kissed her breasts all over, from the full swells of them to the hard, aroused nipples. He sucked the nipples into his mouth, tasting them, finding them sweet beyond measure, aware that they hardened even more at his passionate attention.

Totally, incredibly abandoned, as no woman he had ever known had been, she began wriggling, moving on his lap—much to his own sensual agony—until she sat straddling him, her head thrown back, still clutching him against her, keeping his hungry mouth at her breasts. He felt the cove of her womanhood through the barrier of the stirrup pants she still wore. She was pressed right against his hardness. He was sure he would explode—without having done more than kiss her breasts and feel the slim, soft length of her rubbing against him.

But then she was pushing him backward on the bed, and he gave in to her willingly, dropping back against the quilt.

She sat up, straddling him, and he opened his eyes to see her—wildly sensual, and yet innocent—smiling that secret smile of hers.

She put her hands on his chest, touching him hungrily in an erotic massage. He groaned, recalling in a fragmented sort of way what he had decided earlier—that he would surrender to her. So he lifted his arms and raised them over his head, dropping them back against the quilt, giving his body up to her.

His angel took instant advantage of what he offered, sliding her hands up his arms, until she held him, by each wrist, against the quilt. She lowered her mouth, kissing him, her soft breasts teasing his chest.

Burnett groaned as she kissed him deeply. But then she was pulling away. With a hungry growl, he lifted his head toward her when he lost the tender torment of her lips. But she was only slanting her mouth the other way. And she instantly lowered her lips again to kiss him some more.

"I want to kiss you everywhere..." she promised against his mouth. And then she did what she wanted, kissing a burning trail over his chin, down the straining column of his neck, and over his belly, which he couldn't keep from jerking convulsively when the delicate tip of her tongue teased his navel.

He held his breath at what she did next, unsnapping the fly of his jeans and sliding them down his hips. After that, she slipped off his socks, and then her hands were at his waist again, pulling at the elastic of the briefs he wore.

He felt her slight hesitation, then, as if she couldn't quite bring herself to reveal so blatantly the entirety of him. So he helped her, by closing his eyes and flinging an arm over them, letting her see him as willing to give himself up to her tender hands without reluctance. Letting her do as she would.

And she did.

She stripped the last of his protection away, and she touched him. He groaned, and lifted himself off the bed, sure he was going to go over the edge then. But somehow, he held out.

For more of the same. So that later, when he could think again, he didn't know how he had kept himself from coming completely apart. Because she stroked him and made love to him, until he thought he would die of the incredible pleasure she so freely gave. Finally she loved him with her mouth and tongue, until he cried out in erotic agony. Until, at last, he could remain passive no more.

She gave a little husky cry of alarm and of need as he rolled, suddenly, from beneath her, gaining himself the top position. His eyes capturing hers, he stripped away her slacks and panties, and even the thick red socks. At last nothing, no slightest scrap of clothing, kept her from his sight. He gazed down at her. She stared up at him, her beautiful pale body beckoning him, her breasts rising and falling with each agitated breath she took.

He thought—as much as he could think at that moment—of freedom. That with her, as a penniless nobody she'd pulled out of the snow, he was free at last. No longer bound to the treadmill that demanded he buffer himself with money and success in order to protect himself from loss. He was nobody with nothing. And she wanted him that way.

"Ned..." She breathed the name so tenderly, and she reached up a hand to touch his face. "I love you."

She said it simply, there stretched out nude beneath his hands. And Burnett took the words inside himself, knowing he would treasure them always, the greatest gift anyone had ever given him. Love for himself alone.

Liar, the thought came before he could shut it out. *Not for yourself, but for Ned St. Charles. The man you're pretending to be. She doesn't love you, she loves him....*

Frannie stroked his cheek. "Oh my love," she said, her soft lips caressing the sound. "It's all right. There's no need to say you love me back."

"Frannie..."

"No," she slid her hand behind his head, brought his face down to hers and then spoke against his lips. "Please, Ned. Don't make me sorry I said it, don't freeze me out or pull away."

"I'm not—"

"You're thinking," she chided. "And right now is not the time for thinking. Right now..." She took his hand, and laid it on the curve of one soft, full breast. He gasped, she smiled. "...is time for feeling. The best Christmas gift of all. From us. To us. What it all means can come later. Now, it's enough that I love you and you...care for me." She paused, narrowed those enchanting eyes. "You do *care* for me, at least, don't you Ned?"

"Damn it, Angel. You know I do."

"Good then."

She kissed him. And he was lost. Willingly and completely, in the siren sweetness of her mouth beneath his.

He kissed her back, taking control, though neither of them, by that time, cared in the least who gave in each moment and who it was that received.

He loved her with his body, as she had loved him, from head to toe, with his lips and his hands, until she writhed and pleaded beneath him to have all that he could give. With his hand on her, stroking the core of her, he knew her readiness for him. So he rose over her and nudged apart her slim thighs.

She reached for him, guiding him, taking him within her. She wrapped her legs around him, pulling him deeper, sighing yes. He had that incredible, unbearable feeling once more, as he drove for the first time into her softness—that he wouldn't hold out, that he'd spend himself right then.

And this time, the feeling didn't pass. Instead it grew, expanding and contracting, like the hot sweetness of her surrounding him. He wasn't going over the edge, he was teetering there, reeling in ecstasy. It went on forever. And then he went with it, into a vortex of bliss.

She called out the name that wasn't his name, and he pretended that it was. Because being held within her, moving within her, was the most beautiful thing he'd ever known in his life.

He moved slowly at first, because she sheathed him tightly. But as he felt her full acceptance, and the way she moved excitedly beneath him, he thrust himself within her harder and faster. And she matched him, stroke for stroke, as she clutched his back, the hungry, heated sounds she made coming from deep within her, just like his own.

At last, her release came. He stiffened, giving her all of himself as she writhed and bucked beneath him, crying out in complete abandon, letting herself go. Just before she

went limp, it happened for him. He knew he'd hit his culmination—and this time he was right.

With a deep, rolling groan that seemed ripped from the
deepest part of himself, he thrust into her. And she surged
up to meet him, holding no part of herself back.

He spilled into her, for a moment almost passing out
from the intensity of it, and she cradled him inside herself,
ardent and welcoming, as the world spun away to nothing
and then slowly, like something taking form out of thin air,
revolved back into being once more.

Burnett went limp, then, and her tight hold became
tender. She stroked his back, and his hair, and the side of
his face where it lay tucked tight against her, cradled in the
satiny crook where her shoulder met her neck.

Her touch was so soothing, so wonderfully fine, that he
was flirting with sleep when she spoke.

"Ned?"

"Um?" He lifted his head enough to place a soft kiss on
her shoulder, then lay back down.

She went on stroking his hair. "I'm going to stay here for
the rest of Christmas vacation, until the day before school
starts again—Sunday, the third." Her voice dropped a little, became diffident. "What I'd like more than anything
is for you to stay here with me. Could you—would you do
that, do you think?"

He thought of the promised meeting on Monday. There
was really no way he could get out of it without tossing over
the deal. Tossing over the deal would amount to screwing
over a lot of people who trusted him, and obliterating his
credibility in the business world—not to mention throwing
away several million dollars.

Frannie continued, hesitant and hopeful, "I don't really
know what comes next for us, Ned. And I'd like to have

this, um, special time with you, so that maybe we can figure that out.''

He remembered, with a guilty sigh, that now was the time
he'd intended to tell her the truth about Ned St. Charles.
After they'd made love, when she was supposed to feel
bound to him and thus more receptive to the news that he'd
been pretending to be someone other than himself since the
moment they met.

''Ned?'' She was still stroking his hair.

Her gentle hand felt wonderful. Never in his life had he
felt so satisfied and so at peace.

Maybe, as he'd assumed, she would be more likely to
forgive him now if he told her the truth. But there still remained a chance, and a very real chance, that she wouldn't.
That she'd want him out of her life anyway for what he'd
done.

And now that he'd made love to her, now that he knew
what it was to be buried in her softness, the idea of losing
her scared him all the more.

Silently, Burnett Clinton laughed at himself. His own
strategy had turned on him. He'd made love with her so she
wouldn't send him away when he told her the truth, and
then found himself all the more unwilling to come clean
with her.

''Ned? Are you asleep?'' Frannie whispered against his
hair. And then she sighed and settled him more comfortably against her. He lay still in her arms, suddenly aware of
the little clicking sounds of the electric clock by the bed as
the seconds ticked by.

Soon he felt the even, steady movement of her chest
against his ear. He knew she was asleep. He was reprieved
from giving her an answer until morning.

Sitting up a little, he grabbed the edge of the quilt and
flipped it over them, so they were rolled in it, protected

from the increasing coolness in the little room beneath the eaves.

He thought, as he drifted off, that he hadn't fed the fires downstairs. They would be cold come morning and the old house would be freezing. He'd have to lay the fires all over again.

But it was worth it, he decided, not to leave Frannie's side. Any man who got a chance to sleep with an angel would be a fool to risk losing it, no matter how cold it might be when morning finally came.

"Ned?"

He opened one eye. His angel smiled at him.

He kissed the end of her nose and watched her cheeks turn pink, an enchanting experience, especially since they were both still nude under the blanket, all wrapped up in each other, arms and legs entwined.

"Merry Christmas, Angel," he said, and noticed that, once outside the warm shelter of the quilt, his breath turned to mist. "And the damn fires are out," he added. He moved to throw back the blanket.

"Wait." She shivered and held him close.

He chuckled. "What?"

Her skin colored prettily again. "Nothing." She stroked his back. "I just hate to let you go, I guess."

"I'm going nowhere—except to heat this place up."

"I know." Her arms, which were holding him so close, relaxed a little. She looked past him, perhaps out the tall window on the wall behind him. "I just...I can't believe this has happened, Ned. I never thought this would happen. To me."

"This?" he prompted, his heart eager to hear it, though his mind advised caution until he could decide how to tell her he had to leave her on Monday.

She was suddenly shy. "This. Us. Making love. And what I said last night—it was true." She swallowed, and bravely looked into his eyes once more. "I . . . I love you."

It warmed him to his toes to hear that. He forgot, for a moment, everything but the reality of her slender body against his, her sweet mouth so close. All he had to do was to reach out and cover it with his own.

"Angel," he breathed as his lips found hers. His body hardened, hungry for her. And he decided the heat stoves could wait. He gloried in her eagerness as she readjusted her legs around him, loosing a voluptuous sigh as he found the place he sought.

For Frannie, it was the same. She felt as if they moved as one being, wrapped in their crazy quilt cocoon, sharing heat and passion, oblivious to the cold outside.

Never, ever had she felt like this—with the one boy she'd known intimately as a college girl, or with Kenneth, who had been an expert lover but somehow never touched her soul.

Ned cried out when his completion came, clutching her close and surging powerfully into her. She took what he gave her, avid and hungry as he was, crying out herself as her own satisfaction claimed her in wave after shuddering, delirious wave.

They lay still, at last, holding each other, sharing the last fading pulsations of the greatest ecstasy two people can know.

It was only after he slipped away from her to tend to the fires that she allowed herself to admit the core of sadness at the center of her heart. She had told him she loved him twice—and he had said nothing in return.

She could accept that, she *had* accepted it. He had said he cared for her; he was just unwilling, for some reason, to say he loved her in return. She felt sad, because she understood it was completely possible that he might never truly love her back.

Frannie pushed the sadness away. She would ask him once more, at breakfast, to stay with her through New Year's. Perhaps he'd say yes. And then she'd treasure every moment of the waning year.

Chapter Thirteen

Downstairs, after Burnett had lit the fires, they showered
together, taking turns beneath the ancient shower head in
the old claw-foot tub. They scrubbed each other's backs
and later dried each other playfully. Once dry, they dressed
quickly, since the house was still somewhat cold.

They made breakfast. Burnett grilled bacon and fried a
few eggs. Frannie made toast and coffee and poured the
juice.

They'd just sat down at the table when the tapping came
at the side door. Frannie shot Burnett a quick, grim look.
He glanced toward the ceiling once and then concentrated
on his plate.

"Door's open, Aunt Bonnie!"

Bonnie let herself in and then stood in the doorway for
significant seconds, as if deciding what stance to take in a
touchy situation.

Finally, Frannie said, "Merry Christmas, Aunt Bonnie. There's coffee if you want it."

"Well." Bonnie appeared to give the offer serious consideration. Then she decided. "I suppose just one cup." She helped herself to a cup of coffee. "I thought I would give you my gift later, Frances, at my house," she said, her back to the table as she filled up a mug.

"Fine," Frannie said.

Bonnie turned, cup in hand, and marched to a free chair. She sat down, sipped from her cup, shot a glance at her niece and then at Burnett. At last, she intoned with excruciating cordiality, "It's not a bright day, but I don't think we'll get more snow."

Frannie swallowed a bite of egg and glanced out the window at the ashen sky. "You're probably right."

There was a massive silence. Bonnie's piercing eyes kept shifting from her niece to the man she considered an intruder and back again.

At last she asked tartly, "What about the pies?"

"I made them yesterday." Frannie gestured toward the small pantry by the basement door, where she'd set the pies to cool.

"Well. Good. And the gelatin salad?"

"In the fridge. I checked it a while ago. It set up just fine."

"Good. The bird's in the oven."

"Great."

Silence again. Bonnie sipped from her coffee. Then she seemed to come to some momentous decision. She set her cup down with a little plop, not spilling any only because she'd already swallowed most of it.

She turned to Burnett. "Well, I've called a friend of mine in Graeagle. She knows *everyone* who lives there."

Burnett experienced a sick, sinking feeling in the pit of his stomach. Had this "friend" identified him as who he really was?

He fought to keep his expression composed, while inside he groaned. He should have explained everything last night, no matter if she *had* sent him away. It would have been infinitely better than for her to find out like this . . .

"And my friend tells me," Bonnie went on, "that there actually is a family named Clinton who owns a vacation cabin there."

Burnett cleared his throat, and tried to speak noncommittally. "So?"

"So," Bonnie gave out in a grudging tone, "I suppose you're telling the truth about where you were staying, at least."

"Aunt Bonnie." Frannie's voice held clear warning.

The little woman waved her hand. "I know, I know. You've made it very clear—you don't want me interfering. And I have accepted that, more or less. I'm just trying, if you'll realize it, to get along with him. I'm just doing my best."

Frannie set down her fork and confronted her aunt. "I know what you're doing. You're trying to discredit him."

"Why, I—"

"You're checking up on him. He's my guest. And I won't have it, do you hear?"

"Well, what I found out is in his favor," Bonnie huffed.

"It doesn't matter." Frannie's voice was flat and final. "It's none of your affair."

Burnett, who'd experienced a moment of sharp relief when he realized that the older woman wasn't going to reveal the truth about him after all, was now feeling like a stray dog who'd wandered in from the cold. The two women were doing what they had the last time he'd seen them together—discussing him avidly, as if he were either not there or too stupid to understand what they said. He decided that even Ned would get sick of that after a while.

He cleared his throat again, and spoke in Ned's soft drawl. "Excuse me, ladies..."

"It has to stop, Aunt Bonnie."

"Frances, I only want what's best for you."

"Ladies?"

"What's best for me is up to me."

"Well, I—"

"Ladies..."

"Now, I want your word, Aunt Bonnie—"

"Ladies."

"I only did what anyone who loved you would—"

Burnett had had enough. He put two fingers between his teeth and let out a loud, ear-piercing whistle.

Both women gasped and turned to him.

"I never," Bonnie muttered.

"Ned, what is it?" Frannie exclaimed.

Burnett smiled unassumingly. "Ladies, I don't mean to be rude. But it really gets me down when people talk about me like I'm not even here."

Frannie blushed, realizing, he could see, that she had treated him as less than an equal. "Oh, yes. Of course. I'm sorry, Ned."

"Thank you," he said, humble to the core.

The tough little aunt snorted a few times, and then actually said stiffly, "All right. Perhaps we *were* impolite to ignore you that way. I apologize, as well."

Burnett nodded, and then said to Frannie, "From now on, Angel, I can defend myself." He was completely aware of the way both women stiffened when he uttered the endearment. But he didn't regret using it.

After last night, things had changed between him and Frannie. And even if he couldn't bring himself to reveal who he was to her, he was not going to sneak around behind anybody's back when it came to loving her.

Frannie looked at him levelly, accepting that he refused to hide their new relationship, at the same time as she responded to what he had just said. "You're right, of course, Ned. I won't rescue you again unless you ask me to."

He turned to the aunt. "And as far as what you did, ma'am. Well, I hope you're satisfied now, after what you found out from your friend."

The aunt made a humphing sound. "*Hope* all you want, Mr. Ned St. Charles."

Frannie shot her aunt an irate look, but said nothing.

The aunt relented, then, just a little. "However. Since it's obvious there's nothing I can do at this point about what is going on between you two, we might as well all be civil, at the very least."

Burnett chuckled. Bonnie Lawry was plain ornery, but he did admire her spunk. "Fair enough."

Bonnie stood. "Dinner's at four. I'll expect the both of you around three or so."

"Great," Burnett and Frannie said in unison.

Bonnie carried her cup to the sink and left as she had come, through the side door.

"I'm sorry she's so mean, Ned," Frannie said after the door was closed and her aunt's compact form had disappeared from the porch.

"It's all right," Burnett said. "In a way, I kind of like her. At least you know where you stand with someone like that."

Frannie made a low noise of ironic agreement, and then they finished their cooling breakfast in silence. After that, they cleared up after the meal, still quiet with each other.

Burnett assumed that Frannie was building up her nerve again to approach the subject she'd opened the night before; she was going to ask him to stay until New Year's.

He learned he was right soon enough. They took second cups of coffee into the living room and sat cross-legged before the fire.

"Ned, last night I asked you a question," she began, staring at the flames in the grate.

"Yeah?" he prompted, implying that perhaps he didn't know what she had asked, despising himself once more for the thousand little ways he continued to deceive her in order to protect the central lie of his identity.

She forced herself to face him. "But you were sleeping. And I decided to let it go until today."

"Okay."

"I asked if you would stay here. With me. Beyond tomorrow."

"I see."

"I asked you to stay until New Year's."

"You did?"

"I thought, maybe, it would be a way for us to get to know each other better. To give ourselves some time together. And to see if what we have could end up going anywhere."

"Ah."

She glared at him. *"Ah. I see. Okay. You did?..."* she mimicked his terse responses. "Don't you have *anything* to say beyond that? Do I have to do *all* of this myself?"

She looked so adorable and unsure and vulnerable. He wanted to grab her and kiss her and lay her down on the braided rug before the fireplace. He wanted to undress her slowly, and spread her hair in a fan all around her beautiful face, and to make love to her until she cried for mercy—

and accepted it without the slightest irritation when he told her who he really was.

But she wasn't going to allow him to make love to her right now. Now, she wasn't going to do anything with him until he had dealt with her request. This time, there could be no putting his answer off until later. Though his vague responses might have indicated otherwise, his eyes were open and he was sitting up. She was highly unlikely to believe it if he faked sleep right now.

He searched his mind for a way to explain why he had to leave Monday, and came up blank.

When he said nothing again, she made a low, frustrated sound and looked away. He caught her chin. "Don't turn away."

"Oh, Ned." She pushed his hand away and shook her head. "Don't you understand? This is no picnic for me, either."

"I know," he reassured her.

"You do?" She looked defiant suddenly. "*What* do you know about the way I feel?"

"Well . . . You *have* been making all the moves."

"You noticed." It was a shy whisper.

"And maybe you feel you'd like a little help from me."

Her cheeks colored. "Well, I'd like to know where you *are* on this. How you feel about the two of us. Is it just . . . for a little while? Or could it be something more?"

"Angel . . ."

She put up a hand. "That's sweet, what you call me. And I like it. But sweet names aren't enough. I just want to know what this means to you."

"A lot," he told her firmly. "Maybe everything. Who knows?"

"*You* have to know," she insisted, her eyes filling, though he could see she was trying her damnedest not to cry. "You have to know what you want from me, with me, before we can decide what to do next. It seems like you're *hedging*, Ned. That you're avoiding deciding whether or not to stay with me for the time I asked."

"I'm not hedging," he said, though that was exactly what he *was* doing—for a completely different reason than she assumed.

"Oh, Ned." She shook her head sadly, and wiped away the two traitorous tears that had escaped the dam of her lids. Then she sniffed a little and straightened her shoulders. "Ned," she said, reticent but determined, "I think you have to look at your behavior here."

Burnett blinked. "Huh?" He had no idea what she was getting at.

"I'm afraid," she went on, her sweet face a portrait of gentle understanding, "that the way you're acting with me right now could be symptomatic of all your problems."

She didn't know how right she was. He asked, "How so?"

"You're a wonderful man, Ned. You're tender and kind..."

"Right. And funny and patient and vulnerable and sensitive. Get to the point."

"I don't want to hurt you."

"Frannie. Just say it."

"But you're... wishy-washy. I'm sorry, but I think you have trouble making decisions. And maybe commitments, as well."

Burnett, who had taken on the burdens of a man at eleven, felt irritation rise—then wash right over him and away. She wasn't talking about *him*, after all. She was talking about Ned. And she was actually criticizing Ned, saying things that, if she thought about it, she might recall he himself had pointed out to her the other day.

He was aware of a little thrill of triumph to hear that maybe she at last was discovering that poor, noble Ned had a downside, after all. And then he felt confused, as he realized that he'd been thinking of Ned as a rival—when Ned didn't even really exist.

Frannie was shaking her head. "I have. I've hurt you. I can tell by your silence."

Burnett bestirred himself. "No, it's all right."

"It isn't."

"Yes, it is," he insisted. "And stop apologizing. You've made a good point."

"Oh," she said, somewhat nonplussed at his ready acceptance of her critical words. "Well, it's something to think about anyway."

"Yeah, it sure is."

"And speaking of evasions..."

He grimly said, "Yeah?"

"Are you *ever* going to answer my question? Will you stay here through New Year's or not?"

Here it was again. Back full circle to the original question. And he still had no idea what to say. "Frannie, I would like nothing better than to do that..."

"An answer," she demanded. "Yes or No. Now."

"Yes," he said firmly. Then, "More or less..."

She stared at him with her mouth open for a minute, then she muttered through clenched teeth, "That's it. I have had it." She started to rise.

He put his hands on her shoulders and held her there. "Listen. Just let me explain."

"Either you will or you won't."

"I will."

"Good."

"Sort of."

"Argh." She wriggled her shoulders. "Let me up. Before I kill you."

"Not until you hear me out."

"Let go of me."

"Will you stay put?"

"All right. Just get your hands off."

He released her cautiously, ready to grab her again if she tried to escape. Her expression vitriolic, she backed away and leaned against the couch. "Go ahead, then," she said. "Explain. I'm listening."

"Okay." He looked away and took a deep breath. He let it out.

This is it, he thought. I just can't keep this up any longer. I'm going to tell her the truth...

But then he turned back and looked at her.

If he told her now, it could be the end of it. She could simply kick him out that door over there by the tree...

"Okay," he said again, and forged ahead. "Yesterday, while you were shopping, I..."

"Yes?"

"... I got in touch with..."

"Who?"

"Burnett." The die was cast. He was off and lying once again. "Burnett Clinton."

"Your ex-boss, the one who let you stay at his cabin?"

"Right."

"And?"

"I wanted to check in with him, you know? Because he *has* been really good to me over the years. I wanted to let him know that I left the cabin locked up and everything. And that I'd be back right after New Year's as planned."

"And how did he seem?"

Burnett sought an appropriate ambiguous word. "Receptive," he said. "Very receptive. As a matter of fact—"

"Yes?"

"He really does have a manager's position opening up for me the first week in January."

"Well, that's wonderful, Ned."

"But..."

"What?"

"He, um, wants to meet with me on Monday."

"*This* Monday?"

"Yeah. At eight sharp. He wants to go over a few things with me, he says."

She looked at him narrowly. He wondered if she was about to tell him she didn't believe a single word he said. "Are you sure about that?"

"Er, what?"

"That all he's after is to go over a few things?"

"Well..." He faded off, relieved that it wasn't Ned she doubted, and gambling that his angel would have a better explanation for what Ned's boss was up to than he could dream up right then.

"It's more likely," Frannie told him, "that what he really wants is to check you out. To see if you're back on your feet again, so he can get someone else if he has to."

"Hmm," Burnett said. "You may just have a point."

Frannie gazed at him. "Well? *Are* you, Ned?"

"What?"

"Back on your feet again."

He lifted his chin. "You're damned right."

"Good. So you'll see him on Monday, and you'll have your job back—now what was so mysterious about that, that you couldn't just explain it to me right away?"

I didn't think of it quickly enough, he thought. "I didn't want you to think I didn't want to stay," he said.

"Then you do? Want to stay?"

"More than anything."

"But you have to be in Sacramento on Monday?"

"Exactly."

She sighed, but she was smiling tenderly. "Oh, Ned. It's all right. You can stay till Sunday night, at least. And maybe even come back for New Year's, if all he wants is to see that you're going to be capable of handling the job."

Burnett blinked as he realized she was absolutely right. He'd been so busy trying to figure out how to tell her he had to leave on Monday, that he hadn't let himself think beyond it. He and Jordan McSwain might do a little haggling about the terms of their agreement, but most of it had been hashed out already. It should all be handled in a day—two at the most. After that, there was no reason he couldn't head right back here to welcome the New Year in his angel's arms.

"You know, Angel," he said, allowing his lips to curl in a smile. "You are absolutely right."

"Oh, Ned," she said, then, her eyes misting a little. "Does that mean you'll stay until Sunday, at least? And maybe come back if you can?"

"You'd better believe it." He scooted over to where she sat against the couch.

"I'm glad," she told him, letting her head fall back.

He loomed over her. "Last night, I wanted to lay you back on this couch."

"And do what?" Her voice was husky.

"Guess."

"I have a better idea."

"Yeah?"

"Why don't you show me." She pulled on the collar of his shirt. His mouth covered hers.

They kissed for a long time, and when he pulled away to give them both a breath, she murmured, gesturing at the front window. "We still have a privacy problem." He groaned, but then she added, "We could simply close the curtains, you know."

It seemed a fabulous idea to him. He stood up and closed them. Then he laid her back on the couch as he'd promised and showed her exactly what he'd wanted to do with her there the night before.

Afterward, Frannie held him and stroked his hair. Burnett told himself that though the moment of truth would come eventually, he didn't give a damn about that. Now he could hold her and love her and pretend this joy would never end.

They showered again, and then went out to the front yard, where Burnett shoveled the walk and Frannie built a snowman and they ended up throwing snowballs like children. When Frannie hit him in the face with one, he chased her around to the back of the house and brought her down by the back fence. There they wrestled, laughing, in the snow.

Soon enough, three o'clock arrived, and it was time for dinner at Aunt Bonnie's house. Frannie wore a red wool dress and Burnett his new red shirt.

Bonnie surprised both of them by keeping her promise and behaving with charming civility. She and Frannie exchanged gifts and then her guests began to arrive. Bonnie actually urged Frannie to introduce him to her friends.

After a few minutes shaking hands and murmuring modest hellos, Burnett wandered into the kitchen. He struck up a conversation with one of the ladies he'd seen in the church the night before and was actually beginning to relax enough to enjoy himself when Frannie grabbed his arm and towed him through a short hall into the living room at the front of the house.

"Ned, I want you to meet my dad's favorite teacher, Marlon Everly. Mr. Everly!" she called.

And Burnett looked toward the front door to see the old man he'd met yesterday at the phone kiosk turning in response to his name.

Chapter Fourteen

Burnett experienced a dropping sensation in his stomach as he watched the old man toddle toward them. There was a pleasant, rather innocuous smile on the creased face, a smile belied by the alertness in the slightly watery eyes. Frannie introduced them, explaining to Burnett, "Mr. Everly taught my dad and Aunt Bonnie in school."

"So we meet again, son," the old man cackled—a little too gleefully, Burnett thought. "How's the world of high finance?"

"Fine," Burnett answered, taking the veiny extended hand. "Just fine."

"High finance?" Frannie asked.

"Little private joke." Marlon Everly cackled some more. "I saw your young fellow over town yesterday. He was working out some big business deal on the pay phone by Yo-Ho's."

Burnett wondered grimly how he was going to get out of this one. But, as luck would have it, he kept his mouth shut long enough that Frannie did it for him.

"Oh, I get it," she said, "When you called Burnett, right?"

"Uh, yeah. Right. You got it." He sounded like an idiot, but he was so relieved, he didn't much care. "When I called Burnett."

Frannie said to Marlon Everly, "He was talking to his boss."

Marlon Everly smiled and nodded—and then looked puzzled. "His boss?" He said the two words slowly, as if, in his mind, he were turning them, studying them from all sides.

Burnett's nervousness returned. He knew he hadn't sounded much like an employee yesterday on the phone.

Marlon, meanwhile, was squinting his rheumy eyes at Burnett and feeling beneath the breast of the old tweed jacket he wore. The veiny hands came out with a cigarette and he started to put it to his lips. "Your boss? Hmm..."

From across the room, Bonnie commanded, "Marlon Everly, don't you dare light that smelly thing in my living room!"

The old man looked over his shoulder. "Now Bonnie—"

"Outside with that. I mean it." Bonnie's face wore one of her tight little frowns.

Marlon turned back to Frannie and Burnett and shrugged. "Smokers have no rights anymore. The world is not what it used to be. Excuse me." He moved toward the door, and Burnett allowed himself to relax once more.

The rest of the afternoon and evening Burnett simply avoided Marlon Everly, and the subject of what he'd really been doing on the phone the day before never came up again.

There was only one other incident of note, to Burnett's mind.

Some time after the huge turkey dinner had been eaten, and before the pies were served, the phone rang. They were all in the living room, and Bonnie went to the kitchen to get it. In a few moments she returned.

"It's your mother," Bonnie said to Frannie, her expression so noncommittal that it was almost comical.

"Thank you," Frannie said, her face as blank as her aunt's.

Frannie rose from the seat beside Burnett and disappeared into the other room. When she returned a few minutes later, Burnett gave her a questioning look. "Is anything wrong?"

Frannie counterfeited a smile. "Oh no, no. She just called to wish me a Merry Christmas."

Burnett thought then that perhaps Ned St. Charles wasn't the only one keeping secrets.

Later that night, after making long and tender love, they lay side by side in Frannie's bed upstairs, talking about the evening and Aunt Bonnie's friends.

Frannie told Burnett that Marlon Everly had been one of the town's favorite high school teachers, until his retirement several years ago. For a while after that, he'd been a substitute teacher. Now he was working on a "novel of murder and suspense" because, he used to tell his students, "The vagaries of human nature have always fascinated me."

Marlon had certain eccentricities. He refused to even consider giving up his "smokes," and he had never owned a phone in his life. He made all his calls from the pay phones in town.

"He's a sweet old guy," Frannie concluded. "My dad always admired him. My father loved to read, and he always said that Marlon Everly was most of the reason why. Marlon had a way of making the world of the printed page come alive, my dad said. I used to look forward to being old enough to be in Mr. Everly's English class."

Burnett canted up on an elbow and looked down into her eyes. "You were a daddy's girl all the way, weren't you?"

Frannie laughed. "It's that obvious, huh?"

He traced the delicate, winged shape of her collarbone with a finger. "No more obvious than the nose on your face."

"My dad was good. A good man. A helpful man, with an aura of, I don't know, warmth and contentment about him. When he died, it seemed like my whole world turned dark and lonely."

He kissed the tip of her nose. "And you've never forgiven your mother for rushing off to Tulsa like that, for taking you away from everything familiar just when you felt you needed familiar things most?"

"Partly." The word was bleak. "But it's more than that." She stirred in his arms, fitfully. "Oh, Ned. It's all in the past. And there are so many more pleasant things we could talk about. Let's just let it go for now."

He shook his head, holding her close against his side, so she couldn't turn away. "What we're supposed to be doing, remember, is getting to know all about each other?" A little pang of guilt pierced him, since all he'd told her about himself was more or less a lie. But he continued anyway, ignoring the pang, digging for the source of her pain when she spoke of her mother. "I want to understand, Angel," he said. "I want to *know* you, as much as one person can know another. And the way for me to do that is for you to share with me all that makes you who you are.''

He fell silent, then, looking into her eyes, wondering with half his mind where he—Burnett Clinton, who always froze up like an iceberg when it came to intimate talk—had ever found such tender words, wondering if they were his words at all, or if perhaps they were Ned's.

Frannie said, "It's all kind of complicated.''

"It's okay," he coaxed. "I can handle it.''

"I mean it's *confusing*.''

"Come on, Angel. Just tell me.''

"Oh, all right. The truth is, my dad wasn't my real father. My *stepfather* is.''

"Huh?'' Burnett pulled away a little.

"I told you." She made a groaning noise. "I hate even trying to explain it. It's like some . . . comedy of errors, or something. And it's my life.''

Burnett repeated what she'd said, trying to make it make sense. "You father wasn't your father?''

"Right. See, my mother was pregnant with me when she married the man I thought was my father. She was pregnant by a man from her hometown, who was already married.''

"The man who eventually became your stepfather, you mean?''

"Yes. She ran away to California when she found out she was pregnant. She met Stanley Lawry and he knew she was pregnant, but he wanted to marry her anyway. She agreed, and for ten years the three of us were a family. And then when my dad died, she took me and went back to Tulsa, because my natural father's wife had died by then, too.''

"And so, by then, your natural father was willing to marry your mother?''

"Yes. They got married, and they had more daughters. My sisters. It should have all been fine. I mean, it all worked out, didn't it? After over ten years, he finally made it legal with her. Except that to me, he's just not my father. To me, Stanley Lawry is my father. Stanley Lawry left everything he had to me. And he was there for me from the beginning.

"And worst of all," Frannie said, "she never told me. I had to find it out for myself, when she took me to Oklahoma and introduced me to a stranger and I saw my own eyes looking back at me. I ran away right after that. They brought me back. And *then,* when it was too late to mean anything, she told me the truth."

Frannie cuddled into his shoulder, and confessed the rest. "She wanted me to forget all about our life in California. She said Tulsa was my home now. I didn't argue with her, but in my heart, Tulsa was never home to me. She talked at first about my natural father adopting me, but she dropped that soon enough when I told her that she would never see me again if she tried something like that. I waited until I was eighteen, and then I came back to California and have stayed here ever since.

"My mother and I keep in touch, with calls at Christmas and presents through the mail. But we've never been close since then. I just don't really trust her anymore, I guess."

Frannie laughed, a little raggedly, the sound muffled by his shoulder. "I love her, I do. We're just not close."

"Does your aunt know?"

"Does she ever." Frannie sighed and rolled onto her back. "After I left Kenneth, she and I finally talked about it."

"And?"

"She was relieved to have it out in the open. In fact, since then she takes every opportunity she gets to try to talk me into spending more time with my mother. See, Aunt Bonnie suspected from the first that her brother wasn't my father, because I came along only six months after they were married. They hadn't even *known* each other long enough for him to be my natural father. But Aunt Bonnie never challenged my mother about it or anything. Aunt Bonnie's bossy, but she's got a lot of tolerance, really. Once she saw that my mother treated my dad well, she let it be. And, also, Aunt Bonnie felt the way I did, that in the ways that matter, Stanley Lawry was my dad. To her, I'm her niece just as much as if we shared the same genes."

Burnett found he was feeling great sympathy for Frannie's erring mother. Probably because he understood too well that he had a lot in common with her: both of them had trouble telling difficult truths.

He said, "You know, you might try to see it from your mother's point of view. Maybe she could never quite figure out how to tell you the truth. Maybe what she was really trying hardest to do was not to hurt you, or lose your love."

"Well, I can see that. I can. But she did hurt me—much worse than if she'd been honest. And...I do still love her." Frannie's voice was sad and distant. "She lied, that's all, for the first ten years of my life. About something that meant the world to me. I guess that's one thing I just have a hard time with. That someone I love and trust could lie to me about what matters most."

Though Frannie spoke gently, her words hit Burnett as if they were stones. He felt bone-weary, suddenly, and trapped by his own deceptions. The more his angel revealed to him of the secrets of her heart, the more he believed that there was no way she could possibly continue loving him once she knew who he really was.

Two things she rejected: liars and domineering men. He filled the bill on both counts.

"Ned?" she whispered against his shoulder.

"What is it, Angel?"

"I didn't want to go into all that. But I'm glad I did. I'm glad you know."

He made a vague noise of agreement and settled her close against him.

"Tired?" she asked, her own voice soft and drowsy.

"Um." He closed his eyes and drifted off to a place of velvet darkness, a place of peace, where lies were unnecessary and his angel loved him as he really was.

Somehow, Monday arrived without his telling her the truth.

She walked him out to his Jeep in the predawn hours, down the frozen stones of the walkway that he had shoveled free of snow on Christmas Day. Her wild hair was still tangled from sleep, and she wore her red coat over a heavy flannel nightgown. She held tight to his arm, her body warm and soft against his.

Beyond the gate, beside the Jeep, they embraced and shared a long, slow kiss that was all the sweeter because they knew they would soon be apart.

He pulled away reluctantly. "I could be back as early as tonight. At the latest, I'll be here New Year's Eve. And if something comes up, I'll call your aunt's house."

Her voice had a frantic edge to it when she spoke. "I wish you would leave me a number, Ned. I don't like this. I have no way to reach you."

He felt like a jerk. Back in the house, she'd chided him again about driving without his license. "What if something happens?'' she reproached him. ''They won't even know who you are.'' He'd made soothing noises in response, quieting her fears, all the time knowing that he did have his license, right in his back pocket. And that what the license said was he was not the man she thought he was.

He cupped her sweet face in his hands. ''Angel. I will call. I promise. Please believe me.''

''I don't like it,'' she said again. Her breath came out on a silver plume, just as it had that first evening when she'd found him in the snow.

The memory of seeing her that first time pierced his heart, because it reminded him that their magical time together, one way or another, was coming to a close. Even if he never told her the truth about himself, the real world would interfere. They would both return to their day-to-day lives in Sacramento soon enough. And the fabric of deception he'd woven for her would unravel of itself, much too flimsy a thing to hold up under the hard use of everyday life.

''Please, Angel,'' he told her, his voice a hoarse thread that had to fight its way around the tightness in his throat. ''I know I haven't made everything clear. I know it isn't fair to you. But I swear, one way or another, I'll come back before New Year's. And we'll get all this straightened out. I'll . . . tell you everything I've been holding back. There'll be nothing but honesty between us. I promise you.''

She smiled then, her angel's smile. ''Why is it I believe you?'' she asked, as she'd asked on the night she'd agreed he could stay until Christmas.

He answered as before. ''Because, about this, I'm telling the absolute truth.''

And he was, he realized. When he returned, the first thing he'd do would be to explain everything, though he was almost certain he would lose her then. But he'd had his heavenly Christmas with his angel at his side. And now it was time to come back to earth. Better she hear it from him, than to find out some other way, whatever the cost.

Her light-within-dark eyes gazed into his. "I wasn't going to say this again, until you said it first."

He wanted to hear it. "Tell me."

"I love you, Ned St. Charles."

He opened his mouth to give the words back to her. But then he thought, *No. Damned if it will be Ned who'll say those words first.*

He whispered, "I'm glad."

The light in her eyes dimmed for a moment, but she kept her smile in place. "Come back to me."

"I swear it."

He kissed her once more and then climbed into the Jeep.

Chapter Fifteen

Frannie stood to watch him drive away, hugging her elbows against the cold. The Jeep started with difficulty, and when he pulled away from the sidewalk, he had to drive up to the bend that led out of town toward Reno to turn around.

It was a torment for her, to watch the Jeep disappear around the corner and then reappear a moment later. She waved, forcing a smile, as he went by once more, crossing the bridge and vanishing at the turn to Main Street.

Frannie had a terrible premonition, then. For a moment she was absolutely positive that she would never see Ned St. Charles again. But then she shook herself and told herself she was being ridiculous, letting her unfounded fears get the better of good sense.

The basis of love always had to be trust. Ned still had secrets he was keeping from her, she knew that. But he'd sworn he would explain everything when he returned. Because she loved him, she would trust what he'd told her. He *would* return, and he would explain everything then.

Straightening her shoulders, she hurried back to the warmth of her house.

When she entered the kitchen, the clock on the wall said just past four. She considered going back upstairs to try to sleep a few more hours. But she knew that would be futile. She was too keyed up. Besides, if she went up there and slipped beneath the sheets, all she'd do would be to mourn the absence of Ned's body curled around hers.

So she brewed up a pot of coffee and sat at the table and thought about the miracle that had happened to her. She reminded herself once more that soon enough, Ned would return. All the mysteries would be cleared up.

And she was sure that then he would tell her he loved her. Something—perhaps having to do with those last secrets he had yet to reveal—was holding him back from saying it aloud. But she was positive she'd seen it in his eyes. Felt it in his kiss. And experienced it in the hungry touch of his hands on her skin.

And when he returned, he would say it. She knew that, as she knew that the slight graying of the blackness beyond the windows meant dawn was on its way.

She thought, too, as she sat there watching the daylight come, of all she'd learned from him. Of the things he'd helped her see about herself and who she was.

And she thought of what he'd said about her mother: *Maybe she could never quite figure out how to tell you the truth. Maybe what she was really trying hardest to do was not to hurt you, or lose your love...*

Seen in that light, her mother's actions suddenly lost their selfish cruelty. Frannie still did not consider what her mother had done to be *right*. But she started to wonder if her mother's wrongness really mattered anymore, now that

Frannie herself was no longer a grieving, confused little girl.

And then there was Kenneth. In talking about him with Ned, Frannie had been able to actually feel sorry for him, to pity him his inability to really love another person. She'd been a scared little girl still looking for her lost father with Kenneth. But since the night she'd decided to let Ned stay, she hadn't once heard Kenneth's castigating voice in her mind. She didn't need him anymore, not even his imaginary voice, to help her decide how to run her life.

Smiling to herself, Frannie went into the bathroom and took a long, hot shower. Then she made herself some hot cereal and toast, and sat down for breakfast.

When her meal was done, it was just past nine o'clock. She'd made up her mind about something while she ate, so she put on her jacket and went out the side door.

"So. He's gone," Bonnie said when she answered her door.

Frannie nodded. "He'll be back for New Year's."

"Well, don't stand there in the cold until your boots freeze to the porch. Come on in."

"Thanks, Aunt Bonnie." Frannie went inside. "Would it be all right if I used your phone? It's a long-distance call, but I'll pay you back."

Bonnie gestured toward the kitchen. "Help yourself."

Not giving herself any time to back out, Frannie went straight to the old phone on the wall and dialed her mother's number in Oklahoma.

Her youngest sister, Adele, answered the phone.

"Frannie?" Adele sounded completely disbelieving. "You okay?"

"I'm fine, Adele. Just calling to, um, say hello."

"But it's no special day, just Monday. Not Christmas or anything," Adele murmured, stymied. Then, "You *sure* you're all right?"

"I'm fine. Really." Strange, Frannie thought, how awkward it was, trying to talk to her own sister, since she'd spent so many years keeping everyone in Tulsa at a safe, polite distance.

"You want to talk to Mom?"

"In a minute, yes. But first, tell me how you've been."

Adele was silent. At last she said, "Fine."

"Are you still playing, um, football?"

"Soccer. I play soccer. And yeah. I'm playing forward this year."

"You enjoy it?"

"Yeah," Adele answered in a tone that told Frannie she really ought to come up with an intelligent question soon— or stop wasting her sixteen-year-old sister's valuable time.

"Okay, Adele," Frannie laughed. "You can put Mom on now."

"Just a minute," Adele said. Then she put the handset slightly away from her mouth and bellowed, "Mom!"

After a moment her mother's voice asked anxiously, "Frannie? Is that you?"

"Yes, Mom."

"You're all right?"

"Fine, Mom. I just, well, I realize I haven't really been keeping in touch with you. I, um, missed you, and I thought I'd call and tell you…"

"Yes?"

"I love you, Mom."

There was a silence from the other end of the line.

"Mom, are you there?"

"I'm here. And I love you, too, honey. Very much."

"I'd like to come visit, maybe during spring break, if that would be okay—"

"That would be wonderful." Her mother's voice was eager, lighter suddenly. "I would love that. *We* would love that. We truly would."

"Okay, great. We'll call it a date."

"Yes. A date," Alicia Lawry Anderson said.

There was another silence.

"Mom?"

"Yes, honey?"

"Is Father there?"

"Yes," her mother answered in a voice so full of hope, it almost broke Frannie's heart. "Yes, it just so happens he is." She rushed on, explaining what didn't need to be explained, "Would you believe it, he's down with a cold? Isn't that wonderful—I mean, well, since you called and all... Oh, what is wrong with me? You hang on. I'll get him."

Frannie waited. At last the deep, reticent voice said, "Hello, Frannie."

She talked to him for only a few moments, exchanging pleasantries and promising him, as she had her mother, that she would come for a visit in the spring.

At the end, her mother came back on the line briefly. "Oh, honey," she said. "I am so glad you called..."

Frannie said she was, too, and then they said goodbye.

She looked up to see her aunt in the doorway.

"Well," Bonnie said. "Looks to me like my favorite niece is finally *really* growing up."

"It was about time," Frannie said.

"You'll get no argument from me on that," her aunt responded.

After that, they sat in Bonnie's kitchen and Frannie drank more coffee and Bonnie allowed that sometimes, on a Monday like this, she missed her job down at the courthouse. She'd retired just a year before.

"And that's why," Bonnie went on, "I always keep a few projects on a back burner, for days like today, when I don't want to be sitting around staring at the wall, feeling old and useless."

Frannie, who'd been wondering how she was going to fill the hours that stretched out like a wasteland without Ned at her side, asked immediately, "So what's the project for today?"

"Painting the guest room upstairs. Want to help?"

Frannie jumped at the chance. In half an hour, she and Bonnie were upstairs spreading butter-colored latex on the walls.

The paint job took up half the day. And after that, Frannie returned to her house and cleaned a few closets. Then, since Bonnie had invited her, she went back over there for dinner.

From the moment Ned drove away until she finally fell asleep alone in her bed, Frannie kept herself busy. Still she found herself wondering over and over what Ned was doing now....

At twelve-thirty that afternoon, Burnett and Leland Fairgrove were washing their hands in the restroom of the Sutter Club, where Sacramento's most successful businessmen regularly went for lunch.

"I got the advertising people in on this," Leland said. "They've worked up a nice little piece to send over to the *Bee*. Do you want to take a look at it?"

Burnett took a snow-white towel from the little shelf above the basin and dried his hands, deciding that the last thing he wanted to do today was read about the franchise deal. He'd just spent the entire morning talking about it in detail. After lunch they would return to Leland's offices and, he fervently hoped, it would finally be time to put his name on the dotted line.

"Have you seen it?" Burnett asked about the work the PR firm had done.

"You bet. It's terrific." Leland smoothed his hair.

"Fine. Then approve it." Burnett tossed his towel in the bin. "And let's get back to the table, before Jordan runs off with the waitress and we *never* get that damned thing signed."

"They'll have a photographer there this afternoon," Leland said from behind him as they went through the doors to the hall. "Just a shot or two, of you and Jordan and myself while the agreement's being signed."

"Fine, no problem," Burnett said, eager to get it all over and done. They hurried to their table in the dining room upstairs. There Jordan, true to form, was ordering champagne for a beautiful woman across the room and planning where they'd go to celebrate when their business was concluded.

At a little after two, they at last returned to Fairgrave and Associates. But Jordan still wasn't satisfied with the wording of the agreement. Though this was only a preliminary document aimed at reassuring the man responsible for twelve precise locations, Jordan wanted it to say that all of southern California, Arizona and New Mexico would be franchised out through him and his group.

"Come on, Jordan," Burnett said, "that wasn't what we talked about and you know it damn well."

Jordan gave one of his famous guileless smiles. "Well, hey, Clinton. Let's talk about it now."

Leland asked his secretary for two aspirins and some spring water—and the negotiations began all over again.

It was well after six when Jordan finally agreed to accept the title of Franchise Coordinator for Chilly Lilly's Inc. That would give him the leeway to approach potential franchise owners—with the stipulation that after preliminary proposals, he would get an okay from Burnett before proceeding further.

Even Leland was happy with this solution. Everybody won. Burnett lost none of his control over his company—and yet Jordan was within his rights to warm up new franchise buyers on his own. For every buyer Jordan found—and Burnett approved—Jordan would get a nice cut of the buy-in fee.

The PR photographer set up the shot, and Burnett signed the agreement, with a beaming Jordan and Leland at his side.

"Now we celebrate," Jordan announced. "How about Frank Fat's for dinner? And then maybe over to Dawson's. And after that, who knows?"

Burnett almost said no. He wanted to see Frannie. Since leaving her, he'd felt on edge. He wanted to go back to his big empty house, put on the jeans and shirt that she had bought him, and return to the mountains where she waited for him. He wanted to hold her and kiss her once more—before he revealed the hardest truth of all.

But then he thought of how Jordan had rearranged his schedule just because Burnett had asked him to. It seemed that the least he could do was buy the man dinner to show his appreciation. And Burnett also knew he should spend tomorrow at his own office, to check that everything was going well. And then there was his nephew, Mike, who had saved a gift for him wrapped in three kinds of paper.

Jordan McSwain was grinning at him. "Well, what do you say, buddy?"

"Okay, Jordan. Let's go celebrate."

* * *

In Downieville, Tuesday dawned clear and bright.

Frannie's second cousin, Andy, came over and asked her if she wanted to go up to the summit and ride snowmobiles. She went, crammed between Andy and his wife and their two daughters, in the cab of their big pickup truck.

They rode the motor-driven sleds in the deep, powdery snow, and ate lunch off the bed of the trailer on which the sleds had been towed up the steep and winding road.

They didn't come home until almost dark, riding down from Sierra City, packed tight in the cab, singing rock and roll songs from the fifties at the top of their lungs and laughing when they forgot what line came next.

Frannie felt anticipation building as they approached the limits of town. There was a rising feeling in her throat, an excitement and an expectant joy.

What if Ned were there when she arrived at her house? Or what if he'd called Aunt Bonnie?

She tried not to indulge her disappointment when neither possibility turned out to be true. She watched her aunt's favorite game show with her, and then returned to her own house, where she discovered her nose was sunburned—and the fires were both cold.

Stomping down to the freezing basement to get more wood, she realized she'd grown spoiled having Ned with her. She hadn't even thought about the fires while he had stayed in her house.

She tucked herself in early, cuddling up with a novel of romantic suspense. She read the whole thing before she fell asleep, because she just didn't like sleeping without Ned at her side anymore.

* * *

In Sacramento, Burnett went through his mail and got a rundown from his secretary. Everything at Chilly Lilly's Inc. had been going along fine.

He went to his brother's for dinner, where he passed out the gifts he'd rushed around in the afternoon buying. He received his present from his nephew—a computer game called Combat Chess, at which Mike promptly slaughtered him.

After Mike went to bed, and Joanna, an artist, disappeared into her studio, Casey wanted to know how things had gone with *the angel.*

"I'm going back tomorrow, for New Year's."

"Did you tell her the truth?"

"Not yet."

"Not good, Big Brother."

"I know."

"Well then?"

"I'll tell her tomorrow."

"Good."

Burnett went to the big French doors that looked out on the pool. "I don't know, Casey," he said, staring at his own shadowy reflection in the glass of the door. "I'm afraid I'll lose her the minute I tell her."

"It's a risk," Casey reluctantly agreed from behind him. "But it'll be a hell of a lot worse if she finds out from somebody else."

"I know," Burnett said, turning back to the spacious room. "How about another Scotch and soda?"

"Help yourself."

Wednesday morning in Downieville, Frannie looked out her window on a gunmetal sky. Another storm was on the way.

She rose and fed the fires and decided to go over to the Downieville Bakery, on the other side of the bridge, for her morning coffee and a sweet roll. She just wasn't in the mood to have breakfast alone—especially when she knew she could be snowed in by noon.

She pulled on a heavy blue sweater and some jeans, and tucked her hair beneath a big cashmere tam that her mother had sent her in the mail Christmas before last. Wearing the matching scarf and her red jacket, she went out into the gray, blustery morning. She paused at her front gate to wrap her scarf closer about her and turn her collar up. Then she started down the street, pushing against the harsh wind all the way.

The bakery, housed in the historic Craycroft building, which also contained Yo-Ho's store, was doing a brisk business when Frannie arrived. She got in line in the small area where the glass cases displayed doughnuts and sweet rolls and muffins and such. After her turn to order came, she took her coffee and the paper-lined basket containing a huge apple fritter into the adjacent dining room.

She saw Marlon Everly immediately. He sat at a table in the corner. There was a cup of coffee at his elbow, and he puffed on one of his ever-present cigarettes. Before him was a newspaper, which he appeared to be scanning with extreme avidity.

Frannie hesitated for a moment before joining him. He looked completely absorbed in his paper. But she really did want to chat with someone, to share a little neighborly conversation before she returned to the house to wait out the storm. And Marlon Everly seemed capable enough of speaking up if he wanted to be alone.

She strolled over to him. "Want some company, Mr. Everly?"

His head jerked up. "Eh?" He narrowed his eyes at her. "Frannie!" he said—and then quickly folded the paper over on itself. "Please. Have a seat."

Frannie slid into the chair beside him, wondering at his strained expression and the furtive way he seemed to be hiding the paper from her. "Is everything all right?"

"Eh? Certainly. Everything is fine."

"You look so . . . strange, Mr. Everly."

He chuckled. "Well, I am strange, child. Anyone who lives to be past eighty tends to get a little strange."

Frannie wasn't buying. "What are you reading?"

"Hmm? Eh?"

"In the paper? Is there something in the paper?"

"Something?" he asked, sounding like a bad recording. "In the paper? Why . . ."

Frannie looked at him. And he looked back. And then he shrugged and took another puff from his cigarette. He lifted his arm off the newspaper and pushed it over in front of her.

Frannie looked down at the paper. And then she gave a nervous, unconvincing laugh. What in the world could be in there that would make Marlon Everly behave so oddly?

Frannie flipped open the paper. She saw that it was the Metro section of the *Sacramento Bee*. She also saw a color photograph of Ned.

Frannie blinked. But when she opened her eyes again, the picture was still there. In it, Ned was shaking hands with a big blond man while a thin, serious fellow looked on. All three men were immaculately dressed.

The caption read: Ice-Cream King Closes Sweet Deal.

"You must understand, my dear," Marlon Everly was murmuring in an apprehensive tone. "You introduced him as . . . Ned, wasn't it? And just now, you surprised me. When

I looked up and saw you, my first instinct was to protect you, because I thought perhaps you didn't know..."

Frannie didn't look up. She couldn't take her eyes off the picture. She was trying desperately to assimilate what such a thing might mean. A picture of her raggedy man, all dressed up in a fine suit. Looking supremely comfortable, utterly confident. Looking distant and domineering.

A man just like Kenneth had been. The kind of man she had sworn never to get anywhere near, ever again.

"Frannie?" Marlon Everly's voice came at her, sounding extremely concerned.

Frannie ignored him. She looked at the caption beneath the picture of Ned and read:

Burnett Clinton, Owner and President of Chilly Lilly's, Inc.

Frannie's mind seemed to have gone numb. She had to strain to comprehend what she saw, what the picture and the words on the paper were trying to tell her.

That Ned was not Ned.

That Ned was the man he had said was his boss.

Burnett Clinton was Ned.

And, in reality, there *was* no Ned. Had never been a Ned. It had all been some awful, cruel, incredible joke...

"Frannie, my dear, are you all right?" Marlon Everly was asking.

Frannie looked up, and made herself smile. It would not be a good idea to break down here, she decided with the part of her mind that continued to function. Not here, in the bakery, with everyone looking on. It simply wouldn't do, as Aunt Bonnie would say.

"Mr. Everly?" Frannie asked brightly. "May I take this paper?"

"Why certainly you may. Of course. But are you sure you're—"

Frannie stood up, clutching the paper against her breast. "I'm fine. Just fine. Only surprised. You're right, you see. I didn't know."

Marlon Everly reached for his cane. "Allow me to walk with you."

Frannie understood his concern. She knew she probably didn't look as "fine" as she insisted she was. "No. Please. I really am all right. I just need . . . I need to be by myself right now."

"Are you sure?"

"Positive."

Marlon Everly reluctantly sank back to his seat. "All right, my dear. If you're sure . . ."

Frannie gave him another forced, wide smile and scooted free of the table and got out of there. She raced across the bridge, the fierce wind at her back. The storm had begun, an angry storm, one that tore at her scarf and stung her cheeks with sleeting snow.

When she reached the partial haven of her porch, she yanked off her boots and went in the side door. She sat down at the kitchen table without even removing her coat or her tam and scarf.

She spread the paper open on the table, and then, very slowly, she read every word of the article that accompanied the picture.

It said that Burnett Clinton had taken a single ice-cream store owned by his family and turned it into a million-dollar corporation. It said that after this franchising operation was successfully completed, Chilly Lilly's Inc.—and Burnett Clinton—would have doubled the number of stores in the chain, and massively increased his company's net worth.

And to Frannie Lawry, it said that she'd fallen for another wheeler-dealer. And one much worse than Kenneth. Kenneth, at least, had never pretended to be other than he was.

Outside the wind and sleet beat against the windows. Frannie was hardly aware of the storm. She sat for a measureless time, staring at the picture that showed the complete and total betrayal of the man she'd allowed herself to love.

She didn't hear the tapping on the side door. Finally her Aunt Bonnie had to let herself in.

"Marlon called me," Bonnie said when she stood beside the table. "He was worried about you."

Frannie looked up into her aunt's round face. "You were right, Aunt Bonnie. You were right all along." She pushed the paper over, nearer where her aunt stood.

Bonnie looked down at it, scanned it at a glance. Then she looked up at Frannie again, those dark eyes that could be so sharp, soft with tender sympathy.

"He lied," Frannie said. "About everything."

For once Bonnie Lawry said nothing. She removed her coat and hung it on the hook by the door. Then she returned to the table and sat down. She scooted her chair next to Frannie's, and put her arms around her niece. At first Frannie stiffened, then she sagged against her aunt's solid strength.

Frannie felt her aunt's hands, removing the tam, pulling loose the scarf, and then cradling her close again, stroking her hair. Frannie sighed.

Bonnie spoke at last. "You'll feel better if you cry."

"I can't."

"It's no good holding it back."

"I'm not. I'm just ... numb. I can't cry right now."

Bonnie continued to stroke her hair.

"I don't know," Frannie said in a flat voice against her aunt's substantial bosom, "if he'll even come back."

"Oh, he'll be back," Bonnie said.

"What do you know about it, Aunt Bonnie?"

"I know enough," Bonnie replied.

"I won't see him."

"You'll see him."

Frannie sighed. "Aunt Bonnie, I get so tired of arguing with you."

"I'm not arguing, Frances. I'm just stating the facts."

Chapter Sixteen

The sky overhead was dangerously dark when Burnett started for Downieville at 8:00 a.m. It rained on and off up through Auburn, and the rain became snow as he neared Grass Valley.

But the real storm caught him after he'd left Nevada City, at the middle fork of the Yuba River just as he crossed the bridge there. It was nothing like the storms he'd known during the days he spent with his angel. Those had been windless, gentle things, where the snow drifted down thick and soft to cover everything in a pristine blanket of white.

This was a blowing, sleety gale of a storm. The snow came at the windshield fiercely, attacking it, pelting it as if it wanted to shatter the glass. He had to slow to a crawl for safety's sake, though the old Jeep did have all-weather tires.

As he climbed the last—and highest—hill before descending into the final canyon and crossing the bridge over the north fork of the Yuba, the sleeting snow became so thick that he could see it building up on the road. Even his snow tires weren't holding. He was afraid he was going to have to pull over and put on the ancient chains that were stored underneath the seat.

But then, behind him, he saw the powerful, beaconlike headlights. And he heard the scraping of the pavement, even through the howling of the storm. It was the snowplow.

Carefully he veered to the side when he found a wide space. He let the plow go by. Then he followed it, traveling at a snail's pace, but safely, for the final fifteen miles.

It took nearly an hour, but he arrived at the point above Downieville without incident. The snowplow turned out at the wide space in the road there, moving in a circle, and then heading back the way it had come.

He waved at the driver. Then he slowly started down into the small valley, where the town lay sleeping, closed in on itself against the wildness of the storm.

"Drink your hot milk," Bonnie instructed.

Frannie obediently lifted the cup to her lips and took a sip. They were sitting in the living room, where Bonnie had sent her after helping her out of her coat. Bonnie had heated the milk, and then joined her here in front of the open fireplace.

"I'm going to be fine, Aunt Bonnie. Really I am."

"Of course you are."

Frannie set her cup aside. She still felt numb. Nothing seemed real. But she was conscious of a vague surprise at the way her aunt was behaving.

"I thought you'd be ranting and raving by now, about him," Frannie said.

"No sense locking up the barn now. The horses have gone."

"What's that supposed to mean?"

"You love him."

"I don't. I don't even know him."

"I liked him. When I got to know him."

"Aunt Bonnie. You didn't know him. He wasn't who he said he was at all."

Bonnie grew pensive. "I think he was a lot who he said he was, *whoever* it turns out he actually is."

If Frannie hadn't felt so dead inside, she might have laughed. "Aunt Bonnie, I don't know what you're talking about."

"Yes, you do, Frances. You understand me just fine."

"He's Kenneth Dayton all over again. Can't you see that?"

"Humph," Bonnie said to that. "No, I can't. I despised Kenneth Dayton from the first minute you introduced us."

"You despised Ned—I mean Burnett, too."

"Yes, I did. But the more I got to know him—"

Frannie wearily waved a hand. "That's enough. Please. I don't want to talk about it anymore."

"Well, fine. Don't cry. Don't talk. I'm sure keeping it all in will do you a world of good. I'm sure your support group would be proud of you."

"Aunt Bonnie—"

But Bonnie was gesturing toward the front window. "Well. What did I tell you? I said he'd be back."

Frannie looked where her aunt pointed. And saw Ned.

No, not Ned. There was no Ned. She saw Burnett. Burnett Clinton coming up her front steps. He seemed to be materializing out of the gale, because the storm was so fierce there was nothing but swirling white from halfway down the yard.

He wore the clothes she'd given him—the boots and jeans and heavy jacket. He held himself hunched against the cruel wind, and he stomped the snow off his boots before he approached the front door and disappeared from her line of sight.

"I'll let myself out the back," Bonnie said.

Frannie hardly heard her. All of her being, her entire self, was focused on the front door.

The knock came, three strong raps on the old brass knocker. Frannie shook herself, registering the fact that Bonnie was gone. She rose from the faded wing chair by the fire and slowly, on unresponsive feet, approached the door.

He knocked again before she got there. And that energized her. She hurried the rest of the way and flung open the door.

And then she couldn't move. She looked at him. The snow, borne on the ruthless, turbulent air, blew in the door and swirled around their feet. She ignored it.

He looked so handsome and solid, standing there in the angry wind. Some traitorous part of her wanted to open her arms to him, pull him close to her, feel his breath warm her face as she lifted her lips to offer a welcoming kiss.

But she stood firm against such dangerous desires. She watched his face, watched it change. From a look of joy and hunger, to puzzlement, to slowly dawning awareness.

In the end, he broke the silence. He said two words, "You know."

She nodded, then stepped out of the way. He entered. She closed out the storm.

"How?" he asked. "Who told you?"

She turned toward the kitchen. He followed her there.

She pointed to the newspaper. He looked at it.

Then he shoved it away, muttering a brief expletive, and sank into a chair. She sat down, as well, after moving her chair a safe distance away.

He looked at the table for a while, then he looked at her once more, his eyes pleading. "Angel—"

"Don't call me that!" The words seemed to explode out of her mouth. "Don't..." She forced herself to breathe, to get herself into some semblance of control. Then she finished with great care, "Don't ever call me that again."

"Damn it, I'm sorry," he said in a hoarse whisper.

"You're sorry." She repeated the words very softly, with utter lack of belief.

"Yes. I wanted to tell you. I tried to tell you. All along. But I knew damn well I'd lose you. Like I'm losing you now."

"Why did you do it?" she asked. "Why did you lie in the first place?"

"I wanted to be anyone that day, anyone but myself."

"St. Charles for the bar?"

"Yeah."

"And Ned? Why Ned?"

"Frannie—"

"Answer me." Her voice was rising again, getting close to going out of control. She forced it back into a flat, even tone and repeated, "You answer me now. I've got a right to the truth, after all of your lies."

"All right. Edward is my first name. I used to be called Ned, when I was a kid."

"What are you trying to make me think? That it wasn't *really* a lie, since Ned *is* your real name?"

"I'm not trying to make you think anything." He sounded tired, beaten. "You asked and I told you."

"Why should I believe you?"

He peered at her very closely then, and she wondered in a strange, scared way, what he saw. He said, "You told me you loved me. If you do—"

She couldn't bear to hear more. She threw up a hand. "I loved *Ned*, remember? Not some stranger. Not you."

His face tightened, as if she'd struck him. "You said you loved me." He spoke so low she barely heard it beneath the howling of the wind.

"No!" The word was ugly, raw with pain. "You're not Ned. You're a fake and a liar. You . . . you made love with me under false pretenses. You let me think you were somebody I could trust, somebody I could count on, somebody . . . *real*."

"I *am* real."

She loosed an ugly short laugh. "You? Real? You're not real. You're just—"

Something seemed to snap in him then. He raised his bent head. "What?" Now his face was expressionless.

"Just—" Frannie cut herself off this time. His dark eyes looked dangerous. She realized she had probably gone too far. "Never mind," she said. "What counts is, it's over."

He stood up. "Oh, really?" He wore that distant look now, the one that he'd worn when he'd posed for the picture in the paper.

She stood up, too, not wanting to have him look down on her. "Yes, it's over." She thought her voice sounded very calm. She congratulated herself on that. Because she didn't feel calm.

Something had happened. Everything had shifted. He'd been behaving like Ned might have, trying to get through to her, to make her understand. But then, at some point, he'd decided he wasn't going to get through to her. He'd given up on being vulnerable. He'd put up stone walls around his emotions. Frannie feared what he might say— or do—next.

"Why is it over?" he asked, still in that distant, coldly curious voice.

Frannie felt outraged that he would even ask such a question. She let her anger show. "What do you mean, why? You're the kind of man I never want anything to do with again. And everything you told me about yourself was a lie."

"I admit I lied," he said.

"And you think that makes everything all right?"

"I lied at first," he went on patiently, "because I was drunk and too out of it to know better. And I kept on lying for an understandable reason."

"What reason?"

"Because I knew you'd kick me out if I told you the truth. Pretending to be Ned was the only way to get close to you."

"I should have kicked you out," she said. "I *would* have kicked you out, you're right. And I would have been entirely justified."

"My point exactly." He stepped toward her. She shrank back. "Ned was the only chance I had with you. I took it. And damned if I'll regret it now." He reached out for her, and pulled her close against him.

Frannie gasped at the sweet fire that coursed through her veins at the feel of his big body against hers. He was bad for her, wrong for her. Yet she still wanted him. She was shamed.

"You wanted me," he said into her flushed face. "You still want me. By any name."

"Let me go."

Immediately he released her. Her knees felt weak. She forced herself not to lean against the back of the chair.

He said, "You used Ned, as much as I did."

"That's absurd," she shot back, her voice suddenly wavering, her throat going dry.

"You're afraid of losing control," he went on, merciless now. "You have some confused idea that any strong man will walk all over you. But you were attracted to me. You wanted me. And as long as I was weak, as long as you knew you could dominate me, you could give yourself permission to desire me, to go to bed with me, to even call what you felt for me love."

The words hurt, they were awful. She didn't want to hear more. "Stop!" she said, the sound raw and torn.

But he did nothing of the kind. "You *liked* the idea that I had nothing, that you bought the clothes I wore, paid for the food I ate, that everything—even that Christmas gift I gave you—came from you first." He took a step toward her. She stepped back. "What was I to you, really? A kind of revenge, maybe? On your precious 'Dad' for dying and leaving you so young, on your ex-husband for making you into the woman of his dreams and then replacing you without a backward glance the minute you turned out to have needs of your own?" He took another step. Frannie didn't move back this time. She stared up into his face, horrified, mesmerized, dying inside.

"I'm not either of them, Frannie—your dad or your ex," he said hoarsely into her upturned face. "And I'm also not your sweet, harmless Ned St. Charles." Suddenly he blinked and shook his head, and all the fury seemed to go out of him.

He said, very softly, "Hell, I don't think I know who I am right now."

He stepped back from her, seeming almost to fade away. "I *am* sorry, Frannie," he said in a tender voice. "I only wanted to love you, I swear. But I just never was any good at that. Not any good at all."

She realized then that he was planning to leave, which was exactly what she wanted—a few minutes ago. He was already in the door to the dining room before she called out.

"Wait. You can't go now." Like a coward, she added lamely, "The storm..."

He shook his head. "I'll follow the plow. It's perfectly safe."

"Oh, please," she cried. He stopped. "Ned—" The word was past her lips before she remembered to hold it back.

He turned then, and looked at her. He let out a sad chuckle. "You've got the wrong guy," he said. And then he was gone.

Chapter Seventeen

Had she? Frannie wondered. Had she got the wrong guy?

She stood staring at the doorway to the dining room after he was gone from it. She heard the outside door open, allowing brief entry to the wrathful wind. And then she heard it close.

Had she got the wrong guy?

Very loud, then, someone shouted, "No!"

And she was halfway to the front door before she realized it had been herself. She raced through the dining room, and then across the front room rug to the door.

She flung open the door and shouted, "Burnett! Wait!"

But there was only the thick, spinning snow and the howling wind and—seemingly a thousand miles away—the sound of an engine starting up.

Oblivious to the cold and wind, she raced out onto the porch in her stockinged feet. "Damn you, Burnett! You get back here!"

No answer came, of course. That distant engine was pulling away. Frannie shot off the porch and into the high drifts in the yard. She struggled, pushing and fighting with all her strength, out into the thick, blind force of the storm.

Somehow she made it to the front gate. Her feet were freezing, so cold they burned. If she stayed out in this much longer, she knew, they wouldn't hurt at all. And that would be bad indeed.

But she was less than a hundred feet from her own house, she reminded herself staunchly. And all she had to do was somehow get out into the road and flag Burnett down after he went up the street to turn around. She knew she could do it. She knew she wouldn't damage her poor feet that badly, just from a few minutes out in this freezing gale.

She got the iron gate open, burning her hands on the frozen metal of it. And then she pushed on, out onto what she assumed was the sidewalk, so covered with snow now that there was no clear place where it ended and the street began.

She shielded her eyes with a hand, squinting against the storm—and made out the taillights of the Jeep just as they were swallowed by the swirling snow. It took her a moment to orient herself enough to realize what she'd seen.

This time he hadn't gone up the highway to turn around. This time he'd backed toward the bridge and turned onto Pearl Street. That meant he'd go to the end of that, turn left at the bridge there, and leave town by coming back down Main.

He'd escaped her.

And her feet were *freezing*.

She raced back to her house, floundering twice in the yard, crazily almost losing her way less than thirty feet from the front door. At last, she lumbered up the porch steps, her feet feeling like huge lead clubs attached to her aching ankles.

She fell in the door—and confronted her aunt.

"Are you insane, Frances Anne?"

Frannie dropped to the rug, tore off her sock, and began massaging one foot. Her aunt dropped down beside her, ripped off the other sock, and worked on the remaining foot.

"I could ask you the same question," Frannie muttered as she rubbed the circulation back into her toes. "You were obviously out in it, too."

"Just between the houses. In the proper clothing. What happened?"

"He left. I was trying to catch him. But he disappeared down Pearl Street. He's probably halfway up to Cannon Point by now."

"What do you intend to do?"

"Go after him. I don't even have a phone number for him. If I don't catch him on the road, I'll have to call one of his ice-cream stores or something to try to track him down."

Bonnie looked up from her concentration on Frannie's foot. "You're okay. Get over by the fire. I'll bring you dry clothes."

"Aunt Bonnie? My truck's out back, buried in the snow..."

"Yes," Bonnie answered, before Frannie even asked. "You may borrow mine. It's parked on the street out front."

An hour later, as Frannie slowly followed in a small caravan of vehicles behind a snowplow, she was forced to admit that she was never going to catch up to him. He'd had too much of a start on her.

An hour after that, when she reached the highway at Nevada City, and the storm began to abate, she considered turning back for Downieville.

Instead she veered off at Brunswick Road and found a gas station where she could call her aunt. Bonnie promised to close up the house for her, and Frannie said she'd return the truck within a few days.

Frannie drove on to Sacramento, to her two-bedroom condominium not far from the college. Once inside, she turned on the heat and brewed a pot of tea.

Then she took the snow bubble Burnett had given her from the pocket of her jacket where she'd stuck it before leaving her house in the mountains. She set it on the counter where she could see it if she faltered, and she got out the phone book.

There was no Burnett Clinton listed in the book. That didn't surprise her. She smiled to herself. He was such a big shot, after all. And big shots didn't put their names in the phone book for just anyone to dial.

She found a main office number for Chilly Lilly's Inc. When she called it, a receptionist answered. The receptionist was perfectly willing to take a number, but had no idea when Mr. Clinton might be in.

After that, Frannie sipped her tea for a few moments, refusing to let herself give up. If she had to, she'd march right over to one of his ice-cream stores. She'd chain herself to a freezer. They wouldn't be able to get rid of her until *Mr. Clinton* agreed to speak to her in person.

She racked her brain for something—anything he might have said during their time together that could provide her with a clue to how to reach him now.

And at last, something came to her. She set down her teacup, and turned the snow bubble upside down once. She stared at the somber angel within.

The brother, she thought as the swirling flakes settled. He'd said he had a brother. A brother named Casey. He'd said Casey was the wild one, who fell in love with his best friend.

And Frannie had never doubted that he was telling the truth.

Because, she decided, he *had* been telling the truth. She would bet the only thing she had left of him now—the snow bubble angel he'd bought her with her own money—that all he had told her about himself and his family had been true. That he'd altered it only enough to fit his identity as Ned.

Frannie opened the phone book again to the C's. If only he'd given her his brother's real name....

It was there. Casey Clinton, just as she'd prayed. Now, if only *this* Casey Clinton had a brother named Burnett.

With shaking hands, she dialed the number, hoping fervently that someone would pick up.

Three rings, then a child's voice.

"Hello?"

"Hello—is Casey Clinton there?"

"Yes," said the child.

"May I speak to him?"

"Um, whom may I say is calling?"

Frannie smiled at the well-trained, polite little voice. "This is Frannie, Frannie Lawry. But wait a moment—"

"Yes?"

"Are you Mike?"

"How'd you know?"

Relief coursed through Frannie, a warm, fine thing. Mike was the nephew. Casey and Burnett had once battled over who would have custody of him. She was reasonably sure now that she'd reached Burnett's brother.

But then she realized she wasn't out of the woods yet. Casey probably had no idea who Frannie Lawry was. She would have to convince him that he should give her a number where his brother might be found.

"I'll get Uncle Casey," Mike was saying.

"Thank you," Frannie answered, her voice sounding faint.

"Hello, Frannie Lawry." The voice was not as deep as Burnett's, but it was undeniably masculine. And there was great humor in it. Frannie had a feeling she would like Burnett's brother very much.

Frannie swallowed. He'd said her name as if he knew her—or at least, knew *of* her. "You know me?" she asked in a silly little squeak.

Casey laughed. "I've heard all about you."

"From Burnett?" She knew the question was silly when she asked it, but it just came out. How else would he have heard about her?

"Yes," Casey answered, an indulgent smile in his voice, "from Burnett. Is there something I can do for you?"

Now came the hard part. "Well, um, I have a little problem."

"Yeah?"

"I seem to have lost him."

"My brother?"

"Yes. And I lost him *before* I got his phone number."

"You did?"

"He left in a blizzard, actually. I chased him out to the road."

"I see."

"But he was already gone."

"Oh."

"So I was wondering . . ."

"Yeah?"

"Do you have a number where I could get a hold of him?"

There was a silence, then Casey asked, "This is your business, I understand. But is everything all right?"

Frannie sighed. "I think maybe it will be. If I can ever *find* him to make it that way."

"Okay," Casey said. "Hold on."

He gave her two phone numbers, and addresses to go with them—for Burnett's house in Sacramento and for his private line at his office. He also explained how to get to the cabin in Graeagle, if the other two numbers turned up nothing.

"Call me back, would you?" Casey asked then. "I mean, if you can't find him."

"I will. And thank you."

Frannie hung up, and then immediately started to dial Burnett's home number. But she didn't complete the call.

She replaced the phone in its cradle. More than likely, she reasoned, he would be at home. He wouldn't have tried for Graeagle in the storm. And it was a little late in the day to be showing up at the office.

She wanted to see him. In person. She didn't want him to have a chance to shut her out on the phone.

Frannie threw on her jacket and grabbed up the keys to the truck and went out the door.

The house was a Colonial-style brick structure, set back from the road on a beautifully landscaped lot. She pulled her aunt's old truck right up into the turnaround driveway in front of a stone fountain.

Frannie stepped out of the truck, slamming the door smartly behind her. Above, the sky was still gray, though it was not raining right then. It was cold. Not as cold as in the mountains. This was a more subtle kind of cold, gray and oppressive, the kind of cold that crept into your bones.

Frannie snuggled her red jacket closer about her and marched up to the front door, which was imposingly tall and framed by white columns. She rang the bell and then waited, looking up at the chandelier above her head—an iron creation on a chain.

She began to doubt he could be inside, since he didn't answer, and she'd detected no trace of life or light through any of the paned, shuttered windows upstairs or down. But then, she thought there was a faint brightening in the window nearest the door, as if perhaps the light in the foyer had been turned on.

The door slowly swung back.

She almost expected to see a poker-faced butler standing there. But instead it was Burnett, still wearing the clothes she'd bought him, minus the boots.

They stared at each other, then he growled. "What the hell are you doing here?"

She growled right back. "I came to finish what we started."

He scowled at her for a moment. And then he stepped back and gestured her inside.

Chapter Eighteen

He led her through the domed foyer, down a wide hall and into a big living room furnished with overstuffed skirted chairs and sofas covered in floral patterns. The tables were brass and glass. The fine rugs, in muted rose-and-blue designs, only brought out the rich depth of the hardwood floor all the more. It was an elegant room—and one with a distinctly feminine touch.

Frannie hesitated in the doorway. "Amanda decorated the whole house?" she asked, reasonably sure of his answer.

"Yes."

"It's beautiful—or at least what I've seen so far is."

"It's perfect," he said, the way another person might have said, *I hate it.*

She responded to his tone, rather than his words. "You could move."

"I intend to."

"That's good."

He turned away from her then, in a quick, frustrated movement. "Damn it, Frannie..."

She ventured into the exquisite room, crossing the soft rugs and the smooth, shining floor. He stood by one of the tall, shuttered windows. She approached him, stopping less than an arm's distance away.

She spoke softly to his back. "Within the lie, it was all true, wasn't it?"

"Yes."

"Amanda's miscarriages, the fight over custody of Mike, all that you said about your family. You even gave me all their real names."

"Yes."

"And last Tuesday *was* the day your divorce was final, and you actually did throw your money and wallet in the river—for exactly the reason you gave me."

He nodded. "I did."

"What was in the pocket of your coat?"

"My driver's license." He gave a humorless chuckle. "Hell, I was drunk. I thought it was brilliant of me to save some identification—at the same time as I was wishing I was anyone else but myself."

"Where did you get those awful clothes?"

"Upstairs in the Graeagle cabin. It was the same thing. I found them comforting. I wanted to be someone else."

"Someone like Ned?"

"Yeah, I guess so." He turned then, and allowed himself to look at her. "I liked being Ned. At the same time as I was jealous as hell of him."

"Why?"

His eyes turned bleak and then he looked away with the slightest twist of his head. "Because you adored him."

She took the step that separated them, and laid her hand on his cheek. She guided his face back to her. "I adored him because he was you. He *is* you."

He captured her hand; his eyes now burned into hers. "You think so?"

"I know so. It was all true, what you said. I let myself be attracted to you as Ned, because you seemed to be someone who would never try to run my life. But I think deep down I knew there was much more to you. I lied to myself as much as you lied to me. I deceived myself so I could let myself love you, so I could put aside my fear of what might happen if I loved a strong man."

"And what exactly was that?"

"That you would dominate me, like you said. That what happened with Kenneth would happen all over again."

"And do you still fear that?"

"No," she answered, the word firm and sure.

"Why?"

"Two reasons. I'm not the confused, lost little girl I once was. And you are not Kenneth Dayton, not by a long shot."

"I'm not?"

"No. You're not."

"How do you know?"

"Because I know you. You revealed your real self to me, even if you cheated a little on the last name."

"I lied."

"Not really, not in your heart. Because you *are* Ned, don't you see? Ned is part of you. The vulnerable, sensitive part. The part that you buried, I think, when your father deserted your family. But you're also strong and determined and ready to take on the world. That's important, too. Otherwise, as you once told me, you would be the kind of man that no self-respecting woman would really be willing to put up with for long."

He raised her captured hand to his lips, and he kissed it very softly. Frannie felt the sweet caress along every nerve. "And when did you realize all of this?" he wondered.

"Four hours ago. When you walked out on me. You said I had the wrong guy when I called you Ned. But I didn't. I had exactly the right guy. And I knew it then. I followed you out in the storm to tell you, but you got away."

"To tell me what, specifically?" He held her hand against his heart. She felt the warmth of him, and the solid strength.

"That I love you, Edward Burnett Clinton. I love all of you, with all my heart."

He dragged in a sharp breath, and then he said softly, "Thank God."

His free arm pulled her close. His mouth closed over hers, and she clung to him, offering all of herself, letting him know with her kiss that there was no lie, no equivocation, in the things she had said.

For a time, in the flawless room there was only the sound of shared sighs.

It was he who at last reluctantly pulled away. "I wanted to tell you, since Christmas Eve, that I loved you. But I didn't want to say it . . ."

"When I only knew you as Ned?"

"Yes."

"And now?" she prompted.

"Now I'll say it."

"Yes?"

"I love you, Frannie Lawry."

She smiled at him. "I'm glad—and Burnett?"

"What?"

"Would it be all right, if every once in a while, I call you Ned?"

He gave a low chuckle. "Why not? If you'll still be my angel."

She thought then of the proud, sad angel he'd given her, trapped in her bubble of glittering snow. She said, "I'm no angel, Burnett."

"Sure you are," he told her, "sometimes. Just like a part of me is Ned. You are my angel." He pulled her close once more, and his lips hovered a breath's distance from hers. "And you're also much more than that."

"I'm glad you noticed."

"Oh, I've noticed . . ." His lips brushed hers.

"What? Tell me."

"You're a hell of a woman."

"Why thank you."

"And there are many things I'd like to call you. Frannie. Angel. Wife."

She pressed herself closer to him. "Yes," she said.

"Is that an answer?"

"Yes."

"You'll marry me?" He looked, right then, as sensitive and vulnerable as he ever had as Ned.

"Absolutely," she told him.

"Right away. Tomorrow," he said, taking charge, making demands, behaving like Burnett Clinton to the core.

Frannie reached up, wrapped her arms around his neck, and pulled his mouth down to hers.

"Yes," she said. "Now kiss me."

And he willingly complied.

They were married in Reno, on New Year's Day. Their first child, a daughter, was born a year later, on the anniversary of the day Frannie glanced out her kitchen window to see a poor, ragged man struggling up the levee in the snow.

They named their daughter Angela.

* * * * *

ANGEL FOR HIRE

To my own Michael,
who is truly one of the very best people I know—
Your Alex is out there, somewhere;
don't ever settle for less than you deserve.

Prologue

*"If this be magic, let it be an art
Lawful as eating."*

—Shakespeare
The Winter's Tale

"**P**lease, help me to not give up."

The clouds swirled as the words drifted along on the wind, arriving with all of their poignancy intact. Words like these were not at all strange to this place, yet these got immediate attention.

"Now, that's a voice we've not often heard."

"True. She so rarely asks for anything."

"The last time, I believe, was with her brother."

"That was the only time, as I recall."

There was a rustling, then the same voice again. "Yes, that was it. Despite all her hardships, only the once."

"Yet she has an exemplary history. She could have asked for anything, and it would have been considered."

"And what she is trying to do is more of the same."

"So we're agreed? We send her the help she needs?"

"Absolutely."

There were nods all around.

"Who?"

"Ah, now there's a problem. We're spread a little thin at the moment."

"Gabriel?"

"No, he's still working on the Alden family. We've got to get that boy to speed things up."

"Yes. Make a note, will you? I'll look into it. Perhaps he needs some extra help. Now, what about Evangeline?"

"Still with that little girl. The child is having a terrible time. And everyone else is equally involved."

A collective sigh rose from the group. No words came for a moment, but all knew they had reached the same inevitable conclusion.

"We promised him a rest."

"I know. But what other choice do we have?"

"He is very tired."

"But she is very special."

"Oh, dear. He was so looking forward to a rest. He more than earned it after that thing with the two brothers."

"I don't blame him. They were horrible. If it hadn't been for their mother, I would have said let them kill each other and be done with it."

"It's just this one more time."

"That's what we told him last time."

"And the time before that."

"And before. But this time he swore he'd hold us to it."

"He wants a rest. A long one. And he deserves it. We've been draining his energy for a long time."

"We could help, give him a little more, a loan, so to speak."

"Too risky. We could burn him out altogether."

"Yes, and what would we do without him?"

"It's all academic. He won't go."

"Quiet, please." The new voice was stern, and hushed the chatter instantly. "You all seem to have forgotten something."

"What, sir?"

"Michael."

"Sir?"

"Perhaps I should say Michael's nature. His heart, the very thing that makes him the best we have."

"But even the greatest of hearts can be strained."

"Yes. But even Michael himself doesn't know his own capacity. He will do it."

"How can you be so sure? Sir," the voice added hastily.

"Simple. We'll just let him meet her."

"That's all?"

"That's all it will take."

One

"Alex! The cow got loose again!"

"Telephone, Alex! It's that awful Mr. Rodney again."

"Alex, what are we going to do? Mark didn't come back last night. He must be out in the woods again."

"Alex, help! There's water spraying all over the kitchen! The tape split open again!"

"Alex—"

"All right! Everybody, quiet for a minute!"

Alexandra Logan took a deep breath and pushed her tousled hair back behind one ear. It had been a long time since she'd been able to afford a professional haircut, and it was currently hacked off more or less evenly an inch or so below her ears. It tended to fall forward over her right eye, but it was Aaron's best effort, and she would never hurt his feelings by saying anything.

"All right," she said again. "Sarah, tell Mr. Rodney I'll be right there, then go ahead and feed the chickens. Kenny, turn Cougar loose and follow him. He'll find Daisy. Matt, would you shut off the water main and tape it up again? And, Wheezer, would you saddle Cricket for me? I'll go look for Mark as soon as I get off the phone.''

They scattered in different directions, and Alex smothered a sigh as she walked back into the house. They needed a new gate that would hold that too-smart bovine, a plumber to fix pipes that were so old they were nearly crumbling, a carpenter with more than Matt's rudimentary skills to fix the chicken coop, the barn, and the roof of the house, and a miracle to handle everything else that was falling apart. But the biggest miracle they needed was a way to get the persistent Mr. Rodney off their backs. She took another deep breath and picked up the phone.

"Hi, Mr. Rodney. Beautiful day, isn't it?''

"It's the twelfth of the month, Miss Logan.''

"And lovely in spite of it,'' Alex said, her grimace at odds with her light tone as she listened to the stern voice.

"Miss Logan, I truly must know what you intend to do about this payment.''

"Pay it, of course.'' So much for hiring a plumber.

"Just when did you have in mind?''

"By the fifteenth. The same terms you gave my father, naturally.''

The pause was barely perceptible, but Alex caught it. She tightened her grip on the receiver, preparing for battle.

"When the property was your father's, Miss Logan, it was a working farm.''

"It still is. And believe me, I know. I've never worked harder in my life.''

"That is not what I meant. What you are running there hardly qualifies as a farm.''

"Just what is your definition of a farm, Mr. Rodney? I was under the impression it was a piece of land on which crops or animals are raised. I think I got that from Webster's dictionary. Do you have a better definition?"

"A true farm is a business, Miss Logan, that engages in selling its product at a profit, not a refuge for—"

"When was the last time you looked at the agricultural price index, Mr. Rodney? The profit went out of farming years ago. We use everything we raise, and we're virtually independent. We like it that way."

"Well, the people in this neighborhood don't like it. They don't like what you're doing out there, and they don't like the idea of those . . . people. Only the respect they have for the memory of your parents has kept them from running you off long ago."

Alex felt anger rippling through her, and it was all she could do not to hang up on the man right then.

"I have never missed a payment on this place, Mr. Rodney. And as long as it stays that way, you have no reason and no right to continue this harassment. I don't care what you or anyone else thinks of me or my friends. And if you think I won't fight back, you just try me."

She did hang up then, fiercely. Maybe I should just have the phone disconnected, she thought. We could use the money, and I wouldn't have to talk to idiots like that. Or the sick ones who call and pour out their filthy suggestions.

She felt suddenly weary, and almost eager to go look for Mark. At least she would be away for a while, and any excuse for a peaceful ride up to the high ground was welcome. She turned, then stopped short, a startled gasp rising from her as she came face-to-face with the total stranger standing inside the front door.

"How did you get in here?" And why didn't I hear anything? Why isn't Cougar barking up a storm?

He looked a little dazed, puzzled almost, as he glanced around. "I'm . . . not sure."

Oh, Lord, Alex thought, not another one. Please, I can't handle another one. We're barely getting by as it is. But as soon as she thought it, she knew there was something wrong with her assessment. For one thing, he was much too young. "Who are you?"

She couldn't help the suspicion in her voice; more than once a ringer had been sent in to try to find some excuse for the local citizens to run her out. But if they thought she was going to believe that this angel-face was—

"Michael. Michael Justice."

Well, at least he knew his name. People had shown up who weren't even sure of that much. Or wouldn't tell her. But he wasn't one of them. She was certain of that. Just as she was certain he was the most beautiful man she'd ever seen.

And, oddly, beautiful was the proper word. Not that he wasn't all male; tall—right at six feet, she guessed—leanly muscled, with a solid jaw and corded tendons in his strong neck. The worn jeans and plain, pale blue T-shirt he wore beneath a battered leather jacket emphasized broad shoulders, a flat belly, and lean, narrow hips. But it was his face that fascinated her.

He was perfect. Every line, every angle, was finely drawn, forehead just high enough, chin just strong enough, nose just narrow and long enough, mouth soft enough to be gentle, yet firm enough to hint at a great strength. His hair was dark, nearly black even in the shaft of sunlight that shot through the window to encircle him. It was cut fairly short and combed neatly back except for a few strands that fell forward over equally dark, perfect brows. His lashes were—inevitably, it seemed—dark, long, and thick. And they surrounded blue eyes that were . . .

It was those eyes, or, rather, the change in them, that derailed her detailed assessment. That dazed look had faded, and he was staring back at her with great interest, interest that told her she had been much too intent on her inspection. She shook herself mentally, telling herself that no matter how perfect he might be, he didn't deserve to have her gaping at him like he'd dropped out of the clouds somewhere.

"Find anything you like?"

Oh, Lord, Alex groaned silently, his voice was perfect, too. Low, vibrant, and with just enough gravel in it to send a shiver up her spine. And blue seemed too tame a word for those eyes, especially now that the puzzled look had gone. They were too vivid, too brilliant, for that mild appellation. They were too alive, as if lit from within rather than by the light streaming through the window.

"If you've ever looked in a mirror, I'm sure you know the answer to that."

She said it simply, with the innate honesty that had more than once been the bane of her existence. He looked startled; then a smile curved his mouth. He had, of course, Alex thought with resignation, a dimple that lit up that perfect face. She forced herself back to the matter at hand before she started another session of cataloguing his assets.

"What I'd really like is an answer. Why are you here?"

The incredible blue eyes rolled heavenward, and Alex got the oddest feeling he was expressing his disgust on a very personal level.

"Apparently," he muttered, "I've been had."

"What?"

"Somebody," he said as his mouth twisted wryly, "knows me too damn well."

He glared upward again, and Alex thought he looked oddly like a little boy purposely tempting fate.

"Waiting for lightning to strike for one little curse?" she asked mildly.

He looked startled, his eyes bright and intent on her. Then he laughed. "Something like that."

"Well, I've got news for you. If we got nailed for every four-letter word that floated around here, there wouldn't be much left."

"Good thing they consider the provocation, then."

"Who?"

"The ones who send the lightning."

"They do?"

"Don't they?"

Her brow furrowed, then cleared. "I guess they must," she said with a laugh, "or we wouldn't be here."

"Sounds like that would suit some people just fine."

She wrinkled her nose. "You heard that, huh?" She couldn't help sighing. "We don't win any popularity contests around here." She suddenly realized he had once again successfully diverted her. "I don't make it a habit of asking a lot of questions, but I like answers to those I do ask." He studied her for a moment; then he glanced around the living room of the small house. He seemed to be waiting for something. Almost absently he raised one hand to finger something that hung around his neck on a golden chain. As he caught it between his thumb and forefinger, his gaze suddenly shot back to her.

"You need some help around here."

"That," she said ruefully, "wouldn't take a genius to see. What does that have to do with why you're here?"

Gold glinted on his chest as he released what looked, she thought in puzzlement, like a set of dog tags. Then he shrugged. "I'm here to help."

"Help . . . with what?"

"Everything. Anything."

"Look—"

"I'm a decent carpenter, plumber, and electrician. I can muddle my way through most other things."

Hope flared in her, but she beat it down. She knew nothing about this man, she couldn't just—

"It's all right. Really. I know you don't know me, but I'd never hurt you. Or your friends."

Suspicion bit again. Deep. "What do you know about my friends?"

"Just that you're trying to help them. In ways no one else will."

Her eyes narrowed even more as she looked at him. "And how do you know that?"

"I just heard it around, I guess." He saw her doubt and added softly, "I . . . didn't fight there, but I know what they went through."

Alex didn't know why, but she believed him. She believed that he knew, somehow, of their hell, that he meant them no harm, even while the part of her that had been soured by her recent contacts with her fellow human beings wondered if she wasn't just being fooled by a pretty face.

"Not judging a book by its cover goes both ways, you know."

Her eyes flew to his face. "Was I so obvious?" That honesty again, she thought ruefully.

He smiled, and her heart turned over. "Don't ever try to play poker."

If she had an ounce of brains, she would send him packing, she thought. He was altogether too dangerous to her equilibrium. Then she realized she wouldn't have to send him; he would go on his own when he realized the situation.

"I'm sorry, but we can't afford any help right now."

"Oh?" He looked around again. "You've got a roof, and it looks like you eat fairly regularly. That's all I need."

"The kind of help I need is worth a lot more than just room and board."

"Not to me."

For one of the few times in her life, Alex wavered, unable to decide. She didn't know anything about this man except for his impossible looks and the fact that he seemed to be able to read her far too easily. He could be on the run for all she knew.

"I'm not in trouble or anything. I just need a place to stay."

"The first thing you have to do," she said dryly, "is stop reading my mind."

The dimple flashed again. "Does that mean I can stay?" He didn't give her a chance to say no. "Thanks. And I don't read your mind, just your face. It's very expressive."

She flushed. "If that's a polite way of saying I'm nothing to write home about, don't bother. I already know that."

Something flashed in his blue eyes, dimming for a moment that strange inner glow. It was surprisingly like pain, although for what Alex couldn't guess.

"Don't you ever look in a mirror yourself?" he asked softly.

Her color deepened. "Not if I can help it." She grimaced. "It's bad enough knowing I look like the world's kid sister without reminding myself of it all the time."

"Looking fifteen at twenty-six might be a nuisance, but looking twenty-six at thirty-seven is surely something to look forward to, isn't it?"

She gaped at him, backing up a step. "How did you know how old I am?"

He closed his eyes, letting out a disgusted sigh. "I told you I was tired," he muttered.

When he opened his eyes again Alex was looking at him warily, backing up another step.

"Look, I just—"

He broke off suddenly and started to turn, but not in time to avoid the hulking man who had come in the door behind him. A huge, bearlike arm came around his neck, a snarl issued from somewhere six inches or so above him, and sunlight glinted off the long, deadly blade at his throat.

"Mark!" Alex cried. The big man had moved so quickly that she hadn't even realized what was happening until it was all over. The huge hunting knife hovered much too close to that strong, corded neck. She didn't dare speak yet, knowing Mark's precarious temper when provoked on her behalf. Please, she begged inwardly, just don't move. He won't hurt you if you don't move. He's just trying to protect me.

As if he'd read her once more, Michael went slack, letting the hand that had been clawing at Mark's arm drop to his side. After a moment the snarling subsided, and the big man looked across at Alex.

"Hurt you?"

"No, Mark."

"Sure? You looked scared."

"Just...surprised." She managed a credible laugh. "He guessed how old I am. You know how rare that is."

Mark loosened his grip a tiny bit. The knife never wavered.

"Didn't hurt you?"

"No. In fact, he came to help."

The grip tightened again. "Help what?"

"Fix things. The gate maybe, and even the pipes. Isn't that right?"

Slowly, tentatively, eyes never leaving the gleaming blade at his throat, Michael nodded. The grip relaxed again.

"Too pretty to be much good."

"And you're too big to be going around scaring the daylights out of people," she said sternly. The knife finally dropped, and Mark stepped back.

"Thought he hurt you."

"I know. It's all right. But you should apologize to Mr. Justice."

The snarl rose again, but it ended in a gruff, "Sorry."

He got a wary nod in return.

"Where were you, Mark? We were worried."

"Walkin'."

"All night?"

"Sat. Watched the stars, listened to the night."

"I understand, Mark. I love to do that, too. But remember what you promised me?"

The huge, bearded man looked incredibly sheepish. "Leave note." Alex nodded. "Forgot." She waited, not speaking. The big man blushed. "Sorry."

She went to him then, throwing her arms around him in as much of a hug as she could manage, given that he towered at least a foot over her own five foot six. Huge arms encircled her with a gentle care that was amazing in a man so strong. Yet it was awkward, as if an unfamiliar action. And what could be seen of his face above the bushy beard was flaming.

"It's okay, Mark. Just remember next time, okay? You've got people who worry about you now."

"Okay."

"Will you go out to the barn? I won't need Cricket saddled after all."

The bearded head bobbed up and down; then the big man turned to go. At the last second he looked back over his shoulder, fixing the man he'd just had in a death grip with a warning look.

"You hurt her, you got big trouble. We take care of her. Die for her, if we have to. Or kill for her."

"I believe you," Michael said softly. It seemed to appease the big man, and he went out the door.

When he looked back at her, Michael had to smother a smile. She was glaring at him, fists clenched, waiting. He didn't need to read her mind; she looked like a tigress defending her cub. As he'd said, her face was very expressive.

"He's . . . very special, isn't he?"

"Yes," she said flatly, searching his face for any sign of sarcasm. She found none.

"I'm glad he's your friend." A smile tugged at one corner of his mouth. "And I'm sure he meant every word he said."

Alex felt the tension drain out of her; she couldn't seem to hang on to her wariness or her doubts when he turned those uncanny eyes on her.

"Mark . . . exaggerates sometimes."

"Everyone does, sometimes. But I don't think he was, not about that." He looked at her steadily. "How many live here? Six?"

She answered before she thought to wonder how he had come so close. She supposed he'd heard about it wherever he'd heard that she needed help.

"Seven, at the moment."

He looked at the small house. "You have room for me?"

"We converted one of the barns into a bunkhouse of sorts. The guys stay there. But you can't."

"I can't?"

"They're very…wary of strangers. Even if you were one of them, you'd have to stay here for a couple of weeks, until they decided if they trusted you or not."

"And since I'm not . . . one of them?"

"It will take even longer. Especially for you."

"Why especially?"

"Well," she said, the corners of her mouth twitching, "you *are* awfully pretty."

He stared at her, grinned, then burst into delighted laughter. The sound washed over her, soothing and invigorating at the same time. It was a sound too rarely heard around here to be taken for granted, and just for a moment she let herself luxuriate in it, let a wide smile that was a little lopsided from lack of use spread across her face.

"Lady," he finally choked out, "if they can stand you being around, I'm sure not going to bother them."

Her smile disappeared. "You don't have to do that. I already said you could stay."

"Do what?"

"We're very careful about the truth around here. That's something you'd better learn."

"Exactly what did I do," he asked carefully, "that brought this on?"

"The people here have no patience with any kind of phoniness, especially false flattery. And that includes me."

"False fla—" He broke off, staring at her. "You mean what I said about you?"

"I know what I look like, Mr. Justice."

"You may look, but I don't think you see."

"Cryptic comments don't go over well here, either."

"You really don't know how lovely you are, do you?"

Her cheeks flamed, and hurt tinged her voice. "If you insist on mocking me, you can leave now."

That oddly pained look flickered in his eyes again. "I'm sorry. I didn't mean that at all." He reached out one hand to lightly touch her arm.

Alex stared at him. The moment his warm fingers had brushed her skin, her embarrassment, her hurt, had vanished. She was filled instead with a sense of calm and peace such as she'd never known.

"I would never try to hurt you," he promised solemnly.

"I . . . I know."

That was ridiculous, Alex thought. How could she know that?

There was a thump at the back of the house, and an odd clattering across the bare wood floor. His eyes flicked in that direction, then back to Alex's face; she was unperturbed. A familiar sound, then. In a moment he saw why.

The dog that gamboled into the room was the size of a small pony. Shaggy, with a huge head and a medium length coat of several shades of brown and tan, he looked of no particular breed, but it was doubtful that anyone would ever hold it against him. The huge animal carefully stationed himself in front of Alex and looked at the room's other occupant suspiciously. Michael looked back wryly.

"What's Cricket, a Clydesdale?"

It took her a moment to realize what he meant. Then she smiled as she realized that, so far, everything he'd seen here had been a little on the large side. The smile became a chuckle, then a laugh. A laugh she hadn't used in so long it felt strange. Even the dog looked askance at her, his half-floppy ears cocked attentively at the unusual sound.

"This," she said through the lingering remnants of her laughter, "is Cougar."

"After the color, the size, or the temperament?"

The laughter came more easily this time. "None of the above. I found him over near Cougar Dam. He'd been hit by a car, and they just left him."

"Oh." He knelt down until he was level with the massive head. The dog stretched out his nose as far as he could without leaving Alex's side. Michael didn't move. Finally the dog did, taking one hesitant step. Then he looked back over his shaggy shoulder at Alex.

"It's okay," she said softly.

The wet nose found his hand then. The moment they touched, the dog went suddenly still; even the tentative wag of the plumed tail stopped. The huge, soulful eyes were fastened on Michael's face, staring intently. Then he spoke to the animal, low and rough.

"Yes."

It was all he said, but the effect was electrifying. An odd sound, half bark, half howl, rose from Cougar's throat as Alex watched the remarkable reaction. She knew the sound as the animal's most joyous greeting, and she'd never heard it directed at anyone but herself before.

When Michael stood up again, she was staring at him.

"I...he's never reacted like that to a stranger before. He's usually very wary."

"And protective? Like Mark?"

Her cheeks pinkened slightly. "Yes."

"I hope you take him with you when you go anywhere."

"Yes." She smiled a little ruefully. "Don't laugh, but I traded my little car for a pickup just so he can ride along. It makes me feel better if I have to go into town."

"I wouldn't laugh." He grinned. "I wouldn't laugh at anybody with a dog that size at their beck and call. And I would never laugh at you."

The sudden seriousness of his tone brought the color back to her cheeks. "I...sometimes I'm a little sensitive."

He started to say something, then stopped.

"I'll show you where you can stay," she said hastily. "Are your things outside?"

"No. They're right here."

He turned around and picked up a large leather knapsack that was as battered as the jacket he wore. Alex's brows furrowed; she hadn't noticed the bag there before. But it had been halfway behind the open front door, so she supposed she could have missed it. She was used to men arriving here with no more than they could carry, so she didn't comment on the apparent meagerness of his possessions.

"The kitchen's in there," she said, gesturing toward a big room visible through an arched passageway. "And the dining room. We tore out a wall to get a table in there big enough for all of us. We usually eat together."

He only nodded. She led him down a narrow hall toward the back of the house, past another door, and to the room at the end. It was small, but it had several large, screened windows that looked out on an expanse of green pasture, making it seem much more spacious. There were inexpensive but effective bamboo shades rolled up at the top of each one.

"It's not much," she began, but he shook his head.

"It's fine. Perfect. I like the windows."

He set the knapsack down on the narrow bed that sat beneath the windows. He looked out at the pasture, noting that the fence, although sturdy enough, badly needed some paint. He could see where repairs had been made and guessed that the money had stretched far enough for essentials, but not for the luxury of paint.

"The bathroom's right down the hall, the first door we passed," she told him. "Feel free. Mine's at the other end of the house."

He looked back over his shoulder at her and nodded. She glanced at her watch.

"Lunch is at eleven. We get started early around here, so we eat early. I'll introduce you to everyone then."

He nodded again.

"Then I'll show you around, if you like."

"I would. Thanks."

She sensed his sudden reserve and backed hastily to the door of the small room. "I'll let you get settled, then."

"Thank you. At lunch you can tell me where you want me to start."

"All right."

"Thanks, Alex."

She didn't see him cross the room after she'd gone, or stand in the doorway as he listened to her footsteps fade away; she was too busy trying to remember when she'd told him her name.

Only when he heard the front door open, then close after her, did Michael close his own door and go back to sit on the edge of the bed. He slipped off the leather jacket and tossed it aside.

Great, he muttered silently. I have most definitely been had. Set up for a fall. Shuffled, shaken, and rolled, coming up in front of a sassy little nose with a sprinkling of freckles, and a pair of green eyes that could convince anybody that the world is really a beautiful place if you look hard enough.

He reached up and tugged the gold chain over his head. For a moment he just sat there, staring at the two tags that dangled from the necklace. One bore only his name and a date in an ornate script, the other a stylized image of a dragon. The boss, he'd decided when he'd first seen it, had a warped sense of humor.

At last his hand wrapped around the two tags. Slowly his eyes closed.

Yes, Michael.

Uh-uh. I want the boss.

Michael—

You heard me. I've had one too many fast ones pulled on me. I want the boss.

We understand you're upset. And we don't blame you. But surely you can understand why we had to do it. You know how crazy things have been, Michael. Michael? Michael, we know you're there. Really, Michael! Such a temper! Oh, all right.

That's better.

His hand tightened around the golden tags.

You rang?

Cute. Just like this little stunt you pulled.

Me?

Save it. It had your fingerprints all over it.

We don't have fingerprints.

Quit tap dancing.

We don't have feet, either. Oh, all right, Michael. You're quite right, it was rather underhanded of me.

I thought you didn't have hands?

I'm glad to see you've regained your sense of humor.

I haven't. I was just checking to see what parts I could imagine slicing off.

Michael, really!

You promised. You guys aren't supposed to break promises.

It wasn't broken. Merely... postponed.

For just a second he let his weariness seep through.

I'm truly sorry, Michael. We have overworked you tremendously, I know. But if you weren't so efficient—

Flattery doesn't become you.

No, I suppose not. It is true, however. But we do realize you're not at your peak right now. So we've arranged a little help. You won't need clearance for the basics. If you need anything extra, just ask.

Is that your subtle way of letting me know there's no way out of this?

Do you really want out, Michael? Now that you've met her?

Now *that* is sneaky! You know I'm a sucker for an innocent against the world.

Yes. That's why you're so good at this. And that, Michael, is not flattery.

He sighed, then accepted it.

All right. But this is it.

I understand.

I'm so tired I nearly blew this already. I've never met a woman less impressed with her own beauty. And you were no help, dumping me in here without a clue.

I know.

After this, I'm through. For a *long* time.

Thank you, Michael.

Right. You have the details for me?

Yes. Whenever you're ready.

One more thing. Is she really as . . . special as she seems?

A pause. Then, *Yes, she is.*

That's what I got from Cougar. She sat up with him for four nights in a row, coaxing him to live.

Yes. She would. And she has done much more for the people she has helped.

I know. I picked it up from Mark. It was a little confused, because he was so angry and also scared for her, but he meant it when he said he'd die for her. Or kill for her.

We must see that he is never confronted with that necessity. He's been hurt too much already. He'll be protected, as well.

All right. I'm ready when you are.

In thirty seconds, then. I wish you good luck, Michael.

You *wish* me? You guys make the luck, remember? You'd damn well better make sure of it.

Michael, your language. I've been meaning to talk to you about that.

But you've been too busy bouncing me around, haven't you? Just send the stuff, will you?

He could have sworn, as he swung his feet up and lay back on the narrow bed, waiting for the flood of communication, that he heard a chuckle.

Two

"And this is Cricket. He's my oldest friend, aren't you, love?" Alex crooned, patting the strong neck.

Michael looked at the flashy black-and-white pinto that had danced eagerly to the fence the moment she whistled. He was marked like a pristine white horse that had had glistening black paint poured over his back; the effect was dramatic.

"Oldest friend? How long have you had him?" he asked, waiting quietly while the horse eyed him warily.

"Since he was a foal. He's almost eleven now."

Michael held out a hand, and the black nose snuffled it as the black-and-white head bobbed. Only then did he lay a hand on the animal's neck. Images, clear and vivid, rippled through the connection. Alex, a fifteen-year-old pixie in fiery red pigtails, so unlike the rich auburn of her hair now, hugging the newborn colt in delight. And a devastated, weeping Alex, huddled in a pile of straw as the tiny animal nudged her urgently. And, later, an older Alex, shadows haunting her eyes, mounting the three-year-old horse for a long, lonely ride into the forested hills.

He knew the meaning behind each of those images now, and he sent the loving animal a quick, reassuring message. *I'm here to help her. I promise. Things will change for her now.*

Alex stared as the paint horse let out an exultant whinny.

"You certainly seem to have a way with animals," she observed, a little warily.

"I give them enough credit," he said simply, "and they know it." With a little help.

She studied him for a moment. "Too bad it doesn't work on people."

He shrugged. It would, if he wanted to use it, but he preferred not to. But he knew what she meant; lunch had been, if not quite unpleasant, strained. He didn't blame the men at the big table. He was the newcomer, the intruder, and above all the one who had shared none of the horrors that had brought them here to this refuge Alex provided.

"You seem awfully calm about it," she said.

He shrugged again. "I didn't expect a rousing welcome, if that's what you mean. I know I'll have to earn a place here with them." He turned around, leaning his back against the fence. "And with you."

One brow, curved into a delicate arc he knew she would deny was beautiful, rose questioningly. His heart twisted inside him. Any other woman would have immediately read some kind of personal invitation into his words; this one was so uncertain of her own appeal that the possibility never occurred to her. He felt something tug, tighten, deep inside, an odd sensation that he couldn't remember ever having felt before. She was so beautiful, he thought, and she didn't see it. He would have to work on that. But for now, he merely went on quietly.

"You still don't trust me completely, either."

He didn't seem upset by it, so Alex didn't bother to deny it. She even admitted to herself that part of her distrust stemmed from his amazing looks. She couldn't quite believe that a man so perfect could possibly be as open and sensitive as he seemed. He should be a snob, arrogant and utterly conceited. He'd no doubt had people—women, she told herself in a determined effort to blunt her unexpected response—cater to him all his life, and it should have shown.

Yet she could find no sign of it. When he looked at her with those glowing blue eyes, she felt odd inside, as if he'd scoured her soul down to its very essence with his gaze. Yet at the same time she felt comforted, as if, just for that moment in time, she could put aside the problems that beset her, as if just for that moment she could rest. And oh, how she would love to rest, just for a while.

"You can trust me, Alex. I'm only here to help. Let me carry some of the burden for a while."

She stared at him, green eyes wide, and he knew he'd once again skated a little too close to the edge with her.

"So tell me, who does what around here?" he asked quickly. "I don't want to compound my problems by stepping on anyone's toes."

It had to be coincidence, Alex thought. Or perhaps she really was such a silly little fool that her every thought showed in her face. She sighed, then set herself to answering him.

"Well, Matt's our fledgling carpenter. He's got the desire and the enthusiasm, but he's a little short on experience. He'd only just begun when he got called up, and he never went back to it. Steven was a medic, so he's our first line of defense when it comes to cuts and bruises. Wheezer works with the animals—"

"Let me guess . . . he's allergic to them? They make him wheeze?"

She nodded. "Dr. Swan gave him some medicine that controls it, but the name had already stuck by then."

"Dr. Swan?" He already knew who the man was, but he wanted to hear her reaction.

"He's the doctor at the clinic in town. And one of the few who doesn't want us all ridden out on a rail."

"Why?"

"He lost his son in Nam. He couldn't help him, so . . ."

Michael nodded. "And you, Alex? Why do you do it?"

She shrugged. "It needs to be done." She continued her discourse briskly. "Now Kenny, he grew up on a small farm in Nebraska. Different kind of country, but the principle's the same, he says. So he directs most of the actual planting and real farm work. Sarah's his wife, and I'd be lost without her. She is, as you probably noticed, a great cook."

He smiled. "Yes."

"Aaron helps me with the paperwork and does his best at haircuts," she went on dryly, tugging at her own thick mop.

He reached out and touched the thick section that tended to flop in front of her eye. "All you need is a little trim here in front. Some bangs, maybe. I like your hair," he added carefully. She couldn't argue with what he liked, could she? "I like the way it lights up in the sun, all red and alive."

"Ol' carrot top, that's me," Alex muttered, trying to shake off the odd feeling his touch gave her.

"Maybe once, when you were younger. But not now, Alex. Your hair looks like all the colors of warmth. Brown, bronze, and a splash of fire."

Alex automatically opened her mouth to protest his compliment but found herself saying instead, "That was . . . rather poetic."

"It's hard to talk of the beauty in the world without sounding that way. Now," he said quickly, "don't go all prickly on me. I just like the color of your hair, all right?"

He drew back his hand, and Alex turned to face the fence, leaning on the top rail for the support she suddenly seemed to need.

"What about Rick?" he asked, as if the interlude had never occurred.

"We don't know much about him. He's only been here three weeks or so. Just moved to the bunkhouse last week. He hasn't talked much, and, as you see, we don't pry. One of the guys who left here last year sent him up from Los Angeles."

"One of your successes?"

"I suppose. He's got a good job now and is trying to put his family back together."

"You're doing a good thing here, Alex."

"Not according to the city fathers," she said, a trace of bitterness in her voice.

"Do you really care what they think?"

"Only because it affects the guys. They know what the people think, that they half expect them to go off on some horrible rampage. If it were me, I'd be half tempted to do it just because I knew they expected it."

"Make it a self-fulfilling prophecy?"

"Something like that," she admitted a little sheepishly. Then the touch of acidity returned. "They see all that crap on television and in the movies, and they think that anybody who was in that stinking war came back a menace to society. I don't blame a lot of guys for giving up and just becoming what everybody thought they were in the first place."

"It was ugly," Michael said softly. "All wars are. But the one they had to fight when they came home was a different kind of ugly. And in many ways worse. In Vietnam, it was their bodies and their spirits that were killed or maimed. Here it was their souls, because this was home, this was the place they'd dreamed of coming back to. It was supposed to be safe."

"And it turned out to be just a different kind of hell."

"Except," Michael said softly, looking around, "for a few small miracles wrought by some very special people." His eyes came back to her face. "You built this for them, Alex. The sanctuary they should have had."

"It's not enough," she whispered.

"You built it, and you've kept it going for eight years. That's a hell of a lot to expect from an eighteen-year-old girl."

Her stunned look told him that he was walking the edge again, told him that only now was she realizing that she had poured out things to him that she rarely told anyone. "How . . . how do you know all this?"

"I just put some bits and pieces together." He changed the subject swiftly. "Where do you want me to start?"

She accepted the switch gratefully. "How good a plumber are you? Can you work miracles?"

His mouth twitched. "Give me a try."

"It'll take one," she said grimly, leading the way back to the house. "These pipes are as old as the house, and it's beginning to show. And replacing them is a long way in the financial future."

"They might just surprise you and hold out a little longer—with some help," he said.

"My luck," she said sourly, "isn't that good."

"Luck," he said with an upward glance, "can change."

"What about this guy, Alex?"

Aaron was looking at her worriedly, glancing out the window to where Michael was tugging chicken wire over the new frame he'd built. He'd done it in one morning, Alex thought in amazement, using the wood from the old coop, most of which she would have sworn was too rotten to be reused. That was why she hadn't asked Matt to try to fix it, knowing they couldn't afford any new lumber. The last of what they owned had gone to repair the fence Cricket had broken down the night they'd had the prowler.

"I mean," Aaron said, "are you sure about him?"

She turned to look at the sandy-haired man whose eyes were blurred behind thick glasses. "As sure as I was about you when you first came here."

He had the grace to blush. "Oops."

"You guys have been pretty hard on him, Aaron. And he's never complained, just takes it and keeps going. And he's accomplished more in a week than we have in a month."

"I guess we have been riding him a bit."

"A bit?"

"Okay, a lot."

"Still think he's nothing but a pretty face?"

Aaron adjusted his glasses, avoiding her gaze. "Been that transparent, has it?"

"Don't feel bad. It was my first reaction too. But now I'm very glad he's here. He managed to fix that leak with that piece of pipe he found God knows where, he found those shingles up in the attic that I didn't even know were there and fixed the roof, not to mention repairing that old ladder of ours so it's usable. He's done a hundred little things none of us have had the time or the talent for, and now he's almost done with the chicken coop.''

''You sure that's . . . all you're glad about?''

''Aaron, don't talk in circles. What are you saying?''

''Just that . . . some of the guys, we were talking. He is a good looking guy, and he *is* about your age. We thought that maybe . . .''

''Maybe what?''

''Well, you know. That you might be glad he was here for other reasons.''

''Other reasons? What are you getting at?''

Aaron looked horribly embarrassed, and his cheeks were red as he took off his glasses and wiped them laboriously on his shirttail.

''You've been here with us a long time, Alex. Since you were just a kid.''

''It's where I wanted to be.''

Her voice was soothing. Aaron had been here since the beginning. He'd been Andrew's best friend ''in country,'' and when he'd shown up one day just before Andrew's death, he'd stayed. At first to help, and then, he later admitted, to get what he needed himself: peace and a sense of purpose.

''We know that. But you're missing out on a life of your own, Alex, stuck out here with a bunch of guys practically old enough to be your father.''

She laughed. ''Matt's the oldest, and he's only forty-eight. That hardly puts any of you in the geriatric category.''

''But you need to see people your own age.''

''Let me worry about that, will you?''

Aaron's eyes flicked to the window again. ''Just be careful, will you? We don't know much about him.''

"Aaron," she said, following the direction of his glance, "what on earth would make you think that a man like him would look twice at someone like me?"

"Don't be so hard on yourself. If you ever took any time for yourself instead of spending it all on us—"

"Relax, Aaron. I'm quite resigned to being a perennial little sister. It doesn't bother me anymore."

But it did, she thought. Or seemed to lately. Why else was she so—what had Michael called it?—prickly about the casual compliments he'd given her? She used to just slough off things like that as the meaningless patter that seemed endemic to the male of the species when confronted with a female, no matter what she looked like. So why was she re-acting this way now? Was she getting restless? Or was it simply because of the source of those compliments?

She smothered a little sigh. Of course it was, she thought as she stared out the window at him. What woman alive could come in contact with a man like Michael Justice and not react?

Although she'd actually seen very little of him since that first day; he'd been up and out at dawn, frequently not finishing whatever chores he'd set for himself until the evening meal.

Meals, she thought ruefully, that were still an ordeal. Instead of the usual good-natured teasing, silence reigned, the only conversation being an occasional gibe at Michael, generally preceded by a derisive, "Hey, pretty boy." Even a seat on one of the long benches at the table was surren-dered to him grudgingly, with barely veiled hostility.

He never reacted, never showed the slightest sign that they were getting to him, while Alex found it all she could do not to get up and rap a couple of stubborn heads to-gether. Only Rick, as usual, stayed silent, and only Mark showed him any kind of politeness, apparently having decided that Alex's acceptance was good enough for him.

She watched him as he nailed down the wire he'd mended and stretched over the frame. He moved so smoothly, his arm coming down in a graceful arc time after time as he swung the hammer. She watched his arm flex beneath the sleeve of his T-shirt, watched the cloth stretch tight as his muscles bunched.

His hair was falling forward over his forehead, and she wondered what it would feel like to brush it back. It would feel like silk, she thought, heavy dark silk. She would brush it back, he would look up at her with those incredible blue eyes, and—

And she would be humiliated out of her mind. He would be embarrassed, and she would slink off and look for a hole to hide in. She could just guess what he would be thinking: All I did was be nice to the girl. She must be really starved for attention. How could she think I would really be interested in someone who looks like a fifteen-year-old tomboy?

Suddenly Michael froze, his arm dropping to his side in midstroke. His head came up, and he looked back over his shoulder. Alex drew back instinctively, even though she knew he couldn't possibly see her from there.

It would serve you right if he could, she scolded herself severely. Wouldn't he just laugh his head off to know the little country girl had been drooling over him?

No, she thought with a sudden certainty she couldn't explain, he wouldn't laugh. He'd said he never would, and she believed him. But he would probably feel sorry for her, and somehow that was much, much worse.

So get yourself together, girl. Just because he happens to be gorgeous and, as Aaron said, closer to your age, is no reason to treat him any differently than any of the other men here. And you'd do well to remember that.

And so, she thought suddenly, would the rest of them. So when the others were gathered around the table that night while Michael was still outside washing up, she found herself trying to make them see it.

"I think," she said casually as she set a plate of biscuits on the table, "that we should all go in and apologize to the whole town at the meeting this month."

"What?"

Seven voices in unison made a powerful noise, she thought wryly. "I just mean that you can't really blame the people for being difficult. I mean, they only know what they see on the surface. What else do they have to judge by?"

"What kind of talk is that? And from you, Alex!" Hurt and indignation were etched on Wheezer's face.

Alex shrugged elaborately. "Well, it's obvious you've all come around to their way of thinking, so I thought now that you're in agreement—"

"Come around to what?" Steve asked angrily, tugging at his thick moustache as he always did when perturbed. "And apologize for what? For being ourselves? For not denying what we are? If they can't see past the surface, it's their problem! And you're the one who taught us that, Alex!"

"Not well enough, apparently."

"What do you mean?" Kenny spoke this time, puzzlement in his voice and hurt in his innocent, farm-boy face.

"Apparently you think it only goes one way. That only you deserve that effort to see past the surface."

"Of course we don't," Matt began protestingly. "We know that—"

"Uh-oh."

Aaron's voice was quiet, but it stopped them all dead.

"Uh-oh what?"

"I think she's got us, boys." His eyes flickered to the porch, where the sound of water at the tap they used for washing up had stopped. "Think about it."

There was, Alex noticed with satisfaction, more than one sheepish look around the table. Her point made, she said no more, just sat down at her place at the head of the table, the place she took at their tacit insistence; whenever she came to sit down, it was the only place left.

There was a moment of silence as Michael came in. Eight pairs of eyes fastened on him, and Alex thought she caught the slightest hint of weariness in those sky blue eyes. She didn't blame him, she thought. He'd been working so hard, and then to have to face this every night... She wondered that he didn't just take his meal and disappear somewhere to eat in peace. Except, she thought, that there wasn't an ounce of quit in him.

She saw his lips tighten for just a second, then saw him let out a short, compressed breath. Then he looked away, tossing the towel he'd used in the laundry basket by the door before he started toward the table. He stopped short, startled, when Kenny slid over on one bench.

"There's room here," he said.

Michael's eyes flicked to Alex, and she had that odd feeling again, as if he could read everything that had happened in the room in her eyes. Slowly he took the proffered seat, eyeing them all a little warily.

"Have a biscuit," Steve said gruffly, holding out the plate. And without a word Matt handed him the glass of ice water he'd just poured and began to pour another for himself.

Michael stared at the glass suspiciously. "Is it laced with anything interesting?"

The sheepish looks reappeared, except for Mark, who, from his seat to Alex's right, guffawed suddenly. All eyes turned to him.

"Don't blame him. Been treating him like they treat us."

"Yes," Aaron said. "Yes, we have. And for that we owe you an apology."

Michael seemed stunned. "I . . . thank you."

"Thank Alex. She made us see it."

His eyes went back to her, searching her face. She blushed and wanted to look away, but she couldn't seem to tear her eyes away from his. After a moment he smiled, as if he'd found what he'd been looking for.

"Thank you," he said softly, and the weariness she'd seen vanished, as if he'd gotten a sudden burst of energy.

Michael settled back as a steady rain of chatter began around the table, a return of what was clearly their normal demeanor. Sarah arrived with a steaming plate of potatoes and pork chops, then took a seat next to her husband.

While Kenny talked about the apple crop and Wheezer sighed over a milking machine they couldn't afford, Michael just sat quietly and savored the unexpected jolt of strength he'd gotten. A small miracle had occurred here, and he'd had absolutely nothing to do with it. It had been Alex who had done it, and with no help other than her own generous heart.

She was indeed as special as she seemed, he thought. That must explain it, this odd, warm feeling he got inside whenever he looked at her. It was a sensation he'd never felt before, and he didn't quite know what to make of it. It unsettled him, and he wasn't used to being unsettled.

"—thanks to Michael."

Alex's voice yanked him back to the present. "I'm sorry. What?"

"I was just saying that you've saved us the money we set aside for the roof and the plumbing. And the lumber for a new coop. We'll actually have something left after I make the payment on the farm this month."

"Oh. Good." He glanced around the table. "I gather everybody kicks in for that?"

"We all have something coming in from the government," Matt said with a grimace, running a hand through thick brown hair flecked with gray. "Deserving veterans that we are."

"We give half of whatever we get to Alex for the payments on the place," Steve explained.

"Oh. I...wish I could help, but—"

"Don't be silly," Alex said quickly. "Didn't I just say that thanks to you we've even got money left? We're just trying to figure out how to spend it. There's not enough for everything, but we thought maybe a new gate—"

"I'm going to fix that tomorrow. It just needs new hinges and a latch that Daisy can't get at. I found some hinges in the toolshed, and I can make the latch."

"I don't remember seeing any hinges in there," Matt said.

"I found 'em in a corner on the floor," Michael answered easily.

"Oh. Well, maybe we can get the stove fixed for Sarah. You know what a pain that thing is, but we haven't been able to afford to have someone come—"

"We don't need to," Sarah interrupted with a smile at Michael. "Michael fixed it this morning. It works fine now. Even that fourth burner that never worked. I think we should get Mark's radio fixed. You know how much he misses listening to his music."

Mark's bearded head came up, and he reached into his jacket pocket and drew out a small portable radio. With a grin he turned a knob and the unmistakable beat of a sixties rock tune filled the room. He grinned as he turned it off.

"Michael," he said simply.

The expressions around the table changed from sheepish to ashamed.

"I feel," Kenny said, "like I've been kicking Lassie."

"Lassie," Michael said composedly, "would have bitten you long ago."

They stared at him, wide-eyed, but when they caught the glint of humor in his eyes, they all burst out laughing. And from that moment on, all enmity was forgotten, and when the friendly heckling began again, he was a victim as much as any of them. Only Rick failed to join in and was heard to mutter, "Still too damned pretty," as he got up to leave. Alex's voice stopped him.

"Rick?"

"What?"

"Your plate?"

He glared at her, but he picked up his dirty dishes and carried them to the kitchen. Michael watched him go, his eyes narrowed. Rick was an angry man, but was he angry enough to be behind the trouble here?

"Teach him manners, if you want," Mark said to Alex, his eyes narrowing as he watched the man go.

"No. Not yet, anyway. We give everybody a month to settle in, remember?" Her eyes flicked to Michael, and she was thinking of how they'd crammed all the testing, the "feeling out" they usually did with a newcomer into such a short period of time. "Sometimes we even give it to them in a week."

Michael grinned at her, and Alex congratulated herself for not showing what that flashing dimple did to her silly insides. The rest of them laughed, still a little abashed, and she knew that meals would be back to normal now. For everyone, that was, but her. Now she had nothing left to worry about except her own stupid reactions to his presence.

"We still haven't decided about the money," she said hastily.

"Maybe we should just save it," Sarah said. "For the next thing that falls apart."

"Maybe we should pay Michael," Steve said seriously.

"That's an idea!" Alex said with enthusiasm, and everyone at the table chimed in in agreement.

"Fine," Michael said. "Consider it my contribution to the cause, then."

"But that puts us right back to square one," Aaron said. "Besides, you've more than earned it. And all of us have something left after we kick in our share, so you should, too."

"Something to spend any way I want, you mean?"

They nodded.

"Okay. Then I want to spend it to send Alex on a vacation."

"What?" It was a startled yelp as she stared at him.

"I know you don't know anything about them," Michael said with mock innocence, "but that's when you go away and let other people take care of you for a change. Relax, go to a movie, have a nice dinner out, room service for breakfast, have your hair done, go shopping—"

"I can't do that!"

"I think it's a great idea," Sarah enthused.

"Me too," Steve agreed. "To some place away from here, where you can just have a good time and not worry."

"But we need that money—"

"We agreed to give it to Michael, remember?" Wheezer said.

"And I told you how I'm going to spend it."

"Doesn't look like you have much choice," Aaron put in with a grin. "There's enough left for a nice weekend in Eugene, or maybe even Portland. What do you say? A movie or a play, a little champagne brunch on Sunday morning?"

"I . . . I can't!"

"Just because you never have?" Matt said. "You work and work, Alex, right alongside us. But at least we take some time off on the weekends. For you, that's just when you start wrestling with the rest of our problems. The bills, the paperwork, fighting with the government when they mess up our checks, deciding what gets done now and what gets put off. You need a break, kid."

"I don't mind. And that's why I can't possibly—"

"Yes, you can." Kenny interrupted. "Matt's right. You do all the things we don't want to do, don't want to bother with. You just do them and do them and never complain. And we—" he looked around at the others "—we never thank you enough."

"Work too damn hard," Mark put in gruffly.

"And most of all," Sarah added softly, "you face those awful people, the ones who hate us and want us to leave. And we let you."

"It's just . . . easier for me. I know them. I can handle them."

"Why?"

She looked startled by Michael's quiet question.

"I . . . because they know me, too, I guess. And they knew my parents. It makes it a little harder for them to be . . . nasty."

"I meant, why do you do it?"

"Why . . . ?"

"Why do you do it at all? Why do you push yourself so hard? It sure isn't for the money, is it?"

"Of course not."

"It's because it makes you feel good, isn't it? Makes you feel like you're contributing, helping?"

"I suppose so—"

"Then quit being so selfish."

She heard the startled movements of the others, but they didn't register as she gaped at him. "What?"

"You think you're the only one who likes feeling good? You want to keep it all to yourself? Let somebody else feel good for a change. Let somebody else do something for you and feel good about it."

Steve laughed suddenly. "All right! Got you, Alex!"

She looked around at all the faces that were grinning at her from around the table. She opened her mouth to speak but couldn't think of a thing to say.

"Nice work, Mike," Matt put in, any lingering doubts about this newcomer to their midst erased now.

"I can't," Alex murmured, a little stunned at how things had been turned around on her. "There's too much to do."

"You can, moppet," Steve said. "We'll manage."

"But I'd feel so...guilty!"

"Just think how guilty you'll feel if you disappoint us," Aaron said, winking at Michael in thanks for finding the only argument that would work with her.

"But..."

"Let somebody do something for you for a change," Michael said softly.

Alex turned her head to look at him. The glowing warmth of his eyes seemed to reach out and envelop her, coaxing her, cajoling her.

"I'll...think about it."

"Don't think. Just do it. This weekend."

"Michael, I can't."

"You pack, you get in the truck, you go. Easy."

"But I can't. My truck needs—"

"A new rotor. Plugs. Valves adjusted. I know. I did it yesterday."

She stared at him. "When did you have ti—"

"It didn't take long. That's your last excuse, Alex."

She couldn't fight him anymore. The power of those glowing blue eyes was too much, the strength in them so much more than hers. As if he were willing her to do it, she slowly nodded.

Later, as she lay in bed, she wondered how it had all happened, how she had managed to let herself get maneuvered into this. The image of all of them, smiling at her from around the table, told her how true Michael's words had been; how could she deny them the pleasure this simple thing seemed to give them?

It was difficult for her; taking was not something she was used to. But they were so intent on it, so determined to carry out this idea Michael had come up with, that she didn't have the heart to say no. And deep inside her, a little kernel of anticipation began to grow.

Two days, free of the burdens that were sometimes so hard, even when carried willingly. Two days out of eight years, that wasn't so much, was it? Two days, just for herself? To be at no one's beck and call, to do as she pleased, relieved of the constant demands on her time and energy?

"Thank you, Michael," she whispered into the darkness, wondering how he'd known how badly she needed this when she hadn't even known it herself. That he'd known and had acted to fulfill that need touched her deeply. And gave rise to thoughts she didn't dare let form, didn't dare dwell upon.

She snuggled into her pillow, sleep beginning to creep in despite the image that lingered in her mind, an image of eyes so searingly blue it was like looking at the sky on a perfect summer day. Two whole days, she thought drowsily. She could—

The sharp jangle of the phone jarred her awake, and she reached for the receiver automatically, before she stopped to think.

"Hello?"

"You haven't learned your lesson yet, have you, bitch? Well, you will. And you'll be sorry you didn't get out when you had the chance. Before someone got hurt."

Three

Michael came awake abruptly, sitting bolt upright in the narrow bed. Fear rippled over him in waves, a fear barely touched with anger. He let his senses stretch, much as a wolf scenting the breeze, and in a moment he had it.

"Alex."

It came out on a harsh breath, and he rolled out of bed and came to his feet in one smooth motion. He grabbed his jeans and yanked them on, then ran barefoot down the hall to the room he'd never seen but knew was hers.

She was sitting up in the big four-poster bed, her hand cramped tightly around the telephone receiver. She was shaking, staring at the instrument as if she'd mistakenly grabbed a snake and now didn't dare let go for fear of being bitten.

"Alex."

He was across the room in one long stride. He sat on the edge of the bed and pried the phone from her fingers. He flipped on the bedside light, its dim bulb casting only a faint glow onto the bed.

"I . . . thought it . . . was over. . . ."

Her teeth were chattering, much more than the slight chill of the room warranted. He felt an odd tightness inside at the sight of her in the big bed, a reaction he didn't understand at all. He pushed it aside; he had to concentrate on the fear that was making her shiver. He hung up the phone and turned back to her.

"What, Alex? You thought what was over?"

"I thought he'd . . . given up. He hadn't called. Not for weeks."

"Who?"

"I don't know. He disguises his voice."

"Alex, what did he say? Was it an obscene call?"

He knew even as he asked it that he was wrong; an obscene caller might upset her, but it wouldn't cause the surge of fear that had reached him. Alex Logan was made of sterner stuff than that.

"Obscene?" She gave a harsh little laugh. "Parts of it, I guess. When he talks about . . . what he imagines I do out here, with seven men."

Michael reached for the gold tags that lay against his chest. Nothing. Either they didn't know, or he was on his own. He reached for her hands.

It hit him in a rush the instant he touched her, the horror of it, and his own anger rose up to meet it. It was all there, the crude suggestions, the lurid imaginings, whispered in an avid, almost eager voice. It was muffled, as if he were hearing it over the phone himself. ". . . all at once, or do you take them on one at a time, slut?"

Her hands were shaking beneath his, and he tightened his hold on her. And then the fear was there, the threat, and he knew why she was so frightened.

"It's more than that, isn't it?" he whispered. "He made some threats, didn't he?"

He felt a tremor ripple through her slender body, then felt her draw on an inner strength whose depth amazed him.

"I'm sorry, Michael. This isn't your problem."

"I'm making it mine. This isn't the first time, is it?"

She avoided his eyes.

"Alex?"

It was uncanny, Alex thought, the way she could feel his eyes on her. She lifted her head to look at him, because she seemed to have no choice.

"Trust me, Alex. I want to help."

She felt that warmth, that undeniable feeling of safety, of gentle protectiveness, once more. Trust him? Of course she trusted him. How could she not?

"Has it always been the same voice?"

She nodded slowly.

"But this call was different?"

"Yes." She shuddered, then steadied herself. "Before it was just...the filth. And saying I'd be sorry if I didn't close down the refuge." She laughed bitterly. "Of course, that's not what he called it. He has his own pet name for us. And for me. Especially for me." She shivered, her glance skipping to the phone again, then away. "It feels...ugly. Vicious. So much hate..."

Michael curled his fingers around hers, sending her reassurance, using the full force of his mind to begin to build the shell of protection around her. When he felt her begin to respond, he spoke again.

"This call, it was different?" he prodded gently.

"This time..." She suppressed a shiver. "This time he said someone would get hurt."

He saw the tremor overtake her again and knew this was going to take more. He swung his feet up and pulled her into his arms. He leaned back against the four-poster's headboard and gently made her relax her tense body against him. She didn't fight him, a measure, he was sure, of her distress.

Something odd was happening, he thought. He wasn't supposed to feel the protection like this. It was supposed to be spun around her, a web of warm support. Yet he was feeling it, too, the succor, the warmth. A warmth that was threatening to become heat where she lay against him. His brows furrowed, puzzlement filling his eyes for a moment. This was truly peculiar, he thought, moving one hand to her chin to gently tilt back her head without really knowing why he did it.

Michael suddenly forgot that he wasn't supposed to get angry. He looked into Alex's wide, frightened green eyes and was tempted, very tempted, to plow a shortcut through this whole mess. Maybe he could get to whoever was behind this before the boss caught on.

Whoa, he thought suddenly. He stared at the top of her head as she at last let it rest on his shoulder. In all the time he'd been doing this, never once had he been tempted to violate the strict and often inexplicable rules that had been set down. Yet something about this woman . . .

"If you want to leave," she said with a little sigh, "I understand. I know you didn't count on this kind of trouble."

He realized she had misinterpreted his silence and the intensity of his gaze.

"An anonymous threat over the phone from some coward? You're not getting rid of me that easily."

"It's not . . . just that." She lifted her head. "We've had some other things happen. Little things, mostly. Fences knocked down, phone line cut, that kind of thing."

"'Mostly?'"

She lowered her eyes. "We had a prowler one night, about three weeks ago."

Three weeks. About when Rick had shown up. Coincidence?

"Did you see him?"

"No. He..." She stopped, and he felt another ripple of emotion go through her. He tightened his arms around her and then he had it: anger. A good, healthy spurt of anger. Atta girl, he thought. After a moment, she went on.

"He went after Cricket. I heard him scream, that wild sound a stallion makes when he's ready to fight. I knew something had to be out there, but before I could get outside, I heard the fence go, and Cricket was out."

"You went outside alone?"

She looked puzzled. "He was trying to hurt my horse."

Of course she'd gone outside alone, idiot. What else would Alex Logan do when one of her own was threatened?

"Besides," she said, "I took Cougar with me. He ran him off. He would have had him, but he had a truck stashed up the road, and he got to it before Cougar could get to him. I would have gone after him, but I had to get Cricket before he got hurt." She grimaced. "I found the rocks he'd thrown at Cricket later."

"Where were the others? Why were you alone?"

"I wasn't. Sarah was here."

"Where?"

"In the house. She and Kenny have a room in the bunkhouse, but she doesn't like to be alone when the guys leave."

"Leave?"

"Go up the hill." She saw his look and explained. "It's something Aaron came up with. A kind of therapy."

"Therapy?"

"When Aaron decided to stay here and help me, he went to school. He's a licensed therapist now. Anyway, they go up into the woods. They make a camp in some place they've never been to, then move on the next night and the next. It sort of simulates the situations they were in in Vietnam. Aaron says it makes it easier for them to talk."

"They leave you alone?"

"It's perfectly safe—"

She broke off at his look. "Okay, so it wasn't, that time. But he hasn't been back."

"Until tonight?" His eyes flicked to the phone.

"It may not even be the same person. Lord knows enough people don't want us here. Besides, I sort of thought that anyone who gets his thrills over the phone wouldn't have the nerve to show up in person."

"He sounds," Michael said dryly, "like exactly the kind of person who would chuck rocks at a horse."

Her eyes widened. "I . . . hadn't thought of that."

No, you wouldn't, Michael thought. You don't know anything about that kind of sick behavior. You're good and clean and honest, and so damn gutsy it makes me want to build a fortress around you to protect you from your own courage.

Hold it there, Justice, he thought. This isn't personal, remember? It never is. You're here to do a job, so get back to it.

"Did you tell anyone about it, when they got back?"

She lowered her eyes.

"That's what I thought. Have you told anyone about the calls?"

"I . . . they would only worry."

"Of course they would. They love you. But they should know, Alex."

"They have enough to think about, just trying to keep themselves together."

"So you carry the burden alone."

"Some of them spent years on the street before they came here, Michael. They had to deal with too much of this kind of thing out there. They came here for peace and a chance to heal. They need that chance."

He hugged her tightly, sending her as much serenity and security as he could. He'd never had to concentrate so hard before, but then, he'd never had this odd, inexplicable heat to deal with before, either.

"You're an amazing woman, Alex Logan. You're right, they need that chance. They deserve it. But think about something for me, will you? Think about the possibility that maybe, just maybe, they might need to be needed even more?"

She went very still. He could almost feel her thinking, feel her considering it.

"You can't protect them from the world, Alex. They're grown men, not children."

She gave a shuddering little sigh. "You're right. I have been, haven't I?"

"You were only trying to help."

"But I was treating them the same way I hate to be treated. Like a child." Her eyes flicked to the quiet telephone. "Although at the moment, that's what I feel like. Maybe they're right. Maybe I am just a silly little—"

"There's not a person here who would ever think of you as a 'silly little' anything," Michael said swiftly, positively. "Aaron has been here since the beginning, and Mark almost that long. You were only eighteen then, Alex. It's only natural that they still think of you that way. And the others take their lead from them, or else they knew of you before they ever got here, as Andrew's little sister."

"I suppose," she sighed.

It never occurred to her to wonder how he had become so well informed when these men were some of the most reticent in the world. They had accepted him now, she knew, and were probably much less wary of talking around him.

"And don't forget something else. Part of the reason they think of you as so young is that they feel so old themselves."

She looked at him. "I hadn't thought of it that way." She gave an embarrassed little laugh. "You'd think I'd be used to it by now. Kid sister to the world, that's me. Or kid brother. At least, it seems they think that, sometimes."

"No man with eyes is ever going to think that, Alex. You may wrap it like a boy, but the package is most definitely female. Very nicely female."

Alex flushed, wishing she could come up with some quick, witty remark. But if she tried, she admitted with rueful self-knowledge, she would say something utterly honest and utterly stupid. Like asking if *he* thought she was "nicely female." So for one of the few times in her life, she wisely decided to remain silent.

But she quickly found that remaining silent had its price. She became all too aware that they were on her bed, that her head was resting on his shoulder. His bare shoulder. He had on only his worn, soft jeans, and her hand was resting smack in the middle of his broad, muscled—naked—chest.

His skin, smooth and free of any hair to interfere with her sense of touch, felt like hot silk stretched taut over hard muscle. The heat of him seemed to infuse her, to make her feel oddly slack, so that she sagged against him. Involuntarily her fingers flexed, curling as the tips slid over that taut flesh.

She wondered what that sleek, smooth skin would feel like if she stroked it, if she let her hand slip down to his flat, hard stomach. She wondered what it would feel like to tangle her fingers in the scattering of hair that began at his navel. She wondered how his skin would feel beneath her lips if she leaned forward to kiss—

Oh, Lord, she thought, immensely grateful that he couldn't see her face. Although, she added in silent humiliation, he probably couldn't help but feel the heat from her flaming cheeks; she could only hope that he wouldn't guess the reason. She couldn't give him time to guess the reason, she thought hastily.

Her gaze fell on the rectangular tags that lay just above her fingertips. Thankful for the distraction, she moved to touch them, not surprised to find them warm from his body. Very warm. Well, not warm, exactly. And they didn't feel like the inflexible, hard metal she'd expected, either. In fact, she couldn't quite describe what they felt like.

"What are these?" she asked, lifting her head to look more closely, trying to ignore their enviable position in the center of his chest. She thought she felt him tense slightly, but he answered easily enough.

"A...family heirloom, sort of."

She lifted the golden tags, seeing that they were indeed the size and shape of dog tags. She tilted one to look at it, but it was hard to read the ornate script in the faint light.

"What does it say?"

"Just my name. And...birthday."

She shifted it closer to the light. Now that she knew, she could make out the sweeping swirls of letters and numbers. Numbers. She raised her eyes to his.

"Michael, this says September 29, 1850."

"There's been a Michael Justice around for a long time."

"And I suppose they've all been born on September twenty-ninth?"

"Of course." His tone was teasing, but there was something oddly serious in his eyes that made her wonder.

"Including you?" she asked.

He shrugged, his muscles flexing beneath her hand. "It's St. Michael's day. When else?"

"Oh. That's why you're Michael?"

"Sure. One day later and I would have been Sam."

She smiled. "But why dog tags?"

"Michael was the leader of the celestial armies, wasn't he?"

"Ouch." She gave a pained chuckle. "Someone has a warped sense of humor."

Michael laughed. My sentiments exactly, he thought.

"But they didn't have dog tags back then, did they?"

Oops. "I don't know. These were just . . . given to me."

"So this Michael Justice was the first one?"

"As far as I know."

"It must be nice, to know where you came from so far back. I don't know—what's this?"

She was holding up the second tag, angling it toward the light as she had the first.

"Why, it's a dragon," she said, answering her own question. She looked at him again. "Let me guess . . . Michael fought one, I suppose?"

"So the legend goes."

"Too bad there are none left," she said whimsically. "You're reduced to minor miracles."

She knew he had tensed this time. "What do you mean?"

"Just look at what you've done around here in only a week. I thought it would take a miracle to get everything done that needed doing, but I was wrong. It just took you."

She felt him relax. "You just need an extra pair of hands. And we're not done yet."

"It won't take long, at the rate you're going. It seems like you manage to do at least three things at once."

He shrugged again and gave her a teasing grin. "What can I do? Like you said, there aren't any dragons left to slay."

"If there were..." she began, but trailed off as she realized she'd been about to make one of her foolishly honest remarks.

"Alex?"

"I was just going to say," she said, her color high again, "that you were named appropriately."

He laughed. "Hardly. Michael was an archangel. I don't even work for the same guys. Couldn't. Angelic I'm not."

She took it as he'd meant her to, as a joke. "Just borrowed the name, huh?"

"Yep. Doesn't fit at all. Not like yours."

"Mine?" She looked startled.

"Yes. Didn't you know?"

"Know what?"

"Alexandra is the feminine form of Alexander, isn't it? It means 'defender of men.'"

"I didn't know." Nor, she thought, did she know how he'd found out her full name; she never used it.

"Now you do. And it fits."

She made a face. "Hardly. I'm not brave enough for that."

"You do an impossible job here, you're being terrorized by some crazy idiot and never say a word to anyone or ask for any help, and you don't think you're brave?"

She grimaced. "He was trying to scare me, and he succeeded admirably. I wouldn't call that particularly brave."

"But you kept going."

"I had to. Things had to be done. I couldn't let everybody down just because I was scared."

"Alex, Alex," he murmured, hugging her, "what do you think courage is?"

"It's not cowering over a couple of phone calls," she said sourly.

"No. It's being scared to death and saddling up anyway."

She blinked at him. "Did you just make that up?"

He grinned. "No. I think it was John Wayne." He was suddenly serious. "But he was right, Alex. Anyone who says he's never been scared is a liar, or a fool. And the ones who keep going in spite of it are the heroes."

Alex gave a shaky little sigh; what he'd said made sense, but she could hardly take the thought of herself as some kind of hero seriously.

"You make everything seem so...clear. You make me look at things in ways I never thought of before."

"That's what friends are for."

Friends. Was he? It certainly felt like it. Perhaps Aaron had been right; perhaps she was hungrier than she had realized for someone her own age.

"I didn't realize how much I needed a friend."

"You've been working too hard. For far too long."

"I had to," she said again. "For Andrew."

"Your brother?"

She nodded, the movement rubbing her cheek against his chest. Heat rippled out from beneath that small patch of skin touching skin. For a moment Michael found it hard to breathe. What was happening to him? Confused, he groped for what he'd been about to say. "Tell me about him," he urged her.

"I loved him," she said simply. "He was fourteen years older than me, but I think that made us closer. My earliest memories are of him playing with me, pulling me around in a wagon, and riding me in front of him on his horse."

"Good memories."

"Yes. There are plenty of those. I try to concentrate on them instead of the others. I was six when he went to Vietnam, and I was crushed. He was my adored big brother who spoiled me rotten, and I missed him terribly. I must have driven my poor parents crazy."

"They waited a long time before having another child," Michael said, carefully not making it a question; she was opening up to him, and he didn't want to force it.

"They didn't think they could. My mother had Andrew when she was nineteen, and then she just couldn't get pregnant again. She was heartbroken. She'd wanted a houseful of kids. When she found out I was on the way, she was ecstatic."

Michael smiled. "There's no joy in the world like that of a child coming to those who want it so badly."

Alex stared at him, the beauty in his simple words catching her off guard. Sometimes, she thought, when those blue eyes are so alive and glowing, he seems so...so young and old at the same time, so wise and yet so innocent....

She realized she was staring again and made herself go on. "Andrew went through a rough period when he found out. He'd been the only child for fourteen years, and then suddenly there was all this chaos about a baby he of course thought his mother was much too old to be having."

"But he took one look at you and fell for you like a ton of bricks."

Alex stared at him. "That's what my mother always said. How did you know?"

"Who wouldn't?"

She blushed, telling herself sternly that he was only teasing. "Anyway, I was devastated when he left. I used to live for his letters, although I don't think I quite understood how far away he was, or why he was there. But I'll never forget the day two years later when my parents got the telegram saying he was missing.''

She shuddered at the memory. He held her tighter.

''We were so happy when he was found alive. We didn't care about anything else. Even when he came home in a wheelchair. He was alive. That was all that really mattered.''

''But Andrew cared.''

She sighed. ''Yes. He hated being in that chair. He'd always been so active. He tried to hide it, especially from Mom and Dad, but—''

''But not from you.''

''He had to have somebody to talk to, and I was there. Dad was working so hard here, and Mom had to go back to work in town, too, because the bills were so high and the government didn't pay for everything they wanted him to have. Andrew knew it was because of him, and he felt awful about it.''

''How awful?'' he asked softly, sending her another wave of reassurance.

''Very. I was only ten when he came home, but I remember gradually getting more and more scared for him. I was afraid to leave him alone, afraid he wouldn't be there when I came back. I didn't realize then, only later, looking back, that I must have sensed what he was thinking.''

''About suicide?''

She nodded, glad this time for his perception. ''Dr. Swan tried to get him to go for help, but he wouldn't. He just kept getting more and more depressed. He just sat for hours, in the room you're in....''

So that was what he'd sensed, Michael thought. He'd felt it that first night, the echoes of pain and surrender that seemed to have soaked into the walls.

"One day I found him with one of Dad's guns. He was just sitting there, looking at it, touching it, but it scared me so badly... I ran in and grabbed it from him. It was loaded, and it could have gone off, and I think that scared him, that I might have been hurt. He never did it again."

Courage, he thought again. When it came to the ones she loved, Alex Logan would never come up short. She would have made a hell of a pioneer, he mused, thinking of the hardy men and women of that time. Then her voice jerked him out of his contemplation.

"Then, when I was about thirteen, he changed. He got the idea of a place, a place for guys who didn't get even the attention he got, because they weren't visibly hurt. A place to live away from the world that hated them—it was so much worse then—to be with others who understood, until they could survive back in the world."

"A dream can do a lot to keep a man going."

"It did," she said softly. "He started thinking of the future again, of what he wanted to do, where he would find the land, how to make it self-sufficient, so that when they dealt with the world it would be by choice, not necessity. He..." She swallowed tightly. "He always talked about how horrible it was to have the power of choice taken away. Theirs had been taken away when they were drafted and never given back."

"What happened?"

He knew, had known since that first day, but her need for the release of talk was strong, and he wouldn't deny her.

"He was doing so well, planning, designing—it's because of all his work that we've survived at all. But then . . . our parents were killed in an accident. It took the heart right out of Andrew. Oh, he held on for a couple of years, for my sake, I think. He didn't want to leave me alone. But he got gradually worse. Finally Dr. Swan had to put him in the hospital. It . . . didn't take long after that.''

There was so much more to it than those simple words, Michael knew. He knew about the horror of a fifteen-year-old child having to identify the bodies of her parents because there was no wheelchair ramp at the small morgue. He knew about her struggle to hold on to the farm that had been her home, trying to work a job to supplement the small insurance policy, finish school, run the farm, and take care of Andrew all at the same time. He knew about a seventeen-year-old girl growing up long before her time as she watched her beloved brother deteriorate before her eyes, crying out to her to help him end the pain.

"So you built his dream for him,'' Michael whispered as he held her close, feeling her exhaustion, willing her to rest. "You built it, and you made it work. He would be so proud of you, Alex.''

"I hope so,'' she murmured. "He wanted it so much, once.'' She didn't understand why her eyes were suddenly so heavy; she only knew that the warm lassitude that was stealing over her was delicious, and very welcome.

"He would be,'' Michael repeated quietly. "Just like all of us. You've done so much for everyone you've helped here.''

He changed the pitch and cadence of his voice to lull, to soothe, feeling her beginning to slip gently into sleep as he went on.

"So you've earned a rest, darlin'. You've done the job, and it's past time for you to stop and realize you're a woman now, and a beautiful one at that. No more thinking you're just a scrawny little tomboy, Lex.''

Yes, Andrew.

Alex thought it hazily as the warm, pleasant fog closed in around her. He seemed so close, his dear voice so real as he talked to her just as he always had, the drawl he always put on for her as thick as ever. She wanted to ask, but she was so sleepy she could only think the words: Are you truly proud, Andrew?

The answer came back, clear and strong and certain, in the voice she loved and remembered so well. "Very proud, Lexie-girl."

The old, familiar nickname, used by no one but her beloved brother, echoed sweetly in her ears. And with a little sigh of contentment she slid into a deep, dreamless sleep.

Michael held her for a long time, listening to her quiet breathing as he studied her finely drawn features: the pert nose with its faint scattering of freckles; the delicate line of her jaw; the twin sweeps of her thick, lowered lashes. He saw weariness in the slight shadow beneath those lashes and determination in the set tilt of her little chin. She tugged at him in a way he'd never known before.

He held her until he realized, with a little jolt of shock, that he was doing it more for himself than for her. And that he was shockingly aware of the fullness of her breasts pressed against him through the thin cloth of the long, worn T-shirt she slept in. And that the heat that had been merely puzzling before was rapidly becoming uncomfortable, making him want to do something to ease it. Making him want to touch, to caress . . .

Stunned, he carefully slipped out of the bed, tucking the covers around her. His mind was racing. What the hell was this? This wasn't supposed to happen. It never did, never had. Instinctively his hand went to the tags. Nothing. What was going on? Had they gone to sleep on him?

And then, just as he was about to send out a bellow that would rattle all their cages—or whatever they lived in—he stopped. He wasn't sure what he wanted to ask, or even *if* he did. And he was even less certain that he wanted an answer. He let the tags fall back on his chest. He stood there for a long time, looking at the slender form curled up in the big bed.

Only the creak of the back door being nudged open and the distinctive sound of Cougar's toenails clicking along the floor as he came back from his nightly rounds brought him out of it. And only when he moved his hand to tickle the big dog's ears did he realize that that hand had been pressed against the spot on his chest where her hand had rested.

"Watch her," he whispered to Cougar, then whirled and strode hastily out of the room. And while he had sent Alex into the peaceful slumber she so desperately needed, he was unable to help himself and lay awake long into the night.

Four

"I can't go, either," Kenny said casually, running a hand through his thinning blond hair. "I have to get to work if we're going to get a third cutting out of that alfalfa."

"I don't need—"

"And I've got a huge stack of mending to do," Sarah said blithely. "So I can't go."

"If you'd just—"

"I have to see to that cut of Daisy's," Wheezer put in. "I—"

"And I'm going to finish the barn door, now that Mike showed me how," Matt said swiftly.

"Guess it's up to you, Mike," Aaron said cheerfully.

"I keep telling you that I don't need—"

Steve cut Alex off easily. "You'll pick up Wheezer's medicine, won't you?"

"Of course. And I'm quite capable of carrying a bottle of pills without help, thank you."

"Remember, you promised never to go into town without at least taking Cougar with you," Steve reminded her. "And he's off with Mark somewhere." He turned innocently to Michael. "You don't mind, do you, Mike?"

Michael knew what they were up to, and it made him smile inwardly. It also made him nervous, but he wasn't quite ready to admit that yet, even to himself.

"Mind standing in for Cougar? Of course not."

Alex blushed. "You don't have to, really. I'll be fine. I'm just going into Riverglen, not Beirut."

"Doesn't seem much different, sometimes," Matt grumbled.

"I don't mind," Michael assured her. "In fact, I'd like to go. I haven't been into town yet."

Alex surrendered then, but grudgingly. She had a feeling they were all up to something, with her and Michael as the pawns in their little game.

"I'm sorry," she said as she steered the truck through the gate. "This really isn't necessary, but they just—"

"Worry about you. Like you do about them."

She sighed. "I know. But it's more than that. I think they maneuvered this whole thing."

"I know."

She glanced at him, startled. "You do?"

"It was a little . . . obvious."

"Oh." Her cheeks flamed.

"Don't be embarrassed, Alex. They care about you, and they feel guilty that you don't spend any time with people your own age."

"Like you?" She was watching the empty road as if it were a busy interstate.

"That seems to be what they've decided," he said carefully.

"I'm sorry."

"Don't be. I'm flattered."

She stared at him then. "Why? You could have anybody!"

His mouth twisted wryly. "Not exactly," he muttered under his breath before he answered her. "You're very precious to them, Alex. I'm flattered that they would trust me with you."

"Oh."

Her eyes went back to the road, and he could feel her withdrawal. He'd hurt her, he thought. Involuntarily his hand came up to reach for her, but a sudden memory of that growing, surging heat he'd felt while holding her stopped him. I'm sorry, Alex, he told her silently. I wish... Hell, I don't know what I wish anymore.

"The truck is really running well," she said in a rush, anxious to fill the gap. "Thank you."

"You're welcome. On a full tank, you should be able to make it to Portland and back without stopping for gas."

That earned him another look. "That's almost three hundred and fifty miles."

"Yes."

"Michael, this truck never went three hundred and fifty miles on a tank of gas in its life."

He shrugged. "I made some adjustments. I think it'll do it now."

She looked doubtful, but Michael noticed that she didn't quibble about whether or not she was going. He smiled inwardly; she was going to enjoy herself more than she realized. He turned to look out at the lovely, green Oregon countryside.

Their time in the little town was neither as bad as he'd feared nor as good as he'd hoped. He saw the looks she got, the cool greetings from those who didn't avoid her altogether, and there were a few nasty grumblings as they passed, but most of the people seemed merely wary, watchful rather than antagonistic, unfriendly rather than malevolent. And the majority of raised eyebrows seemed directed at him rather than her, and he could almost feel them assessing him, trying to figure out how he fit into the image they had of her and what she was doing at the refuge.

They weren't sure, he realized. His hopes rose; as long as their minds weren't set, they could be changed. He began to turn over possibilities in his mind as they walked down the small street.

Alex stopped at the little post office, taking the stack of mail the woman behind the counter handed her with a smile. "Thanks, Lucy."

"You're welcome, dear. How are you?"

Here, at least, was a friendly face, Michael thought, studying the pleasant looking, plump woman in the flowered dress.

"Fine, thanks." Alex introduced Michael, explaining that he would be there for a while.

"Welcome, Michael. I'm Lucy Morgan, town clerk, notary, postmistress, and general gofer." She eyed him curiously, but with none of the speculation or avidness others had. "Will you be expecting any mail?"

"No."

Somehow the single syllable sounded very forlorn, and Michael shifted uncomfortably. He hadn't meant it to sound that way and certainly couldn't be feeling that way. He'd always been alone; he was used to it, and it didn't bother him. Did it?

"—so sorry about what Frank said to you the other day."

The distress in the woman's tone brought Michael out of his musings.

"It's not your fault," Alex said with a little sigh. "I know he doesn't like the idea of the refuge."

"He just believes all those horrible things you hear, you know, about that traumatic stress thing, and people like that going on crazy shooting sprees."

"I know, Lucy. And I can't say it doesn't happen."

"But I remember your brother, Alex, and that sweet Gary Swan, God rest them both. If things had been different, it could have been them out there with you. They would never hurt a soul."

"No, they wouldn't. And neither would the men who are there now. They're just trying to get over a horrible experience they were never allowed to deal with before."

"That's what I try to tell Frank, but you know my husband. He's so stubborn."

"Keep trying, Lucy. He might come around."

"I will. But please believe me, he isn't behind that trouble you're having with the council. He may not like what you're doing, but he wouldn't interfere."

"I know." Alex gathered up the mail. "We have to stop by Dr. Swan's, so we'd better go. Thanks, Lucy."

"What," Michael asked when they were outside and heading for the small grocery store, "did her husband say to you?"

Alex shrugged. "Just the usual. He admits they need a place to go, but he doesn't want it in his backyard."

"That's all?"

Alex looked up at him. "He's not the caller, if that's what you mean. He's stubborn and set in his ways, but there's not a vicious bone in Frank Morgan's body."

Michael shrugged. "Just checking. What did she mean about the town council?"

"Somebody complained, said we should be closed down because we're in an area that's not zoned for what we do."

"What you do is unique. How could there be a zone for it?"

"Exactly." She sighed. "We're going to fight it at the town meeting this month, but I don't know what's going to happen. Mayor Barnum isn't overly fond of us, either."

"Don't worry," he reassured her, his mind racing as he wondered who was behind this attack, and whether it was the same person who was making the calls. "It'll be all right, Lex."

She stopped dead, staring at him. "Why did you call me that?"

Oops, Michael thought. You're getting sloppy here. Or you're just thinking too much about her and not enough about what you're doing. "I . . . heard one of the guys say it. But if you don't like it, I won't—"

"No, I . . . it's just that Andrew used to call me that."

"Oh. Sorry. I didn't realize it was . . . reserved."

"No," she said again, shyly, her cheeks flaming. "I don't mind if you use it."

Had there been an emphasis on that "you?" Maybe, he thought. Even if there was, that's no reason for you to go all mushy inside, he lectured himself. Lord, he was having a hard time with this job. He couldn't seem to pay attention to anything when she turned those green eyes on him. He tightened his jaw, determined to get back in the old, familiar, safe groove. Disquiet flickered through him as he wondered why he'd used the word "safe," but he smothered it as they reached their destination.

He held the door of the small grocery open for her, then wandered around as she gathered her purchases. He thought the woman at the checkout counter watched them a bit too closely, but he was more concerned about a group of boys, no more than thirteen or fourteen years old, who were clustered in one corner.

They eyed Alex avidly and began to have a lively, heated discussion among themselves. Michael saw her react as some of their whispered phrases reached her, saw her cheeks pinken as she handed the thin, middle-aged woman her money.

The woman took it as if it were tainted, handling it with two fingers as she stuffed it into the register. Here, then, was the enmity he'd been warned about. But, he thought, as long as it was only there in a few, it could be overcome. He would see to that. He stopped by the door to wait for her.

One of the boys, backed by his supporters, turned to look at Alex, and when he spoke it was obviously meant for her to hear.

"Hey, look guys, there she is. I'd like some of that, wouldn't you?"

As Alex's color deepened, Michael's head snapped around and he looked at the sniggering group. They didn't look at him, apparently not realizing he was with her.

"Yeah," the same loud voice came again. "My old man says she puts out for all of them out there."

Michael went rigid, then started toward them. Alex hastily gathered up her small bag and ran over to him.

"No, Michael." He turned to look at her, and she saw the fury in his eyes. "He probably doesn't even understand what he's saying. They're just kids."

"So was Jack the Ripper, once," he growled.

"It's not their fault. He's just…repeating what he heard from his parents."

For the briefest of moments her eyes flicked to the woman behind the counter. Michael didn't miss the movement and turned his head to look steadily at the woman. He saw it then, the resemblance in the sulky set of the mouth and the obdurate glint in the dark eyes. The woman glared back at first, her mouth twisted into a smirk as she crossed her arms over her stomach. Then, as Michael's gaze never wavered, she began to look uncertain, then shifted uneasily.

"Please, Michael, I don't want any trouble. It will only make things worse."

The loud-mouthed boy had fallen silent the moment he had realized he wasn't dealing with a lone female. He backed up a step, stopping only when he came up against a large stack of soup cans.

Alex held her breath as she watched Michael. There was something so elementally physical about him as he stood there, every muscle taut, his gaze now locked on the boy who was looking more nervous every second. He looked like what he was at that moment, an angry man ready for a fight and more than capable of winning it. Then she saw him let out a long, compressed breath, and the tension in him eased.

Only the pleading look in Alex's eyes and the youth of the boy stopped him. It had been a long time since he had resorted to physical violence, but he wanted to now. He wanted to pick up that kid by the heels and rattle him. He'd never felt such fury. The fierceness of the need to avenge the insult to her startled him, and he knew he'd better get out before it won.

As he held the door open for Alex, he saw the woman, smirk restored, reach out to close the drawer of her cash register. The boy was slower to react, relief still uppermost in his face as he watched Michael start out the door.

He almost made it. Another two seconds and he would have. But the boy opened his mouth just a fraction of a second too soon, and Michael heard him.

"Guess I told her what we think of her kind!"

Michael waited just long enough so that Alex wouldn't see before he looked back over his shoulder. She never heard the boy's startled yelp as the soup cans tumbled down on him, or the woman's squeal as the cash register drawer slid shut on two of her fingers. And by the time they reached the truck, Michael had his grin under control.

Alex didn't speak until she had pulled the truck into the parking lot of the small twelve-bed clinic on the edge of town. She shut off the engine, then turned to look at him.

"Thank you." There was only the slightest of quivers in her voice.

"For what? Not ripping the little moron's head off?"

"No. For wanting to."

He looked startled; then he laughed, that same full, joyous sound she had reveled in before.

"You're welcome," he said with a grin. "But that doesn't mean I won't do it later if he doesn't grow some brains."

Alex smiled tentatively, somehow not completely certain he was joking. She glanced at the door to the clinic, then back to him.

"Will you come in and meet Dr. Swan?"

"Yes. I'd like to."

She nodded, pleased, but her expression was troubled. "Would you . . . not mention what happened?"

"Why?"

She sighed. "He tries so hard to change the way people think about us. It would upset him to know it isn't working."

"With a couple of people, anyway," he muttered.

"I don't want him to worry about it. He's already done so much for us. He takes care of us when things get beyond Steve. He did all those tests on Wheezer and gave us the medicine for next to nothing. And he was always there for Andrew and me."

"Okay. Not a word."

He reached for the door but stopped when Alex didn't move.

"What's wrong?"

"I . . ." She glanced at him, then away. "It isn't true."

He looked at her blankly. "What isn't?"

"What Billy said."

"Billy?"

"In the store."

He drew back sharply. Anger flooded him, an anger that was tinged, amazingly, with hurt. He didn't stop to think that he wasn't supposed to be feeling things like that; he just reacted.

"I ought to rip *your* head off," he said gruffly. "Do you think I don't know that?"

"I didn't . . . I just wanted . . ."

He reached out to take her hands.

"Shh. It's all right. I understand. But don't be silly anymore. I know who you are, Alex Logan, and what you are. And no idiot kid spouting vicious garbage can change that."

Alex stared at him, then down at his hands covering hers. That sensation of calm, that feeling of peace and security, seeped into her again. She should have known, she thought. She should have trusted him to know. Why did she always feel this way when he touched her, so warm and safe?

And then something changed, shifted. The feel of his hands on hers became something else, something hot and exciting, and she felt her heart begin to race. She looked at his fingers around hers, tan and strong, and a sudden image of them touching her in other places flashed through her mind, making her take a quick, gasping breath.

He jerked his hands away, and she had the craziest feeling that somehow he had known what she was thinking. Color flooded her face, and she whirled around to jump hastily out of the truck.

Michael sat for a moment, shaken. The images had been so real, so vivid. His hands stroking her intimately, caressing her skin, cupping her breasts...

He sucked in a harsh breath. God, they were too vivid to have come from her, weren't they? Had they been his thoughts? Had he transmitted them to her somehow, in some strange glitch that went along with the other crazy feelings he'd been having? And why couldn't he tell where the thoughts had come from? He'd always been able to tell before. Before Alex, he'd never been confused like this.

And you'd damn well better stop it now, he ordered himself fiercely. Pay attention to the job. He slid out of the truck to follow her, forcing his rebellious mind to obey, to stick to the problem at hand.

He wondered if Billy or his malicious mother was behind the attacks on the refuge. Or the father. It seemed possible, especially if the boy had inherited his father's dirty mind and mouth.

Someone was just exiting the inner office as they came in, a young woman who greeted Alex civilly enough and turned a look of interest on Michael. Alex introduced them, refusing to acknowledge the pang she felt when the petite blonde eyed him with a look of pure feminine assessment.

"This is Marcy Thomas," Alex said. "She and I went to school together."

"Well, not exactly *together*," Marcy simpered. "Alex is so much younger than I am." The disdainful look she gave Alex's slightly shaggy hair and plain jeans left no doubt that she meant too young, at least for a man like Michael.

She made it sound like a disease, Alex thought, and it was only two years anyway.

"Where are you from?" Marcy was asking, looking up at Michael from her five-foot height and managing to look helpless and fragile despite the fact that she could, Alex knew, swear like a Hell's Angel and drink several of the men in town under the table. Alex said nothing.

"I know you can't be from around here," Marcy trilled. "I know all the men here, and none of them could hold a candle to you!"

Subtlety, Alex thought wryly, had never been Marcy's strong suit. But the part about all the men she knew was probably true; Marcy had the fastest reputation in town. At least she had until they decided that Alex herself was a more interesting topic, she added bitterly.

Oh, stop being a bitch, she snapped at herself, feeling a rush of sympathy for the girl who had been the center of the town's gossip for so long.

"I came here from Denver," Michael was saying blandly, seemingly unmoved by Marcy's fluttering eyelashes and the way she reached out to touch him. "And before that St. Louis. I get around a lot."

"Oh, that's what I'd like to do, travel, see the world! I'm so tired of this boring little town!"

"I'm sure you are," he said smoothly. "It was nice meeting you, Ms. Thomas. But if you'll excuse me, I have to see the doctor now. Penicillin shot, you know."

He winked broadly at Marcy as Alex smothered a gasp. Marcy stared, wide-eyed, then stammered a hasty goodbye and scampered out the door.

"Michael Justice, you are terrible!" Alex exclaimed. "You know what she thought!"

"Yeah." He grinned crookedly. "I thought she might. Experience, maybe?"

"Michael!"

Alex tried her best to look aghast, but she couldn't quite stop a giggle. She was amazed that she was able to laugh at all. It was because of Michael, she thought. And this time she felt the warmth just by looking at his glowing blue eyes.

"Well, that's a pleasant sound I haven't heard enough of. I thought you'd forgotten how to laugh, young lady."

Alex smiled at the tall, lean, gray-haired man who had stepped out of his office.

"Hi, Doc," she said as she went to give him a swift hug. "This is Michael Justice. He's been our lifesaver this last couple of weeks. He's saved our time, our money, and our spirits more than once. Michael, Dr. Hank Swan, friend to this town, the refuge, and me."

"Doctor." Michael spoke with the quiet respect he used to the men of the refuge. It was sincere, and Dr. Swan sensed it immediately as he took the proffered hand.

"Call me Hank," he urged. "Or Doc, as Alex does."

"Okay, Doc."

"You're helping out at the refuge? Good," he said at Michael's nod. "It's certainly needed." He smiled fondly at Alex. "She can't do it all, no matter how stubborn she is about not admitting it."

"She's done wonders," Michael said.

"Yes, she has. But she needs to lighten the load, get some rest, like she's been promising me for years."

"I will, Doc," Alex said, and before she realized it, she was bubbling over with the news of her trip to Portland.

"Well, well, you *are* a miracle worker." Dr. Swan raised an eyebrow at Michael. "I've been after her since she was fifteen to take some time for herself."

But she wouldn't leave Andrew, and then she wouldn't leave the men at the refuge. Michael heard it as clearly as if the man had said it.

"I just wish it could be longer," he said softly.

"Oh, no," Alex said with an embarrassed laugh. "I feel guilty enough already."

"For taking two days off in eight years?" Michael asked dryly.

"But I—"

"Lex, if they can't last two days without you, you haven't done a very good job there."

Once again he stopped her dead with an argument she couldn't answer. She heard Dr. Swan's approving chuckle and turned to look at him wryly.

"Easy for you to laugh," she grumbled. "He does this to me all the time."

The doctor's clear gray eyes met Michael's for a moment. Then, without being sure why, Swan was nodding. "Good," he said succinctly. "It's about time someone slowed you down. Now," he went on briskly, "I assume you're here for Cyril's medicine?"

She nodded.

"Fine. I'll get it. You can wait in my office. I'll only be a minute."

"Cyril?" Michael whispered as he followed her through the waiting room door. "Wheezer's name is Cyril?"

Alex giggled. "Yep. Now you know why he doesn't complain about being called Wheezer."

"I guess so. I—"

He broke off, stopping dead as they stepped into a short hallway. He glanced around but saw nothing except a tall, thin man, escorted by a nurse, leaving one of the examination rooms. Nothing that explained the sudden prickling at the back of his neck, or the chill that had rippled down his spine.

"Michael? Are you all right?"

"Fine." He answered her automatically as they went into the office, trying to shrug off the eerie feeling; it was weaker in here, but it wouldn't go. Michael began to walk around the room, searching for any clue to the source of the icy sensation. He knew it had nothing to do with the doctor; nothing lay hidden behind those kind, gray eyes.

He came to a stop before a photo on the wall. It was of a young man in military uniform, and even with the difference in age, there was no doubt as to his parentage; the resemblance to Hank Swan was unmistakable. And it wasn't just in looks; after a moment of staring at the photograph, Michael knew two things. One, that the young man in the picture was his father's son in spirit and kindliness as well as appearance, and two, the sad realization that this gentle man had been taken from the world in a cold, ugly way.

Yet his spirit was here in this house, nearly strong enough even now to overcome the odd sense of malignancy he'd felt. Michael knew it was a measure of the love his father still felt for him, keeping him alive in heart and memory. No, the hostile presence in this place did not emanate from here, either, Michael thought.

"He was killed six months after he got shipped out. Near Da Nang. Doc was devastated. Gary was very special, to all of us." She looked at the picture, a sad fondness in her eyes. "He and Andrew were close, and I used to follow them around like a puppy. But Gary never minded. He used to carry me when Andrew got tired, and tell everybody that he was going to wait for me to grow up so he could marry me."

Michael opened his mouth to speak but found he couldn't get any words past the sudden tightness in his throat. Her poignant nostalgia moved him, but what truly bothered him was the odd feeling that settled in the pit of his stomach at what she had said about Gary marrying her when she grew up.

It should have seemed ridiculous, but Michael's mind wouldn't let go of it. It was ridiculous from a twenty-year-old to a six-year-old, but if he'd lived, would it have been so ridiculous from a thirty-four-year-old to a twenty-year-old Alex? Would she even now be settled in with him, with a couple of sassy, bright-eyed children? And why the hell wouldn't this knot in his stomach go away?

"Here we are."

They both turned to face the doctor as he came into the room. His eyes went briefly to the picture they stood in front of, and Michael felt the wave of love and lingering pain and longing that welled out from the man. But he said nothing except, "You tell Cyril I need to see him sometime soon, to make sure this dosage is still appropriate."

"I will, Doc. Thanks." Alex took the bottle.

The outer door was closing as they came out, and Michael caught a glimpse of that same tall, sallow-faced figure in the instant that the feeling hit him again; he felt a crawling sensation that made him shiver. It lingered in the waiting room like the pungent odor of a skunk long after the creature had passed. Was it connected to that disappearing figure, or to the clinic itself? Or someone else who was there, unseen? He shivered again.

Michael was glad to be out of there, glad to be rid of that repellent crawling sensation. A few minutes later he heard Alex groan under her breath as she pulled into the gas station.

"What?"

"Mr. Rodney," she muttered, gesturing toward the big black car parked on the other side of the gas pumps.

Michael turned to look. "And who," he asked, studying the pale, thin man who had several sparse strands of gray hair combed carefully over his shiny pate, "is Mr. Rodney?"

"President of the bank."

He absorbed this. "He's the one you were talking to, wasn't he? The day I arrived?" She nodded. "He's been giving you problems?" He eyed the man with a new suspicion; was he the one? I'm going to need a minute with him, Michael mused, and glanced at the hood of the man's car.

Alex sighed. "Oh, he's not as bad as some of the others. He doesn't like the idea of the refuge, but I think it's more because it offends his sense of tradition. Just like having a woman responsible for a considerable loan at his bank offends his perception of a woman's place."

"Barefoot, pregnant and in the kitchen?"

"'Fraid so."

"His loss."

She looked at him curiously. "Oh?"

"Women are the real strength of the world. The backbone." He grinned. "That's why they have the babies. If you left it to the men, mankind would have died out eons ago. No man could stand it."

She grinned; she couldn't help it. Then, as a muttered exclamation came from the car next to them, they both turned to look.

"Blasted car! Start!"

Mr. Rodney's face was red as he turned the key again. He was rewarded with a few seconds of rough, coughing engine noise, and then silence as the motor shuddered and died. The young attendant stood by scratching his head. There was no sign of Pete Willis, the regular mechanic who ran the station. Alex sighed; if he couldn't get it started, she would be trapped into offering the man a ride. Reluctantly she slid out of the truck.

"Problem, Mr. Rodney?"

The pale man's paler eyes looked her up and down in dismissal. "That's quite obvious, isn't it, Miss Logan?"

Alex rolled her eyes as the man got out of the car, but she kept her voice level. "It sounds kind of like the truck did when I had a couple of spark plug wires loose."

"And just what would you know about it?" Rodney said condescendingly.

"Let her take a look, Mr. Rodney. You might be surprised."

Alex gaped at Michael as the skinny man eyed him suspiciously, obviously trying to remember if he knew him. Michael looked back blandly. The man was petty, tight-lipped, and rigid, but after a moment of intense concentration, Michael knew that he was too wrapped up in his own little world to be the one he was looking for.

"Go ahead, Alex."

Michael winked at her as he urged her forward with a gentle hand at her back. Bewildered, she went, aware as she leaned over the fender that Michael set up a stream of chatter with the equally bewildered Mr. Rodney. She stared at the engine compartment that was much more complicated than her relatively simple truck and wondered what on earth he expected her to do.

At last, for lack of anything else, she reached out and pushed down the spark plug wires, thinking that perhaps one truly was loose. They seemed secure, and she straightened up, looking at Michael in confusion.

"Go ahead and try it now," he urged Mr. Rodney, who wore the smugly disdainful look of a man about to prove a woman's foolishness as he got back into the driver's seat. He turned the key and got the same results; his expression grew even smugger. But before he could voice his complacent superiority, Michael gave the struggling engine a quick look, and it roared to life. Rodney was stunned into silence, gaping at the car as if it had just grown wings. And Alex was looking at it with even more surprise.

"Ah, women," Michael said melodramatically. "Just think what a wonderful world this will be when they run it."

"Never!" Mr. Rodney exclaimed automatically, finding his tongue at last.

"Don't count on it," Michael said, an odd glint in his eyes, as if he were looking at something only he could see.

The older man muttered something unintelligible, and reached to close the car door.

"We'd better be getting along," Michael said lightly. "You can just thank Alex, and then we'll be on our way."

"Michael!" Alex protested. "I didn't—"

"Nice work," he interrupted, reaching out and tugging on her arm to bring her around to face the flustered Mr. Rodney. Then he looked at the man pointedly.

"Er, thank you, Miss Logan." It sounded as if it had nearly choked him, and without another word he shut the door and drove off.

Alex stared after him, then shifted her nonplussed gaze back to Michael.

"I've heard men get teeth pulled with less pain," he said with a grin. "Without anesthetic."

"Michael, I didn't do anything to his car."

He shrugged. "You obviously did something. It sounded like what you said. Maybe it was just a loose wire." He grinned again. "With any luck at all, it'll die on him again. Preferably in the middle of nowhere."

She laughed, the look on Mr. Rodney's face when he had to thank her sweetly fresh in her mind. Her mood lasted as they drove back to the farm, and she even admitted she was looking forward to her trip to Portland.

"You just be careful, and remember you're there to re-lax."

"Yes, sir," she said meekly.

Michael looked at her sharply, then, when he saw the teasing glint in her eyes, burst out laughing. Alex smiled, thinking she would do a lot more than pretend docility to hear that laugh. It comforted her, in an odd sort of way, and not just because it convinced her that he couldn't really have read her earlier, steamy thoughts.

They—or rather Alex—talked easily, Alex marveling at how much she had suddenly found to say and Michael listening intently, encouraging her. They were nearly to the farm when he jerked his head around suddenly, staring ahead.

"What is it?"

He didn't answer right away; he just leaned toward the open window, tilting his head back. He looked, Alex thought, like some wild creature that had scented danger, and she felt an odd shiver go up her spine.

"Michael?"

"Something's wrong," he muttered.

He looked so forbidding that she didn't ask, just tried to control the fear he was instilling in her. He leaned farther out the window, nostrils flaring.

"Something's on fire," he said suddenly.

Alex smothered a little gasp. It had been an unusually dry year; a fire could be disastrous. She sniffed the air, but she could detect nothing. Yet he'd been so positive that she couldn't doubt him.

They went on a little farther, and then she, too, could smell it. Unconsciously she sped up. They made a wide turn, then crested a small rise, and Alex's heart leaped into her throat. Straight ahead, from the direction of her home, rose a black, ominous cloud of smoke.

Five

The smoky pall grew thicker the closer they got to the farm. Tears began to well in her eyes, and she didn't know if they were from the smoke or the fear that was building in her.

"It's all right," Michael said suddenly.

She turned her head to look at him.

"It's not the refuge."

Her eyes widened, then flickered back to the road.

"How...?"

"It's not. Trust me, Alex."

She could feel it, that reassurance stealing over her. She knew that if she looked at him again his eyes would hold that radiance that lit them from within, that glow that made her feel so certain he was right. He would never let anything hurt her, she thought, then wondered where those words, so immediate and sure, had come from.

Yet she didn't question them; she just drove. As the road made another turn the air seemed to clear a little. Although she hadn't doubted him, she was relieved to pull into the long driveway at the farm and see that he was right. The gray, acrid cloud hung in the sky to the west, a safe distance away.

Matt, followed by Steve and Kenny, met them in front of the house.

"Do you know where it's at?" Alex's words tumbled out as she scrambled from the truck.

"No. Aaron drove over to look. He should be back—"

They all turned at the sound of a car and saw Aaron's battered little convertible pulling into the drive.

"It's about five miles over," he said as he dragged his lanky frame out of the low-slung car. "We should be fine."

"What is it?" Alex asked, eyeing the smoke nervously.

"Brush, for now. But it's closing in pretty fast."

"On what?"

Michael was looking at Aaron rather than the cloud or the others who had joined them to hear the report, including a capering Cougar, nudging Alex for attention.

"A couple of the places off the mill road." He pulled his glasses off and wiped them on his shirttail.

Alex's head came around swiftly. "The Morgans'?"

"That the little dairy farm?"

"Yes."

Aaron nodded. "The guy was arguing with the firemen. They want him to evacuate, in case they can't hold."

"But it's only him and his son," Alex said. "He'll never get his stock out."

"That's what they were arguing about. He says he won't go, not unless they help him get his cows out."

"And if they help him, they won't be able to stop the fire. There's not enough of them." Alex looked back at the rising gray haze.

"There could be."

They all looked at Michael. "What?" Matt said.

"If we helped."

"Us?" Kenny looked startled.

"Why?" Steve said, a little bitterly. "They'd be sitting back cheering if it was us."

"Exactly."

Aaron looked thoughtful, the others dubious.

"They think the worst. Give them the best instead." Michael concentrated on Aaron, knowing his best target. "Make them think."

Slowly, Aaron nodded. "Guilt can be a powerful thing." He looked around at the others. "You all know that."

"Guilt?" Sarah asked, puzzled.

"How would you feel if someone you'd judged without really giving them a chance did something good for you?"

"Guilty," she admitted.

"And," Aaron went on, "what would you do afterward?"

"I don't know. Wonder if I'd misjudged them, I suppose."

Aaron let her words stand as he glanced at Michael, who nodded in approval. Then he looked at the others.

"Well?"

"Do you really think it might work?" Kenny asked doubtfully.

"It can't hurt."

For a moment they wavered. Then Alex spoke. "I'm going to change into my jeans and boots." They all looked at her. "I've always wanted to know if Cricket had any cow horse in him. Cougar—'' she bent to the big dog ''—find Mark, boy. Go find Mark.''

The dog let out a yelp and took off, Alex straightened up, and it was suddenly decided.

''I'll get our shovels,'' Matt said.

''I'll get my gear,'' Steve said. ''Might need it.''

''Alex, you got my pills?'' She nodded and handed Wheezer the bottle from her pocket. ''Good. Then I can help with the cows.''

''Me, too,'' Aaron said quickly.

They scattered in all directions, even, after a moment of grudging hesitation, Rick. Alex turned toward the house but stopped when Michael reached out to touch her arm.

''I'll saddle Cricket for you,'' was all he said, but there was the warmth of a salute in his sky blue eyes.

''Thanks,'' she said, wondering why her voice sounded so funny.

When she came back out the others were gathered on the drive, loading shovels, blankets, and anything else they thought might be useful into the back of the truck. Sarah had filled several containers with water, and she put them in along with some plastic cups. Cricket was dancing, testing Michael's grip on the reins, sensing that something unusual was afoot.

''I'll take the back way,'' Alex said as she steadied the animal with a pat on the neck. ''I should get there about the time you do.''

Michael nodded and handed her the reins. They heard a ringing bark and looked around to see Cougar racing toward them, Mark hot on his heels.

''I'll explain to him,'' Michael said. ''You take Cougar with you.''

She nodded and swung up into the saddle with a smooth, graceful movement. Cricket snorted and gave a little crow hop, but Alex brought him down easily.

"Easy now, love," she crooned, stroking the black-and-white neck. The horse arched into her touch and whickered softly. An odd quiver went through Michael, followed by a blast of that persistent heat he couldn't understand or seem to avoid. He felt his muscles tense, ripple, as if they, too, wanted to feel the stroking caress of her hand. He clenched his jaw. He was going to have to have help with this, he thought. He didn't know what was going wrong, but he couldn't deal with it much longer.

Alex looked at him for a long moment, as if puzzled, then whirled the horse on his hindquarters and was gone.

When the men arrived at the mill road, now blocked off by parked fire trucks, the beleaguered, sweat- and ash-covered young fireman there took one look at them and the equipment they'd brought and welcomed them openly.

"Boy, can we use you! We're holding the line but just barely. And that old coot won't budge without his damn cows."

"We'll help there, too, and more's on the way," Michael said. "You need a ride back up?"

The man nodded and joined the others in the back of the truck. He gratefully accepted the water Sarah poured for him, then looked around at them as he drank.

"You're from the Logan place, aren't you?"

Matt eyed the man warily. "Yeah. So?"

"Nothing." The man finished the water, then met Matt's gaze. "My dad died in the Tet offensive," he said simply.

After a moment Matt nodded in acknowledgment. "I was there. But I was luckier."

"Supposedly," the man said, and a look of understanding passed between them.

It was followed by an odd look of speculation on Matt's face, a look that Michael noted with interest. That's it, he thought. Think about it, Matt. There are more like him around. Just give them a chance.

When they arrived at the fire line, there was no time for any more talk. The flames were creeping closer, feeding voraciously on brush that was all too ready to burn after the uncommonly dry spell. The man in the white fire-captain's helmet who was directing the desperate efforts to hold back the tide of flame welcomed them without question.

"We've got four with shovels, one medic, and two to help with the animals, plus a rider on the way," Michael reported quickly. "And I'll fill in wherever you need me."

The man nodded gratefully and snapped out some quick directions. They scattered to do as ordered, and the battle began. It was hot, horrible work, and breathing the acrid, stinging air seared their lungs. They dug a firebreak, then had to drop back and dig another when the first was jumped by the racing flames. Steve was busy with several minor injuries, and Michael barely had time to look up now and then and check on Alex.

She made a dramatic picture as she rode the black-and-white horse through the milling black-and-white Holsteins. The animals were restless, agitated by the smoke and the crackle of the flames that were closing in. Several times they tried to break away, but she always seemed to be there to stop them.

Cricket the cow horse, he thought with a grin. And Cougar the cow dog, he added as the big animal raced after a bolting cow and herded her back to the main group that Alex was urging out onto the road.

She rode with a supple grace that fascinated Michael and a daring that made him afraid for her; one misstep by the dancing stallion and she could go down beneath the scrambling hooves of the cows. He had to force himself back to his own task of scouting the flank of the fire and marking the path for the firebreak they were trying desperately to get done before the flames reached the buildings.

He didn't know how long he'd been driving the flat-bladed shovel into the dirt when he looked up from his digging to see a gray-haired man in soot-stained overalls desperately spraying the sides of the barn with a small hose. The roof was already ablaze, sending embers up into the breeze. It was hopeless; the fire captain had ceded the barn in the effort to save the house, but the man refused to quit.

Michael was ahead of the others, changing the course of the firebreak to protect the house, when something made him look back at the barn once more. At first he saw nothing but the stocky figure of Frank Morgan, still fighting a lost battle. Then he heard an ominous crack, and as clearly as if it were outside instead of hidden in the flaming building, he saw the main beam give way.

Without a second's thought he dropped his shovel and launched himself toward the now-engulfed barn. He covered the twenty yards in less than two seconds.

Frank Morgan let out a startled shout as he was hit by a hundred and ninety-five pounds of solid muscle. They went down hard, Michael rolling until the man was beneath him.

"Hey! Stop, I—"

It seemed as if all the fires of hell were raining down on them as the beam gave way and the roof caved in. The air was thick with smoke and ash and flame. Michael felt a thud across his back and shoulders, felt the pressure, the heat, but no pain. He hunched over the man protectively, sensing rather than seeing the embers drifting down over them.

"Michael!"

He heard Alex's scream, a terrified, heartrending sound that made him shiver to the bone despite the fierce heat radiating around them. He could feel the thud of Cricket's hooves through the earth, then felt them come to a sudden halt.

"Michael! Oh, God, Michael!"

The sheer dread in her voice galvanized him. He braced his hands on the ground and lifted, feeling a heavy weight sliding away. He rolled to one side, off of Frank Morgan's overall-clad form. Then Alex was there, her arms going around him as he sat up.

"Michael," she said breathlessly. "God, I saw the roof go. I thought you were . . ."

She shuddered violently. His eyes met hers, and he read the lingering fear there, fear for him. Something knotted up inside him, tightening as he watched her eyes go over him, felt her hands touching him, as if she couldn't believe he had escaped unscathed.

"I'm fine," he managed to get out. Please, he thought dazedly, don't touch me. It feels too . . . too . . .

"You're really all right? That beam was right on top of you. I thought sure—"

"I'm fine," he repeated, more steadily this time.

Her hands had come up to cup his face, her eyes searching his. Her lips were parted for her quick, short breaths, and he felt a heat more intense than the fire begin to uncurl deep inside him.

He had to stop this, he thought a little dizzily. He lifted his hands to tug hers away, to stop that touch that felt so good. Instead he found himself pressing against them, holding her soft palms to his face.

"Michael," she breathed, her tongue coming out to wet lips dried by panic. He heard an odd, choked sound; it was a moment before he realized it was his own groan.

"What the . . . ?"

They pulled apart at the dazed sound of Frank Morgan's voice. As she recovered her composure, Alex's gaze went to the man as he gingerly sat upright, staring at the still-smoking crossbeam that lay next to him. His eyes went to the fallen roof of the barn, and his wonder that he wasn't dead showed plainly on his face.

"Are you all right, Mr. Morgan?" Alex asked quickly.

"Yes," he muttered, obviously still shaken. "Thanks to him." His eyes had shifted to Michael, then focused on Alex. "Alex?" His ash-smeared brow furrowed. "What are you doing here?"

"We came to help."

He stared, then looked around at the other men who were digging furiously and hosing down the roof of the house under the direction of the fire captain.

"Those men . . . they're from your place?"

She nodded.

"Why?" he asked, stunned anew.

Her eyes went to Michael as she opened her mouth to give him the credit, but he forestalled her with his own simple words.

"We're neighbors." He scrambled to his feet and held out a hand to the still dazed man. "Better go to the first-aid station and get checked out."

Nodding somewhat numbly, he walked off. Alex turned her attention back to Michael, staring at the numerous holes that had been burnt into his shirt. There was a wide, black, charred stripe across his back, where the beam had fallen, but he appeared unhurt.

"Are you sure—"

"Alex, I'm fine," he said patiently. Then he went on, his carefully even expression denying the moment that had just happened between them. "You got the cows moved?"

He could almost feel the effort she made to shake off the lingering effects of those moments of terror. And of that frozen, electric instant in time. He could almost see her shoving away the turmoil, could almost hear her silent self-lecture.

"Yes, we did. They're all penned up down the road." She managed a smile. "You'd swear Cricket had been doing it all his life. And Cougar had a ball. Got to chase cows without getting in trouble."

He smiled back at her then, warmth returning to his eyes and banishing the last of her fright.

"I think they've got the upper hand now," he said, glancing over his shoulder. "Looks like the house is safe."

"Thank goodness. Lucy would have been devastated."

"I'm glad, then, for her sake." I'd be glad for anyone who was decent to you, he thought. "I saw her earlier, taking some things out of the house. Somebody must have called her."

"I want to go find her, see if there's anything she needs."

"If she saw her husband, she's probably at the first-aid station."

Alex nodded. She meant to go but couldn't quite relinquish the sight of him yet.

"Looks like you had a close call here."

They turned to look at the weary man in the white fire helmet.

"I wouldn't want to make a habit of it," Michael said wryly.

"I wanted to thank you. You people turned the tide for us. I don't doubt that we would have lost the house if you hadn't shown up."

Those words came back to Alex that night as they all sat around the table. They looked tired but quietly pleased with themselves. Even Rick wore a slight smile, although, as usual, he said nothing. They knew they'd done something good, she thought. They'd been needed, and they'd responded, thanks to Michael's nudging.

Michael. He'd been so right. They needed that feeling. They had needed to be needed. Not to be appreciated or thanked, just needed. Her eyes went to him, savoring the sight of him, remembering that heart-stopping moment when she'd been afraid he lay dead beneath that flaming, crushing beam. And the heart-starting instant when they had been locked in some frozen twist of time, touching with their eyes as much as their hands.

It was foolish to dwell on that moment, she told herself. And foolhardy to think it had been anything more than a fierce reaction to survival. Michael Justice had bigger and better things to do than waste his time with some naive country girl who was spellbound by him. The thought brought on a tightness in her chest that made it difficult to breathe. Involuntarily, she looked at him.

He was laughing at something Wheezer had said, his eyes alight and the dimple flashing. He'd become a part of them, a part of their lives so thoroughly now that it was hard to remember when he hadn't been here. And impossible for her to think of a time when he would be here no longer. She lowered her gaze to her plate, blinking rapidly.

"I heard the Morgans don't have enough insurance to rebuild the barn."

Alex looked up as Michael spoke; she knew that tone. It was the same one she heard just before he made her think of something she never had before, or think in a new way.

"That's rough," Aaron said.

"They have enough for the material but not the labor."

He left it at that, but the seeds he had planted today found nourishment in the good feelings they were enjoying, and Matt's grin was only slightly wry as he met Michael's eyes.

"And I suppose you figure we ought to volunteer?"

Michael shrugged. "Did I say that?"

"No," Kenny said dryly. "But you do have a less than subtle way of hinting."

"Me?"

Michael struggled to look innocent and failed utterly. Wheezer laughed and tossed a biscuit at him. Then they all laughed, and Alex had to blink against the brimming of her eyes again at how completely they had accepted him.

"Gonna build a barn?"

They all laughed at Mark's reduction of things to the essentials. Then Matt glanced around the table at everyone, one by one. The answer was obvious.

"I guess we are, buddy."

"—and then we'll start the . . . Alex, are you listening to any of this?"

Alex jerked her attention back to Sarah, her cheeks tinged with pink. She knew she'd been staring, but she couldn't seem to help it. She wished she weren't so helpless with a hammer, although she thought that maybe some pounded fingers would be worth the distraction.

"I can't blame you," Sarah said with a little laugh as she looked over to where the framework of the new barn now rose above the newly leveled and graded spot that had held the ashes of the old one. "Even though I'm crazy about Kenny, I wouldn't deny myself the pleasure of looking at that."

Alex's color went from pink to red. She busied herself with setting lunch out on the table, but it didn't matter. The image she'd looked so hastily away from was burned into her mind.

It was an unusually warm day, and as the work proceeded many of the men had pulled off their shirts. Including, to Alex's heart-pounding dismay, Michael. She had begun by staring in fascination at the flex and play of the muscles in his back and shoulders as he worked on one of the walls they would soon raise. Then, when the wall went up, so did her blood pressure, as Michael turned around to help lift the framework.

His worn jeans rode low on his narrow hips, emphasizing the broadness of his chest. She stared at the sweat-sheened smoothness of his skin, swallowing tightly when a bead of perspiration trickled down his chest, through the sparse trail of hair at his navel, then down below his waistband.

Only when Sarah's words had teased her out of her rapt entrancement did she realize that all he would have had to do was look at her and everything she was feeling would no doubt be written all over that silly face he found it so easy to read.

"Don't be embarrassed, girl," Sarah said kindly. "You need a little excitement in your life. And that," she glanced back at Michael, "is enough excitement for any woman."

Alex couldn't help the little sigh that escaped her. Sarah was kind, gentle, and loving, and had been her closest female friend for a long time despite the difference in their ages, but she had probably never suffered a moment of the kind of uncertainty Alex was feeling. She had loved Kenny since they were children, had married him when she was sixteen, and had stood by him through thick and thin, war and the shaky peace that followed.

"Now, what was that for? You can't tell me you haven't thought about it, child. I've seen you looking at him."

Alex carefully lined up the silverware. "And looking is as close as I'll get," she muttered.

"What do you mean?"

She sighed. "Look at him, Sarah. He could have any woman in the world with a snap of his fingers."

"What's wrong with that, as long as it's you?"

Alex flushed again. "Why on earth would it be?"

"Oh, so that's it, is it? Well, I've got news for you, dear. As much time as you spend sneaking peeks at him, he spends watching you when you're not looking."

Alex made a small sound of disbelief, but the descent of the men hungry for lunch stopped any further discussion. Alex kept her eyes carefully on her plate as she ate; Michael, still shirtless, was sitting next to her, and she didn't dare risk looking at him for fear of what silly thing she might say or do. But she did look up at last, when Frank Morgan stood up at the head of the long table they'd set out under the trees in the front yard.

"Er, I'd like to say something. My wife tells me I'm as stubborn as a Missouri mule, and maybe that's true. But when I know I'm wrong, I admit it." He coughed. "Well, I was wrong about you folks, and I'm sorry. And I'm downright glad you're my neighbors."

He sat down quickly, as if embarrassed. He didn't need to worry; all the eyes at the table were on Michael. He just smiled, not even the slightest touch of "I told you so" in his expression.

The barn was done by the time Saturday dawned. All of them gathered around as Alex was getting ready to leave for her weekend away, postponing their busy day long enough to say goodbye to her. They had beaten down all her protests about leaving them to catch up with all the work that

had piled up while they'd been working on the barn,
threatening to kick her out if she didn't go voluntarily.

"The reservations are all made, so get moving," Steve
told her gruffly.

"Yeah," Matt said. "We don't want to see this ugly
truck again until Sunday night."

"Fun, Alex," Mark said as he restrained a confused
Cougar. "Have fun."

She sighed.

"Don't worry," Michael said. "This is for you. Don't
worry. Don't even think about anything but yourself for a
change."

He reached for the truck door at the same time she did,
and their hands met on the handle. The moment she felt his
touch, the anticipation she'd lost in the face of all the work
she was leaving behind returned.

"Be careful," he said softly. She looked up at him, and
for a long, silent moment their eyes locked.

"You gonna kiss her goodbye or what?"

Alex colored at Steve's remark, but Michael just smiled
gently as he leaned forward to press his lips on her forehead. Alex's blush deepened again at the casual touch; a
kid sister kiss, she thought, dispirited.

"Aw, come on, Mike! If you're gonna kiss her, kiss
her!"

Alex could have cheerfully strangled Kenny at that moment. She lifted her head to say something, anything, to get
out of this horribly awkward situation, but before she could
speak, Michael moved.

She caught a fleeting glimpse of the battle in his eyes, but
before she could decide what it meant, his mouth was on
hers. Searing, piercing heat shot through her, melting away
her embarrassment and her resistance. His lips were soft
and gentle on hers, and she felt his hands come up to cup

her face. His fingers threaded through her hair as he tilted her head back, and she heard an odd sound come from him at the same time that she felt his muscles tense, as if he were trying to back away and failing.

Then she was pulled hard against him, and his kiss became suddenly hot, fierce. Her head reeled as he ignited flames as blistering as those he'd fought, and she sagged against him.

"All right!"

"Whoooie!"

The assorted whistles and exclamations broke the spell, and Michael broke the kiss. Alex stared at him, her face flushed with a heat that had nothing to do with embarrassment. His own breath was coming quickly, and she could see the pulse beating rapidly in the hollow of his throat.

"Alex," he said thickly, shaking his head slowly.

She saw the pain in his troubled eyes and felt a sudden, frantic need to escape before he could say something that would shatter the sweetness of that kiss. She wanted to cling to it, savor it. She would face reality when she came back, but for now she wanted to hug this memory to her with the desperation of someone who thought it was the only thing she would ever have. She followed that instinctive urge and scrambled into the cab of the truck.

Michael stared after her as she drove away, heavy swallows alternating with his harsh breathing. He felt them all looking at him and started to move. He nearly staggered but kept going; he had to get away, had to calm down, had to think. His steps quickened; then he broke into a run. He didn't stop until he was into the trees behind the house, safe from curious eyes. He found a small, grassy clearing and sank to his knees. He knew he was shaking, but he couldn't seem to stop.

Michael?

A throttled sound of protest broke from him. *Not now. I can't handle this now.*

Michael, are you there?

They weren't going to go away. He knew that, because the signal wasn't usually this strong without direct contact. He grabbed the golden tags.

Go away.

Ah, you are there. We got the oddest signal a few minutes ago. A burst of static.

They'd felt it. They just hadn't figured it out yet. He barely managed to drop the tags before the memory blazed through his mind. The feel of Alex's soft lips, the unexpected jolt of pure, sizzling pleasure that had rocketed through him as she went warm and pliant in his hands.

Michael? Are you still there?

He took a deep breath and grabbed the tags again. And sent the message again.

Go away.

Go away? Really, Michael, we haven't heard from you—

I've been busy.

Well, of course you have. But there are such things as regular reports, remember?

Right. Sorry.

Something wrong, Michael? You sound . . . odd.

He dropped the tags again. He had to get a grip, he told himself severely. He didn't understand what the hell was happening, and until he did, he wasn't about to let anybody know about it.

Michael? There is something wrong, isn't there? Do you need some extra help?

He laughed harshly. *I need help period.*

We keep losing you, Michael. Are you having transmission problems?

Steadying himself, he grasped the tags again.

No.

That's much better. A pause. *We don't mean to bother you, Michael, but we were concerned. You're usually so punctual about checking in. What have you been doing?*

Fighting fires. Building barns.

Puzzlement came through. *Commendable, certainly, but—*

Never mind. I'll give you a report.

All right. Ready when you are.

He tightened his grip on the tags and sent it to them. Carefully edited. He'd never done that before; he could only hope it worked. It seemed to, for he got a calm answer when he was done.

Congratulations, Michael. You've accomplished more than we expected so soon. When do you think you'll be done?

Pain, sharp, biting, and instantaneous, grabbed him.

Heavens, what was that? Are you all right?

No, damn it, I'm not.

For once they ignored the curse. *What is it? Something's very wrong, isn't it?*

Forget it.

But, Michael—

Forget it. Please.

Please? From you?

I'll keep on top of the reports from now on.

Michael—

Later.

He let the tags fall back to his chest, then let out a tremendous, shuddering sigh. He should have told them, he thought. He should have asked what the hell was happening to him. He'd quit counting the years that he'd been doing this, but never in all that time had he felt anything like this. Maybe something was wrong with him. Maybe he needed a recharge or something.

Or maybe he was just plain worn out. Did people like him retire? It had never come up, and he'd never asked. But he supposed it couldn't go on forever. Nothing did. But he'd never thought about it until now. Just like he'd never thought about the fact that he never stayed when the job was done. Or that when he moved on he was alone. Always alone. It never bothered him. It wasn't supposed to bother him. They'd promised him that. They'd promised him...

He sat in the shadowed little clearing for a long time, the image of Alex in his mind and the feel of her on his lips.

Six

Michael's head shot up, and he nearly dropped the cross-bar he'd been nailing on the new barn door when he heard the sound of a car in the drive. Alex? Had she changed her mind? Come back?

He was out the door and halfway around the building when he skidded to a halt. Of course she hadn't. He would have known. He started to walk again, slower this time, but came to a halt again as he rounded the corner of the barn.

A police car? He blinked, but it didn't go away. And neither did the man in uniform standing beside it, talking to Matt. Michael eyed him curiously as he slowly walked the rest of the way.

The man was about thirty, tall and spare, with medium brown hair showing under his hat. A rather scraggly moustache shadowed his upper lip. He was pleasant looking enough, with light brown eyes that seemed oddly ingenuous, considering his profession.

Matt introduced him as Deputy Walt Howard. There was wariness in Matt's demeanor but no outright dislike, and when Michael shook the deputy's hand, he knew that the artless openheartedness was genuine.

"Anyway, like I was saying," Matt went on, "she took a trip up to Portland."

"Alex? But she never goes anywhere."

"Well, she did this time." Matt's eyes flicked to Michael, noticing how his casual scrutiny of the deputy had suddenly become more intense. "I'll tell her you stopped by."

"Do that, thanks. But actually, there's something else I needed to talk to her about."

"Anything I can help you with?"

Walt considered for a moment. "Maybe. Been a few livestock killings, last week or so. Looks like an animal brought 'em down."

"Sorry to hear that, but we haven't lost anything."

The man looked uncomfortable. "Well, some people sort of mentioned, not accusing, you understand, that big dog of hers."

"Cougar?" Matt laughed. "He'd never hurt a fly, unless it was hurting Alex."

Howard shifted his feet and didn't meet Matt's eyes. "Well, that's what I told him—"

"Who?" Matt asked.

The deputy's head came up. "Well, now, I couldn't exactly tell you that."

Matt looked at the man narrowly. "Doesn't Alex have a right to know who's running around accusing her dog of things like that?"

"Sure, but—"

"Who said it?"

They were the first words Michael had spoken, and something in his tone made the deputy meet his eyes. The man swallowed, looking as if he wanted to turn away but couldn't.

"Who?" Michael repeated softly.

Howard stared as if mesmerized, and when he spoke, it was as if the words were being dragged from him.

"Willis," he said slowly.

Michael's brow furrowed as he reached for the memory, knowing he'd heard the name somewhere.

"Henry? He's the one who said this?" Matt sounded not at all surprised.

Then Michael had it, the image of Alex mentioning the Mr. Willis who ran the gas station where they had encountered the grumpy bank president.

"Not exactly," Walt was saying. "He just said it would take an animal the size of that dog to bring down those calves and sheep." He coughed and, looking decidedly ill at ease, muttered something, then climbed back into the marked car and started the engine.

"Is he talking about the guy who owns the gas station in town?" Michael asked as he watched the car drive off.

"Not Pete. He's okay. It's his son. Henry." There was the slightest sour emphasis on the name.

"You sound like you don't like him much."

Matt grimaced. "Don't mind me. I don't care for a lot of people around here. Only came here because of..."

He trailed off, and Michael read the look in his eyes easily; pain, sadness, and regret rose in a swamping wave.

"Gary Swan?" he finished quietly.

"Yeah. Gary."

"You knew him pretty well, didn't you?"

"Yes. He was in my unit 'in country.' When I finally decided to get my life together, one of the first things I did was come here to see his father." Matt's eyes went oddly distant. "I was there when he died. I thought his father might want to know about it."

Michael reached out and touched Matt's arm gently. He maintained the contact, watching Matt's face until the far-off, haunted look disappeared. Slowly, Matt's head turned, and the look he gave Michael was calm and slightly bemused.

"You all right?" Michael asked.

"Yeah." He looked puzzled. "I feel...strange. But good. I don't usually talk about that." He shook his head. "Anyway, that's when I heard about what Alex was doing." He smiled. "I already knew about her, though. Gary kept talking about this little pixie back home. Said keeping the world safe for kids like her was the only thing worth fighting for."

"He was right."

"Yes, he was. So, I came out here. For his dad, and to see how she'd turned out, for Gary, sort of." He looked puzzled, as if wondering why he was telling this man so much. He ended the story rather abruptly. "And I stayed."

Michael nodded slowly, then tried to gently nudge Matt back to the subject of Walt's visit. "I gather this... Henry is not one of the reasons why."

Matt shrugged. "I don't know him that well, but Alex has known him all her life. She... dislikes him intensely."

"Hates him?"

"Alex doesn't hate anybody. But Henry Willis is about as close as she'll ever come to it."

"Why?"

"I don't know. I've asked, but she won't talk about it. I get the idea it's a long-time thing, though. And that's good enough for me."

Was that the answer? Michael wondered. Was it some long-held grudge that was behind what was happening here? Was it aimed specifically at Alex, rather than the refuge in general? No, he thought. It couldn't be. Alex could never do anything to inspire that kind of hatred.

Matt was watching Michael thoughtfully. "Long-time thing," he repeated. "Like Alex and the deputy, there."

"What?" Michael snapped back to the present.

"He's been trailing after her for three, four years now," Matt said casually.

"Trailing after her...?"

"Yep. Ever since he got assigned to this part of the county. Asks her out at least once a week."

Michael turned to stare back down the road. "How... does she feel about him?"

"Oh, she likes him well enough," Matt answered, his eyes trained on Michael's face. "Kinda keeps him at a distance, though. But then, maybe that's our fault, for keeping her so busy here."

Michael's gaze went back to Matt but darted away quickly. He usually had no problem with people reading his thoughts, but his faith in the ones he worked for was a little shaky at the moment. Besides, the knot in his stomach was so big he was afraid anyone with eyes could see he was messed up.

"Now that you're here to help, maybe she'll have more time free for him."

Michael jerked, his gaze snapping back to Matt's face; it was blandly innocent. "Right," he muttered, and stalked back to the barn, uncharacteristically unaware of Matt's grin behind him.

He went back to pounding nails into the crossbar with much more force than was necessary. What was wrong with him? He'd just been handed the answer to his dilemma. He knew Alex was becoming too attached to him, and what better way to solve the problem than by finding someone else for her?

He slammed the last nail home with a single furious blow.

Michael yawned despite the steady flow of chatter at the table; he'd spent a long, restless night. Sleep had eluded him in this place that seemed to echo hollowly, devoid of the bright spirit that made it live. Alex.

He'd spent the dark hours wondering if things were going as planned and what she was doing. Except for the frequent moments when he felt a soft, warm breath of air against his skin and knew what she was doing: she was thinking of him.

He'd tried to smother his chaotic feelings, but it was impossible in this place. In the hour just before dawn he had at last gotten up and made his way down the hall to her room. Cougar, sprawled disconsolately on the floor beside the bed, had raised his head to look at him, then lowered it with a heartfelt canine sigh.

"Yeah," Michael had muttered.

He'd sat down on the edge of the bed. Even here, where her presence was so strong, it felt empty. The way this house felt empty. The way he felt empty.

One hand had crept up toward the tags on his chest. He had to know what was happening, why were they letting it happen. But before his fingers reached the tags, they'd curled back against his palm. He'd sat there for a long, long time, only slightly comforted by Cougar when the dog got up and laid his big head on Michael's knee.

He'd nearly jumped when they'd called him.

Michael.

He grabbed the tags angrily. What?

No need to sound so testy, Michael. You promised regular reports, remember.

Fine. Here.

He sent them what he had, again edited.

Thank you. You're doing fine.

Sure I am.

Something bothering you, Michael?

I'm tired. You want twenty-four hour service, you should have fixed it so I wouldn't get tired.

We tried. It would have been much more practical if you didn't have to rely on sleep, or food. But, unfortunately, there are some things that even we can't arrange.

Pity.

You seem to be awfully cranky on this case, Michael. Are you sure there isn't something wrong?

Everything is just peachy. Good night.

He dropped the tags and shut his mind to them. And he'd spent the rest of the minutes before light began to fill the room wishing he could shut his mind to the images of Alex as easily.

And now he yawned again, pushing the remains of his dinner around on his plate. He was contemplating the glass of milk—part of the regular deliveries that had begun, unannounced, from Frank Morgan's small dairy farm—when a sweet, honeyed warmth began to spread through him. His head came up, tilting to one side as he stretched for the heat. Then he had it, and he couldn't help the smile that spread across his face.

"Hey, Mike, what's with you? You look like somebody just left you a million bucks."

He looked up at Steve and shrugged. "Nothing."

He turned his attention back to his meal, appetite a little stronger now. He had finished the last of his milk when they heard Cougar's joyous howl and, moments later, the sound of Alex's truck.

As they all poured out the door, Matt flipped on the outside light, casting a bright, golden circle into the yard where Alex had pulled to a halt. She seemed to hesitate inside the cab for a moment, and Matt went to pull open the door with a flourish.

"Welcome back, kid," he said melodramatically, bowing as she at last slid out and into the golden circle of light. "We missed—"

His words broke off sharply, and a muffled gasp rose from the rest of them as they stared at her. But Alex looked for only one pair of eyes. Bright, glowing, sky blue eyes. She found them, and they didn't let her down. More than just appreciation of her appearance, they held a teasing glint of "I told you so" and, without a trace of conceit, the fact that he had known it all along. The rest was hidden, locked away from her, but she was too excited to mind just then.

"Wow," Wheezer finally said.

"Yeah, wow," Steve echoed.

"Beautiful," Mark said gruffly, and Rick stood there staring as if he'd never seen her before.

Alex blushed, but she was pleased with their reactions. Her hair had been trimmed and shaped into a smooth, neck-length sweep, tucked demurely behind one ear and falling sexily instead of raggedly over her other eye. Long, lacy gold earrings dangled from her ears, accenting the delicate lines of her jaw and neck. The minimum of makeup, skillfully applied thanks to a couple of hours of practice, highlighted her cheekbones and the thick fringe of her lashes.

She'd found the dress she wore, a smooth, graceful knit that accentuated her slenderly curved figure without clinging, in a small shop in the hotel. She'd fallen in love with it immediately, especially when she'd tried it on and seen how the deep jade color made her eyes stand out with startling vividness.

She had sadly gone to put it back on the rack, knowing its price was far out of her reach, when the clerk had come to her, wearing the oddest expression, and told her it should have been on the half-price rack. Alex had crushed her qualms and bought it before her conscience could talk her out of it. And also the matching pair of shoes that she had, with incredible luck, found the same day in a small shop a few blocks away. They were high-heeled and utterly impractical, and she loved the way they accentuated her legs in their unfamiliar, sheer hose. She felt deliciously feminine with the soft skirt swirling about her knees and the delicate gold earrings dancing against her neck. Kid sister, huh? She laughed inwardly.

"Well, are you going to let me come in? I have presents for everybody."

She reached back into the truck and brought out a large, gaily colored shopping bag. Matt scrambled for her small suitcase as Aaron hastily went to hold the door open for her.

"You were supposed to spend that money on yourself," Aaron said sternly.

"Oh, I did, mostly." She laughed. "But it seemed like everything I wanted was on sale. Now, sit down, all of you."

With all of them there they were short of seating, so Mark lowered himself to the floor. Michael sat on the hearth, where he busied himself starting the fire to ward off the evening's chill.

"Where's Cougar?" Alex asked.

Aaron coughed, and Matt looked uncomfortable.

"He's in the barn," Michael said quickly. "There's been some livestock killed, and I thought he'd be safer there until they find out what's doing it."

"Oh." A troubled line appeared between her brows.

"Don't worry about it now, Alex."

"Yeah," Matt chimed in hastily, managing to sound like a little boy on Christmas morning. "What did you bring?"

Alex smiled. "Sarah, you first," she said happily as she drew out a bright silk scarf in shades of gold and yellow that did wonders for Sarah's pale blond hair and caramel-colored eyes. Sarah exclaimed in delight; such things had long been beyond their limited budget. Mark crowed with pleasure as he opened the headphones she had given him so he could listen to his music anytime without disturbing the others. A stack of paperback mysteries went to Wheezer, who had a weakness for them, and a huge bag of gourmet jelly beans to Kenny, whose sweet tooth was legend. For Matt, a frustrated photography buff, came a book on the subject, and for Aaron a psychology text he'd been lusting after for months.

She hesitated for a moment, then reached into the bag again. She drew out a small, slim volume and walked over to Rick.

"I wasn't sure what you'd like," she said shyly. "But I know you were in the First Cav, and this was written by a First Cav captain. I thought they were wonderful. I hope you like them."

Rick stared at the book of poetry she held out to him, then looked back at her. His expression was very odd, and his voice more so as he at last moved to take the book. "I . . . thank you."

Michael looked up at his tone. For the first time the man's guard was down, and he could see what he needed to see. Whatever was going on around here, Michael didn't think Rick was behind it. Rick was merely what he appeared: a haunted man with a scarred soul who was trying to heal. Michael turned back to the fire, adding another stick of kindling as he narrowed his list of suspects once more.

Alex went back to the bag one last time, conscious of everyone's eyes on her. They seemed to have an inordinate amount of interest in this last gift, she thought wryly. She lifted out the four-inch square box and carried it over to the fireplace. She sat down on the hearth and carefully put the box down between them.

Michael looked up, startled. He wasn't one of the group here, not really; he hadn't expected her to buy him anything. Then he met her eyes, and he knew that she had spent more time and care choosing this than anything else. That knot in his gut tightened another notch. He stared at the box for a moment. Then, with a hand that was none too steady, he reached for it.

The box opened to reveal a base of rough, jagged pewter. Atop it sat a three-inch crystal dragon, its tail curved into a flaring arch, each scale on its body cut in exquisite detail.

He reached out a tentative finger and touched the tiny beast, sensing through the polished facets that were flashing in the flickering light of the fire exactly what had gone into her choice of this gift. That knot leaped from his stomach to his throat, and Michael found himself blinking rapidly at the sudden stinging in his eyes.

Alex watched him a little breathlessly. She'd had no practice in this kind of thing; she only knew that when she'd seen the little crystal dragon she'd had to get it for him.

"Is it...all right?" She hated the way she sounded, but she couldn't help it.

He looked up then, and she saw the sheen of moisture in his eyes; he didn't try to hide it. "It's perfect," he said softly.

He meant it. He wasn't supposed to care about things; they weren't supposed to mean anything to him. That made it easier for him, they said. Well, if this was easy, he didn't want anything to do with hard. And to hell with their little rules; this tiny crystal creature was going to stay with him for a long, long time.

"We may have lost the little sister we all adopted," Aaron was saying softly, "but we gained a beautiful, extraordinary woman."

"We've taken you for granted for far too long," Matt added. "But not anymore."

Mark suddenly rose from the floor and engulfed her in a hug. "Beautiful inside and out, Alex."

Michael was still awake in his narrow bed when the rain started. He hadn't even tried to close his eyes, knowing that sleep would evade him again. Last night it had been because the house was so empty of her; tonight it was because the house—and his heart—were so full of her.

He'd always seen the beauty hidden behind the tomboyish exterior, but her transformation had stunned even him. She had been radiant in the rich green dress, alive with a newly discovered femininity. A femininity that called to something so deeply buried inside him that he wasn't even certain what it was.

He turned his head restlessly on the pillow, his gaze coming to rest on the tiny dragon on the table beside him. It seemed to glow even in the darkness, to sparkle with an inner light. He stared at it until the morning light, turned gray by the pouring rain, came through the window.

The rain kept on, as if trying to make up for its long absence all at once. By late morning they were stepping over rushing streams everywhere; by afternoon they'd given up on that and sloshed through the small rivers that crisscrossed the farm.

"Cougar's miserable," Alex said, listening to the dog's mournful howl as she helped Aaron spread a sheet of plastic over the chicken coop. "He hates being caged up like that."

"Mike's right, though," Aaron grunted as he secured one end of the plastic. "With whatever it is running loose killing livestock, he's better off locked in the barn."

Reluctantly agreeing, Alex moved to secure the other end. The dress had been traded for the necessary jeans, shirt, and boots, but the haircut remained, along with a slight touch of makeup and tiny gold earrings. She had, to her surprise, been able to hang on to the feeling her makeover had given her, in no small part due to the new way they all were looking at her. Maybe she wasn't forever doomed to be the world's little sister after all, she thought.

The downpour slackened to a gently steady rain by late afternoon, soft and pleasant. Chores done for the moment, Michael walked to the small clearing he'd found before. He found the spot soothing, and that was something he seemed to need a lot of lately. It was an unaccustomed feeling for him, and he didn't know how to deal with it.

He sat down for a moment, heedless of the wet ground and trying to think only of the clean, fresh feel of the rain on his face. The white-trunked alder tree offered scant shelter, often dousing him with larger drops that had collected on its round leaves, but he didn't care. The rain distracted him, although nothing seemed to keep his mind off a vibrant, slim girl in a clinging, tempting green dress.

Alex. God, what was wrong with him? How could she do it? How could she tie him up in knots like this? It had never happened before, not in all his years on the job, and he didn't know why it was happening now. Over the years he'd dealt with women who were, he supposed, more beautiful than Alex, and they'd had no effect at all on him. He'd wondered about it at first, that odd feeling not so much of something missing as something he should—but didn't— miss. Then he had come to realize the wisdom of it and to be thankful for the lack of emotional involvement. And now Alex had blown it all to bits, and he didn't know how.

At that instant she appeared, so quietly that he wondered for a moment if he'd discovered some heretofore unknown power to conjure up reality out of his own wandering thoughts. She seemed unaware of his presence as she walked slowly, her face turned up to the gentle rain. Michael could only stare at her, fascinated by the drops of liquid crystal lingering on her thick, dark lashes, by the fortunate raindrops that beaded on her skin and then darted downward, over her soft cheek, her delicate neck, down her silken smooth skin to disappear in the vee of her open-necked shirt just above the swell of her breasts. He wanted to follow that path, wanted to trace the rain's course with his fingers, with his lips, with his tongue. . . .

Alex turned sharply, and he knew she'd heard the sound he'd strangled in his throat. Quickly he tried to compose his expression, knowing that all his tangled emotions, all the untoward heat and hunger he was feeling, had to be showing on his face.

"You're getting wet," he said quickly.

"So are you."

She said no more, just looked at him, as if she knew exactly what he wanted. But she couldn't know, not when he didn't know himself, not when he didn't have the slightest idea why this was happening to him, or what to do to fight it. Or even if he wanted to fight it.

Did he? Or did he really, deep down, want to give up this battle he'd never expected to have to fight? The one they'd promised him he would never face? Didn't he want to throw it all away and forget the rules? Didn't he want to grab her and kiss her senseless, until they both went down like melting wax from the heat of it? Didn't he want to touch, stroke, and kiss every sweet inch of her, and—God help him—have her do the same to him?

He shuddered under the force of the images that swamped him then; he couldn't help it. He staggered to his feet. He had to get back in control, he thought grimly, feeling perilously close to losing his grip altogether.

"You'd better go inside," Alex said quietly. "You're shivering."

"Right," he muttered, but he wasn't about to argue with her, not when she was barely inches away, not when he could smell the sweet scent of her, could almost feel her skin beneath his fingers. Damn them, he ground out silently, why were they letting this happen? He made his way across the soggy ground to the house, every cell, every nerve ending in his body, aware that she was just behind him.

That night, their traditional evening spent around the fire in the living room seemed unusually short as one by one the others left for the bunkhouse, claiming weariness after a day full of work.

Michael knew what they were doing; he'd sensed their plot to leave him alone with Alex in this romantic setting, with a cozy fire inside and rain outside. He fought the urge to run, to avoid this, but when she sat down in front of the fire to dry her still damp hair, just a scant two feet away, he couldn't seem to move.

The light from the fire brought out the flames in her hair, the thick silk of it gleaming as she brushed it into the smooth cap of her new haircut. The sight of it, and the graceful movements of her arm as she lifted the brush, seemed to hypnotize him.

She stopped suddenly, looking up to find him staring at her. Her eyes widened, and her lips parted as she looked back.

"Michael . . . ?"

If he'd had more practice, he might have been able to resist the need that overtook him then. But in an instant he was back to where he'd been in the clearing, trying to battle something he had no weapons to fight, something that had never happened to him before, at least not in the memory they had left him. And when she looked at him, all wide-eyed and wondering, he never had a chance.

"Alex."

It came out on a gasping breath, and then she was in his arms. His mouth came down on hers hungrily, demanding the sweetness he'd barely tasted before. She yielded to him gladly, eagerly, her lips parting for his tongue the moment it flicked over them.

A low groan broke from him, and he pulled her hard against him as he plunged his tongue deep into the warm recesses of her mouth. He felt her move, felt her slender fingers tangle in her hair, heard the tiny sigh of pleasure she made as he crushed her mouth with his.

That sound ignited him, and his arms went tight around her as he took them both to the floor in front of the hearth. She was soft and warm and pliant beneath him, her fingers digging into the muscles of his shoulders as she clung to him. He deepened the kiss, probing, tasting, his head spinning with new sensations, his heart pounding a rapid cadence.

She moaned, her body rippling beneath him. He choked out a gasp as her breasts were crushed against his chest, then nearly stopped breathing altogether when her hips pressed against his. Involuntarily he jerked, grinding himself against her.

He realized then, through the haze, that the unbearable ache he'd been feeling was the unexpected, violent response of his body to the feel of her. His body was surging to life with a fierce swiftness that stunned him. He was hot and hard and ready, and he didn't know why.

He'd seen others in this state, although right now he couldn't believe he'd ever seen anything happen so hot and fast. He had even, at times, been part of bringing those people together. But he'd never experienced it himself, and he didn't know how to deal with it. He was way out of his depth, and with his last ounce of sanity he knew it.

"Alex," he gasped, lifting himself off her with a greater effort than he'd ever made in his life.

"No," she whispered, trying to pull him back, needing his heat, his mouth on hers.

"Alex, no," he choked out. "I can't. God, I can't."

He rolled away, his breath coming in short, sharp pants.

"Michael . . ."

"No!"

He jerked away from her outstretched hand, knowing that if she touched him, he would be lost. Alex recoiled, paling at his rejection. With a choking little sound she scrambled to her feet, and without a word she ran out into the dark and the rain.

"Alex!"

Michael struggled to get up, his body seeming to have forgotten all its ordinary functions in the wave of new, unfamiliar sensations. He staggered to the window just in time to see her disappear into the barn, Cougar at her heels.

He sagged back to the floor, propping himself against the hearth, his back to the dancing flames. His body was screaming; his mind was in turmoil. He had to have some answers, and he had to have them now. This time, when he reached for the tags, he didn't stop.

My word, Michael, what's wrong? We've never heard—

Get me the boss, damn it.

Really, Mi—

Shut up and get me the boss. I want some answers, and I want them fast.

But he's unavailable at the moment. He—

I don't give a damn where he is. Get him.

A moment of silence. *Michael, are you in trouble? Please, tell me.*

Even in his angry distress, Michael caught the difference. Tell me. Not us, me. Except for the big boss, they never used the first person. He must have rattled their cage. Or Alex had, with what she'd done to him.

You're right, I'm in trouble. You said this would never happen. You promised that it would never be a problem. You even asked if I could handle it that way.

Michael, please, calm down.

Calm down? It's eating me alive, and you tell me to calm down?

What is? It was nearly a shout, as close as he'd ever heard them come to an emotional outburst.

I love her, damn it!

Silence, stretching out, drawing his strained nerves even tighter. Then, at last, *Oh, dear.*

Oh, great. That's a lot of help. What the hell is going on up there, anyway?

I don't know, Michael. This has never happened before.

That doesn't make me feel any better.

I can't answer you Michael. I'll have to find the boss.

As I recall, that's what I asked for in the first place.

He knew it was bitterly sour, but he didn't care. Nothing mattered anymore except what was happening to him. And, more importantly, what was happening to Alex. He was hurting her, the very last thing he wanted to do. The very thing he'd been sent here to avert.

Michael, please, just hang on. We'll find out, I promise.

Right. Pardon me if I'm not real excited about your promises at the moment.

I understand. Soon, Michael.

And then they were gone, leaving him to fight the battle of his newly awakened senses alone.

Seven

Alex shivered, but not from the cold. She was warm enough in her bed of straw, with Cougar beside her and Cricket above her radiating their body heat. She sat with her knees drawn up in front of her and her arms clasped around them, trying to control her shaking.

She'd done many things in her short life, she thought, but never had she so completely made a fool of herself. She'd thought she had herself under control, but when he'd looked at her like that she'd forgotten all of her lectures to herself at the first glimpse of the heat in his eyes.

On her trip to Portland, in the quiet hours alone, she had admitted, both fearfully and ruefully, that she loved him. She'd known it inwardly, although she had fought the knowledge, the moment she had seen him go down beneath that crashing, flaming beam. Her heart had screamed a protest that was immutable proof of what her mind had tried to deny.

She had also, in those hours alone, sworn that he would never know. That look of pain and guilt she had seen in his eyes when he had broken that unexpectedly hot and potent goodbye kiss had been seared into her mind, and she could think of only one explanation: he didn't want to hurt her. He knew the foolish little girl had fallen for him, and he was trying to be gentle. That was the kind of man he was, and she had sworn she would never put him in that position again.

So what had she done, within days of coming home? She had virtually thrown herself at him, practically begged him to kiss her. And he had. Oh, Lord, had he kissed her. She'd never known anything like that kiss, never felt anything like that total disruption of her senses.

Not that her experience was so great. There had only been a few chaste kisses from Walt Howard that had left her feeling a mildly pleasant warmth, nothing more. And that one, ugly experience that seemed so long ago that it could almost have happened to someone else. What had happened with Michael was so far removed from either of those that it was impossible to compare. Never in her life had she responded like that.

And it had affected him, too. Color flooded her cheeks as she remembered the rigid feel of him pressed so intimately against her. Surely that wouldn't have happened if he hadn't wanted her in return? Or was she being incredibly naive to think that it mattered, that it was her instead of just a willing female in general?

She didn't know. She almost laughed at the irony of it. She'd lived with anywhere from three to ten men at a time for the last eight years, been accused behind her back of everything from running some kind of sexual cult to indulging in one-woman orgies with all of them, and here she was at a total loss to understand one man's sexual reaction.

Some woman you are, she said to herself harshly. Can't even tell if a man wants *you* or just wants sex. Or...

Maybe that was it, she thought. He wanted it, but not with her. Not with her because he knew this was only a brief stop in his path, and he was too honorable to take her when he knew he would hurt her when he left, or...

Or he didn't want her, period. Much more likely, she thought bitterly. Just because she'd done as he said and discovered that she wasn't just the ragged little tomboy she'd always been didn't mean someone like him was going to fall at her feet. Sure, the guys had been bowled over by her new look, but they loved her already. Michael didn't. Why should he, when he could take his pick of all the women in the world?

In the end, she supposed, it didn't really matter. The result was the same, a deep, tearing pain that dug into some dark, protected corner of her soul.

"Oh, Cougar," she moaned. "What am I going to do?"

The dog lifted her head and licked her tear-stained cheek. She hugged him, burying her face in his thick fur.

Michael didn't know that it was already too late to avoid hurting her, she thought. He would be worried about that; he was too kind a man not to be. He would feel horrible if he knew how deeply she'd already been hurt, even though it was her own foolish fault. She could save him that, if she tried hard enough.

She would try. It would tear her up inside, but life had done that before and she'd kept on; she would do it again now. He deserved that much in return for all he'd done for them, if nothing else.

Tomorrow, she thought. She would begin tomorrow. Somehow she would face him as if this night had never happened. Tomorrow she would let him think it had meant nothing to her, freeing him from any responsibility he might feel. Tomorrow she would keep her head up and her eyes dry, no matter how much effort it took. But to-night...

Cougar whined his distress as his mistress wept dismally against him.

As it turned out, it was easier than she'd expected. For two days Alex saw Michael only at meals. She had to make very little effort to avoid him; he didn't ever seem to be around, no matter where she was. Because he's avoiding you, she told herself acidly. What did you expect?

Therefore she found it curious that he appeared just as Walt Howard drove up to the house.

"Hi, Alex," Walt said with a fond smile, getting out to give her a hug.

"Hi, Walt."

She restrained her instinctive desire to pull away from him; Walt was her friend, and she wasn't going to let a foolish infatuation with a man who wanted nothing to do with her ruin that.

"You look...different." Walt backed up to look at her.

Different. Yes, she supposed that was all she had really accomplished. She just looked different. She was still that same naive country girl, just with a different wrapping. Michael had proved that to her quite thoroughly.

She was too aware of Michael's presence, and of the fact that he was watching them. She spoke hastily. "What brings you out here?"

"I wanted to let you know that a lot of people think it was a good thing you all did, helping the Morgans that way."

"Oh?" She smiled wryly. "I didn't think there was anything we could do that would impress Riverglen."

"Well, people are talking a little differently now."

Trying not to look at Michael, she lifted an eyebrow at Walt. "You came all the way out here to tell me that?"

"Not just that."

"What else, then?"

Walt coughed, then shifted his feet. "Why, to see you, of course. I thought you might have lunch with me."

"I can't," she answered automatically. "I have too much to do today. I have to clean up Cricket—he got so muddy after the rain—and I need to treat his feet. He's been standing in a lot of mud lately."

"I'll do it," Michael said suddenly.

Alex flushed. "But I have to bathe Cougar."

"I'll do that, too. Go ahead and go."

Pain tore through her, but Alex set her jaw and brought her head up proudly. "All right."

Emotion flared in a pair of sky blue eyes—pain, resignation, and a spark of pride at her courage. None of it made any sense to Alex.

"Good," Walt said brightly. "And thanks," he added to Michael. "Oh, speaking of Cougar, you are keeping him tied up or inside, aren't you?"

"What?" Alex looked at him blankly.

"Well, we've had two more animals killed. Like I told Matt, I don't think he had anything to do with it, but there are still some rumblings going around."

"Cougar? Something to do with it?" Her eyes shot to Michael's face. "That's not what you told me!"

"You know it's not true," he said. "He's been locked up since—"

"Yes, but I had a right to know somebody thinks it is!"

"I...didn't want you to worry."

Alex was angry now. "How can I protect him when I don't know? I thought at least *you* weren't treating me like a child, but I guess I was wrong. I seem to be making a habit of it lately!"

Michael winced, and Walt spoke hastily.

"Alex—"

She whirled on him. "Who thinks Cougar did it?"

"Only one person, and nobody's really listening. It seems things are changing in town."

"But—"

"Let's go, Alex. We'll talk about it later."

Alex turned to look back at Michael; he was gone. Battling tears, she let Walt lead her around to the passenger side of his car.

Aaron stood watching Michael watching Walt drive away.

"Interesting, isn't it? Walt can't decide if he wants to pursue her or not, until the town begins to decide maybe we're not so horrible after all."

Michael clenched his jaw. "He's a decent guy."

"Sure," Aaron agreed easily. "Nice enough, if a little wishy-washy. When the town wanted her and us out, he was really careful about who knew he came to see her. Now, all of sudden he shows up to take her out in public."

Michael muttered something unintelligible and stalked off. When he got into the toolshed, he slammed down the plane he'd been using to fit the new barn door. His stomach was churning, and he had to bite back a string of angry, vicious curses. Nonchalantly sending her off with Walt Howard had ripped at him so fiercely he was surprised he wasn't bleeding. Maybe he was, inside, he thought grimly.

He didn't even bother to reach for the tags; he'd had no help or even contact from them since his last explosive message. Either they were giving him time to calm down, or they didn't know what was happening, either. Or perhaps they had abandoned him entirely, he thought suddenly. Was that what they did when somebody got out of line, out of synch? He'd done some things they hadn't totally approved of now and then, but he'd never gone completely haywire on them before.

What if they had abandoned him? He'd been working for them for so long, he didn't know anything else. What would he do? The answer came from someplace deep inside him, fully formed and definite. He would spend the rest of his life with Alex, trying to make up for being such a bastard to her. If, of course, they left him a life.

"Come on in, Mike," Matt called effusively. "You can help us ward off this disaster."

Alex looked up in time to see him hesitate in the doorway of the house. She and Matt and Aaron were at the small coffee table in the living room, some papers and a notepad spread before them.

"I just came back for my gloves," he said and started to walk past them toward the kitchen, where Sarah was washing the lunch dishes.

"Well, give us a hand anyway," Aaron said. "We decided to all go to the town meeting tonight. You know people, maybe you can come up with the arguments we need."

"You mean that Alex needs," Matt said. "She's going to have to do this." He put a hand on her shoulder. "Sorry, honey, but you're the only one they'll listen to."

Alex saw Michael look toward her, and she dropped her gaze to the notepad in front of her before their eyes could meet.

"You'll manage," Michael said tightly, then walked on into the kitchen.

Matt stared after him, then looked at Alex. "You two have a fight or something?"

Alex's grip on her pencil tightened. "What would we have to fight about?" she asked evenly.

Matt's eyes met Aaron's over her bowed head. They glanced toward the kitchen; then Aaron shrugged in disavowal of any understanding.

"Can we get on with this?" Alex asked a little sharply.

"Sure, I just—"

Matt broke off as two things happened: Michael came back in, tugging on his heavy work gloves, and as he passed it, the phone rang.

Michael nearly jumped. Aaron's eyes widened; he'd never seen Michael startled by anything. He must really be on edge, Aaron thought, his eyes flicking back to Alex's bowed head.

"Get that, would you, Mike?" Matt called out, and as Aaron's gaze lifted to Matt's face, he knew that Matt had sensed the same thing. And had asked Michael to get the phone on purpose, to keep him from leaving.

Michael knew he couldn't very well refuse, so he picked up the receiver. He answered, listened for a moment, spoke briefly, then hung up. The others were watching him, including Sarah, who had come in from the kitchen. He looked at her, at Matt, at Aaron, at everyone but Alex, as his words came out in short, choppy bursts.

"That was Mayor Barnum. There's a kid lost. Somewhere up in the hills above the east end of town. They figure he's been gone nearly fourteen hours."

"They figure?" Aaron asked.

"He snuck out last night. With a friend. The friend came home this morning. Said they got separated in the woods and he'd been looking all night."

"That's terrible!" Sarah exclaimed. Their only daughter was grown up and married now, but Sarah and Kenny had never lost their soft spot for children. "Poor child."

"Maybe," Michael muttered. And at last his eyes met Alex's. "It's Billy Peterson."

Alex held his gaze, although it took every bit of her will to look into those sky blue eyes and say evenly, "The sins of the father? I think not. He's still a boy." Her eyes flicked to Matt. "I'll take Cricket. I can cover more ground that way."

God, I love her, Michael thought. She's got more nerve and brains and goodness than anyone I've ever met. He had to look away; his faith in his ability to hide his thoughts from her was shaky beside the strength of his feelings.

Matt was speaking rapidly. "I'll get the truck. Aaron, round up Wheezer and Mark and Rick. Steve and Kenny aren't back from Eugene yet, though."

"I'll leave them a note," Sarah said, and hastened off to do so.

Alex watched them go, smiling softly. They'd never hesitated this time. They were becoming part of this community they had once held themselves so far apart from. And the community was accepting them at last. What she'd tried to accomplish in eight years had been done in less than a month. Thanks to Michael.

She realized then that he was still there, watching her. She tried to steel herself, to ignore him, but she couldn't deny him what he'd earned. She turned to look at him.

"Thank you," she said softly, hoping he would understand all she meant. The blue eyes lost their guarded look and went warm and soft with that inner glow, and she knew he had.

"Take Cougar with you," he said after a moment. Memory flashed in her eyes, destroying the momentary warmth and striking at him like a blow.

"I thought I was supposed to keep him tied up?"

He cringed inwardly at the memory of that day he had sent her off with Walt Howard, but he kept his expression even. "He might be able to help."

"Right."

She turned on her heel and left him standing there. He let out a long breath. He hadn't known it was possible to hurt like this. Or if he ever had, he'd forgotten. It was a moment before he could make himself move to join the others in the truck.

They easily found the makeshift command post Walt Howard had set up. Walt was speaking to the group of people gathered around his sheriff's unit.

"—haven't located the boy by dark, we'll call in outside help. There are trackers, dogs, and people trained in this sort of thing that we can call on. We'll find him."

Off to one side, Michael saw the woman from the store, Billy's mother, weeping in the arms of a heavy, ponderous looking man with a band of white skin above a tanned face, indicating he rarely went without wearing the rather grubby looking cap he held.

Michael stared at him, concentrating. He got the chaos of worry, anger, and frustration, the almost nauseating vibrations of a mean, shriveled spirit, but not the dangerous radiations of evil; he moved the man down lower on his ever-shortening list of suspects.

He still had his abilities, so they hadn't abandoned him after all, he thought in passing as he narrowed his focus, willing the man to turn.

"Uh-oh," Steve muttered. "Old man Peterson's spotted us. That won't make him happy."

"Nothing makes that man happy," Aaron said grimly. "But we make him particularly unhappy."

It was true, Michael thought, as he kept his eyes on the man. He was one of those who was not happy being happy. But although his eyes narrowed at the sight of them, the worry over his son outweighed his dislike, and he turned away without doing anything. Good, Michael thought. There was hope.

Alex rode up just as Walt spread a map out on the hood of his car. The young deputy gave her a smile, then handed her one of the whistles he'd been giving everyone else.

Michael caught a glimpse of someone on the edge of the crowd, someone whose attention was riveted not on the sheriff but on the group from the refuge. About the same age as Aaron and the others, the man seemed familiar somehow, yet he didn't recognize the face. He was tall, thin, and sallow looking, and something about him set Michael's teeth on edge. He looked at Aaron.

"Who is that?"

Aaron glanced toward the man. "Ray Claridge," he said shortly.

"Is he a local?"

Michael saw a muscle jump in Aaron's jaw but heard only a careful evenness in his voice. "Sort of. He grew up here, but he . . . left for several years. He came back a few years ago. Alex knows him better than I do."

Michael stared at the tall man, wishing he could make the connection. Under the force of his gaze, although that hadn't really been his intent, the man suddenly turned and moved away. Something in the way he walked struck home, and in that moment Michael knew where he'd seen him before. Dr. Swan's office. His gaze narrowed.

"Has he given you any problems?"

"No."

Michael sensed there was more, but before he could ask, Walt was giving directions and Aaron had turned to listen.

"We'll divide up the area to be searched. From what the other boy told us, we need to concentrate on that area, there." He gestured toward a thick belt of trees to his right. "We'll make the area between the river and the mill road one. I'll take that, along with the mayor's team."

Nice choice, Walt, Michael thought sourly. Run for office someday; you've got the moves. He turned to stare up at the low ridge that ran along the edge of town, concentrating, stretching, searching....

"Area two will be between the mill road and the start of the north ridge line. Sam, you and your group take that. Area three will be the ridge line. It will be tough, because of the terrain, so—"

"We'll take it," Michael said suddenly. All eyes shifted to him and the group of men standing beside him.

"That's rough ground," Walt began, glancing at Alex.

"We'll do it," she said. "I know the area, Walt, and so does Cougar. And Cricket. And the guys can handle the terrain."

After a moment Walt nodded. "The signal will be three long blasts on the whistle, all right?" They all nodded and began to scatter.

The men from the refuge clustered around Michael. He took charge so naturally, Alex thought. And they all listened to him, these gruff, war-toughened men who seemed to have forgotten they had ever doubted this man.

"Aaron, you and Rick start up the west boundary of this section," Michael said.

They both nodded, even Rick. Another transformation since Michael had come, Alex thought. Something cold seemed to squeeze her heart, but she forced it out of her mind.

"Mark, you and Wheezer take the section from the base of that rock up."

They looked over at the boulder he indicated and nodded. Michael knew he was dealing with men who understood searching unfamiliar country; they didn't need him to tell them how to do it. He paired himself up with Matt, then turned to Alex.

"I saved the best for you, Lexie," he said softly. "It'll be easier for you and Cricket to check the gorge trail."

She blushed at the nickname but only nodded, not taking time to wonder how he had managed to become so familiar with the countryside. The gorge trail was a narrow track that made its way up the ridge in a single straight line; it was steep but not necessarily treacherous if you took your time.

Alex whistled for Cougar and started off, ignoring the looks the big dog drew from some of the gathered crowd. If they were too blind to see the brave, fearless, honest heart of the big animal, it was their problem, she thought angrily.

They had been slogging through the brush-covered, still soggy landscape for nearly three hours when Michael suddenly came up short, his head cocked as if listening. Matt stopped behind him.

"What's wrong?"

It took a second for Michael to make the switch back to his actual surroundings. "Er, I'm a little tired. Let's take a break."

"You?" Matt chuckled. "Aren't you the guy who's been running me ragged all afternoon?"

"So I ran myself ragged, too." He found a relatively dry log and sat down. Matt followed suit gratefully, reaching for the canteen he was carrying for a quick drink.

Michael leaned back against an upthrust branch, closing his eyes. He let his surroundings slip away, let his senses expand, and after a moment he had it.

It unrolled against his eyelids as clearly as a piece of film. Cougar, ears suddenly upright, scampering off into the brush, Alex pulling Cricket to a halt on the trail, waiting. Then the excited barking of the big dog, and a faint wailing cry.

Alex wheeled the big horse on the narrow trail and sent him into the brush after Cougar. She shouted, and the cry came again, a little stronger this time.

Careful, Alex! Michael sent it to her on the wind, a sharp, short warning. His hands tightened into fists, relaxing only when she looked up, startled, and he knew she'd gotten it. Just in time, she pulled the paint to a halt. His hooves sent a little slide of rain-drenched soil down the sharp drop that loomed in front of them, hidden by a particularly heavy growth of brush.

"Down here! I'm down here!"

Cougar was barking furiously, and Alex listened, trying to judge how far down he was.

"Hang on, Billy! I'll be right there!"

She slid off the big horse and took down the rope that was fastened to the saddle. She looped the end over the saddle horn and tossed the rest over the drop. She yanked a pair of gloves out of her saddlebag and pulled them on, then took a brief moment to steady the horse.

"Easy now, love," she crooned. "Steady. Don't be dancin' around now, darlin'."

A mile away Michael smiled; she sounded like Andrew with his exaggerated drawl.

She went over the drop without hesitation, hand over hand down the rope, her boot heels digging into the damp earth. Cricket never moved; he stood like a statue of black-

and-white marble, the only motion his ears as they swiveled, listening.

She found the boy wedged between a rock and a fallen tree, with Cougar crouched over him, licking his ear in an effort to comfort him. Billy's left ankle was twisted painfully, caught beneath a branch of the tree. A pair of frightened eyes in a dirty, tear-stained face widened when he recognized her, but surprise didn't stop him from clinging to her when she reached him.

"It's okay," she soothed. "We'll get you out of here right away."

She freed his foot, moving with exquisite gentleness when the boy cried out.

"I know it hurts, Billy, and we'll fix it real soon, but we've got to get up the hill first."

"I f-fell," he stammered. "The ground sl-slipped. And I was so c-cold."

"I know, Billy, but it's all over now. You'll be home in no time."

She had the rope secured around them now and sent a sharp whistle upward. "Cricket! Back, Cricket, back!"

The response was immediate as the well-trained stallion began to move, his muscled hindquarters breaking a pathway through the brush. Slowly, with Alex shouting encouragement, the big horse lifted them up the steep slope as Cougar raced up and down, barking excitedly.

"That's it, Billy, we're okay now," she told him as they came up over the top. She called to Cricket, and the horse's black-and-white head soon poked through the brush. She got the first-aid kit she'd stuck in the other saddlebag and quickly taped up the boy's injured ankle. Only then did she think to reach for the whistle around her neck and give the signal.

"There," she said soothingly as the echo of the whistle faded away. "Now your folks know you're found. Let's go home, okay?"

She helped him up into the saddle, cradling his sore ankle until he was settled. She was about to climb up behind him when he spoke, soft and wondering.

"You came after me."

"Of course."

"But I was so mean to you, I said those things—"

She stopped then and stood looking up at him. "I won't say it didn't hurt, Billy, because it did. Lies always hurt someone. But you're still young, and maybe you don't know any better yet."

"I'm sorry."

A tear trailed down his grubby cheek. He bore no resemblance to the cocky boy she had seen in the store that day; now he looked like what he was, a frightened child.

"Just remember that next time you feel like calling somebody names."

"I will," he promised fervently. Alex mounted behind him and held him carefully as they started down the hill.

"Michael! Wake up, man! Didn't you hear the whistle? They've found the kid."

Michael's eyes opened slowly. "Yes," he said softly. "I know."

Most of the searchers were back by the time the big paint horse came walking out of the woods. Mrs. Peterson gave a glad cry and ran forward, her smile changing her entire appearance. Her husband followed more slowly, joy lighting his face, but confusion in his eyes, the confusion of a man feeling a tremendous gratitude toward someone he didn't want to like.

"Cougar found me, and Alex came right down the side of the cliff. She was awful brave! And then Cricket pulled us up—"

Billy was engulfed in his weeping mother's arms as Alex helped him slide out of the saddle.

"Careful," she cautioned. "His ankle is hurt. It might be broken."

Myra Peterson looked up at the woman on the horse, her eyes still streaming. "Bless you. I don't know why you did this for us, we've been . . ." She faltered and hugged Billy even tighter.

Her husband laid an unexpectedly gentle hand on his son's head, then looked at Alex as she slid off Cricket's back.

"Thank you for my son," he said gruffly, holding out his other hand. Alex took it without hesitation.

"You're welcome," she said. "I'm glad we could help. But you'd better get him over to Doc's, to look at that ankle."

"Wait!" Billy cried. "I want to thank Cougar."

At the mention of his name the big dog scampered up to the boy and began to lick his face sloppily. Billy giggled and threw his arms around the shaggy neck; the animal fairly wriggled in delight. Alex was aware of the looks coming from several among the gathered townspeople—the ones who had suspected the big dog of the murderous livestock raids, she guessed—but her eyes stayed on Billy as he looked up at her.

"Do you think I could come and play with him sometime?"

Alex knelt beside the pair. "I think he'd like that," she said solemnly. "As long as it's all right with your parents."

"Can I Mom? Dad? Please?"

522   ANGEL FOR HIRE

"Well . . ." George Peterson began doubtfully.

"I have to, Dad! Alex might never have found me if Cougar hadn't found me first!"

"Of course you can," his mother said suddenly, unexpectedly. "But now you need to go see Dr. Swan."

Billy made a face. "But I can't walk, Mom," he said, looking at the clinic about a hundred yards away.

"Carry you, if you want," Mark said.

Billy eyed the big, bearded man warily. But when he saw how Cougar rubbed up against the big man's leg, and the way Cricket nuzzled him familiarly, he nodded suddenly.

"Okay."

George Peterson looked as if he wanted to protest, but his son was too big for him to carry, so he subsided. Mark lifted him easily, cradling the boy carefully against his broad chest.

"Wow!" Billy exclaimed. "You're really tall!"

"You too someday."

Billy's eyes widened. "You think so?"

"Don't fall off mountain anymore," Mark said sternly.

Laughter rippled through the onlookers. Genuine, friendly laughter, not the rude, contemptuous sound Mark had been subjected to so many times before. He knew the difference, and when a smile split his bearded face, it transformed him. Alex surreptitiously wiped at her eyes; she loved that big man dearly.

"Atta girl, Alex!"

"Way to go!"

The cries rang out from all through the crowd as Mark carried the boy into the clinic. Alex smiled a little vaguely.

"Good work, Alex," Walt slipped an arm around her. "How about dinner tonight? The biggest steak in town for our heroine."

"No thanks, Walt. I appreciate it, but all I really want is a long, hot bath. I have to be back for the town meeting tonight."

"Another time then." Walt seemed to accept her refusal gracefully and left to go back to the milling group. Alex turned to remount Cricket and head home but stopped when a furtive movement from behind the clinic caught her eye. She saw who it was, and her mouth twisted with distaste.

"Alex? What is it?" Michael had appeared suddenly, but she was too tired to be startled.

"Nothing." She reached past him for the stirrup.

"Who was that?"

"Henry Willis."

Michael wheeled around to stare, remembering what Matt had told him, what Walt had said about the man's insidious suggestion about Cougar. Alex took advantage of his movement to swing up into the saddle.

"What is it, Alex?" Michael asked at last. "Why do you dislike him so?"

If she hadn't been so tired, she never would have said it. But she *was* tired, physically and emotionally. The intensity of the search had drained her. She'd been battered by Michael's rejection and her own uncertainty, and the specter of the threat to the refuge that hung over them tonight. Her guard was down, in tatters, and it slipped out.

"No big reason," she said acidly. "I just don't care for so-called men who molest children."

She whirled Cricket and put her heels to him, leaving Michael staring after her in shock.

Eight

The church auditorium that was used as the town hall was filled to overflowing. Alex nervously smoothed down the skirt of the simple, button-front dress she'd worn. She had been to a few of these meetings, but never had she seen so many people at one. Did it have something to do with them? she wondered. Did so many people still hate them, that they had joined together to try and get them out?

Alex turned to look at Aaron, needing the reassurance of the wiry, kind man who had been with her since the beginning. Instead she found Michael sitting next to her, and she drew back in surprise.

She had refused to talk to him after leaving him that afternoon, already regretting what she'd said. He'd tried to get more out of her, knocking on the bathroom door while she was cleaning off the remnants of her trip down the side of the ridge, and later on the bedroom door after she'd locked herself in. She'd ignored him, although it had more than once taken her teeth clamped on her lower lip to do it.

When they had gathered to leave, she had taken refuge in the middle of the group and gratefully accepted Aaron's offer to drive her in his little convertible. He put up the worn top and handed her in as if it were a chariot; Alex felt more like it should have been a jeep, carting the losing general off to the battle.

"It's going to be all right," Michael said softly.

She tried to look away, but his eyes drew her with that odd power that she couldn't seem to resist. It filled her again, that calm peace, that feeling of security, and she wondered how it was possible for him to make her feel this way at the same time that he was tearing her apart.

"Ahem, ladies and gentlemen." Mayor Barnum had taken the dais and was tapping the podium with the gavel. "I have an announcement to make. In view of the events of this afternoon, it has been moved, seconded, and passed in chambers that this meeting be limited to only one item of business tonight."

Alex's shoulders sagged; she hadn't wanted to do this at all, but she had been set for it tonight and didn't look forward to having it drag on for another month.

"That one item was also passed unanimously. It is, in short, an acceptance of the voluntary withdrawal of a complaint requesting an investigation into a possible zoning violation."

Alex's head shot up. Mayor Barnum was looking straight at her and smiling.

"I think today—this past week, in fact—has proved quite clearly that Alex Logan and her friends are a part of this community. A valuable part. And I thank Mr. Peterson for withdrawing his complaint."

All their heads swiveled around toward the red-faced man who sat off to one side.

"And with that I declare this meeting adjourned!"

A round of applause broke out around the room, and a dazed Alex was enveloped in congratulatory hugs.

"How about that?" Aaron crowed.

"All right!" Matt laughed.

"Safe now," Mark said, practically lifting her off the floor with his embrace.

"Let's go celebrate!" Steve exclaimed.

Alex shook her head. "You go," she said numbly. "I'm going home." She tried visibly to steady herself, then looked at them all. "Don't thank me," she whispered. "Thank Michael. He did it."

Aaron nodded slowly, then grinned. "Uh, unaccustomed as I am to public speaking," he began with a laugh, to a round of boos and hisses. "Seriously, there is something I wanted to say. Something happened tonight that has never happened since Alex started the refuge. This town made an overt gesture of friendship to us. And I think it's clear to all of us that we have one person to thank for it."

They all nodded.

"So," Aaron went on. "From all of us, thank you, Michael. You shamed us into doing what we should have been doing all along."

"You just needed a nudge in the right direction. You've all been fighting for so long, you forgot how to make peace."

A strangled little sound broke from Alex. Then she whirled and ran toward the door, although her progress was impeded by several newly gained well-wishers. The others turned to look at Michael, who was watching her go, looking oddly pale. He took a hesitant step, as if to start after her, then stopped.

"Here," Aaron said, holding out the keys to his precious convertible. "Go take her home. She's wiped out. We'll get home in the truck."

Michael stared for a moment; then, as Alex finally made it out the door, he grabbed the keys and ran.

He was surprised that she didn't fight him until he took her elbow to help her into the little car. He realized then that she was utterly drained, like a soldier who had drawn on the last of his reserves for the fiercest fight and then found it was over before it began.

He started to lower himself into the driver's seat when a chilly blast of air struck the back of his neck. The gust startled him, since there was no wind tonight, but when he whirled around to look, he thought he understood. For there in the doorway of the auditorium, standing next to the tall, gangly figure of Ray Claridge, was Henry Willis.

He was torn for a moment, but the chance to probe at his prime suspect seemed insignificant compared to the need to get Alex home. He turned away and got into the car.

She said nothing all the way home, and nothing as they went inside. She stopped in the living room doorway, while Michael went to build up the fire, stoking it gently until it was crackling, sending waves of heat into the room. They needed a heat pump to recirculate the heated air, he thought. Or a wood stove designed for heating. It would keep the little house much warmer with less wood.

He turned to see her still standing in the same spot, her hands clasped tightly in front of her chin. They were trembling.

He crossed the room and swept her up into his arms. She made a tiny sound of protest, but there was no force in it, and he ignored it. He carried her to her bedroom and set her down on the bed as he flicked on the light.

"No," she murmured as he knelt to slip off her shoes, but her voice, too, held no conviction.

"Shh," he murmured. "You need to rest, Lex. That's all, just rest."

He clamped on controls he'd never had to use before when he began to unbutton the pale green dress. Controls that slipped several notches at once when the dress slipped off her slender shoulders and revealed a skimpy swath of emerald green silk beneath.

He sucked in his breath. He'd been prepared for practical underwear—all, he was sure, she had ever been able to afford. This was a stunning, breath-stealing surprise, this silky, sexy little teddy. She must have bought it in Portland, he thought, and tonight she had needed the way it made her feel.

He knew he was trying desperately to keep his mind on things like that, to keep it off of how incredibly beautiful she was. Gone was any trace of the shaggy tomboy. This was a slim, lusciously curved, long-legged woman, with a burnished sweep of russet hair and a pair of wide green eyes that looked bottomless in the faint light from the bedside table.

"You need rest," he muttered harshly, more to remind himself than to convince her. It was the hardest thing he'd ever done to leave her there.

He was still wide awake, battling the resurgence and unfamiliar hardness of his body, when the phone rang. He'd heard the men and Sarah come home, their off-key singing telling him that the celebration had been a success. He'd tried to sleep, but, as it had done so many times before, it had eluded him. When the ring finally came, he knew he'd been expecting it.

He sat bolt upright before the echo died away and was on his feet, pulling on his jeans, before the second ring was cut off as she answered. He didn't wonder if it was the phantom caller again; he knew. He stopped at her closed door, spreading his fingers on the wood, closing his eyes.

"... Think you're set now, don't you, bitch? Got the town eating out of your hand now, right? All your problems are over?" A string of filthy, crude words followed. "They're just starting, slut. We haven't all been blinded by a few good deeds. You'll leave, and you'll be sorry you didn't listen to us before."

She said nothing, just hung up the phone with a quiet care that said a great deal about her state of mind.

"Alex!"

Nothing. He tried the door; she'd locked it.

"Alex, let me in!"

"No."

"Damn it, Alex—"

"Go away."

He hesitated, glancing at the tags that hung against his chest, but he didn't expect any help. They generally left him alone to do what he had to, but they'd never been this absent before. He took a breath, clenched his jaw and put his hand back on the knob. He stared at it, then tightened his grip until he heard the quiet click. It turned, and the door swung open.

Alex jerked upright. "I . . . I locked that."

"It didn't catch." He strode across the room and sat down beside her. "I know it was him, Alex."

"I . . . it doesn't matter. They're just phone calls."

Just phone calls. From someone who knew enough to call at night, knew that she was generally in the house alone then, knew that she would be the one to answer the phone.

But he didn't say it; she was frightened enough already, no matter how bravely she tried to deny it.

"Alex—"

"Please," she whispered, shivering. "I don't want to talk about it."

"Alex, please. I know I've hurt you—"

"Not your fault," she said quickly, through teeth that were chattering. "I should have known better."

He felt her chill and moved to hold her. She tried to pull away, and he slid up beside her on the bed to stop her.

"Know better than what, Alex?" he asked softly.

She sagged, giving up the protest she didn't have the strength to make in the first place. "Than to think you might... want me."

"Oh, God, Alex," he said on a shuddering breath. "I do. I can't, I shouldn't, it's crazy, but I do. But—"

"No. Please. Just... leave it. I understand."

He wanted to explain, to tell her, but he couldn't find the words. He was having trouble just breathing, with her so close in his arms in that shimmering little thing that did so little to conceal the full curves of her breasts.

He wondered if the boss was blocking him, knowing how close he was to breaking the most important rule ever laid down for him. He thought it might be true, for the other words came easily enough.

"Tell me about Henry Willis."

She twisted in his arms, but he didn't let her go. "I shouldn't have said anything. It was a long time ago, and it doesn't matter anymore."

"Tell me." He lifted a finger to tilt her chin back and made her meet his eyes. "Tell me, Alex."

She shuddered, dropping her head as soon as he released her. He pressed her face to his shoulder, knowing the truth would come now.

"It was after my parents were killed," she said slowly. "I felt so...lost. Andrew tried to help, but he was hurting as much as I was. I started going for long walks. It helped a little. I ran into Henry one day, fishing down at the river."

She drew a shaky breath before going on. "He started hanging around, walking with me. He was older, twenty-five then, but I didn't realize it was a little strange that he had so much time for a fifteen-year-old. He seemed nice about it. He listened to me and never said much. I thought he was...trying to help."

She trembled again, and Michael pulled her around so that he could slip his other arm around her, too, to hold her more securely against the tide of ugly memories.

"One night...it was after Andrew had a really bad day...I had to go get a tire fixed at the gas station. Pete was gone, but Henry was there, and we talked for a while. But when I tried to leave..." She bit back a sob.

"Let it out, Alex," Michael whispered. "You've held it in for so long."

"He...grabbed me. I didn't realize what he was doing at first, until he threw me down on the floor and started ripping my shirt. Then he...hit me."

Michael fought back the tide of fury that rose in him; he had to concentrate on Alex now.

"I screamed, but he just laughed. He wouldn't stop. I tried...I clawed at him, I kicked, but he was so much bigger than me...."

A twenty-five-year-old man against a fifteen-year-old girl. Michael was getting the images from her, broken, ugly pictures, ragged around the edges from being suppressed for so long in the innermost recesses of her mind. She'd had the memory buried so deep even his bosses hadn't found it. Fury surged in him again, and again he beat it back. He tightened his hold on her.

"What happened, Alex?"

"He...made me touch him. Through his pants." Her head came up then. "I did." The barest ghost of a smile flitted across her pale, strained face. "Hard. I got away then."

He got it then, the image of a slim girl fighting back the only way she could, with slender but strong fingers driving to do damage where it would hurt the most. Pride welled up in him, pride in her. He nearly laughed with the force of it.

"Oh, God, Alex, you're the most incredible woman I've ever known." He gathered himself when he saw her staring at him, wide-eyed. "You never told anyone."

Her eyes dropped to the quilt that was tangled around them now. "I couldn't. Henry knew that. It would have hurt Andrew terribly. He just would have felt even more helpless, knowing he couldn't even defend his little sister."

"So you carried it all alone, all this time."

"I just stayed away from him. And after Andrew died, I told him that if he ever came near me, or if I heard of him pulling that on anyone else, I'd go straight to the sheriff."

She saw Michael's eyes flick to the phone.

"No," she said slowly. "It can't be. He's left me alone for years now."

He wasn't sure, but he said nothing. He held her for a long time, whispering to her, telling her how brave and good and wonderful she was, softly blocking her automatic denials. She gradually relaxed and snuggled closer to him. He thought she had slipped into sleep when she spoke, in a tiny little voice that made a quiver run up his spine.

"Michael? Did you really...want me to go with Walt the other day?"

Oh God. "He's a good man, Alex."

"That's not what I asked."

"He's better for you."

"That isn't it, either."

"No. No, damn it, I didn't. I hated it. It shouldn't make one damn bit of difference to me, but I hated it!"

She moved then, sitting up so quickly it startled him. Her hair was tousled, her eyes wide as she looked at him. The covers dropped to her waist, and he could see the ripe swell of her breasts, the tips pressing tautly against the thin covering of emerald silk. His newly awakened body roused to the sight with a rush, and he groaned under the force of it.

"Alex..."

She lifted one arm, reaching out to lay her hand flat against his chest in the V formed by the golden chain.

"Alex, don't do this."

"You said you wanted me...."

"But I can't—"

He broke off as, cheeks flaming, her eyes dropped to the zipper of his jeans and the unmistakable bulge behind it.

"God, Alex, you don't understand. This isn't right. Something's wrong, and I don't know what it is, but this shouldn't be happening."

"Why?" she asked in sudden fear. "Did you leave a wife behind somewhere?"

"No." He groaned again as her hand flexed on his chest, her fingers stroking his skin, sending heat out in rippling circles.

"It's all right," she whispered huskily. "I know that you don't...I don't expect anything."

"You should," he said harshly. "You should. You're too good for somebody who'll just move on, Alex."

A little stunned by her own boldness, Alex leaned forward. She knew what she was risking, knew that another rejection from him would shatter her fragile confidence. But she couldn't seem to care, and she bent to press her lips to his chest.

His muscles convulsed, his back arching involuntarily to press his chest against her mouth. In that second, when heat and sensation sizzled along every nerve in his body, he knew he was lost. It didn't matter anymore that this shouldn't, couldn't, be happening. The years he'd gone without feeling a thing didn't matter. It didn't matter what rules he was breaking, or what they would do to him. Nothing mattered except this woman and this moment.

He came up off the bed and rolled her beneath him. His mouth darted to hers, taking it hungrily, furiously, as if all those years alone had been damming something up somewhere inside him. She welcomed him, opened for him, and he drove his tongue into her sweet warmth.

Her arms went around him, and her nails dug into the muscles of his back as she clung to him, a low moan of pleasure rising from her throat. It coalesced into a breathy whisper of his name, and heat crackled through him like wildfire.

Her hands slid up his back to tangle in the thick hair at his nape. Her fingers caught the gold chain, and Michael's head came up suddenly. He moved a hand, caught the gold chain on one finger and tugged it over his head.

Alex watched him, her eyes puzzled.

"I don't want an audience," he growled, tossing the tags onto the nightstand.

Before Alex could even try to make sense out of that, his mouth was on hers again. She greeted his returning heat joyously, sending her own tongue daringly in search of his. They met, twirled, danced, and Alex felt herself shifting, changing, as if muscle and bone had melted into some golden, flowing liquid that was capable of feeling only pleasure.

Every touch expanded the heat; every movement of his body over hers made her less certain where the boundaries between them were. The solid wall of his chest crushed her breasts, and she reveled in it, arching herself against him to increase the pressure, twisting sinuously to rub her throbbing nipples harder against him.

Michael's breath left him in a rush, and he bore down on her with his full weight, wanting to feel every inch of her as she moved beneath him. He lowered his head and trailed a path of quick, hot kisses down the line of her jaw, the side of her throat.

Alex gasped, moaning his name again as his lips reached the high swell of her breasts. She'd never felt this, never known such a burning need. She felt the rippling movement of her body begin, the consecutive convulsions of muscles that had found a new purpose: bringing her body closer to his. Her hips, then her stomach, then her breasts, all arching, seeking, wanting him.

"Alex," he whispered thickly, "what are you doing to me?"

He slid his hands down her shoulders slowly, following his hands with his mouth. He was moving with a sureness that almost surprised him. He was vaguely aware of the fact that this was different, that this certainty was coming not from some source outside his own consciousness but from deep within him, from some long-forgotten place of ancient, primitive instinct that was rusty from disuse.

He moved to cup her breasts, and his body fairly sizzled as he lifted the full, feminine weight, as the soft flesh rounded into his palms. She gasped, lifting herself to him instinctively, and he couldn't resist the unspoken plea. His mouth went to one breast, his lips seeking, finding, the taut thrust of the tingling nipple beneath the thin silk. The sheer fabric was no barrier to his suckling kiss as he wet it with his tongue.

Her cry of shocked pleasure raced along his singing nerves. The crest tightened under his tongue, urging him on, and his body clenched fiercely around a white-hot shaft of need. He felt her hands slide down his chest to his stomach, and every muscle there contracted at her touch. Her fingers slipped down to his waistband to caress his belly. He groaned, low and deep, at the thought of what it would feel like if she moved her hand just a little farther.

He felt the sweet, hot pressure of her lips as she lifted her head to blaze a trail down his throat, lingering to flick her tongue in the hollow at its base.

He had to know. He had to feel her touch. He shifted his weight and gently grasped one delicate wrist. A throttled groan broke from him as he carefully moved her hand that last critical distance and pressed it lightly over the swollen flesh begging to be freed from the too-tight jeans.

He nearly gasped at the hot, brilliant flash of pleasure that shot through him. But he choked off the sound when he realized she had gone utterly still. Comprehension flooded him, and he let out a harsh breath as guilt rose up and kicked him in the gut.

"Oh, God, Alex, I'm sorry! I didn't think... Damn, and after you just told me what that bastard did."

"No," she whispered as she looked up at him, her eyes holding none of the fear, repulsion, or condemnation he'd expected. The green depths were full only of an awed wonder. "It's just...how different it is, how wonderful... when it's someone you love."

Her hand moved, flexed caressingly, and fire shot through him in a fierce burst. He shuddered, trying desperately to rein in his soaring senses, knowing she didn't even realize what she'd admitted.

She loved him. It didn't surprise him; he supposed he'd known it on some subconscious level for a long time. But it stopped him. He couldn't do this, not to Alex, not when she didn't truly know what she was doing.

God, it should be so easy! He loved her. She loved him. Hadn't he orchestrated this for others hundreds, maybe even thousands, of times? So why was it killing him, ripping him apart?

"Alex," he moaned, his head dropping to rest in the sweet valley between her breasts. "What am I doing?"

"Michael?"

She shook as his name escaped her, terrified that he was going to reject her once more. His head came up, and he took a long, slow breath as he looked at her.

"There's something I have to tell you."

"Now?" Her voice was tiny, strained.

"I have to. Before we . . . go any further. You have the right to know."

"You're scaring me, Michael. To know what?"

He reached for the tags on the nightstand. They glinted in the dim light. "Who I am," he said softly.

"But I know all I need—"

She jerked in response to the loud crack of sound, a startled cry breaking from her. Michael's head snapped around as they waited, frozen.

"That was—"

"—a shot. I know," Michael said grimly.

"Was it as close as it sounded?" she asked, trembling as she stared into the darkness.

"Afraid so."

He was on his feet and moving, tugging the gold chain and tags back over his head. He grabbed his socks and battered boots and yanked them on hurriedly as Alex tugged on her own jeans and boots. She reached for a heavy sweater, quashing a little pang as she pulled it down over the teddy that was still damp from his mouth.

The others were spilling out of the bunkhouse, and they met in the yard. They wasted no time on preliminaries; they all knew that hauntingly familiar sound too well.

"How far, you think?" Aaron asked.

"Hundred yards, maybe, depending on the gun," Matt answered grimly.

Michael nodded. "Up there, I think," he said, looking toward the hill behind the orchard. They nodded back.

"Where's Cougar?" Alex asked suddenly. The big dog had been nowhere in sight when they'd gotten home, she realized now. "Oh, God, what if somebody saw him out and thought he was—"

"Easy, Alex," Michael murmured. "He's in the barn. He was under house arrest until tonight, remember?"

Steve glanced around suddenly. "Mark's gone."

Michael's head came up sharply. "You're sure?"

Steve nodded. "I saw his bunk was empty. I thought he was already out here."

"We'd better find him." Wheezer said. "Let's each head—"

"No!" Michael snapped. "Nobody goes alone."

"He's right," Rick said suddenly, unexpectedly. "There's still somebody out there with a gun."

"Rick, Aaron, Steve, check along the road. Matt, you take Wheezer and Kenny and check the trees around the pasture. Then we'll all check the hill."

No one questioned his rapid orders, but Matt raised an eyebrow as he said, "That leaves you alone, Mike."

"I'll catch up. There's something I have to do first."

They hesitated, then went, as Rick reminded them of the need for haste. Alex stood stock still, looking at Michael.

"You're going alone, aren't you?"

He shrugged off her question. "Alex, listen. You've got to think. You know Mark better than anyone. Where does he go when he takes off like this?"

"Lots of places. Sometimes he just walks. It makes him feel better."

"What if he's already feeling good? Like tonight?"

Her eyes widened. "He goes to the rock," she whispered.

"The rock?" He looked over his shoulder and up the hill. "You mean the shelf up there?"

She nodded, not even wondering anymore how he knew about the big outcropping of rock that jutted out of the hill and gave an expansive view of the farm. Michael started off at a run but stopped when he heard her behind him.

"Stay here."

"Don't even start. I'm not sitting around waiting."

"Alex," he said tightly, "there's somebody out there shooting."

"Nobody goes alone. That's what you said."

He gripped her shoulders. "Alex—"

"I'll just follow you," she insisted.

He held her tight, staring into her eyes. Even in the dark she could see the warmth steal into the sky blue. "You are the stubbornest . . ."

Her chin came up defiantly. Michael laughed, hugged her swiftly, and said no more when she matched him stride for stride as he started up the hill.

They were about halfway up when the back of his neck began to prickle, the hair standing up as his muscles tensed. He looked around, but nothing moved. They kept on.

Ten yards later he stopped. Alex looked up at him questioningly, but before she could speak he held a finger to her lips and shook his head slightly. Then he backed up a step, lifting his head and closing his eyes.

"Michael?"

"He's still here. With the gun. I can feel it."

Alex paled. She never thought to doubt him; the certainty in his voice was undeniable. She shivered as they resumed the climb to the big rock that was Mark's favorite place, and it had nothing to do with the cold.

"Please," she murmured, not sure to whom. "Not Mark. He's been hurt so much already."

"I know, Lexie."

"All those years he was in the VA hospital...they thought that shrapnel had made him an...an idiot. And all it had done was damage his speech center. He was fine, his mind was fine, but he just couldn't talk to tell them."

"We'll find him, Alex."

"We have to. He's so special...and he's changed so much since the first week he came to us and realized he could talk the best he could and no one would laugh at him."

She couldn't stop the sharp, startled cry that slipped out when Michael whirled, then went rigidly tense.

"Him," he muttered, fury and realization in his voice.

He dived through the brush to their left. She followed, frightened but determined. He looked like a predator on the hunt, his eyes trained into the distance even though she knew he couldn't possibly see anything. Once, far ahead, she thought she heard another, heavier, clumsier movement, and her heart began to hammer.

And then he stopped. A short, muttered oath broke through the stillness. She came up hard against his back and staggered. She saw him give one last, angry look in the direction they'd been going; then he took two long steps to the right and went down on his knees.

Only then did she see Mark. Sprawled on his back, one hand on his chest, his bearded head thrown uncomfortably back.

"No!" Alex went down beside him, reaching for that limp hand. Then she drew her own hand back, staring at the ominous sticky redness. "Oh, God! Mark!"

Michael moved swiftly, his fingers feeling desperately for some sign of life. He found a faint, thready pulse, fading even as he felt it. "Damn."

"No!"

She shuddered violently as the word broke from her, and Michael saw in her eyes the crumbling of a valiant spirit. No, he echoed to himself. And he reached for the tags.

Michael, we've been trying to reach—

Later. This is more important. Mark's hurt. You promised he wasn't to get hurt.

Yes, but—

No buts. You're going to help me help him.

Michael, you don't mean—

Damn right I do. And right now.

But the risk! If you fail, it could kill you both!

Damn the risk. If I don't, he's dead for sure. There's no time to argue. You've blown a lot of promises lately but not this one.

You're quite right. All right, Michael. Good luck.

He caught a glimpse of Alex looking at him oddly as he dropped the tags, but he had no time to deal with her now. Every second mattered. He leaned over and gripped Mark's brawny shoulders.

Alex stared at him. She saw the change overtake him, saw him go pale, sweat beading up on his face and glistening in the dappled moonlight coming through the trees. His eyes closed, his face contorted sharply, and a hissing breath escaped through his clenched teeth.

When the first sound broke from him, Alex cried out his name. She'd never heard anything like it, never heard a sound so full of pure, burning agony. He was doubled over, his breath coming in short, choppy pants, the knuckles of both hands white with strain as he held on to Mark as if trying to lift his full, huge weight with just his fingers.

The sound came again, ripping, tearing. Then again and again, short, horrible chunks of sound. Tears streamed from Alex's eyes. She didn't understand what was happening, but she knew Michael was in agony. His beautiful face was twisted in such pain that it was almost unrecognizable. She was seized with a clawing fear that she was about to lose both of them, a fear that was a glowing hot blade slowly piercing her heart.

"Please no, please," she moaned over and over, feeling so utterly helpless that she wanted to cower and hide.

Suddenly Michael moved sharply, his lean body curling inward as a harsh, rasping breath burst from him. And then he went slack, like a puppet with all the strings cut at once. He crumpled, sliding off Mark's limp form and onto his back, the rise and fall of his chest so shallow that Alex was barely certain he was breathing at all. She just sat there, shaking, stunned beyond any understanding. Michael looked so pale, his skin almost translucent in the silver light, his eyes dark and bruised looking in his exhausted face. He looked, she thought in torment, as close to death as Mark.

Her eyes strayed to that beloved, bearded face. She reached out to touch his cheek, knowing she would find it cold and lifeless. And then, incredibly, Mark opened his eyes. And smiled at her.

Nine

Michael felt the warmth, saw the light through his closed eyelids. Instinctively he turned toward it, tilting his head as if he could absorb some of the radiant energy. He needed it; he felt more drained and weak than he could ever remember.

He nestled into the pillow, wishing he had the strength to turn over and shut out the light so he could go back to sleep. But there was something he needed to do, wasn't there? No, it could wait. It had to wait. He was so tired, and just lying here felt so good. Too good. When had the narrow little bed become so comfortable?

He pried open one eye, then the other, then blinked at the flood of light. Alex's bed? He jerked himself up on one elbow, startled. And found himself looking right into a pair of emerald eyes.

Memory snapped back with a sharpness that was almost audible, sending weariness flying before the burst of adrenaline, like leaves before a hurricane. He searched her face, looking for some sign of what she was thinking. But for the first time he couldn't read her. The wide, innocent green eyes were shuttered against him.

Which told him what she was thinking, he supposed wearily, as clearly as if he *had* been able to read her. He sank back on the pillow. How many times had they told him? People didn't deal well with things they didn't understand, with things—or people—that weren't...normal. He had thought, had dared to hope, that Alex might be different. But it was too much to ask; it always had been.

He knew it wouldn't matter to her in the long run. The rule was only to make sure the job got done without interference, because in the end, when he left, it would all be taken care of. They would see to that. But he had hoped...

Had hoped what? For a miracle? He nearly laughed at the irony of it; he was in the business of making them, not getting them. A sick feeling, making his entire body ache and his gut twist violently, rose inside him.

Alex moved then, leaning forward in the chair she had pulled up beside the bed. Reflexively his eyes went to her, even though the last thing he wanted was to see that flat, shuttered look again.

"That was what you were going to tell me, wasn't it?"

Her voice was as expressionless as her face.

He let out a long, tired breath. Slowly, he nodded.

"Will you tell me now?"

Now. Now that she'd been frightened, repulsed by what she'd seen. Now that she knew he was not, in the usual sense, normal. He was different. Very different. Inhuman, from a human point of view. Desperately he tried to dodge what he knew was coming.

"Mark...?" he began.

"He's fine." Alex looked at him steadily, as if she realized he was stalling. When she went on, it was in the short, clipped tone of a person getting a required report out of the way so she could get on to what she really wanted.

"Mark doesn't remember much. Or else he isn't saying. The guys got you both down the hill. I told them you fell getting to Mark. They put you to bed. Doc was here. He said Mark would be fine. He didn't understand how. He didn't understand what was wrong with you, either. He wanted you at the clinic for tests. I told him to wait. We were to call him if you didn't wake up by noon. Which is when he's going to call the sheriff. He has to, for any gunshot wound. But he gave us until then. Because I asked him to wait."

She'd handled it perfectly. She'd done everything he would have done, if he'd been able to. He let out a sigh as the weariness began to creep back into his body, into his very bones.

"Well?"

His eyes snapped open. The words, strained and tight, slipped out despite his efforts to stop them. "What's the point? You've already made up your mind, haven't you?"

"Yes," she said quietly, sending a dart of searing pain through a heart that wasn't supposed to be able to feel things like that. "But I still want to know."

"You want the whole story, right?" he asked bitterly.

"You told me I had the right to know."

The pain again, fierce, stabbing. "That was..."

He trailed off. The reason she had the right to know—because she loved him—obviously didn't exist anymore. It had been destroyed in a few desperate moments on a dark hillside. He was a freak now, something to be stared at, to be avoided.

"Help me understand."

For the first time a hint of emotion slipped into her voice. Michael drew a deep breath. Still he hesitated. But what did it matter? It was all going to be over soon anyway.

"Why not?" he muttered. "I've already broken every other rule."

"Rule?"

His eyes flicked to her again. Then he shifted, moving the pillows to prop himself against the headboard of the bed.

"Rules," he said at last, training his eyes on her. She looked so very vulnerable, huddled in the worn terry cloth robe she wore. He had to do this, he thought. He had to at least try and make her understand. She might not love him anymore, but he couldn't stand the idea that she found him repulsive.

"Whose rules?"

He began, speaking low and clear, using every ounce of energy he had left to will her into understanding.

"It started a long, long time ago, Alex. A group of... people, for lack of a better word, stumbled across a place inhabited by a developing race of creatures they found fascinating. They saw potential there, and the seeds of disaster as well. For a long time they just studied those creatures, watching them change, grow. Sometimes not for the better."

She was listening, but he sensed the impatience in her.

"Stay with me, Alex. It's a long story." He realized his hands had curled into fists and consciously relaxed them. "These... people, their own laws wouldn't let them interfere. But they found a way around that. They started... recruiting people, people from this place."

"Michael, if this is supposed to be an explanation, it isn't working. I want to know about you."

He sighed. "All right, all right. Me." He took another breath. "It started in a coal mine. In Kentucky. There was an explosion and a cave-in. Twenty men died, the rest were dying. There wasn't any hope anyone would get there in time. The place was full of poisonous gas."

His eyes had gone strangely hollow. She saw a shiver ripple through him, and he took a quick, gulping breath, as if he hadn't been sure he could. Alex's eyes widened with realization; he had been one of those men. But before she could dwell on that, he was speaking again.

"One of those men who was left alive—barely—well, he started to hallucinate. At least, that's what he thought. A man seemed to appear in front of him. Just sat there, like there was all the air in the world. Then he offered the guy a way out. A job, so to speak, if he agreed to all the conditions."

"A job?"

"To do the interfering they couldn't do. To go where something was about to go sour and straighten it out for people who deserved it. They'd give him the knowledge he needed and a little...help to nudge things in the right direction."

His mouth twisted wryly. "Well, this guy, he figured he was dead anyway, so he said yes. What did it matter, since it was only a hallucination anyway? Except it wasn't."

"Michael—"

"I know it sounds crazy. But that guy, the next thing he knew, he was outside. In the sun. Breathing." He drew another gulp of air. "He spent a week, in their time, learning the rules."

"Their time?"

"Yeah. Their time is a lot different. A month here is about a day to them."

Her eyes narrowed, but she let it pass. "The rules?"

He smiled wryly, ticking them off like a child reciting a lesson. "No violence. No lying, except by omission. No interference in anything that doesn't have a direct bearing on the job you're sent to do. And above all, no one finds out who—or what—you are."

He could see the doubt in her eyes, warring with the memory of the incontrovertible evidence she had seen last night.

"I know, Alex. I didn't believe it, either, at first."

"You... were the man in that mine?"

He nodded.

"Michael... when was that?"

Here it came, he thought. She would be sure he was crazy now. "September twenty-ninth."

Something flared in her eyes as her dilemma deepened. "What year, Michael?" she asked softly.

"I think you already know that."

Her eyes fell to the golden tags that lay on his chest. "But that was over a hundred years ago."

"I told you their time was different. That was part of what they gave me."

"Part?"

"They gave me vision. Second sight, if you like. The power of will, and the ability to extend it to others, to plant ideas, to make things happen. The power to read people, even past the masks they wear. And, when necessary, some powers I can't quite explain."

Alex paled. "You mean like... warning people from a mile away?"

Slowly, wondering if she was going to be able to accept this, he nodded.

"I... I heard you," she said shakily. "I would have ridden right over that drop. I thought later I'd been hearing things, but—"

"You weren't."

She just sat there, and he could see her trying to absorb it all. At last she met his eyes. "That first day, when you came here..."

"I was due for a vacation. Overdue. They owed it to me, but they dropped me here instead."

"Why?" This was crazy. *She* was crazy, for even listening.

"Because you asked for help."

She sat up straight. "I what?"

"Help not to give up the fight for the refuge."

"I..." She faltered, remembering the day that weary plea had escaped her battered heart. Her head was reeling, her common sense screaming that this was all insane, but there was too much that she couldn't explain away.

"All the things you fixed...the wood that shouldn't have been usable...the shingles you found...my truck...and you weren't hurt in the fire, when you should have been dead...oh, God, and Mark..."

"Yes. They gave me that, too."

Her eyes fell on the tags once more. "Those are..."

"My connection with them."

"Oh, Michael."

"I'm sorry, Alex. None of this was supposed to happen."

"But you said they helped you control things...." Lord, when had she started to believe all this craziness?

"They blew it," he said flatly.

She stared at him.

"In all those years, I've never gotten...personally involved. It was part of the deal. They weren't...human, but they understood human nature. That it would eventually kill a man to come to...care about the people he was helping, and yet always have to leave them behind. To have them all die, eventually, while he went on. They took care of that. I don't know how they numbed that capacity to feel, but they did. I've never felt any personal attachment, ever. Until you."

Alex was gaping at him now.

"I don't know what happened. It wasn't supposed to. It never has." He glanced at the tags. "I don't think they know, either. It really shook them up, when I told them."

"Told them . . . what?"

With the greatest effort of his life, he held her gaze. "That I love you."

Alex gasped, then stifled a tiny cry. The shutters that had blocked her soul from him fell away, and light leaped into the green depths of her eyes. She came out of the chair in a rush, scrambling down beside him on the bed.

"Oh, Michael, I love you, too."

His hands shot up to grip her shoulders, and he held her up and away from him as he stared at her, stunned.

"You . . . do? I know you thought you did, before, but—"

"Of course I do!"

"But I thought . . . you said you'd already made up your mind . . . after last night. . . ."

"Oh, God, Michael, I meant that I'd already made up my mind that I still love you, no matter what the explanation was for what I saw."

"Alex . . ." His voice was suddenly thick. "I know I'm . . . different, Alex, and you looked at me like I was . . . Your eyes were so . . . cold."

"Because I didn't understand. I thought you . . . didn't trust me, because you hadn't told me. Oh, I don't mean I understand now—it all sounds so crazy—but all that matters is that I love you."

She turned her head to kiss the fingers of the hands that held her. He shivered.

"Alex, stop. You *don't* understand. That's why I had to...stop last night. When you're safe, when my job is done here, I—"

"You'll leave."

"I have to. It's one of the rules."

"But you said...they owe you a vacation." She lowered her eyes to the tags, caught between her breasts as she lay on his chest. "Don't you get to choose where you take it?"

"Alex," he breathed. "Oh, God, Alex, don't you get it? Even if I could stay for a while, I'd still have to leave. I can't promise you the future you deserve. And I can't just...make love to you, knowing that."

"*You* don't understand, Michael. I'd rather have one day with you, if that's all I'm allowed, than the rest of my life with anyone else." She lifted one slender hand to brush back his tousled hair. "Besides," she said with the barest flicker of a grin, "how could a girl resist a man who's waited for her for a hundred years?"

He gaped at her, stunned. Then, welling up from so deep inside him that she could feel it before she heard it, he laughed. Long and deep and joyous, it washed over her like warm, soft rain, soothing away all the ache and hurt. He moved to cup her face in his hands.

"A hundred years," he said solemnly, "could make a guy a little rusty."

She blushed. "I didn't notice a problem last night."

"Now that you mention it," he said, sky blue eyes sparkling, "neither did I. There's a lot to be said for instinct, I guess."

"Too much."

"What?"

"Too much to be said. Please don't."

Again he laughed, and she thought that despite all the times she's seen his eyes gleam with that uncanny glow, she'd never seen them alight like this.

"Just what would you suggest I do instead?"

She reached down and lifted the golden tags. "Get rid of our audience."

Still chuckling, he tugged them off, but as he tossed them on the nightstand once more, Alex looked uneasy.

"Will they . . . will you get in trouble?"

"They never thought it would happen, so they never gave me any rules about this. They never counted on you, Alexandra."

She didn't even mind the name, not the way he said it, drawn out as if it were something regal. He pulled her down to him, his mouth seeking hers. She gave a glad little cry and met him, lips soft and warm, the nerves in her scalp tingling as his strong fingers threaded through her hair. His heat flooded her as his tongue invaded her mouth, stroking the ridge of her teeth, probing into every secret place.

Her own tongue sought his, teasing, dancing over the hot, rough velvet. He groaned low in his throat at her eager responsiveness and crushed her lips as he deepened the kiss.

He shoved the pillows aside, keeping her carefully atop him. He lifted himself slightly, savoring the slight weight of her. She went slack, letting herself press downward as if she'd read his need and echoed it.

"Lex," he murmured, trailing his mouth down the side of her throat. She threw her head back, baring the slender arc for his lips. The movement pressed her against him through the cloth of her robe. With a low, throttled sound he slid his hands down from her shoulders to cup the outer curves of her breasts.

She gave a muffled cry, and in an instinctive response, she braced her hands on his chest and raised herself over him. The movement freed her breasts, and the sight of them swaying beneath the pale green robe as she hovered there sent a blast of undeniable need through him. He slipped the worn cloth from her shoulders, then down her arms, baring the full, tempting curves, each tipped with a perfect pink crest.

Alex moaned, feeling her already tingling nipples contract as he looked at her. Michael echoed that groan as he saw the pink deepen to rose and the soft flesh tighten and peak under just his gaze. He moved his hands to cup the feminine softness, lifting the sweet weight, heat cascading through him at the feel of her filling his hands, at the sight of those taut nipples going rigid at the first touch of his hands on her flesh. A pulsing, throbbing heat settled somewhere low and deep inside him, hardening him in a single, fierce rush.

Those two beckoning crests were a temptation too great for him to resist, and he lifted his head to flick his tongue over them, savoring Alex's tiny cry as she arched toward him, letting her head loll back as she closed her eyes. The movement pressed her hips hard against his, her stomach against his eager, demanding flesh.

It might have been a long time, and that time buried in what primal memory they had let him keep, but his body remembered perfectly, and it was hot and hard and aching. He looked up at her, at the slender curve of her throat, the quivering of her breasts as she thrust them toward him, and at her glistening nipples, wet from his mouth.

He gave a hoarse groan as his head shot upward, capturing and tugging at one of the begging peaks with his lips. He suckled softly, then deeply, feeling Alex's response in the exclamation that broke from her on a breathless gasp, in the eager bowing of her body to give him more of the honeyed sweetness of her breasts, and the way her fingers dug into the muscles of his chest. His aching flesh pressed against her, trapped in a sweet caress between them. Convulsively his hips jerked as he moved to her other breast, drawing the taut nipple deeply into his mouth and flicking it with his tongue.

"Michael," she gasped. "Oh, Michael!"

"I know, Lexie, I know," he muttered.

He was on fire, sizzling with the heat that erupted anew with every touch, with every sliding of skin over skin, with every eager shiver of response that he drew from her. He tugged at the tangled robe, and with a quick little shake of her shoulders, she helped him. It slid to the floor, forgotten. He tugged off his briefs, then nudged her gently to one side as he kicked the covers away, needing the feel of her naked body against his with an urgency that stunned him.

Alex cried out in shocked pleasure as he rolled her beneath him, startled by how good it felt to have his weight bearing down on her. She could feel the column of aroused male flesh hard against her own softness, starting a hollow ache she'd never known before in some deep, private place inside her.

He was so hot and strong and solid, and her body ached to be even closer. Her arms went around him, her hands stroking over the muscles of his back, loving the feel of his skin, smooth and sleek as it slid over rock-hard muscle. She remembered the day they'd built the barn, remembered the way she'd felt as she'd watched him move, watched the flex and play of the muscles in his back, chest, and belly. And now that beautiful body, naked and fully aroused, was in her arms, setting her on fire in a way she'd never dreamed of. She tried, in broken little phrases, to tell him.

"No, Alex. It's you who's beautiful." His mouth lingered over one breast, and she felt the erotic brush of his breath as he spoke. "You know that now, don't you?"

"I know you make me feel beautiful," she whispered, unable to stop herself from arching her back again, thrusting her breast to him until the aching, beseeching nipple brushed his lips.

"You are," he murmured, letting the vibration of his voice tickle the tingling peak. "Inside and out, Alex." Then he took her nipple fiercely, making her cry out with the sudden burst of sweet, rippling sensation.

She felt his knee slide between hers, urging her legs apart. She opened for him eagerly, shuddering with pleasure as he slipped between her parted thighs. Her hands slid down his back to cup the tightly muscled curve of his buttocks, trying to draw him closer. She did it without thinking, only knowing that she couldn't bear this aching emptiness inside any longer, and only he could end it. Only he could ease the ache; only he could fill the hollowness inside her with the sweet, hot gift of himself.

"Alex," Michael said thickly, "Alex, are you sure?"

"Yes," she gasped, twisting sinuously beneath him. "I need you, Michael."

He groaned, burying his face in the soft curve of her neck and shoulder. "I want . . . I don't know how slow I can go—"

"It's all right," she whispered. "I know it will hurt at first—"

"Hurt?" He lifted his head to stare down into her eyes. "Alex you mean you've never . . . ?" He closed his eyes as the truth that should have been obvious hit him. "Of course you haven't," he said, his voice rough. "After what that bastard did to you . . ."

"Michael, no. It doesn't matter. It has nothing to do with this, with us."

"No. No, it doesn't."

He lowered his head to kiss her lips softly. A virgin. Lord, what now? He didn't want to hurt her; she'd been hurt so much already. A thought came to him, and he paused, considering. He didn't like the idea, didn't want it, but if it would save her pain. . . .

"Alex? I can . . . make it not hurt."

It took a moment for his meaning to penetrate the hot haze of pleasure that surrounded her. Her answer came quickly, unhesitantly.

"No, Michael," she whispered. "I don't want that between us. We're together here and now. It's real, and I don't want anything but that reality. Just you and me."

It was as if she'd reached into his soul and pulled out the very essence of his reluctance, and he shivered a little as he hugged her fiercely. He began to kiss her, soft little suckling kisses that left a line of fire up and down her body, down the line of her shoulder, over the full rise of her breasts, lingering at the throbbing nipples, down over the concave curve of her stomach, over the point of her hip to the soft flesh of her thigh.

When he lifted her to his mouth, parting the soft auburn curls with his tongue, Alex cried out as the intimate kiss sent flaring, crackling sparks through her in a fountain of golden heat. He tortured her with quick, darting caresses, until she was bucking with wild abandon.

At the moment when she cried out to him that she couldn't bear any more, he moved over her, his eager demanding flesh seeking the heat he'd created in her with all the urgency he'd fought so hard to suppress.

A low, harsh rasp of sound broke from him at the first touch of her slick heat as her body yielded to his. She was rippling in his arms, tiny little cries rising from her, her hands raking over his back. He tried to go slow, every muscle in his body standing out with the strain. Then she lifted her hips, taking him deeper, until he could feel the resistance of that fragile barrier.

"Please, Michael," she gasped.

The breathy little plea sent him careering out of control, and with one convulsive jerk of his hips, he thrust forward, deep and home.

Alex gave one small cry of pain, but it was forgotten as soon as it left her lips, lost in the wonder of the feel of him deep and full inside her. She felt him shudder, heard her name escape him in a voice so thick and husky with pleasure it was barely recognizable, felt the throbbing of that swollen male flesh that had so sweetly invaded her body. He had filled her beyond all expectation, erasing that hollowness as if it had never been, stretching her to an exquisite tightness.

Then, with a ragged groan, he began to move. He began with long, slow strokes, measuring his rigid length in her again and again. Then she began to move with him, lifting her hips to meet his thrusts, and he exploded into frantic action. Alex went flying with him, soaring, her only connection to the earth that had always held her was the sound of her name in that deep, husky voice.

"Alex," he gasped, his hands gripping her shoulders as he drove deep into her again. "I . . . can't . . . wait. . . ."

Her nails dug into his back, and she nipped lightly at his shoulder with a boldness that would have startled her had she been able to feel anything except her body racing toward an explosion she couldn't even imagine. And then she was there, every part of her erupting into a spray of heat and fire and spinning light. She cried out his name, a touch of fear in her voice as she lost her hold on the earth. But he was there with her, holding her so very tightly, so very sweetly, her name breaking from him in a choking shout as he exploded within her, pouring all the yearnings of years into her sweet, hot depths.

"Alex?" he murmured much later, as he lay with her cradled in his arms, their legs still entwined.

"Mmm?"

"Those hundred years? This was worth every minute."

She giggled, a low, carefree sound that sent a ripple of delight up his spine. "I'm afraid I can only claim twenty-six years of waiting, but I'm very glad I did."

"So am I," he whispered. "Did I hurt you very much?"

"I don't remember," she said, snuggling closer.

He smiled, nuzzling her hair with his lips. "I'm glad."

After a while she said softly, "Michael?"

"Hmm?"

"Why did they pick you?"

He chuckled. "I'd like to say that it was because I was such a great guy, but that ain't it. I just happened to meet their qualifications."

"What do you mean?"

He shrugged. "I was alone, basically. Not that it would have made any difference to anyone I might have left behind, since I would have died anyway, but it would have been harder on me if there had been someone I'd left, someone that I would have had to walk away from and never see again...."

He faltered, knowing that that was exactly the position he was in now.

Alex read him immediately. "Not now. We won't think about it now."

She pressed a kiss on his cheek, then let her head settle back onto his shoulder. Her arm, stretched across his chest, tightened for a moment in a fierce hug. Then she went on as if the painful subject had never been mentioned.

"What I really meant was, why did they send you here? There are...more of you, aren't there?"

"A few." He reached up and tweaked her pert nose. "They sent me because they knew I'm a sucker for big green eyes and sassy noses."

"Michael," she said with a mock sternness belied by the twinkle of pleasure in her eyes.

"They sent me," he said with sudden seriousness, "because they knew that once I met you, I'd forget about how mad I was that they'd reneged on their promise that I'd get a break."

"Why? Why would you forget?"

"Because they've infected me, I suppose. I can't stand the thought of injustice, especially when it's against innocence and goodness and honesty and integrity. And you're all of that, Alexandra."

She blushed. "Michael, no, I just—"

"You are, Alex. Take it from an expert."

She had to accept it; he wouldn't listen to any protest. She settled down beside him with a sigh of contentment. She had known it would be sweet, but she had never dreamed it would be so all-consuming. She'd never known anything could be.

She lay there for a long time, savoring the feel of his muscled shoulder beneath her cheek, the steady beat of his heart beneath her hand splayed on his chest, the feel of his hair-roughened thigh between hers. Then, tentatively, she began to explore, her hands moving slowly, then more boldly when he didn't protest.

Her hand slid over the muscled wall of his chest. She felt him jerk sharply, heard his quick intake of breath when her fingers found one of his flat, male nipples. Experimentally she let her hand drift to the other brown nub of flesh, this time feeling a spurt of heat shoot through her own body at his response to her touch.

Her hand slid down over his belly, feeling the deep muscles there ripple beneath her touch. The tiny spark flickered and caught; how potent it was, she thought in wonder, to be wanted in return. How powerful a feeling, to know that she could do this to him.

As if of its own volition, her hand moved downward, then paused as her fingertips reached the thicket of dark, curly hair at the base of his belly. Shyness suddenly swept over her, and she began to pull back. Then his hand was there, over hers, holding it there.

"Anything you want, Alex," he whispered thickly.

Color flooded her cheeks, but the magnet was irresistible, and her fingers crept down to touch that male flesh that was already fiercely responding to her caresses. It was slower this time, but no less sweet, and, in the end, no less urgent, just as the explosion was no less shattering.

Michael was loath to disrupt the sweet silence that followed, but he knew it was time. Still, he couldn't quite stifle a sigh.

"What, love?" she asked softly.

Reflexively his arms tightened around her at the sweetness of the word. But still he couldn't beat back the hovering cloud of things yet to be done, and at last he spoke heavily. "We have to call the sheriff."

She lifted her head to look at him. "Can we? I mean, we can't exactly explain what happened last night."

"They don't need the details. But Mark was shot, and the guy who did it is still out walking around."

She sighed in turn. "I know. But they won't be able to find anything. Matt and Steve went over that hill with a fine-toothed comb. There wasn't a trace."

"I know."

"He's long gone, whoever it was."

"Long, but not far."

Her eyes widened. "Michael? Why did you say it like that? Like you . . . knew?"

His eyes met hers then.

"Because I do," he said softly.

Ten

"Why did you wait so long?" Walt asked with an air of mild exasperation.

"We were too worried about Mark," Alex said, and left it at that.

They'd given the young deputy the basics, including the phone calls, but no more.

"You're sure you don't know who it is?" he asked Alex.

Her eyes flicked to Michael. He said nothing, so she answered carefully, "*I* don't have any idea. Except that it has to be the caller."

"We can't prove that," Walt said warningly.

"But he said someone would get hurt—"

"I know, Alex," Walt said. "And you're probably right. I just don't know how we'll prove it. *If* we ever find him."

Alex opened her mouth to speak, then shut it again. She couldn't doubt Michael when he'd said he knew who it was.

She remembered too clearly that moment in the woods when she had sensed the wave of realization that had swept him. But he'd told her gently that he couldn't tell her who it was.

"It might affect what happens, Alex. You might act differently around the wrong person. He has to believe no one knows, that you're still scared, or he might run."

She'd laughed a little ruefully. "I *am* still scared."

"Don't be. Nothing will happen to you."

"Like nothing happened to Mark?"

"That was a promise my bosses didn't keep. This one is from me."

An icy determination unlike anything she'd ever seen glowed in the sky blue eyes, and she knew he meant exactly what he said. He would go to any lengths to protect her. It was a new, strange feeling to Alex, and she treasured it even as she wondered at it.

She was yanked back to the present by Michael's unexpected words.

"Where were the animals found?"

Walt gaped at Michael, startled by his seeming non sequitur. "What?"

"The animals that were killed. Where were they found?"

"Three or four different places," Walt said, clearly puzzled. "One on the road near the Morgan place, one out in back of the feed store in town, one down by the river, near the swimming hole—"

"All places where they'd be found almost immediately."

"Well..."

"And all in unusual places for livestock to be found."

"I suppose so, but—"

"Was there blood?"

Walt gaped again. "What?"

"Where they were found."

"Well, no, now that you mention it. Not like you'd expect, anyway. But they could have been wounded and just wandered that far. Look, what has that got to do with—"

"It wasn't Cougar," Alex said suddenly.

"Sure, Alex," Walt said soothingly. "I don't think anyone believes that anymore, no matter what Henry says. Not after seeing the way he was with Billy Peterson. Besides, you said you've kept him locked up."

"What if it wasn't an animal at all?" Michael asked.

Walt wheeled around to stare at Michael again. "What?" he said for the third time.

"What if it was someone who wanted everyone to think it was Cougar? To cause more trouble for Alex and the refuge."

"You mean . . . the caller?"

"And the shooter."

"But—"

"It would explain it, wouldn't it? If the animals were killed in one place, then moved to another? It wouldn't take much to make the wounds look ragged, like an animal bite. Especially if he thought no one would look too closely."

After a long moment Walt nodded. "I suppose. But we're back to who again, aren't we? And up until recently, I can think of a dozen people who might have had an interest in shutting this place down."

"We only need one."

Walt looked thoughtful. "Maybe I should talk to Henry," he began.

Michael glanced at Alex, glad to see that no haunting memories shadowed the green eyes at the mention of the name. He had done that, at least, he thought, exorcised

that awful demon she'd buried so deep. He turned back to
Walt.

"You're a good cop, Walt. And smart enough to look
beyond the obvious."

Now that she knew, Alex could almost see it happening.
She saw that incredible gleam growing in the clear blue
eyes, saw the slightly dazed look come over Walt's face. For
several long, silent moments it went on, until at last Michael spoke again, quietly.

"You'll find him, Walt. Just go with your instinct."

"Uh . . . yeah." Walt shook his head, looking a little like
a wide-eyed owl waking up after a day's sleep. "Sure. I'd
better get started."

When he was gone, Alex looked at Michael curiously.
"Couldn't you just . . . tell him?"

"I could. But it's better if he finds it himself. He'll believe it more if he has to work at it a little."

"But you . . . told him where to start, didn't you?"

He didn't deny it. "I gave him a nudge in the right direction."

"You seem to do a lot of that."

He shrugged. "Most people want to go in the right direction. Sometimes they just need a little help finding it."
He grimaced. "So do I sometimes. I had the wrong guy for
a while, because I had something personal against him. But
Walt will have the right one, soon."

Alex's eyes went to the golden tags he'd put back on this
morning when Walt had arrived, then back to his face.

"You've seen such wonders, haven't you, Michael?" she
said in a hushed tone. "I wish—" She stopped, dropping
her gaze.

"What, Alex?"

"Nothing."

"Tell me."

Her head came up. "I wish we...had time. I'd like to hear about things you've seen."

"Time." It came out flatly, sourly. "Time," he repeated. "We're going to get that time, Alex." He stopped, looking at her steadily. "If you're sure you want it. But it might make it worse, in the end." His voice dropped, pained. "And it has to end, Alex. I can't quit."

He hated saying it, but he couldn't let her hope, not when it was impossible. She met his gaze unflinchingly.

"I know that. And I told you, I'd rather have whatever time they allow me with you than all the time I have left with someone else. I love you, Michael."

He pulled her into his arms. "Oh, God, Alex. I love you, too." He held her for a long moment before he gripped her shoulders and looked down into her face. "I guess I'd better talk to the bosses."

"Now?"

He nodded. She stepped back, her eyes fastened on the gold tags a little warily.

"If they're mad, tell them it's their own fault."

He smiled. "I will." He studied her for a moment. "Will you come with me?"

"Can I?"

For answer he took her hand, then began to walk toward the quiet little clearing he'd come to use as a refuge of his own.

"Michael?"

"What?"

"What if they had kept you from...feeling anything for me? Do you think I would have still—" She broke off, then answered her own question. "Of course I would have. How could I not love you?"

His hand tightened around hers. "Thank you. But I think it . . . I don't know. It's like there's been some kind of barrier, all these years, that everyone could sense even if they didn't understand it. It kept them all away. Until you found a way through it." He grinned at her. "You were just too much for them, Alexandra Logan."

They reached the small clearing and sat down on the cool grass. He gave her a quick look of reassurance, and then his hand went to the tags.

Michael! Are you all right? We've been very concerned.

Fine.

You're certain? We felt the drain. We were afraid we'd lost you.

I'm fine. Thank you.

Thank you? For what?

For the help. Mark is going to be okay.

Good. Michael, are you sure you're all right? You sound very odd.

Yes, I am. But I'm very tired.

We realize that, Michael. And we realize that we've been unfair with you. We've put you under too much strain. It's only natural that you should imagine a fondness for—

It's not a "fondness," and I'm not imagining it.

I understand how strong these . . . urges are in humans. Perhaps we underestimated the power of such a strong attraction. But it can be fixed.

This is not something you can "fix." I don't know what went wrong—or right—but I love her.

Michael, you know that's impossible.

It's true, nevertheless.

But we made certain that something like this would never happen. I—

Goofed. And she says to tell you it's all your own fault.

A silence, stunned this time; Michael wasn't sure how he could tell, but he knew. He answered the unspoken question wryly.

Yes, I broke that rule, too. She saw me with Mark. She had to know. And it won't matter, later.

That, Michael thought with amazement, was a sigh. First they drop that damn royal "we," and now they're sighing.

I suppose you're right. Then, indignantly, *Did she really say that?*

Yes.

A pause. *She believed you, then.*

Yes.

Unusual.

So is she.

Yes. Hmm. Well, we could bring you back here for some readjustment, I suppose. Perhaps that's all that's wrong.

No. It's not a matter of adjustment.

But for all of these years of yours—

It worked. But it only worked for one reason.

What?

Because I hadn't met Alex.

A pause.

You said she was as special as she seemed. It was an understatement. Don't blame me if I see it, too.

We don't blame you, Michael. We just don't quite know what to do.

I'll tell you what you're going to do.

I beg your pardon?

You're going to give me that vacation you owe me.

Well of course we are. As soon as you're done. It will be soon, won't it?

Very.

Good. Now, where would you like to go?

Nowhere.

But you just said . . .

I'm staying here.

Another pause. *You know we can't allow that.*

Then I quit.

You can't do that, either.

Watch me.

You know what that means, Michael.

Yes.

It means that much to you? You'd go back to that awful hole in the ground, knowing the result?

I'd be just as dead if I walked away from her now.

You'd be giving yourself just that many more memories to live with later. Is it worth that price to you?

It's worth any price.

They didn't answer. He clutched the tags tighter, waiting. Still nothing. He knew he was bargaining with his life, but he also knew that they wouldn't pull him before his job was done. No matter what their decision, he would have that much time. After that, if they made him leave, it wouldn't matter. Nothing would. He waited.

Still nothing. A sudden rush of uncharacteristic anger filled him. He'd done everything they asked, all this time. He'd been all over the world for years on end. He'd seen more tragedies than anyone should ever have to look upon. And never once, until now, had he even asked for a break, let alone anything for himself.

He scrambled to his feet, tearing the tags over his head. He let the full force of his temper go through, not caring anymore. He leaned back, cocked his arm and, with all his strength, flung the golden tags up and away from him.

They twirled in midair, soaring up out of the shadows of the trees and into the sun, catching the light in golden glints. And then, in a sudden flare of brilliant golden sparks, they disappeared.

Michael closed his eyes as he sank back to the grass; his strength had drained away the minute the tags had been claimed by their true owners. So this was it, he thought, his head spinning as he gasped for air. He'd been wrong. They'd decided to pull him anyway. When he opened his eyes, if he lasted that long, he'd be back in the dark, his lungs on fire as he tried to eke out a last few seconds of life.

He shuddered, but he made himself do it. And opened his eyes to the dappled sun and Alex's face. Stunned, he sat up.

"I'm still here," he whispered. "I thought they'd put me back."

"Back?"

Alex barely managed to get it out; believing what he'd told her and seeing the incontrovertible proof of it with her own eyes were two different things, she discovered.

"To the mine. I thought… That's what was supposed to happen. If I quit."

She looked at him, wide-eyed. When he'd told her he couldn't quit, she hadn't realized that the reason was that it would cost him his life. Alex paled.

"They wouldn't! Not after all you've done!"

He was a little steadier now. "It was one of the conditions, Alex. If I quit, they had to put me back. It didn't seem too bad at the time, compared to the alternative."

"You did that, risked that… to stay with me?"

"I had no choice," he said simply. "I love you. I didn't know what they'd do, but I had to try."

"But what if they—"

"I know." He pulled her into his arms as he let out a sigh. "Whatever it is they've done, all this time, it's worked well up to now. It never mattered to me before, being alone. Not feeling any real emotion for anyone. Not needing anyone. Not loving anyone. It made sense. It was the only way it could work. But now..."

"What will they do?"

He laughed wryly. "You mean now that you've come along and blown all their calculations to bits? I don't know. They still can't figure out what happened."

"But..." She hugged him tightly, even as a shudder went through her at the idea of him, even as a bluff, thinking of going back to that death trap. "You're still here."

"Yes." He went suddenly tense, cocking his head. Then his eyes fluttered closed as he swallowed tightly.

"Michael?"

When he opened his eyes, it was to give her a tenderly joyous look. "We've got a month," he whispered.

Her eyes widened. "Oh, Michael," she breathed as she hugged him fiercely again.

He held her close, pressing his lips against her hair. "It's not forever, Alex. I wish it could be."

"Any time at all is more of a gift than I ever expected in my life," she said softly.

She meant it, and in the days that followed she tried to live it. It took one of the greatest efforts of her life, but Alex put the shadow hovering over them out of her mind. She was determined to make the most of these precious days, determined to store up as many sweet, honeyed memories as she could for the long, lonely time to come.

The others seemed to blithely accept the changes in her, the way she bloomed before their eyes. They never commented on the fact that Michael had changed his sleeping quarters, or that every time anyone found them together, they were in each other's arms. And they silently took over many of her chores, giving her more free time than she'd ever had.

Mark came home from the clinic, weak but healing rapidly. He claimed to remember nothing that had happened after he'd been shot, but Alex had seen something flicker in his eyes when he shook Michael's hand.

"Knew you were special," was all he said.

Every day seemed more beautiful than the last, and Alex hummed happily as she groomed Cricket, brushing his black-and-white coat until it gleamed like the wet hide of a killer whale. They had taken to riding double on the big stallion whenever they had a free moment, savoring the deep pine scents and crisp air of her beloved Oregon countryside.

Michael had laughed at first, telling her that his only riding experience was longer ago than he cared to remember. But he'd grown to love it as much as she did, and this day was no different.

"Want to drive?" she asked as she led the big horse outside.

"No thanks," he said with a wicked grin. "I like having my hands free."

Alex blushed furiously and took a teasing swipe at him with the reins. He laughed and gave her a leg up onto the horse's broad back. He leapt up behind her and settled into his accustomed spot, with her nestled closely between his strong thighs. His arms came around her, locking beneath her breasts and pulling her even tighter against him.

Alex felt the warmth that was so familiar to her now begin to radiate through her body from beneath his hands. Every day it seemed that it took less time for that aching need to build in her; sometimes it took only a look from him to bring it to life, full-grown and demanding.

She let out a tiny sigh and heard Michael chuckle behind her. He let his hands slip downward and pulled her hips back against him, letting her feel the instant effect her closeness had on him.

"Wonder how far we'll get this time?" he asked her huskily as he leaned around to nibble her ear.

The sound she made was half laugh, half gasp. So many times their rides had come to an abrupt end when the desire that seemed to be always simmering just under the surface came to a boil so suddenly and fiercely that it couldn't be ignored.

Alex blushed as she thought of the unlikely places they'd made love: a clearing near the bank of the river, on a bed of pine needles up the hill near home, and once, when the need had grown too great too quickly, in the hayloft over Cricket's stall. The need for quiet then had somehow added to their fervency, as if the feelings they couldn't vent with their voices were transferred to their bodies, making their gasping, silent climax even more shattering.

Michael's thoughts were apparently going along the same lines, for his hands became more urgent as they moved over her, pressing against the flat of her stomach, then rising to cup and lift her breasts.

When they were out of sight of the farm, up in the trees on the hill, Alex dropped the reins and let Cricket go where he wanted. She lifted her hands back over her shoulders to lock behind Michael's neck and draw him down to her. The movement arched her back, moving her breasts against his hands. He groaned low in his throat, and his fingers fumbled with the buttons of her shirt.

Alex felt the insistent pressure of his aroused flesh against the curve of her buttocks and reflexively moved against him. Then she could feel nothing but hot, pulsing pleasure as he freed her breasts for his hands.

They made it as far as a quiet, shaded clearing near where they had found Mark before they tumbled from Cricket's back to the grassy carpet. They tugged at each other's clothes, kissing and caressing every inch of skin they exposed, until at last they could wait no longer.

Michael rolled to his back and pulled Alex over him. She had lost the last of her shyness days ago and straddled him eagerly, lowering herself to take him in with a glad cry. He reached up to caress her taut nipples as she rocked on him, the tiny sounds of pleasure she made blending with his low murmuring of her name.

She felt it begin, that rising, swirling tide, and her slow pace became urgent. Michael felt the change, and his body responded with the swiftness he'd come to expect with her. Soon he was moving her, arching up into her with all his strength, loving the cries that broke from her and the way her fingers curled desperately into his shoulders as she rode him so sweetly. The first rippling contractions of her body around his were his undoing, and he felt himself erupt inside her in wave after wave of hot, fierce pleasure.

"Alex . . . Lex . . . Lexieee . . ."

He shuddered as she collapsed, trembling, atop him, his name coming from her on a long, shivery breath.

"God, I love you," he said fervently when he could speak again. "All these years, I've watched people . . . I knew that it worked. Love, I mean. I knew how it worked, what it did to people . . . but I never knew how it felt. That it could be so hot, so sweet."

For a time, just for a while, Alex let herself think that it would never end. That they could go on like this forever, that the beautiful dream would never stop. Then, when three weeks of their precious month had gone, the outside world came crashing back in with shocking force.

They came back from a ride to find Walt's unit parked in front of the house. Walt was leaning against the fender, but he straightened as soon as he saw them coming. Alex could feel his eyes going over them speculatively. By the time she slid off Cricket's back in front of him, the young deputy wore the expression of a man who had just reached an unexpected conclusion and was not too happy about it. But his voice was amiable enough.

"We got him, Alex."

Alex let out a long breath. "Thank God." Then, after a moment, apprehensively, "Was it Henry?"

"No."

Alex let out a sigh of relief. She hadn't liked the idea of having to tell the world why Henry had disliked her enough to do all this.

"I thought it was, at first," Walt said, "but then I thought maybe I just didn't like the guy."

Alex gave a little start as a memory clicked into place. She turned to stare at Michael. "I had the wrong guy for a while," he'd said, "because I had something personal against him." Now she understood; it was Henry he'd been talking about, and the something personal was what he'd done to her so long ago.

"Anyway," Walt went on, drawing her attention once more, "something kept nagging at me to check some other things out." He glanced at Michael with a look that was curiously puzzled. "That instinct you mentioned, I guess."

Michael shrugged. "I knew you had it."

"Well," Walt said, pleased with himself, "you must be right. Only thing I can think of that made me pull Ray over."

"Ray?" Alex asked. Walt nodded.

"Yep. Ray Claridge. I found the knife he used on the animals, blood in the back of his truck . . . and a pistol under the seat."

"A gun?" Alex's breath caught. "Mark?"

Walt nodded again. "Haven't got the ballistics back yet, but it's the same caliber. Besides, Ray copped out when he realized I'd found the gun and could match it with the bullet Doc took out of Mark. He admitted the phone calls, too."

"But . . . why?" Alex stared at the deputy. "He's never been one of the complainers. He never acted like he cared one way or the other if we were here."

"He was afraid that if the town came to accept you, they might look at him and start remembering."

"Remembering?"

Walt looked uncomfortable. "He . . . I guess you were too young at the time . . ."

"Walt, what are you talking about? Why on earth would Ray want to hurt us?"

Michael put his hands on her shoulders comfortingly. "Do you remember him?" he asked.

"Not really. I remember he and my brother never got along. Ray was always trying to bad-mouth Andrew behind his back. But he left town when I was young to take a job up north. He's only been back a few years."

"He didn't leave for a job," Walt said.

"He didn't?" She turned away from Michael to look at Walt. "But his father said he was—"

"He left because he'd been drafted."

Alex's eyes widened. Michael nodded.

"He went to Canada. He came back under the amnesty program," Walt went on.

"But—"

"He was afraid that if the town started to see the men at the refuge as the brave men they are, they might change their minds about accepting what he had done. He'd always insisted it was because he objected to the war, but I think he knew not very many believed that. Besides, he'd always hated your brother. And Gary Swan," Walt finished.

"But why?"

Michael gave her a gentle smile. "Because everyone else liked and admired them. He was jealous of them both when they were alive, and more so after they died. Then Henry told him, one night when they'd been out drinking, what he'd done to you."

Alex flushed and glanced at Walt. He'd been staring in surprise at Michael, but when he looked up, he quickly averted his eyes. She knew then that he knew, and embarrassment filled her. But Michael took her hand and it faded away. He went on softly.

"Ray never had the nerve to fight face-to-face, so he concocted this plan to scare you off and get Henry blamed for it. And Henry only helped by mouthing off about Cougar. Not only did Ray hope it would close down the refuge, it was his way of getting back at Andrew. And Gary, too, in a way, because he loved both you and Andrew so much. He figured you were vulnerable, and he had a hold on Henry because of what he knew. But it got out of hand when Mark found him skulking around the farm, and Ray shot him."

Michael stopped as he realized Walt was gaping at him, his surprise turned to shock.

"How did you find all that out? I only figured it all out yesterday."

"I . . . just put two and two together."

"Maybe you should be a cop."

"No thanks. I don't have the fortitude." He held out a hand. "Nice work, Walt," he said evenly, holding Walt's gaze unflinchingly.

"Er, yeah." An odd expression came over Walt's face as he shook Michael's hand. Then his mouth twisted wryly. "I'm still not sure how it happened, though. I just seemed to keep heading in that direction."

"A good cop has good instincts, Walt. You just followed them."

Diverted, Walt muttered a thank you.

Only when he'd gone did the significance of the morning's revelations hit Alex. They were walking toward the barn when she stopped dead, staring up at him.

"It's . . . done now, isn't it? Your job here?"

He took a long, slow breath and nodded.

She cringed inwardly, pain flaring in her eyes. Michael reached for her and she clung to him, fighting tears.

"We still have a week," she said fiercely. "They promised."

"I know, love. We still have a week."

Alex seemed determined to cram as much as she could into that precious time. They rarely slept. They talked, walked for hours, rode for hours more, and made sweet lingering love until they were both spent. And one night, driven by the demons of the hovering future, Michael made love to her time after time, until she was quivering, until one shuddering explosion blended into the next and into the next and she collapsed in limp, sated exhaustion in his arms.

When she woke up, it was to the dreaded sight of the golden tags once more around his neck.

"No!" she cried. "No, not yet!"

"Alex," he began, reaching for her. She jerked out of his reach, and, pulling on her clothes as she went, she ran out of the room, out of the house, tears streaming down her face.

He found her in the clearing behind the house, sitting on the small patch of soft grass. Her cheeks were still damp, but the stream of tears had stopped. She looked up as he dropped down beside her.

"I'm sorry, Michael," she said in a tightly controlled voice. "I thought I was prepared, but I wasn't."

He pulled her into his arms. "I know, Lexie-girl, I know. Neither was I."

"You knew, didn't you? Last night?"

"Not really. Sensed it, maybe." He gave a sigh so weary that it frightened her. He flicked the golden tags with one finger. "I should have known I hadn't seen the last of them." She felt him tremble, knew this was as hard for him as it was for her. "I love you, Alex. I'll love you forever."

"You will, won't you?" Her voice caught at the ironic truth of his words. "I love you, Michael. I'll always love you."

"I know."

"You can't . . . ever come back?"

"No. Never."

"Then I'll live on the memories," she whispered. "I . . . they're sweeter than most people's lives."

He went very still. "Alex . . ."

"What, love?"

"There won't . . . be any memories."

She pulled back to look at him. "What do you mean?"

"When I go . . . you'll forget."

"I could never forget, Michael."

"You will. Everyone will. You'll remember what happened, but not my part in it. You won't remember me at all."

"Michael, no!"

"Yes, Alex. It's the way it works. And it's better that way. Really."

Alex stared at him, horrified. "How can you say that?"

He sat up and took her hands, holding them tightly. He wished he hadn't begun this at all; he hadn't meant to. But now that he had, he had to explain. "Listen to me. What we've had is . . . special. Different. You said it yourself. It's sweeter than anything most people ever have in their lives. If they left you with those memories, you'd spend the rest of your life looking for something to match them. It would never happen, Alex, and you'd be alone forever. You weren't meant to be alone."

"No," she moaned. "Please, Michael, no. They're all I'll have of you."

"I can't, Alex. It's not negotiable."

"It will be like we never were," she cried softly. "Like I'd never met you, or you'd never met me—"

His eyes darted away but not swiftly enough. "Michael?"

He wouldn't look at her, and that gave her her answer.

"You'll remember, won't you?" she whispered hoarsely. "Michael?"

Her hand went to his chin to turn him to face her, and she read in his eyes the knowledge of the long years of torture ahead, years of remembering, yet being able to do nothing, of longing yet having to stay away, and, ultimately, of knowing, years from now, of her death and still having to go on endlessly.

"*No!*" she cried out in a voice fiercer, more ringing, than it had been in her own pain. "They can't do this to you! They can't expect you to go through such hell! They can't!"

"Alex—"

"No! If they're these wonderful, kind beings you say they are, they would never do this! There must be a way!"

"A way to what?" he asked gently, his heart aching as he looked at her agonized, tear-stained face.

"To make you forget, too," she said hoarsely, brokenly.

Michael stared at her. "You *want* me to forget you?"

"I can't bear the thought of you hurting like that," she choked out, fighting the sobs that threatened to take over. "I'd rather lose everything, the refuge, my home... I'd rather Ray had gotten me with that gun than to have you hurt like that. There has to be a way they can make you forget."

"Oh, God, Alex," he murmured, pulling her hard and close against him. He'd never felt so humbled as he did now, faced with the power of this woman's love. He rocked her, cradled her, even as his arms shook with his pain and hers.

"What?"

He looked at her as she lifted her head. "What, Alex?"

Her brows furrowed over reddened eyes. "What did you say?"

"I didn't say anything."

"But I heard—" She paled suddenly, putting a hand to her head. "There it is again. It *wasn't* you!" Her head jerked around as she scanned the trees around them frantically.

"Alex—"

"I heard it," she insisted. "It was my name. I—"

Michael swore softly. He grabbed the tags, and the connection was so immediate that he knew he'd been right.

It *was* you. Knock it off, you're scaring her.

Sorry, Michael. Can you bring her in?

He couldn't help being suspicious.

Why?

Please, Michael.

He sighed. With an effort he withdrew part of his consciousness from the contact and turned it to Alex's wide-eyed face.

"They want to talk to you," he said. "It's up to you."

She recovered quickly. "Good," she snapped, some of her battered spirit returning. "I've got a few words for them."

Michael smothered a smile. This, he thought, should be interesting. "Hold up your hand." She did, and he laced his fingers with hers, the gold tags caught between their palms. "Close your eyes," he urged. "It makes it easier. Just think the words."

Alex?

She tried it.

Yes.

Good. We wanted to—

I don't care what you want.

A startled pause. I beg your pardon?

What I want is for you to live up to your billing. To the faith Michael has in you.

Live up to...?

If you were everything he thinks you are, you would never put him through what you know is coming.

My, she is a little... feisty, isn't she?

Michael chuckled. Don't say you weren't warned.

Yes. Quite. Then, to Alex, although she wasn't sure how she knew. *You meant what you said? That you'd rather he forgot you?*

Yes.

From our observations over time, it's most unusual for a woman to want to be forgotten. Why?

Because I love him. And I'd rather be forgotten than cause him pain.

I see.

A new voice then, and one that made Michael stiffen with surprise. The big boss, he communicated to Alex swiftly.

You were always exceptional, Michael.

Were?

Michael "said" it a little shakily; the voice ignored him.

Your choice of a mate is only further proof of that. She is as extraordinary as you are.

Michael gulped.

But then, it would take an extraordinary woman to make a man give up immortality, wouldn't it?

Alex gasped as Michael gathered his nerve to go on.

Am I?

So it seems. You've had a grand run, my boy. You've more than earned this, if it is what you want.

The yes he sent them was resounding, without hesitation or doubt.

Good luck, then, Michael. To both of you.

Alex's mind was too stunned to make much sense, but they seemed to understand.

You've won, my dear. And, may I say, never have I taken more joy in losing a battle. If Michael hadn't chosen you for his own, I would have looked into recruiting you, if the chance ever arose. Goodbye, children.

The connection was gone, leaving them both dazed by the sudden exit. Then Alex's vision cleared as the tags between their hands began to glow, to shimmer with a golden light. And then they were gone, as if they'd never been.

Slowly Michael flexed his hand, feeling an odd weight, as if the tags were still there. Then he looked, and in his palm rested two plain, gold rings that seemed to shimmer with a strange light. Alex gasped, her eyes flicking around as if there would be some trace of their benefactors.

"A final gift," Michael murmured as he held up the rings. "Will you wear my ring, Alex? Will you marry me?"

"Of course," she whispered, her eyes glistening. "How could I turn down the man who literally gave up immortality for me?"

And as they joined together in that little clearing, somewhere far away a pleased laugh floated on the wind.

*　*　*　*　*

HOW TO UNEXPECTEDLY MEET
MR. MARRIAGEABLE DURING
THE HOLIDAYS:

♥ Sell kisses for a dollar behind a booth at a Texas Christmas fair

♥ Challenge an anonymous Santa to deliver him by December 25th

In December Yours Truly has two holiday treats:

CHRISTMAS KISSES FOR A DOLLAR
by Laurie Paige

Anne's selling kiss after chaste kiss for a dollar at the Christmas fair—until a gorgeous rancher's hot lips have her swooning in his arms. Now Anne's in love—with a man she can't ever hope to marry!

HOLIDAY HUSBAND
by Hayley Gardner

Single scroogey Sharon challenges an anonymous Santa to deliver the man of her dreams by Christmas. There won't really be a tall, dark and handsome, red-ribbon-wrapped gift under the tree—right?

Love—when you least expect it!

YT1295

Three brothers...
Three proud, strong men who live—and love—by

THE CODE OF THE WEST

Meet the Tanner brothers—Robert, Luke, and
now, Noah—in Anne McAllister's

COWBOYS DON'T STAY
(December, Desire #969)

Tess Montgomery had fallen for Noah Tanner
years ago—but he left her with a broken heart *and*
a baby. Now he was back, but could he convince
her that sometimes cowboys do stay?

Only from

SILHOUETTE®

Desire

CHRISTMAS WEDDING
by Pamela Macaluso

JUST MARRIED

Don't miss JUST MARRIED, a fun-filled miniseries by Pamela Macaluso about three men with wealth, power and looks to die for. These bad boys had everything—except the love of a good woman.

***

"Will you pretend *to be my fiancée?"* Holly Bryant knew millionaire Jesse Tyler was the most eligible bachelor around—not that a hunk with attitude was her idea of husband material. But then, she and Jesse weren't really engaged, and his steamy mistletoe kisses were just part of the charade...weren't they?

Find out in *Christmas Wedding,* book three of the JUST MARRIED series, coming to you in December... only from

SILHOUETTE®

Desire®

Coming in 1996 from

SILHOUETTE®

Desire®

SONS AND *Lovers*

A new series by three of romance's hottest authors

January—LUCAS: THE LONER by Cindy Gerard

February—REESE: THE UNTAMED by Susan Connell

March—RIDGE: THE AVENGER by Leanne Banks

SONS AND *Lovers* : Three brothers denied a father's name, but granted the gift of love from three special women.

"For the best mini-series of the decade, tune into SONS AND LOVERS, a magnificent trilogy created by three of romance's most gifted talents."

—Harriet Klausner
Affaire de Coeur